WAY OF THE DEAD

ASHRAF MOVED MORE swiftly then, knowing that he had to hide himself before the goblins discovered him. He had to find somewhere in the crowded temple where he could put as many of his enemies down before they combined forces to rush and overwhelm him.

He knew that his prospects of long-term survival were relatively poor, and they did not seem to have improved when the situation became still more complicated. The goblins were being followed by a scaly and skeletal monster – half-crocodile and half-human – walking on its hind legs. – *from* **The Road to Damnation** *by Brian Craig*

ANGELIKA TOOK HER knife and placed it on the back of Potocki's neck. She leapt up, then fell, so that her entire weight pressed on the blade. She opened a gash in Potocki's neck that went clear to the bone and kept hacking; there was no blood, and the dried flesh came off in chunks. – *from* **Head Hunting** *by Robin D. Laws*

IN THE DARK *and gothic Warhammer world, the foul magic of Chaos is everywhere, its corrupting and mutating powers twisting man and beast alike. From the south, the dark armies of the undead attack the realms of man, thirsting to drain all life from the civilised lands. From the north, the endless tide of Chaos sweeps down to kill and capture in the name of the Dark Gods. From the pages of Inferno! magazine, this collection of fantasy stories follows man's fight for survival in these desperate times.*

More Warhammer from the Black Library

WARHAMMER FANTASY SHORT STORIES

REALM OF CHAOS
eds. Marc Gascoigne & Andy Jones

LORDS OF VALOUR
eds. Marc Gascoigne & Christian Dunn

THE LAUGHTER OF DARK GODS
ed. David Pringle

WARHAMMER NOVELS

RIDERS OF THE DEAD by Dan Abnett
MARK OF DAMNATION by James Wallis
BLOOD MONEY by C. L. Werner
THE DEAD AND THE DAMNED by Jonathan Green
STAR OF ERENGRAD by Neil McIntosh
THE CLAWS OF CHAOS by Gav Thorpe
ZAVANT by Gordon Rennie
HAMMERS OF ULRIC by Dan Abnett,
Nik Vincent & James Wallis
GILEAD'S BLOOD by Dan Abnett & Nik Vincent
THE WINE OF DREAMS by Brian Craig

GOTREK & FELIX by William King

TROLLSLAYER • SKAVENSLAYER
DAEMONSLAYER • DRAGONSLAYER • BEASTSLAYER
VAMPIRESLAYER • GIANTSLAYER

THE VAMPIRE GENEVIEVE NOVELS
by Jack Yeovil

DRACHENFELS • GENEVIEVE UNDEAD
BEASTS IN VELVET • SILVER NAILS

THE TALES OF ORFEO by Brian Craig

ZARAGOZ • PLAGUE DAEMON • STORM WARRIORS

THE KONRAD TRILOGY

KONRAD • SHADOWBREED • WARBLADE

WARHAMMER FANTASY STORIES

WAY OF THE DEAD

Edited by Marc Gascoigne
& Christian Dunn

A BLACK LIBRARY PUBLICATION

First published in Great Britain in 2003
by BL Publishing,
Games Workshop Ltd.,
Willow Road, Nottingham,
NG7 2WS, UK

10 9 8 7 6 5 4 3 2 1

Cover illustration by Karl Kopinski

© Games Workshop Limited 2003. All rights reserved.

Black Library, the Black Library logo, Black Flame, BL Publishing, Games Workshop, the Games Workshop logo and all associated marks, names, characters, illustrations and images from the Warhammer universe are either ®, TM and/or © Games Workshop Ltd 2000-2003, variably registered in the UK and other countries around the world. All rights reserved.

A CIP record for this book
is available from the British Library

ISBN 1 84416 013 0

Set in ITC Giovanni

Printed and bound in Great Britain by
Cox & Wyman Ltd, Reading, Berkshire.

No part of this publication may be reproduced, stored in a retrieval system, or transmitted in any form or by any means, electronic, mechanical, photocopying, recording or otherwise, without the prior permission of the publishers.

This book is sold subject to the condition that it shall not, by way of trade or otherwise, be lent, re-sold, hired out or otherwise circulated without the publisher's prior consent in any form of binding or cover other than that in which it is published and without a similar condition including this condition being imposed on the subsequent purchaser.

See the Black Library on the Internet at
www.blacklibrary.com

Find out more about Games Workshop
and the world of Warhammer at
www.games-workshop.com

THIS IS A DARK age, a bloody age, an age of daemons and of sorcery. It is an age of battle and death, and of the world's ending. Amidst all of the fire, flame and fury it is a time, too, of mighty heroes, of bold deeds and great courage.

AT THE HEART of the Old World sprawls the Empire, the largest and most powerful of the human realms. Known for its engineers, sorcerers, traders and soldiers, it is a land of great mountains, mighty rivers, dark forests and vast cities. And from his throne in Altdorf reigns the Emperor Karl-Franz, sacred descendent of the founder of these lands, Sigmar, and wielder of his magical warhammer.

BUT THESE ARE far from civilised times. Across the length and breadth of the Old World, from the knightly palaces of Bretonnia to ice-bound Kislev in the far north, come rumblings of war. In the towering World's Edge Mountains, the orc tribes are gathering for another assault. Bandits and renegades harry the wild southern lands of the Border Princes. There are rumours of rat-things, the skaven, emerging from the sewers and swamps across the land. And from the northern wildernesses there is the ever-present threat of Chaos, of daemons and beastmen corrupted by the foul powers of the Dark Gods.

As the time of battle draws ever near,
the Empire needs heroes
like never before.

CONTENTS

Glow *by Simon Spurrier*	9
Head Hunting *by Robin D. Laws*	33
The Small Ones *by C. L. Werner*	55
Three Knights *by Graham McNeill*	93
The Road to Damnation *by Brian Craig*	115
Mark of the Beast *by Jonathan Green*	169
Jahama's Lesson *by Matt Farrer*	193
A Good Thief *by Simon Jowett*	219
What Price Vengeance *by C. L. Werner*	249

GLOW
by Simon Spurrier

AUTUMN IN TALABHEIM. Cloying mists rose languidly from sultry canals, stretching ethereal tentacles along streets and alleyways. Wind-banked leaves withered in papery necrosis and fat crows sulked on wet roof tiles, cawing their hungry indignation at the carrion-free cobbles below.

Autumn too, in the slums. A time of shadows and footsteps, rippling puddles and the *drip-drip-drip* of ill-weathering architecture. A time for unwelcome visitors.

'Should I knock first, captain?'

'Mm. Knock hard, Kubler, if you know what I mean.'

Wood splintered with a resounding *crack*! Echoes from the blow flitted through the mist; startled crows launched from the rooftops. Dark figures tumbled through a shattered doorway.

'Up! Up! Get up, scum, or by Sigmar's wrath I'll–'

'That'll do, Holst. Our host seems positively catatonic... No sense in dirtying one's boot.'

The invaders' ebony forms seemed almost unreal beside the tattered rags of the building's solitary inhabitant who lay curled uncomfortably on the sagging floorboards, snoring in intoxication. The tallest of the black cloaks, crowned with an austere wide-brimmed hat, squatted athletically to examine the sleeper's mud-smeared countenance.

'Drunk, captain?' another dark figure enquired.

'No... No, I should say not.' The gloved hand rummaged briefly within the shapeless rags and reappeared grasping a crude earthen pillbox. A deft movement and the box opened to reveal a cluster of green tablets within.

'Hmm.'

'Sleep analeptics, captain? My brother swears by 'em.'

'Perhaps. Apothecary nonsense, of course.' The tall man stood, examining the room. He sighed. 'Turn it over, gentlemen. Anything untoward, I want to know about it.'

Several of the black cloaks stooped to their task, unsettling mould-strewn furniture. Presently another of them turned to the hat wearer with a frown. 'No sign of a Taint, sir.'

'Mm.'

'The heretic yesterday practically screamed the address.'

'I daresay the flames of righteousness will do that to a fellow, Kubler... I don't detect any Dark Powers at work here – just the usual city filth.'

The slumbering form fidgeted with a guttural groan.

'Captain...' one of the cloaks quavered uncertainly, 'h-his eyes!'

The men drew back from the rag-strewn bundle that was suddenly thrashing with comatose fury. Sure enough, its eyes flickered and wept, an unnatural glow ebbing forth from the lidded irises. Bubble-flecked spittle collected in the corner of the man's mouth.

'Hmm,' said the hat-wearer. 'I stand corrected...'

The sleeper lurched to its feet, rough skin bulging and twisting, frothing in a paroxysm of internal anguish. The jaw creaked open in a ghoulish smile; serrated canines erupted from writhing gums like impatient saplings, human tongue curling in extended, prehensile distortion. And finally the eyes opened fully, a ghastly light smouldering from their scorched sockets. It fixed its vision on the pillbox and reached out a shaking hand.

'G-give... gg...'

The thing made an attempt to articulate, pulsating arteries disturbing its swollen larynx, unfamiliar tongue unable to form sounds easily. 'Give back... guh. Glow. W-want.'

But the transformation was incomplete, and already the skin was tightening cadaverously, already the ridges of brow and cheek were ossifying further, bony protrusions appearing with tectonic certainty. With a wet snap of elasticity the skin burst from within, peeling back in reptilian folds, splitting like overripe fruit.

'Want it nowwwww!' it gurgled, insane eyes rolling. 'Give Glow or I ki–'

Boom.

The beast's twisted features dissolved beneath a grisly haze of airborne ichor. A pistol crack shuddered angrily about the room, acrid smoke oozing lazily from the hat-wearer's outstretched weapon.

Time stagnated for one long moment, then returned explosively as the chaos-thing tumbled downward, ruptured skull spewing viscous fluids that splattered and coagulated across the dismal room. It thrashed and jerked.

'In the name of Sigmar I purge thee,' the hat-wearer intoned, fingers tracing the Holy Hammer in the air.

Reality coalesced. The other Templars, aghast at the suddenness of the creature's transformation – and grateful for their leader's adroit response – breathed again. The corpse twitched then lay still, a sludge of liquefying tissues dribbling from its wound.

A deep silence settled.

One of the witch hunters mumbled, nodding at the pillbox in the hat-wearer's hand. 'Y-you... uh... you still think they're sleep analeptics, captain?'

'On balance, Heinrich... I suspect not.'

Witch Hunter Captain Richt Karver squinted at the tablets in his gloved hand and pursed his thin dry lips in thought.

Rain unfurled across the city like the casting of a vast net. All across the poor quarter it pelted, shivering along the merchant streets, dousing what scant illumination had been created against the drawing in of the night. The mist dissipated beneath the barrage, puddles formed and ran together, rusted gutters overflowed, cascading their moss striated contents earthwards.

The crows ruffled themselves in self pity, beady eyes scowling at the indignity of such bedraggelment.

Even the mighty Temple of Sigmar, implacable in its domination of the brooding skyline, was forced to surrender a fraction of its haughty demeanour to the torrents that assailed its towers and buttresses. And yet deep, deep below that drenched edifice existed a world of stale air and flickering light that no rain could penetrate.

Richt Karver cast off his hat with characteristic aplomb and sank into a straight-backed chair. His well polished pistols were hung casually across the furniture's wooden frame, intricately decorated powder bag dumped unceremoniously upon a tabletop and his ebony walking cane – never absent from his side – was twiddled distractedly in his perfectly manicured hands.

'Bring it in,' he muttered after a moment's thought.

The other hunters entered in a gaggle, dragging with them an awkward bundle. Wrapped in stained sheets and bound with what few scraps of crude twine could be plundered from the slum, the oily fluids of the mutant's body were already blemishing the linen.

Karver rubbed his chin for a moment, a habitual motion that his acolytes had learned to recognise as a sign of deep thought, and took pains not to interrupt. 'Let's see what we can find out about this... what did he call it?... ah – "Glow", shall we? Holst, you cover the slums. Loose talk in taverns, that sort of thing. You have the face for it, old boy. Lars, the estates in the west quarter. I daresay these things are equally at home amongst affluence as effluence. Heinrich, see if the militia's heard anything – oh, and take Spielmunn with you, he might learn something. And

Kubler, you can find me that little worm Vassek. If anyone knows anything about this it'll be him, you can count on it.'

'Keep your eyes and ears open, gentlemen. Whatever this stuff is, I want it out of my city. Report back when you have something.'

Kubler nodded and hefted the corpse. 'What about this, captain?'

'Little point in burning it in the platz, I suppose.' Karver grumbled. 'Nobody wants to see the righteous flames of purity claiming a heretic who's already dead... Not that we could start a fire in this weather anyway.'

Spielmunn, the youngest of Karver's Templars, piped up nervously. 'A spike at the city gates, captain? Haven't been many heads up there recently.'

'Mm,' Karver grunted. 'The displaying of a head does rather require that the body has one. Our unfortunate subject is somewhat lacking in that respect.'

Kubler resettled the shape on his wide shoulder. 'The Heap then?'

Karver nodded slowly. 'Yes. Yes, I suppose so. Seal it carefully, mind you. I think in the spring we'll have to see about clearing it out down there. There must be – what – a dozen bodies festering away, now?'

Holst frowned, 'Don't see why we don't just dump 'em in the river.'

'Because, you idiot,' Kubler snapped, 'we'd end up with a water supply full of tainted flesh. Would you drink it?'

'Can't be worse than Bretonnian ale,' muttered Karver, dispelling the emerging confrontation with a forced chuckle – but sparing a private nod for Kubler. The boy would go far, Sigmar willing. 'No, I'm afraid that onto the Heap it goes. Recite the Prayer to Banish Uncleanliness at the doorway and we'll be fine. The best kind of dead heretic, gentlemen, is one that stays dead.'

Kubler nodded and dragged the corpse to the head of a convoluted stairway, beginning the descent that would terminate eventually at the vault where the remains of mutants lay putrefying. Karver listened to the gradually fading percussion of the body being manhandled indelicately until the gloomy depths swallowed the sounds of their passage. The other Templars, perhaps sensing Karver's disquiet, dispersed upon their respective errands in silence.

Karver paused for a moment, then passed through the heavy doorway to his workrooms.

THE CREATURE HISSED at his approach, filth-matted hackles rising in a peristaltic wave, short forelimbs bunching with muscular alertness. Its single remaining eye rolled uncontrollably, spastic orbits reflecting the imbalance of the beast's mind.

It leapt with a shriek, slavering jaw gnashing, prominent incisors wielded for action.

Only at the very pinnacle of its lunge, when its jaws seemed inescapable, did the iron chain about its neck jarringly arrest its movement. It lurched to a halt with a pitiable squeal and dropped to the floor, gagging and retching in frustration.

Richt Karver hadn't flinched once.

'And how are we today, my little horror?' he cooed to the vast rat, which scrabbled its dagger claws on the stones as if imagining its captor's hated face within its grasp. 'Not too hungry, I trust?'

He'd captured the creature the previous year – an expedition into the unexplored tunnels beneath the city had resulted in an encounter with the repugnant skaven. The nest had been purified, Sigmar be praised, but not before two of his Templars had been carried, screaming, into the nightmare labyrinths below. He'd purged twenty ratmen in Sigmar's name that day, and captured several more for 'interrogatory purposes'. They'd died, shrieking and cursing, manacled to the walls of the very room that their insane pet now guarded. It gave Karver some small measure of satisfaction to imagine their revolting bodies, defeated and mutilated, rotting away in the Pit far below his feet.

The witch hunter strolled into the ruddy half-light of his workroom, humming under his breath. He sagged into a chair, fingers rapping on the armrest. Presently, he turned to the rat that lurked silent in the shadows by the doorway. It watched him – as always – with a malevolence compounded by cyclopic asymmetry, its single beady eye glistening. The Templar made a decision.

'Dinnertime, vermin...' he trilled, reaching into a pocket for the confiscated pills.

TIME PASSED. WINTER reached Talabheim, an icy breath squalling from the north.

The few remaining leaves, already revealing their spidery skeletons to the onset of seasonal decomposition, quit their lofty positions and were borne away by the chill. Puddles crystallised treacherously, the ruts and grooves of cobbled streets no escape from the gathering ice.

The crows shivered and puffed themselves up, miniature spheres of black indignation. They eyed each other distrustfully, aware that a starving scavenger was just as ample a meal to its brethren as any other.

In his workroom, Richt Karver warmed his hands over a well stoked fire and ignored the stream of groans and curses from the nearby wall. The whole place reeked of overcooked meat.

'...rrnnn... nnneeed medicine... glow glow glow...'

Karver sighed, pushing the branding iron back into the fire to re-heat. 'Spare me, Villhelm. I have a headache.'

'...glow glow glow...'

Muttering, Karver turned to the figure manacled on the wall. A burn mark already blistering across his chest, the man's contorted form writhed uselessly: swollen muscles spasmed, tumourous growths pock marking his flaccid skin. A dappled blemish coiled colourfully across his shoulders and chest, just one of the gaudy signs of his Taint.

Unmoved by such alterations, Karver leaned in close. His expression – far from the contempt one might expect –

instead mirrored the countenance of a disappointed parent whose child has been disobedient once too often.

'Now come on, Villhelm. You know I don't enjoy doing this to you. Just tell me where you bought those tablets, eh? It's for your own good.'

Such was the sincerity in the Templar's voice, such was the element of concern, that the mutant paused incredulously in its cursing to stare at its tormentor.

At which point Karver placed the firebrand against the creature's flesh and pushed. Smoke rose, flesh curled and charred, and the chaos-thing screamed and screamed and screamed. The pain overcame it rapidly; its jagged head sagged forwards in a dead faint.

Karver returned to warming his hands, grumbling quietly to himself: 'A bit of bloody quiet, Sigmar be praised.'

It didn't last.

Within moments there came a thumping at the door and a muffled voice beyond. In the gloom of its alcove, the chained rat slunk to its feet.

'It's me, captain – Kubler!' came the call. 'I've found Vassek! I've got him right here!'

'Very good, Kubler. Send him in, please.'

The door inched open slightly and unseen hands propelled a small, greasy man into the room. Karver mentally placed himself in the sweaty individual's unenviable position as first reactions were gauged.

The smell hit him first; assailing his nostrils, the miasmic stench of charred skin made him gag and spin on his axis, whereupon he was faced with the limp mutant, hanging scarred and smoking from the wall. Attempting to repress the biliousness that rose in his belly at such horrors, the man twisted away and sunk to his knees...

Coming face-to-face with hissing, snarling death.

The rat had changed. Since the autumn, when its diet of Glow had begun in earnest, a dreadful transformation had occurred. Now its one eye glowed with an internal fire, no longer rotating with insane misdirection. Its lank fur hung loose and decaying in infected strips, the corpulent flesh beneath glistening in decay. Weird ridges and sores pockmarked its ulcerous skin and its long tail had sprouted a forest of spines in between the weeping lesions that punctuated its length.

It opened its cadaverous mouth and shrieked in the small man's face, straining against its chain.

Vassek DuWurz emptied his bladder and blubbed like a baby.

Karver hauled him upright and dumped him bodily in an empty chair, where he sat quivering with eyes like dinner plates.

'Hello, Vassek.' The witch hunter smiled, his friendliness utterly incongruous with his dismal surroundings. 'We've been looking for you for quite a while. How have you been?'

'D-damn you, Karver! What's all this about?'

'I just wanted a chat, really. It's so rare that I get to see old friends, these days.'

'Don't start that! Don't start that "friendly" rubbish! I've been down here before, remember? I know the routine!'

'Oh, come now! I'm too much maligned, old fellow. Surely a conversation isn't too much to ask?'

'Too bloody right, it is! Unless you've a reason for keeping me here, I'm leaving right no–'

There was a cold, metallic hiss. Vassek, suddenly frozen, examined the glittering blade that had materialised at his throat. Karver's ebony cane lay hollow on the floor, its secret contents exposed.

Karver's voice was quiet, but no less friendly. 'How's that... what did you call it last time we met.... that "birthmark", Vassek? Covers half of your back, I seem to recall. Most unusual.'

'J-juhst a... hkkk... buhhthmrrk!...' the porcine man choked.

'Mm. Maybe. It's funny, you know, how many of my, ah, "patients" say that.'

'Whtt d'y wnnt?' Vassek burbled.

'Ah, that's more like it...' Karver smiled happily, releasing the pressure on the quivering man's throat. 'That's much more like it.' He settled back into his chair, delicately fingering the blade. 'I know you like to... how can I put this?... "listen" to things, Vassek. Now that we're friends again, how about you tell me everything you've heard about this.'

In his hand lay a pile of Glow tablets. Over by the door, the rat-creature began howling and hissing, straining at its chain. Vassek shuddered in horror.

Karver winked conspiratorially, 'Oh, don't worry about him – he just wants his supper. Between you and me... I think he has an addiction problem.'

KARVER STRODE FROM his workshop purposefully, buckling on his pistol belt. The other Templars jerked to informal attention.

'We have an address!' he exclaimed, donning his hat with a theatrical flourish. 'Come, come, gentlemen! We have holy work to attend to!'

'Sir! You trust the word of that maggot?' Kubler grunted, nodding towards Vassek, who was edging his way past the snarling rat-beast.

'Oh, there's no harm in him. He keeps poor company – but he remembers things and seems, now at least, keen to keep me informed. I dare say he's more use to us at large, as it were. Let's reacquaint him with the outside world, shall we? We have far greater fish to fry! Besides... I think Herr DuWurtz knows only too well what'll happen if we can't trust him.'

In a tangle of billowing black fabric, dragging Vassek DuWurtz behind them, the Templars passed from the catacombs like a malignant storm cloud.

DESPITE THE FILTH and the poverty, the people of the city's working quarter walked with heads held high. Possessed of a ridiculous quality of embittered imperiousness, their indomitable pride glimmered in their demeanour. We may be poor, their expressions contrived to announce, but by Sigmar we'll not show it!

This was a world of starched clothing, of saving up for a rainy day, of keeping up appearances, and of fierce, unconditional piety.

In the lowliest of places does Sigmar find his champions, thought Karver with a sad smile, passing along the cobbled streets. He hated entering this district – not out of any great distaste at wallowing in conditions below his station, but rather for the reactions that such visits earned. These people weren't witches or heretics, they'd sooner kill themselves than invite the Taint into their disinfected little world – and yet still they lowered their gaze, still they clutched at their hammer pendants silently, still they sweated in cold, guilty fear at the passing of a witch hunter.

These people didn't deserve to be afraid of him, Karver knew, and he hated himself because they were.

The Templars passed into a side alley, leaving the wide eyes and the whispers behind. They gathered around their leader, who nodded towards an ill fitting door at the alley's end. 'There.'

'They have such fear of us,' Spielmunn whispered, peering back over his shoulder at the thronged street, where already rumours would be breeding and accusations cast.

Karver smiled sadly. 'Mm. You'll quickly learn that fear can be a powerful weapon, my boy. Then again, it can also be a great hindrance. An innocent man has no need to fear the Templar's knock upon his door, but he fears it anyway... What, then, is the hunter's other greatest weapon?'

Spielmunn's smooth features contorted in uncertainty, cheeks already blushing red. Holst sniggered and hefted his pistol, caressing its barrel.

'Put it away, Holst,' Karver muttered, one exquisite eyebrow arching. 'A man who reveres such clumsy things has no right to them in the first place. No, Spielmunn? Any ideas, the rest of you?' The teacher-to-class routine came easily, and Karver, in his secret soul, basked in his acolytes' reverence.

'Kubler? I daresay you know the answer.'

Kubler thought for a moment, then nodded. 'A templar's greatest weapon, captain – besides fear – is an open and smiling face.'

'Correct. The man who is reticent when threatened may well be loose tongued in the face of simple friendliness.'

Holst spat in disappointment. He preferred his gun.

Karver went on with a flourish, 'The Templar must be, above all else, a gentleman! He walks with poise, is polite at all times and strives to bring light – be it the light of purity, of truth, or of refinement – into places of darkness.' The Templars, in varying degrees of understanding and accordance, nodded.

'Look at Kubler, if you will.' Karver grinned, reinforcing his point and embarrassing his star pupil in one deft move. 'He's clean – well, mostly clean – his boots are well shined; why, his face is so open one could walk through it and exit the other side!' The Templars sniggered, enjoying the street theatre. Karver could sense their anxiety at the forthcoming raid and knew exactly how to coax their relaxation. 'See here,' he said, pointing at Kubler's ebony-swathed chest, 'he even wears a brooch in his buttonhole! Quite the Bretonnian court dandy today, isn't he?' Karver's gloved hand darted out and snatched up the bauble, inspecting its bright emerald surface. 'A most exquisite jewel too, I'd say. Where did you find it?'

Kubler squirmed, clearly uncomfortable with the attention, 'I... ah... I bought it, sir. Got it from a peddler up in the platz. All different sorts, she had.'

'Well next time you visit your peddler, my boy, you be sure to purchase enough of these trinkets for all of us, you hear?' Smiling benignly, Karver handed the token back to Kubler. 'And now gentlemen,' he nodded, twiddling his cane, 'if we've all quite finished admiring this blushing model of Talabheim sophistication, what do you say to a little exercise?'

An element of apprehension returned to the group, but Karver could sense their calm professionalism. It was an altogether better prepared squad that turned as one towards the door at the foot of the alleyway.

Karver drew his pistol.

Boom.

A flare of light and a vicious geyser of smoke.

The decayed timber erupted in a maelstrom of whirligig splinters and corroded bolts. Messily bisected planks slumped mournfully in their dislocated bindings, the dismal light from beyond the ruined door spilling into the gloom within.

Dust motes capered in a flurry of concentric eddies as a gloved hand, ebony sleeve avoiding snags on the jagged wood, hastily reached into the room and tore back the deadbolt holding the door closed.

In the darkness someone – or something – moaned dolefully.

The door lurched open, hinges squealing in protest at the twisted wreckage of their load. Cold air rushed into the room like the surge of a broken dam, and again something within keened to itself.

Richt Karver strode into the gloom, pistol in one hand and swordstick in the other. Squinting into the shadows, he braced himself for whatever evils might be lurking within – tensing the muscles of his leading leg, preparing for combat.

Nothing moved.

Accosting him from the cloying darkness was an exotic melange of herbaceous aromas, strange and tantalising scents, carrying with them visions of distant lands and wondrous flora. Holst spat, shattering the silence. 'Stinks like a privy in here.'

Rows of bundled herbs hung drying from the ceiling, an inverted forest of miasmic odours. The chamber – poorly lit as it was – looked for all the world like an apothecary's workroom.

Again came that low murmuring moan, and instantly the Templars tensed, weapons levelled, eyes desperate to penetrate the darkness. Karver cocked his head, owl like, attempting to locate the source of the sound. Gradually, like a sundial's shadow point, he pivoted around the room, coming to rest with all his formidable attention focused upon a wide, flat topped cabinet.

'Show yourself,' he growled.

Something moved fractionally in the gloom, curled under the low top of the table. It began to draw itself upright, tattered rags hanging around it like dead flesh, a distinct metallic chiming accompanying its stiff movements. A heavy hood shadowed the thing's face, a few errant strands of blond hair hanging loose.

Quivering, it groaned horrendously. The Templars spread out across the room, blocking the twitching creature's escape.

'Come out in the open,' Karver grunted. His command was ignored. Frowning, Karver slowly lifted a leg and stamped down hard on the floor. The resulting thump had the desired effect.

Like a startled rodent, the hooded head snapped around to regard the black clad apparition blotting the light from the door. 'Muaa...' it gurgled.

'Come out into the open,' Karver repeated, gesturing with his pistol. 'Understand?'

Again, a moment of recognition – perhaps even a half nod – and Karver felt sure that he could hear the thing breathing, sharp, panicked intakes of breath.

And then, with lightning rapidity the figure twisted to reach for something hidden from view beyond the cabinet. Karver felt a hot rush of adrenaline pulsing through him, senses surging ahead so that glacial slowness seemed to clutch at his movement.

'Weapon!' yelled Kubler in astonishment. All around the room the Templars were reacting, eyes wide – slow, too slow!

Karver didn't even think. His finger tightened fractionally on the trigger and the world went white.

Only when the echoes of the pistol crack had fled from the chamber did time appear to flow freely again. Dry fragments of cloth capered briefly in the air, blown clear of the shambling figure by the force of the impact. The creature itself had folded away neatly: no whalespout of chaotic fluids followed its descent, no mad thrashing of limbs and gnashing of teeth. It collapsed with a strangled yelp, the clink of metal upon metal, and lay still.

Karver inched forwards cautiously. Finally convinced of its death, he stooped to peel back the ragged hood. He instantly understood his horrible mistake.

It was a girl – perhaps twelve – and she had been insane.

Her eyes betrayed her madness; not the volatile, explosive insanity of the Taint, but rather a wide eyed horror, an expression of untold hardships barely endured that had robbed her of her sanity and replaced it instead with an endless fount of terror.

Her lips were open in a silent moan, betraying the mutilated flesh within.

'Her tongue's gone,' he murmured quietly.

And then, with morbid curiosity, Karver allowed his eyes to travel along her outstretched arm to whatever she had been twisting to grab in her final moments of life. Cold reflected light on metal glimmered beneath the rags festooning her frailty, and, horrified, Karver understood his error.

A thick manacle was set around her bruised and bloody leg – a manacle securing her, by means of an iron chain, to an immovable stanchion cemented into the floor. She had been reaching to expose the chain – a mute explanation for her inability to comply with Karver's order to move out into the open.

This girl had been a prisoner. A voiceless innocent, mutilated and abused by her captor, held here for who knew what reason. And Karver had killed her. He felt sick.

'Get out,' he hissed, teeth grinding together.

'But s-sir,' Lars stammered, 'you couldn't have kno–'

'Get out.'

Exchanging glances, the witch hunters withdrew, leaving their leader with the grim trophy of his error. Hunched over, he closed his eyes and hissed a litany, forcing down the bile in his stomach.

'...Sigmar forgive me... Sigmar forgive...'

Silence sank gradually into the room. Slowly, precariously, struggling all the way, Karver allowed a sense of resolution into his mind. Witch hunters were predators. They weeded out the weak and the defective and felt no remorse at the execution of their holy work: holy work, Karver knew, that could brook no inner guilt. No guilt! A commandment that shrieked through his skull and demanded acquiescence.

He'd killed before. Oh, countless times. So many bodies gathered at his feet, so much blood spilled on his polished boots, so many vengeful bullets fired in Sigmar's name. How many fires had he lit in the communal platz? How often had he heard screams of denial turn to anguished, meaningless shrieks of admission in the stygian dungeons of the Temple?

Compared to such overwhelming carnage – he lied smoothly to himself – what did the accidental extinguishing of one tiny, innocent life truly matter?

Something happened to Richt Karver's eyes, then. A minor change, to be sure, but a change nonetheless. Some fractional glimmer within his steely blue irises dimmed, hardened with new crystalline certainty, and when finally he straightened, it was a minutely different man who arose.

The echoes of an ancient text rattled in his mind – a fragment of dialogue, written by some long dead bard, recited in the dry lecture halls of his youth.

I am in blood stepped in so far, that should I wade no more, returning were as tedious as to go o'er.

All trace of sentiment removed from his bearing, Karver peered about the room intently, halting his gaze upon the surface of the cabinet. Piled carefully upon a stone tile, surrounded by pestles, mortars and racks of spherical tablet moulds, lay a pyramid of finely formed powder. Well within reach of the girl, the Templar noted, bending to scrutinise the substance.

Nodding with newfound certainty, he glanced about for a container. Nothing seemed available – the room was as spartan as it was gloomy – and Karver grimly peeled off one leather glove and, careful not to touch it with his bare skin, scooped a portion of the powder inside.

Then he ran his gaze around the chamber quickly, dipped his hat in farewell as if to cauterise whatever wounds festered therein, and stalked out into the cold city.

THE VENERABLE HERR Ehlbeck – Graduate of the College of Magic in Altdorf; Initiate of the Jade Order; specialist in herbology; much sought after purveyor of balms and healing potions – tugged on his beard and fumed quietly to himself.

Around him graceful glass vessels bubbled and boiled, fluted beakers frothed in multicoloured agitation and thick smoke was shooed through an open window by a gaggle of fan wielding assistants. A flickering flame turned from yellow to green, coating the sorcerer's eyeglasses in an oily frosting and causing him to sneeze explosively. He felt positively light headed – which only added to his growing sense of indignation – and murmured a quick incantation to ward off the intoxicating effects of the vapour.

The cheek of the man! Storming in without so much as a by your leave! Stomping around, knocking over equipment, making demands as if he were the Supreme Patriarch himself! And then, having delivered a justifiable refusal to cooperate with this madman, to have been threatened by him; a Practitioner of the Secret Arts, threatened like some low-born thug in a tavern! It was too much to bear!

Ehlbeck forced down an image of that decorative pistol being thrust forcibly into his rosy swollen nose and told himself that the only reason he'd relented was to get the odious man out of his workshop.

Contenting himself with considering what cutting responses he could have supplied had he wanted to, Herr

Ehlbeck bent down to his task with all the false bravado of a man who knows he's been defeated but refuses to acknowledge it.

In an adjoining chamber, Richt Karver slumped on an uncomfortable bench and attempted to relax. As defender of Sigmar's Inviolable Faith the very notion of relying upon the suspect talents of a wizard seemed questionable. He'd balked when the idea first came to him, but after a forced inspection of the facilities he was as convinced as he could be that no Taint existed here. The ease with which the frail old man had been terrorised had been most gratifying.

The various other citizens sitting patiently in Ehlbeck's waiting room had long since dispersed, with as much nonchalance as they could muster. The presence of a witch hunter was more than enough to dissuade them from pursuing the incantations and healing potions they sought. In such small ways was the sanctity of Sigmar preserved.

Eventually Herr Ehlbeck came bustling from his workroom, green robes flowing behind him and snagging clumsily on the assorted twigs and branches festooning the room. He came to rest before Karver – who regarded him dispassionately – muttering excitedly to himself and fiddling with his eyeglasses, all former hostility forgotten.

Finally, twitching like a rodent and tapping his fingers together, he turned to Karver. 'Where... ah... where did you find this powder?'

'I don't think that's really any of your concern,' Karver responded. 'Is it Glow?'

'Oh – Oh yes. No doubt about that. I mean, I compared the powder with the tablet form exhaustively. Exhaustively, I say. Same results, all the way through, bam-bam-bam, just like that. Definitely the same stuff. Whatever it is.'

'And what is it?'

'Ha. Quite.' The wizard scratched his nose distractedly, 'I was rather hoping you might tell me, actually...'

'Listen.' Karver grunted, annoyed. 'This... substance, whatever it is, am I correct in assuming it to be some physical form of–'

'Magic?' The wizard breathed, eyes twinkling behind his glasses. 'Oh, absolutely. Mixed with all sorts of herbs, of course, but essentially it's... well... I'd go so far as to say that if Chaos–' and here Ehlbeck noted Karver's narrowing eyes and added quickly: 'thrice damned that it is, of course – if Chaos were distilled into material form, then this would be the result.'

Karver glared acerbically at Ehlbeck for a moment. Men had died burning in the platz for showing less of an interest in the Taint than this skinny little bundle of nerves before him, but it occurred to him that a tame wizard was perhaps a valuable resource... 'Mm.' he grunted eventually. 'Chaos dust, eh?'

'Haha – quite,' the wizard laughed nervously. Karver treated him to a glance of unequivocal disdain.

'Very well.' The Templar muttered to himself, 'I suppose I must discover where the wretched stuff comes from...' He nodded perfunctorily at the wizard – the only thanks the venerable man would get – and turned to leave.

'There... ah... there is one other thing...' Ehlbeck said, polishing his glasses distractedly. 'Whilst I was conducting the tests, I... well, that is to say... I was a touch... distracted by the tenseness of the situation and, ah, to start with I tested the wrong thing...'

Karver's eyes narrowed. 'Go on.'

'Well, you see... Y-you asked me to test the powder in the glove against the Glow tablet, yes? Um, whereas, t-to start with, I tested the specks I found on the glove. I-I realised my mistake quickly and repeated the test on the stuff inside – w-which are the results I've been giving you – but, you see, it wouldn't have made any difference anyway because the stuff on the outside was exactly the same, chemically speaking.' The old man was twittering now, embarrassed at his mistake.

'The powder on the glove?' Karver repeated, perplexed.

'Y-yes. Just a few green fragments. Quite pretty, in fact, haha. Um.'

'I didn't touch any powder. I scooped it up inside.'

The wizard shrugged wretchedly, desperate to get the terrible man away from his premises.

'Mm,' Karver grunted again, and then stepped through the door into the street.

As he walked, he thought. And as he thought, a revelation began to form.

A DARK PLACE. A place where no light ever penetrated, save the sputtering, tortured firebrand placed carefully in a corner. Its limited luminescence served merely to stress the depths of those dark corners it failed to penetrate.

Something moved. Someone hunkered close down to the uneven floor of the chamber, hefting energetically at something corpulent and foul, from which the last vestiges of lank fur hung in sparse clumps, putrification peeling back its skin in thick gelatinous folds. The man, unconcerned by the dead fluids oozing from the vile corpse, thrust a hand deep into the folds of cloth wrapping that covered it. His fingers found a worn leather pouch and pushed deep inside, snatching up a handful of green jewels from within, glowing with hypnotic beauty in the gloom.

The man giggled, emptying the warpstone into his pocket. He'd lost one Glow producing slave, certainly – but there were others. Other terrified children, snatched away in the night, forced to labour in hidden workrooms, terrified into compliance. Production would continue. The money would flow. The Taint would spread.

The man walked upon a floor of rotting corpses, collecting his malevolent harvest.

The fire flickered in its alcove.

And then some subtle sense, not wholly natural, made him jerk upright. Something was comi–

The door ripped open like a thunderclap and something reared in the doorway, billowing like a storm cloud, ebony undulations coursing through its extremities. Despite himself, the man in the dark moaned in fear.

Boom.

The lead shot hit him in the chest and sent him crashing to the floor. He gasped in pain and began to shudder, uncontrollable spasms rippling across him. Gradually the pain subsided.

Blood coursing down his chin, the man smiled revoltingly.

'How did... gkkh... you know?'

The storm cloud stepped into the room, robes settling, and the light threw Richt Karver's features into gruesome relief. 'The brooch,' he growled. 'I took it from your buttonhole, remember? It left a trace.' The hunter held a leather glove between pinched fingers, flinging it disgustedly to the floor.

'Hehehekkgh...' Kubler chuckled, coughing more blood. 'A nice touch, I thought. Hidden in plain sight, like you always say.'

'Arrogance, Kubler.' Karver grimaced, shaking his head, smoking gun still levelled. 'I can't begin to tell you how disappointed I am.'

'Spare me the lecture, old man... kkh... let's not pretend I'm one of your bloody smiling gentlemen any more, eh? You made me drag those skaven bodies down here last year. Remember that? It would've been such a waste to leave them rotting without checking for... heh... valuables.'

'It's twisted your mind, Kubler. That stuff. It's made you insane.'

'Hekkh. Is it so wrong to make people feel... hnnk... happy? You should try some Glow, old man. You never know – heh – you might like it.'

Kubler coughed, more blood dribbling thickly from his lips.

'You're dying,' Karver intoned, pistol unwavering. His calm exterior required an effort to control. Inside, he howled at the betrayal, raging against his own weakness for not noting the Taint seducing his disciple sooner.

'Isn't... nn.... isn't everyone?' Kubler chuckled, lugubrious breaths growing more and more strained. He pushed a quivering hand into his pocket and extracted a pillbox, clicking it open. 'Such... hkk... such pain... w-wouldn't begrudge me my medicine, would you?'

'Kubler...' Karver warned, too late. The dying Templar, fluids draining across the Heap like a warm slick of oil, upended the box. Green spheres rattled lightly against his teeth. He swallowed heavily, gagged on air for a moment, then slowly, clumsily, sagged. His face froze, lips drawn back, blood oozing across slick teeth.

And then he moved. Fast. Twisting impossibly, rising vertically in one long, terrifying lurch. Karver's hand blossomed with pain and the pistol skittered away into the dark, echoing.

Kubler stood back and leered. With a creak his jaw ratcheted forwards, his brow sloped back in a graceful arc and his eyes snapped open to reveal a yellow iridescence below. His neck distended noisily, the vertebrae concealed below rising like swelling bruises in a series of fluted spines. His fingers flexed then began to writhe, curling back onto themselves like a fistful of pink, fleshy maggots.

'Sssssssssss...' the thing hissed through a rapturous smile. Its features were slipping away to be replaced by new and deadlier forms, its skin writhed, its patterning moulded. Kubler's body shivered and jerked, a humanoid representation of amorphous, viscous, and constant change.

It moved with the effortlessness and speed of lightning, and before his eyes registered any attack Karver was bleeding, thrown back against the embrasure of the thick doorway with a long gash across his arm.

'U-unclean thing!' the Templar stammered, aware of the blood oozing across his clothing. 'Sigmar damn you!'

The creature smiled, and when it spoke it was still Kubler's voice – soft and undemonstrative – that left its wormlike lips. 'Oh, please, captain. I think we can dispense with that... Don't feel too bad – it's a poor novice that fails to excel his master.'

The sword was flung away, clattering against the wall in a flurry of sparks and shattering metal. Karver, consciousness beginning to ebb with the flow of blood from his wound, barely even saw the creature move.

And then it advanced, a reptile sneer the only constant upon a face of writhing parts. Karver reached out to the wall for support, feeling blindly into the darkness of the stairwell outside the catacomb, every movement agony.

'Mmmm...' Kubler trilled. 'Stagger away, old man. Where are your lessons now? Eh? Where's your faith? It's about time you realised, "captain"... You've nothing left to teach me.'

Karver's quivering hand fell upon a cold metal hook, cemented into the wall of the stairwell. His questing fingers – growing weaker with every heartbeat – encountered a thick loop of chain, planted over the stanchion. He grinned feebly. 'I've a lesson or two left in me yet, my boy.'

Then he pulled the chain, straining against its placement, off the hook.

The rat barrelled from the shadows of the stairs like a comet. Trailing its own useless guts, discarding flesh and flaccid fur in its magnificent arc, gimlet eyes glowing in anticipated victory. Kubler never knew what hit him.

Starving and insane, chained there in the shadows moments ago, it had been treated to a perfect view of the writhing figure within the chamber consuming enough of what it wanted, what it must have, to last it a lifetime.

It struck Kubler at waist height and dug.

Kubler's amorphous form reacted admirably – seething around the invading monstrosity, spreading forth tentacles to seal up the crater into which the beast had vanished, rocking as it attempted to ascertain what damage might have been caused.

Kubler's grin froze, and then vanished. His eyes bulged. His fingers flexed.

He sank to his knees and doubled up, a slow but enormous retch building in his throat.

Richt Karver, weak and barely conscious, opened his eyes and forced himself to watch.

Like volcanic forces long dormant reaching a critical pressure deep within the living earth, Kubler erupted.

His chest cavity detonated, mutant flesh flexing and palpitating in the air, shattered bone scything outwards, fabric and reptile skin hanging limpid in stunned clouds around the fragmenting form.

Kubler – or, rather, the thing that had once been him – gave a final disbelieving giggle and died.

The rat-creature tumbled from the organic wreckage, body hopelessly shredded, sliced and dissolved by whatever internal attacks Kubler's doomed innards had attempted in its final moments. The fierce light of triumph burnt in its one remaining eye, and – unaware that its viscera were long gone, it gobbled hungrily upon the semi-digested Glow that Kubler had swallowed.

'Dinner time, vermin...' Karver whispered. Then he snatched up the firebrand and tossed it onto the Heap.

Months' old bodies, mummified by the dryness of their subterranean tomb, ignited like paper. The rat screamed as it died, and Karver watched it until it stopped, too charred to draw breath any longer.

He sat on the stairs of the Heap until the others arrived in a gaggle of excitement and confusion. He sat until the fire burnt itself out, leaving nothing but soot and ash. He sat until every last trace of Kubler – his greatest novice, his greatest enemy – had been obliterated.

He was trying to decide how he felt. Somehow he understood that deep, personal grief would be the natural response to this episode. Further, he felt that – until recently – his reaction to this situation would have been just that.

But not any more. Too much had changed.

Sitting there on the step, surrounded by devastation and death, Richt Karver – Witch Hunter Captain of Talabheim City – was fighting the urge to grin in triumph.

Outside, in the bitter air, the crows ruffled their feathers against the cold and waited for spring.

HEAD HUNTING
An Angelika Fleischer story
by Robin D. Laws

THE SOUND OF screaming crows drew Angelika Fleischer onward and downward, deeper into the ravine. Where the birds fed, she would find her quarry. She threaded her way through mossy trees, their trunks riddled with rot. Pounding rain had given way to half-hearted drizzle; on dying branches, the water formed itself into heavy drops. Angelika, thin of limb, high of cheekbone, sharp of jaw, reached up to push a grasping branch out of her way. Her hair was a damp, dark mop. She wore black leggings under a soiled grey tunic, which was too long for her, and tied at her waist so its tails became a skirt. High boots, worn but sound, hugged her calves. An old brown jacket clung to her back, its scarred and cracking leather stretched tightly between her shoulders' sharp blades.

The branch she'd moved snapped back to smack the forehead of the young man struggling to follow her. Franziskus cried out in protest, wiping rainwater from his fine and noble features. He wore the sad vestiges of a junior officer's uniform from rustic Stirland's armies but his once-fine coat had lost much of its golden threading; several roughly-patched holes, as well as the dark remnants of well-scrubbed bloodstains, marred its green fabric. His face was handsome but still slightly round and boyish, and his blondish hair, once impeccably groomed, now dangled long and lank from his large, aristocratic head. The rain had plastered a curling ringlet to the middle of his brow.

Angelika paid no heed to the young man's voiceless protests. She'd warned him not to come. He'd make a nuisance of himself when she got where she was going. He was, at least, smart enough not to complain aloud to her. She ducked under another damp branch, sending it flying incidentally backwards. This time she heard no wet thwack of branch making impact; Franziskus was getting better at dodging.

The cawing grew louder. Behind her, Franziskus slipped, his boot twisting and sliding along rain-slicked grass. Angelika twisted his way, raising a finger to her lips. Franziskus grabbed onto a young tree's thin trunk and arrested his slide.

'Stay here,' she hissed, turning from him and advancing into a skiff of fog. Carrion birds, perched on logs and branches, eyed her jealously.

No need for fear, she thought; the spoils I seek are not the same as yours. She looked down and there was a dead hand under her foot. She lifted it to survey the entire, mud-spattered body. It was human. Its face stared up, still shocked at what had befallen it. She could tell from the ragtag uniform that the man had been a mercenary. Angelika crouched down to make sure that the only movements around her were those of the crows. Satisfied, she rose to examine the other bodies. They, too, appeared to be dogs of war. This boded well. Though their clothing was shabby, sell-swords such as these were the likeliest to have gold hidden in their boots or gems glinting in their teeth.

She beckoned Franziskus to join her, though she didn't care if he took her up on the invitation. He'd made his self-righteous aversion to her livelihood more than evident in the weeks since she'd rescued him, lying like one of these corpses, on a field of battle a little further down the throat of the Blackfire Pass. He stepped fastidiously toward her. Abruptly, a crow rose from a dark, wet rock and flapped its wings at the young man's face.

'Sigmar's eyes!' he cried, taking in vain the name of his Imperial deity. He defended himself from the bird with windmilling arms. Having made its territorial point, the crow circled in victory and lighted again deeper into the stand of corpses. It found an eyeball that the others had missed, plucked it from its socket, and let it roll down the length of its beak and into its gullet.

Franziskus stood beside Angelika and shuddered. He shook his head with the theatrical sorrow of a novice priest. 'Nothing good will come of this consort with the dead.'

'I beg to differ,' Angelika replied, squatting over the first body she'd found. She pulled on the dead man's right boot. It held to its master's leg with a miser's tightness. Angelika strained. She fell into the mud, on her behind. Boot in hand, she looked up at Franziskus, to catch him mocking her. But no, he was too great a stick in the mud for that; his expression was merely pained. She scrabbled up onto her haunches and over to the foot she'd exposed. Sure enough, there was booty there: a large ring, made of incised silver, with a trio of red gems mounted in it encircled the mercenary's big toe. There was still plenty of play between ring and toe; it must have originally been forged for some thick-fingered dwarf she decided. It slipped easily off and into the leather pouch that hung on Angelika's bony hip. 'We've found ourselves a rich haul today. You can see who these men are.'

'Mercenaries. The pass crawls with them. They fight to honour neither god nor empire, but merely to line their greasy purses.'

'Which, for our purposes, is a fine and splendid thing. Men who fight for money often die with money on them.'

She felt the first corpse for a purse, coming up with a muck-encrusted pouch. She withdrew from it four Imperial schillings, and a few coins from far-off Tilea. 'We'll dine well on the final fruits of this one's martial labours.'

Franziskus wrinkled his finely-sculpted nose. 'I won't sup on dead man's coin.'

'Suit yourself,' Angelika said, 'but I don't notice you doing anything much to secure your next meal. Perhaps this is something you should give some thought to. Forgive me for noticing, but your purse grows steadily leaner.'

'I am here not to profit from the slain, but to discharge my debt to you, by extending you my protection.'

Scanning the ground for the next body, she laughed a breathy laugh. 'Would I be rid of you if I told you that your protection is a hindrance, and that your debt exists only in your imaginings? If you mean to make me regret the foolish lapse that made me rescue you from those orcs, I can tell you: you've succeeded.'

He stiffened to attention, as if observed by some distant field marshal. 'I appreciate your effort to release me, but honour demands that I do my duty.'

They heard a noise, and silenced themselves. Though it reverberated across the rocky ravine and through the darkened trees, the nature of the low thwocking sound was immediately recognizable to both of them: it was that of a heavy blade hitting flesh and cracking into bone. An axe, perhaps.

Angelika held a hand out to Franziskus, urging quiet. She pointed ahead, showing him she meant to investigate. Franziskus opened his mouth to argue, but the chill in her expression stopped his words. Shamefaced, he regarded his boots. A dead man's crow-pecked face returned his gaze, eyeless and reproving. Franziskus shifted his position and looked up into the sky instead, where grey clouds mixed with white ones.

Angelika was gone for what seemed like an age. Then Franziskus heard whistling. He knew the tune: it was a children's skipping song. He crouched behind a boulder. The whistling grew louder until eventually a tall figure stepped through the fog. It was a man, wearing monkish robes, frayed at the hem. He swung an axe in his right hand and held the end of a large sack, slung over his shoulder, in his left. A long woollen scarf hung around his neck, like a stole. Crude shoes protected his feet. His head was long and narrow: its slightly pointed crown was naked, but a fringe of wiry chestnut hair ran around the back and covered his ears. Creases of veiny skin lay under beady, deep-set eyes. His upper lip protruded at the middle, driven outwards by a pair of oversized incisors. His demeanour was one of bland contentedness.

Unusually for a person one might meet on the slopes of the Blackfire Pass, his face was washed clean, though his hands were spattered in muck, and dark droplets of blood speckled the lower portions of his robe. The head of his axe was bloody, too.

Franziskus sank lower behind the rock, drawing his short blade from its scabbard. He would wait until the man approached, then leap up and, surprising him, get his dagger in past the reach of his axe. If the man was fool enough to resist, Franziskus would–

He heard rushing footsteps and then Angelika's voice: 'Drop the axe!' she said. Franziskus rose, to see Angelika standing behind the man, her knife at his back. The man's eyes rolled up to the heavens, and he wobbled; for a moment, Franziskus thought the fellow might faint. He held both of his arms out to his side and dropped both the weapon and the sack. It fell heavily into the mud.

'If you want to make yourself useful,' Angelika called out to Franziskus, 'then come here and help me keep watch on this person.'

Franziskus moved toward them, picking his fastidious way through the corpses. As a unit, the crows retreated to the surrounding trees. They cawed their annoyance at him for disturbing their meal.

Finally the man spoke, sputtering out his words: 'I am not a person who requires to be kept watch upon. Rather, it seems to me that it is you who are the brigands and bandits here.'

'Identify yourself,' she said, jabbing him in the back. She used her thumb, but he jumped as if she'd stabbed him.

'It is Victor Schreber, the noted doctor of philosophy, whom you impertinently manhandle.'

Angelika looked to Franziskus. 'Have you heard of this man?'

Franziskus shrugged. 'My tutors pressed many books of philosophy into my arms, but your name is unknown to me, sir.'

'You are an individual of quality, then? In that case, I demand immediate release.' Schreber stepped toward Franziskus, but Angelika stopped him short, grabbing him by the collar of his robe. He made an undignified choking noise.

'Unfortunately for you, the individual of quality isn't the one with the blade at your back. What's in the bag?'

Schreber pointed his long nose to the clouds and sniffed. 'I merely collect samples for my scientific researches. Though of surpassing value to me, its contents are worthless to the non-specialist. See for yourself.'

'Franziskus...' Angelika ordered, indicating the bag with a shake of her head. Reluctantly, he made his way to it. He opened it up and immediately closed it, his face flushing with green revulsion. He gasped for air.

'What is it?' she asked him.

'Heads,' he said, eyes watering. 'Human heads.'

'Of course, human!' Schreber exclaimed. 'Why, the science of phrenology is at present in its barest infancy. We have barely scratched the surface of human physiognomy. It is much too early to even begin to contemplate the skulls of dwarfs, elves or halflings! Strict rigours must be observed!'

He had turned toward her, without permission, but Angelika shrugged. He was well on the way to proving himself a harmless fool. 'So you collect these heads as scientific specimens?' she clarified.

'Indeed, indeed!'

'A ghastly and unwholesome practice!' Franziskus said, fists tight.

Schreber's eyes swept from Angelika to Franziskus and back again, as if evaluating which of his captors posed the greater threat. 'But good sir, it is vitally important to understand the mysteries of the human organism. By studying anatomy, we can one day perhaps cure deadly maladies. Or, by good breeding, wipe out idiocy and the propensity toward mutation.'

Franziskus crossed his arms. 'It is obscene and against the ways of Sigmar.'

'I don't know, Franziskus,' Angelika said. 'It strikes me as no more useless than any other form of scholarship.'

'More than that!' Schreber said, stooping down to pick up the bag. He rustled around in it, pulling out a bloodied globe of flesh. Franziskus recoiled; Angelika succeeded in maintaining her composure. 'This, for example,' Schreber continued, 'represents a find of the rarest order. It is a Type Nine, with a notably prominent mandibular archway. Do you know what that means?'

'Humour us with an explanation.'

'A person of this type is known to be of a poetic bent, devoted more to feeling than to reason, and with tendencies towards pessimism and melancholy.'

'Especially now.'

The scholar ignored her jape. He reached into the bag for another sample. She held her palm out to stop him.

'You needn't trouble yourself any further, Dr. Schreber. The subtleties of your lecture are no doubt lost on us.'

He stammered, directing his attention once more to the sharp point of Angelika's dagger. 'Ah, then. You will see, then, that I offer neither threat to you, nor competition to your looting efforts. It is specimens I seek, not coins or baubles.'

Angelika looked meaningfully at his pouch, which was fat.

'Ah yes. It is true, though, that I have picked up the occasional item of value, which lay on the ground in plain sight, in order to fund my researches, which can be expensive.' His lips were flecked with spittle. 'Sometimes, you see, I have call to commission the collection of certain specimens which are known to me, but which require the – I see that I bore you, however. You wish me to hand over to you the contents of my purse, is that not it?' He handed it to her.

She threw it back at him. It hit him in the chest and bounced to the muck at his feet.

'What makes you think I'm some kind of common thief?' she demanded.

He gestured at the corpses all around them.

'Those aren't living victims, are they? I may take from those who no longer need their earthly goods, but I'm no back-alley robber!'

Franziskus chuckled but realized too late that she truly meant it, that this distinction was no joke to her. She narrowed her eyes and glared at him. He felt his face burning.

'Then I am free to go?' Schreber asked her, bowing experimentally to pick up the purse and the head bag.

'Leave the axe. I think I believe your words, but in these parts, trust can be a costly thing.'

'I quite understand,' said Schreber, bending low, exposing his teeth in a courtier's smile. He picked up his dropped items. He turned to go, then stopped. 'But wait,' he said. 'Now that I know you both not to be miscreants, but honest scavengers, a thought occurs.'

Angelika planted a foot on a large stone and crossed her arms. 'Let me guess. You're thinking of a specimen you'd like us to procure for you.'

Schreber bobbed his head up and down. 'Indeed, indeed. North of here, in the mouth of the pass, lies a village – a trading post, really – named Verldorf. Its people are redoubtable, surviving as they do in this terrible place without paying homage to elector count or border prince. Yet the anxieties of their precarious existence have clouded their judgment, so that they sometimes mistake friends for scoundrels.'

'You've been there, I take it, and secured a hostile welcome for yourself?'

Schreber's nods became slow and pensive. 'Aye. It was most distressing. They thought me some kind of ghoul.'

'A shocking error.'

This time the doctor's thick eyebrows twitched, as if on the verge of detecting irony. 'Indeed. I merely sought to relieve them of a burden, and at a generous price. Yet their hostility was such that I was forced to depart with haste, lest I submit myself to bodily harm.'

Franziskus put his hand on his dagger's hilt. 'You wished to loot their graveyard, for the heads of their relations?'

'No, no, not relatives – Potocki! Recently they caught and executed the dread and notorious murderer of that name, who for many years preyed upon the posts and fortresses hereabouts.'

Angelika had heard the name before; the locals associated it with a succession of crimes, from brigandage to child murder. No one person could have committed them all. 'You're sure it was Potocki?'

Schreber placed a thoughtful hand on the side of his face. 'To be truthful, no. But this is immaterial – I seek his head, not in vengeance for his misdeeds, but because he exhibits the most pronounced triple occipital ridge I have ever had the pleasure to lay eyes upon. I simply must add it to my collection. They have no further use for it, and I will pay you two hundred schillings if you bring it to my cottage, inside the walls of the Castello del Dimenticato.'

Angelika knew the Castello; it was a fortress town to the south, lorded over by one of the self-styled border princes.

'A tempting sum,' said Angelika, turning so she couldn't see Franziskus, who was pleadingly shaking his head. 'Why so high?'

The scholar tugged at his collar. 'As I said, the villagers are a surly lot and no doubt they will seek to thwart you. Potocki's corpse dangles in a cage, across from the village tavern. The best course is to sneak in at night, open the cage, and remove the head. Naturally this involves risk – hence the generosity of my offer.'

Franziskus took a haughty pace in his direction. 'We are not grave robbers!'

Angelika stopped him, the back of her hand against his chest. She asked Schreber: 'You can direct us to Verldorf?'

The philosopher led them over a rise, where he'd tied a mule to a spindly beech tree. It was laden with packs; he rummaged in one until he found a quill, an inkpot, and a scrap of parchment. He scratched out a clumsy map to Verldorf, with the Castello del Dimenticato marked on it for reference. Their destination appeared to lie about eight leagues to the north, meaning a day's travel through the valley, two days if they kept to the forested shelter of the ravine on either side. Then it would take another half-day to reach Schreber's place and lay hands on his gold.

'Anything else we need to know?' Angelika asked him.

'The salient facts have been well covered.'

She walked away, waving farewell in the stiff-armed manner of a countess. 'Then go home and prepare your schillings, doctor of philosophy.'

'But wait,' Schreber said, loping after them. He cradled something in his hands. Angelika stopped; he handed her an iron box, with a hinged lid. She opened it; it was lined with velvet.

'We deal with no ordinary cranium,' Schreber puffed, out of breath. 'Not like the common ones I gather here, which I bang together in my carrying sack. Potocki's skull has already been mistreated, and may be in fragile condition. Transport it in this, to ensure that it arrives intact. Be warned: a shattered skull earns you no pay.' He took the liberty of wagging a finger at Angelika, but halted himself in mid-gesture when he saw her reaction. He turned and proceeded quickly back to his mule, muttering inaudible goodbyes. They stood and watched as he clambered up on the mule and guided it down to the valley.

'We aren't even sure,' said Franziskus, pushing damp hair out of his face, 'that he'll reach the Castello alive.'

'Maybe not,' said Angelika, 'but he seems to know his way around. And for two hundred schillings, I'll risk the waste of a day or two.' She handed the iron box to him. Its heft surprised him; he nearly dropped it. 'You have room in your pack for this,' she said, 'don't you?'

Attitude stoic, he slipped his pack from his shoulders. 'And why such a cumbersome container?'

'You heard him: he wants the head in one piece.'

'Then why this?' He opened the box to show her: resting on its velvet lining was a key and a padlock.

VERLDORF SMELLED OF sheep dung and burning wood. The place consisted of cottages, a stable and a tavern. The buildings were made of mud-daub, with sagging, thatched roofs. Bleating livestock filled large corrals; animals warranted more space than people in this part of the world. A wooden palisade, its pointed timbers grey and deteriorating, served as the village's main defence. Its gate was flimsy and its gateman drunken.

In the event of a serious assault, the place would be pounded to matchsticks. The locals, it was clear, relied on the fact that the orc armies rarely got this far up into the pass. And when they did, Angelika surmised, they'd be too eager to smash through the Imperial borderlands to bother with this blemish of a settlement. The gateman hadn't even challenged them on their way in.

As the scholar had suggested, Potocki was not hard to find. A cage swung from a freshly built gibbet in the irregular expanse of muddy ground that played the role of village square. Inside, propped standing against the cage's bars, stood a mangled corpse. Its head lolled off to one side. Its lower leg was bent in two. The body's entire surface was blackened by fire. Angelika looked around, and, seeing no one, stepped closer to the cage. One of Potocki's hands was crushed to an unrecognisable pulp. His downturned face was frozen into a hostile grimace; lips, burned away, bared long and yellowy teeth.

Franziskus cleared his throat: a man had appeared on the porch of a shop across the way. From a rickety awning hung a painted sign, depicting a sheep's head and a flagon. This would be the tavern; the man wore an apron and a worried look, and had to be its proprietor. He had bushy eyebrows and a swaddle of fat around his chin, though the rest of him seemed lean enough. Angelika made her examination of Potocki less conspicuous.

'Welcome to our poor, benighted village,' the barkeep said. His voice was soft; his speech, halting. 'My name is Ralf. We offer only poor shelter, but this is, after all, the Blackfire Pass, and I hope you will find my bunks better than none.'

'Greetings, Ralf,' said Angelika. 'It is refreshing to find an innkeep who does not over-praise his amenities.'

The taverner's anxious demeanour did not lift. 'Travellers in this part of the world can be quick to seek violent remedy, so I have found it prudent to prepare my guests for disappointment. Please, step inside, and relieve yourself of the weight of your packs.'

Angelika and Franziskus clomped up onto Ralf's wooden porch, which creaked loudly under them. Angelika adopted her blandest posture and hiked a thumb back at the caged corpse. 'Your display there – the impression it creates is unwelcoming.'

Ralf beckoned them into the tavern's darkness. He spoke in a lowered tone. 'It is an accursed thing. Do not speak of it.'

Angelika remained in the doorway. She watched Ralf's eyes flutter nervously over her shoulder, to the gibbet. 'But, Ralf, it's hard to concentrate on anything else.'

He put his hand on her elbow and gently guided her inside. He slid shut a canvas curtain, erasing the cage from view. 'I do not speak colourfully. We are forced to labour under its curse, but if you pay it no mind, it can have no hold on you. I know it is difficult, with such a thing, but I urge you to dampen all curiosity, leave early tomorrow, and expunge it utterly from all your thoughts.' He clapped his hands together. 'We have no private rooms, I am afraid, just a small sleeping hall with cots. It is unsuitable to a person of the tender sex, madam, but there is no better choice.' He gestured to the room's few tables, only one of which was occupied, by a woman who lay snoring on it, head in hands. 'Tonight we have gravy soup, and ale.'

Later, as they finished the meagre meal Ralf served them, the tavern filled with locals, eager for the soup. Angelika eavesdropped but heard no mention of Potocki, just talk of sheep and troop movements. More Imperial forces were said to be venturing into the pass, to disperse the massing orcs down south. Franziskus's pallor deepened; he'd been part of that campaign, but had since made no effort to return to his superiors for reassignment. Angelika was tempted to tweak him on the subject, but couldn't summon up the required cruelty. With a turn of her head, she informed him that she was heading into the bunk room. They were tired from the trail, and a few hours of sleep would better prepare them for their robbery.

ANGELIKA'S EYES OPENED. She rose from her stinking cot. Franziskus was already sitting up on the edge of his. She peered into the long, dark room to see if any other guests had joined them. She stood and checked each bed; there was no one. The village was quiet. All they heard were croaking frogs. She crept out to the open archway that led back to the tavern room. A gaunt villager, lightly wheezing, slept in a sitting position, propped up near the exit. Angelika winced. She retreated into the bunk hall, motioning Franziskus over to a small window mounted about a yard off the floor. It was shuttered. Gently, she tested it. It wouldn't open. She peered through the crack between the shutters; they had been tied tightly shut, from the outside, by a cord of some kind.

'Hold both of them, so they don't rattle in the frame,' she told Franziskus, her mouth close to his ear. She drew her knife from her boot and sawed at the cord. It was tough and springy, like leather. Angelika heard a faint sound, of metal hitting metal, and stopped. 'There's something dangling from the cord.' She thought for a moment, shrugged, and started up again. 'When I nod my head, open both shutters, quick as you can. But keep hold of them, so they don't slam into the wall.'

She kept sawing; finally the cord snapped through. Franziskus opened the shutters and Angelika shot her hand out and caught the cord. She held it in her outstretched hand. Suspended from it were half a dozen pieces of scrap iron, tied on with short lengths of twine. Franziskus looked puzzled. She craned her head out of the window, pointing to the ground below. A sheet of tin, pounded flat, waited beneath. Franziskus nodded his comprehension: it was a makeshift alarm, intended to send a clattering noise echoing around the town if any of Ralf's guests chose to exit through the window.

'Making sure we don't sneak off without paying?' he asked her.

'We paid in advance,' she noted.

Angelika crawled headfirst through the window, eyes alert for additional traps. She hit the ground palms-first and rolled to a soft landing. She got to her feet, reached out for Franziskus, and helped him wiggle through. They stepped lightly across the muddy square to the gibbet. The wind had picked up, and hissed its cold way through Verldorf's thatched cottages.

Angelika put her hands behind her back and stood thinking of the best way to get the head out of the cage. A large padlock hung from the cage bottom, keeping its hinged door securely in place. She was no lockpick, so it would remain shut. But the bars of the cage were widely spaced: if she could get the head off the corpse's shoulders, she could then probably work it through the bars and be off with it. She inspected the gibbet, pulling on its central post to test it for give. Stony concrete had been poured around it; it was not a pretty job, but the gibbet would take her weight, which was nothing compared to that of the iron cage.

'Boost me up,' she told Franziskus. She handed him her blade. He got down on one knee for her, and she used him as her step-stool. She wrapped slim hands around the bars of the cage, right behind the body's head. The gibbet gave off a wooden groan as it swung on its chain and Franziskus steadied it with his shoulder. Hanging one-handed from the cage, Angelika reached out for her knife; Franziskus moved to place it in her palm.

Then Potocki's corpse jolted into action. It lunged at Angelika, clawing at her throat with its one intact hand. Franziskus dropped the dagger; he dove to the ground to recover it. Angelika let go of the cage, but the creature seized her jacket and yanked on it, sending her head pitching into the metal bars. She got her elbow between her face and the cage, cushioning the blow. With jagged fingernails, the undead beast raked at her arm. He tore open the fabric of her jacket. He seized it; she struggled free. The cage swung violently, clipping a kneeling Franziskus on the back and sending him sprawling into the mud. Angelika hung from the cage like a marionette; she got her free arm out of its jacket sleeve, and now worked to wrench herself out of the one the monster held. She jerked and twisted as the creature snapped at her with its teeth. Finally she dropped free, crashing to the ground.

She sat there, looking up at the beast, grateful at least that it wasn't screaming. Maybe she could get her jacket away from it and sneak back into the bunk room, so none of the villagers would know. Or perhaps they should just clear out, and forget their two hundred schillings. One thing was certain: if she did get the head, her price was going up. Schreber should have warned her. She could have been killed. The creature opened its mouth wide, and Angelika saw why it couldn't alert the locals – they'd cut its tongue out.

It hurled itself against the bars, rattling the chain that held cage to gibbet. The sound echoed. Villagers poured from their huts, armed with crooks and hayforks. Franziskus leapt up, but Angelika stayed seated on the cold dirt. The Verldorfers pointed the tines of their forks at her throat and chest, or stood ready to bash her with their crooks. They surrounded Franziskus, too; he held his hands out beside him, far from the scabbards of his dagger and rapier.

Angelika shook her head. She blinked. 'Where am I? What has happened?' She hoped Franziskus was clever enough to follow suit.

A gaunt woman with dusky skin thrust the blunt end of a pole at her; she might be considered beautiful, were she equipped with a few more teeth. 'You know where you are, harlot! It is Verldorf, and you do the Dark Gods' work!'

Angelika rubbed her forehead. 'Verldorf – why, yes, I begin to remember...' The villagers looked to one another for guidance; a few stepped back. Angelika smelled guilty consciences. Even the toothless woman moved a pace to the rear. 'I slept, in there!' Angelika cried, pointing at the open shutters, which provided punctuation by banging in the wind. 'Then I thought I dreamed–' She regarded Potocki, who was still, but had shifted position. 'Yes, this thing, this beast, it is alive! It beckoned to me!'

Without warning, she sprang up, seizing Ralf the innkeeper by the tunic and sticking her blade to his throat. 'Why did you not warn me of this foul thing's sorcery? It stole into my dreams and lured me nearly to my death!' The others sidled back, making a wide ring around her. Off to the side, she noted that Franziskus stood with eyes shut and head down.

'I beg pardon, madam!' Ralf cried, struggling to kneel, though her tight hold on his shirt brought him short. He clasped his hands in supplication. 'We should have warned you, it is true! Forgive us – we are afraid to speak its name, or even think of it. It haunts us; we are cursed!'

'Tell me of this thing, and I'll decide if forgiveness is warranted.'

'For decades it has stalked us! We cannot kill it! First, it sent minions: cripples, gypsies, madmen! They waylaid our shepherds, put hands on our children. One by one, we slew them. Then the beast itself came. It could leap over a house or break a man's neck with its empty hands! It ambushed our headmen; it set us against one another. Sometimes it even stole our blood, to drink!'

A few of the onlookers joined together to underscore Ralf's words with a rising wail of lamentation; it prickled the fine hairs on the back of Angelika's neck. She released him.

Ralf shook his head. 'Many times he came, and many times we fought him. We pierced him with sharpened stakes, and he dug himself up from the grave we made him. We burned his flesh, yet still he walked. We drowned him. We broke his bones. He casts spells on us if we lapse in diligence, and fail to keep his tongue trimmed down. The only safe place for him is in that cage. And now we see that, even with his tongue out, he can still creep into the minds of unprepared strangers. Please absolve us of our ignorant crime of omission!'

Franziskus caught her gaze; he was cocking an eyebrow at her.

'Very well,' Angelika said. 'In the face of such implacable evil, your error is understandable. What was it that first brought Potocki's wrath on you?'

'Our grandfathers could tell you, perhaps. Some say one of our ancestors offended him. Others claim he came here in search of an ancient text, abandoned here by a mysterious traveller. Which we did not have, because one of us had foolishly burned it, as kindling.' He stooped to pick up a stone, which he pitched at the cage; it went between the bars but missed Potocki. Through the creature's jagged teeth, a hiss escaped.

In an exaggerated gesture, Angelika craned her neck to gaze into the lightless sky. 'We would leave immediately, but night travel is too dangerous. We'll retire to your bunks for now, though I doubt either of us will sleep.'

'Shall we stay up and stand guard?'

'Please don't; though I've accepted your apology, my anger toward you has not entirely subsided.'

Ralf nodded. He spotted the metal alarm for the shutter doors, lying near the cage. While seeming to look the other way, Angelika watched him pick it up.

Angelika and Franziskus headed into the bunk room again; Ralf and his fellow villagers formed an escort. Once inside, she stationed herself beside the window. She listened as Ralf, back outside the building, replaced the shutter's alarm device.

'You've made me an accomplice in dark deception,' Franziskus said.

'That's the sort of thing that happens when you decide to follow a person like me.'

She sat and waited until snores reverberated between the hovels of Verldorf. She reached out to cut the alarm cord. Again, Franziskus opened the shutters and she caught the bits of metal. She slid out of the window. He followed. She crept to the cage. From her pouch, she withdrew a large key, which she'd liberated from Ralf's pocket as she'd held him at knifepoint. She slid it into the lock at the bottom of Potocki's cage, turned it and swung the cage door open. She stood her ground and bared her teeth. Potocki leapt out at her. She sidestepped. Potocki hit the dirt where she'd been, landing on his face. She dove onto his back. Franziskus jumped to seize his kicking legs. She grabbed the corpse's matted hair and pushed his head into the mud. He bucked powerfully.

Angelika took her knife and placed it on the back of Potocki's neck. She leapt up, then fell, so that her entire weight pressed on the blade. She opened a gash in Potocki's neck that went clear to the bone and kept hacking; there was no blood, and the dried flesh came off in chunks. Franziskus fell back as Potocki kicked him in the chest. The head came off. Verldorfers streamed forth from their doorways. Angelika seized the head by the hair and jumped to her feet. The villagers roared angrily. Franziskus gasped as Potocki's legs scissored around his chest. Angelika grabbed his collar and hauled him upright.

A rock, thrown by the toothless woman, sailed past her head. She and Franziskus turned and ran. Potocki pushed himself up and sent his headless form charging at the loudest sound, the howling of the people of Verldorf. They shrieked. They pounded the undead creature with their clubs. Angelika did not look back.

The head, held by its hair, snapped at her. 'The box!' she said. Franziskus wrestled it out of his pack. He held it open as Angelika dropped Potocki's head into it. He slammed it shut. The head rattled and bumped inside it. 'A good thing the box is well-lined,' she said.

SKULLS LINED THE walls of Schreber's cottage. Some sat on shelves, but most were simply stacked in precariously vertical piles. The skulls of halflings, or children, which were the smallest, formed the top rows of each stack. The philosopher's axe leaned casually against the pile nearest the doorway.

Schreber leaned against a short cabinet of polished teak; he had positioned himself so that it shielded him from Angelika and Franziskus, who faced him. Angelika held the iron box.

Angelika sniffed the air, taking in the delicious aroma of roasting meat. 'Preparing a feast of welcome for us, Schreber?'

'Ah,' he said, looking furtively at the open entranceway to his back room, 'that smell is in fact my cooker, where I remove the flesh from my fresher finds.'

'Ah,' said Angelika. 'Then that leaves us only with the exchange of our merchandise for your two hundred schillings.'

Schreber reached into a drawer. 'What kind of miscreant do you take me for? To do business with common grave robbers?' He pulled out a pistol.

'I was afraid you might say that.' Angelika had removed the lock from the iron box. She opened the lid. The head sprang out of the box, at Schreber. His eyes widened. Jaws snapping, the head sailed in a vigorous arc across the room. Its teeth clamped onto the front of Schreber's throat. Bright red blood spattered chalky skulls. Schreber fell, disappearing behind the cabinet. His screams ceased, replaced by the squishing of flesh gnawed by ancient teeth.

Angelika and Franziskus ran to the front doorway. They stepped outside the cottage, slamming the heavy wooden door shut, bracing it with their backs. The flailing noises they heard from inside continued for a surprisingly long time.

Schreber's home stood in a neglected corner of the walled town. The few passers-by they could see were some distance away, in a busier square, where marketers sold gruel and skewered beef from canvas stalls. There was no one to ask them why they leaned so desperately on the scholar's front door.

The thrashing sounds subsided.

'We can't risk its getting out and harming the townspeople,' Franziskus said.

'We can't take the chance of abandoning a possible two hundred schillings!' Angelika replied.

They nodded and burst back through the door. Once inside, Franziskus seized the handle of Schreber's axe. They couldn't see Potocki. They could see the legs and torso of Schreber's lifeless body.

'Here, Potocki...' Angelika said. 'Here, boy...'

The head came bowling out from behind a set of shelves. It barrelled at her feet, across a worn carpet. She leapt aside and ducked down, rolling the rug up over the skull. She kept at it, until the thing was trapped and unable to move. With the axe handle, Franziskus pounded the lump in the carpet. He kept hitting at it until the rug seemed to trap nothing more than a shapeless mush. Gingerly, Angelika unrolled it. Indeed, Franziskus had thumped Potocki's skull to the consistency of porridge. The paste was grey, with a few flecks of pink rippled through it. Franziskus spotted a few pieces of still-solid bone in it. He smacked those as well, until they were as gluey as the rest.

'Enough,' said Angelika. She stepped over to the cabinet, bracing herself against it to roll Schreber's body out of the way, giving her the clearance she needed to open its lower drawers. She started with the top and rifled through it. From the last drawer, she withdrew a purse. It was the one he'd flaunted back at the ravine. She opened it and turned it upside down. Rocks poured out. 'The occasional item of value, my foot,' she said. She gave his remains a dispirited kick. 'I suspect it'll be of little use, but we should search the rest of the place.'

Angelika pawed through all the drawers she could find. She checked under Schreber's bed and inside his mattress, leaving his sleeping quarters strewn with stuffing. She cleared his shelves, opening each of his books to see if it had been hollowed out. Franziskus sorted through the philosopher's cups and bowls, but she thought his inspection less than thorough and went through them herself. She opened the lid of Schreber's cookpot, and grimaced. She even looked inside some of the skulls.

She took the pistol and put it in her belt. 'This is the only portable thing of value here.'

Franziskus stood, hands on knees, peering down at the glob of paste that had been Potocki's head. 'Look at this,' he said.

She looked. She could see nothing.

'See? It has moved. It has travelled several inches, toward the doorway, in just the time you've been searching.'

Angelika nodded. She had to agree; the crushed skull had inched ahead.

'Where does it think it's going?' Franziskus asked.

She straightened, got her bearings, and performed a quick calculation. 'Verldorf,' Angelika Fleischer said. 'It intends to reunite with the rest of him. And, my guess is it will – in about a hundred and twenty-five years.'

She stepped over it and left the cottage, doing nothing further to impede its progress.

THE SMALL ONES
by C. L. Werner

THE SOUND OF squealing laughter echoed across the northernmost of Eugen Duhring's wheat fields. The wide patch of barren ground had been left fallow this season to allow the soil to replenish and revivify itself. Duhring was known as a miserly and mean-spirited man, hateful and bitter about his station in life. Some in the village of Marburg called the wheat farmer 'the Badger' because of his fierceness regarding trespassers on his property. Had Duhring heard the laughter and seen the small shapes scampering across his field, he would have set his brace of dogs on them. If the farmer happened to see who one of the shapes was, the children could have expected a swift and physical reprimand courtesy of a switch broken from one of the nearby trees.

Keren laughed even as she gasped for breath and danced away from the outstretched arms of her pursuer. She was a young girl, long locks of golden hair dancing in the bright sunlight, her white blouse and black dress offsetting the rich colour of her arms and face. The girl's face was pretty, her button nose placed above a pair of pouting lips that were well-versed in the art of forestalling a scolding by means of a simple downward tremble. Her eyes had a slightly mischievous cast to them, the faintest arching of her brow that hinted at a cunning mind. She carried herself with an air of pride, and it would have been apparent to any observer that she considered herself better than her companions, a sense of station more befitting a great lady of some Bretonnian house than the daughter of Marburg's miller.

Still, perhaps the girl was not to blame for her superior attitude. Her father, Bernd Mueller, considered himself something of a petty noble, the closest thing the village of Marburg had to an actual burgomeister. The prosperous miller was banker, landlord and, some would confess in confidence, robber baron to the farmers who made their living in the vicinity of Marburg.

His was the only mill for many leagues in any direction, and Mueller made certain that his monopoly paid well. True, a farmer could take his wheat to some other village, perhaps Fallberg to the north or Giehsehoff to the east, but the expense and time to do so would cost the farmer more than it would to swallow his pride and pay Mueller's extortionate rates.

Mueller openly mocked his patrons, treating them as little better than indentured servants. It was small wonder then that the girl should hold herself as superior to the children of her father's customers and deal with them in a manner befitting her eminent position.

Keren laughed again as Paul lunged for her and danced away from his clumsy attempt to catch her. Paul was a tall, gangly boy, his face still bearing the moon-shaped depressions from the pox that had struck Marburg many years ago. He swore one of the colourful curses he often overheard in his father's tavern and turned to again try and catch his quarry. A safe distance away from the hunter, Therese blushed when she heard the words leaving her playmate's mouth. Beside her, the brawny figure of Kurt remained wary, lest the hunter turn his stumbling steps in his direction.

Keren started to dart away from Paul's clutching hands once more, when suddenly a bright flash of pain tore at the back of her head. A hand slapped the small of her back and Paul's figure pranced away from the girl in triumph.

'Ha, now you have to try and catch us,' the boy laughed as he sauntered toward the advancing Therese and Kurt. Keren dropped to her knees and stroked her long golden locks.

'You pulled my hair, you stupid toad!' the girl snarled in her most indignant tone.

'I caught you,' corrected the boy, noting with some concern the sullen look that had crawled across Kurt's face.

Keren rose from the ground, glaring at Paul, venom in her eyes. 'Doesn't your family teach you any kind of manners? Just because you look like a monster doesn't mean you have to act like one.' The words left the girl's mouth like daggers, her target visibly wilting at the assault.

'Show your betters some respect,' Kurt said in a low, menacing voice as he pushed Paul with a meaty hand. Kurt often helped his brothers in their profession as foresters and his size was quite beyond his years. He was entirely devoted to Keren, and many of the village children had received a beating at his hands when offence or her own malicious spite made Keren call upon the devotion of her brawny protector.

'But I caught her,' protested Paul, retreating from Kurt's glowering form. Therese came to her brother's aid.

'Try and catch us!' she cried, racing away into the woods that bordered the wheat field. Paul took that as an excuse to run away from Kurt and the threat of a short and one-sided fight. Kurt cast a confused look at Keren before deciding that he should hide as well or risk being tagged himself. Devoted or not, the young woodsman had no desire to bear the stigma of playing the hunter, even for Keren's sake. In the matter of a few seconds, Keren was left standing alone in the barren field.

The girl let a few moments pass, trying to compose herself rather than actually intending to give her friends time to conceal themselves. It was humiliating for her to be the hunter. When she had proposed this game, she had never thought that she would ever have the shame of being the searcher. Indeed, if everyone had not already run off, Keren would have haughtily declared that the game was stupid and that they play something else. Now she would have to show these farmers' brats that she was much better at playing the hunter than any of them.

Keren entered the shadowy stand of trees and tried to pierce the dark bushes and bracken with her youthful gaze. She listened carefully for any aberrant sound that her quarry might make in seeking to elude her. Only the chirping of a few birds and the frightened scrambling of a startled squirrel rewarded her efforts. She continued to walk along the narrow game trail, her annoyance rising with every step. How dare these peasants force her down to their level? It was enough that she deigned to play with them at all, why should she endure this indignity? The girl loathed the role of hunter, playing alone, struggling through the bushes whilst having to endure the taunting elusiveness of the others.

It was not for the daughter of Bernd Mueller to have to chase for friends, she thought, as if she really wanted to find a rabble of dirty peasants anyway. Keren had almost made up her mind to leave the others to their stupid play and go home when she heard the rustle of dead leaves behind a patch of bushes a few yards away. A crafty smile crept upon Keren's face as she stalked toward the noise. She had found them much faster than Paul had and she would not be reduced to chasing them out into Duhring's wheat field either.

Slowly, with as much silence as she could manage, the girl made her way to the bushes. With a yell of victory, she jumped around the closest of them. Abruptly, her yell became a shriek as the girl realised what she had found.

It was not one of her friends lying behind the bush; indeed, it was no such creature as Keren had ever seen in her short, isolated life. It looked like a little man, certainly not more than five feet tall had it been standing. Its overall shape was that of a man but where human features should have rested there was the porcine countenance of a farmyard swine, its brutish flesh covered in a soft golden down, almost like the fur of a duckling. The creature was wearing a dark robe and Keren could see that one of its legs was twisted beneath the black fabric at an unnatural angle. As she watched, pale blue eyes stared at her from the swinish head with an almost human look of alarm.

Keren was still staring into those pale orbs when Kurt ran to her side, alarmed by the girl's scream. When he saw the strange creature lying almost at Keren's feet, he halted abruptly, his mind seized by fear. The two still stood there, frozen to the spot, when Paul and his sister joined them. Therese let out a shriek when she saw the beast, the sound seeming to jar the other children out of their paralysed fright. They all ran away from the bestial form, far enough to be out of its reach should it decide to lunge at them. The children were silent, not one daring to speak, though one and all peered through the bush, to make certain that the strange beast was truly there.

Keren caught a hint of the creature's gold fur and looked away in disgust, the memory of the creature in its entirety refreshing itself in her mind. She regarded the other children, noting the faces of her playmates as she did so. They all bore expressions of horror tinged with childish fascination, yet none had the courage to take the lead. Keren forced her own face to curl into a haughty and disdainful sneer, adopting the expression she had seen the elder Mueller adopt on many occasions when addressing some cowed villager. She was not afraid, not like these farm whelps. She would show them what true superiority was.

Keren pushed Kurt toward the bush. The boy resisted her efforts, scrambling back to his original position. The girl glared at the brawny youth. 'Don't tell me you're afraid of a dying pig,' the girl scolded in her most imperious and high-handed tone. Kurt's face reddened and the boy stomped toward the bush, determined to redeem himself. Keren followed the boy, at what she judged to be a safe enough distance. A glare brought Paul and Therese hurrying to be at her side. By degrees, the timid gang advanced upon the bush. At last all four children stood over the twisted, brutish shape once again.

Kurt bent down and picked up a large stick. Timidly, the boy poked the tip of his improvised weapon into the creature's side. A human-sounding groan emerged from the porcine snout.

'Is it a monster?' asked Kurt, his voice trembling.

Keren looked intently at the gruesome, bestial thing. It was hideous, certainly, but as she looked into its gentle, pleading, strangely human eyes, the girl was not so very certain that it was actually dangerous. It was very obviously hurt and weak. She knew, if she wished, she could have it crushed as a beetle. The other children gawped, fearfully, and Keren knew that they were unconsciously waiting for her judgement.

'That's stupid,' she declared, 'monsters are big and fierce. This poor little thing doesn't look like it could scare anybody.' She chose to ignore the sudden shock she had experienced when she had stumbled upon the creature. The others were afraid of it, and that made it all the more important that she showed them that she was not.

'Goblins aren't big,' Paul protested, 'and they're monsters.'

Keren scoffed at the tavern boy's argument. 'Stupid, everybody knows goblins are just baby orcs. That is why they're little.' Keren returned her attention to the little creature, fascination overcoming her lingering horror. The little creature moved one of its delicate, long-fingered hands feebly as she watched it.

'I am going to go get my father,' Paul decided, pulling on his sister's hand. Keren turned on the boy with her most venomous glare.

'Paul Keppler, if you do that I will hate you!' Keren screamed as the boy started to pull his sister away. Paul looked at the girl with an apprehensive gaze. Keren decided to press the attack. 'If you go telling about this, you won't be playing with me or any of my friends ever again!'

The threat was a dire one for any of the children of Marburg. Keren Mueller was the most popular child in the village; her whims of friendship and dislike decided the hierarchy among the children. Those she did not like, like the young bell-ringer at Marburg's Sigmarite chapel, were virtual pariahs, teased and tormented by all the other children at every opportunity. With his scarred features, Paul was already the object of her ridicule; only his sister's close relationship to Keren kept him from being an object of complete scorn. Paul looked at his sister for a moment and then released her hand. Keren's bullying threat had been enough to cow the boy.

'What are you going to do with it?' Paul asked as he returned his gaze to the swine-headed creature.

'He's hurt, maybe sick,' the girl declared. 'If we help him get better, maybe he'll get us presents.' She was now certain that the creature was a bewitched prince and surely a prince would be able to give her gifts if she helped him recover.

'But where will we take him?' Paul asked, hoping yet to foil Keren's plans with reason. There was something horrible about the creature; he could not understand why Keren was not frightened of it. 'What will we do with it? We can't very well take it home; mother would never let that thing sleep in the house!'

Keren thought about the problem for a moment before the light of an idea gleamed in her eyes. 'I know a place!' she declared. The girl swatted Kurt's stomach with one of her dainty hands, rousing the boy from his embarrassed silence. 'Help Paul pick the prince up and follow me,' the girl commanded.

As the boys grabbed his arms and legs, a smile split the porcine features of the sorcerer Thyssen Krotzigk. None of the children noticed that smile, nor its malevolent twisting at the corners of his mouth.

KEREN LET ANOTHER distinctly un-ladylike oath escape her lips as the underbrush grabbed at her dress and scratched at her legs for the umpteenth time. She had not figured on the disused path to the old mill being in such a sorry state. Had she known that getting there would be such a chore, she would never have suggested the ruin. The girl looked over at the two boys, struggling to keep the creature's body high enough to escape the clutching brambles. Their legs were even more scratched and bruised than her own.

An impish smile graced Keren's face as she saw the boys enduring their discomfort simply because she had told them to. Keren looked away from the gasping, sweating pair and looked again at the crumbling wooden structure which was their destination. Once, it had been the business place of Ludwig Troost, the man who had dared to try and end her father's monopoly. Herr Mueller had begun a campaign of sabotage and slander to destroy Marburg's other miller. In the end, friendless and destitute, Troost had crushed himself beneath his own mill wheel. Keren's father liked to talk about his vanquished rival, and he had shown his daughter Troost's abandoned mill many times since the man's suicide. Few other people would come here, believing the place to be haunted. It was the perfect place to hide their strange secret.

The inside of the mill was as decrepit as its exterior. Over the years some of the supporting beams had toppled from the roof to repose in angled pillar-like positions. The floor appeared to be the final resting-place for every dead leaf in the forest, filling the building with a rotting ankle-deep carpet. A brace of crows cawed from the shadowy top of the monstrous mill wheel. A rusted chain dangled from the end of the wooden yoke Troost had once hitched his mule to when working the wheel, swaying slightly in the breeze. Under Keren's direction the children carried their patient to a raised wooden platform that was slightly less debris-laden than the floor proper. They set him down beside a pair of neglected barrels and quickly stepped away.

'Kurt, go and see if you can get some blankets from your brothers,' Keren told the burly boy. Kurt hesitated a moment and then made his way through the ruinous mill to the clean air outside. Keren turned her attention to Paul and Therese.

'He needs some food. Why don't you get some from the tavern?' Keren said to Paul.

'You mean steal it?' the boy's voice was almost incredulous. Keren's eyes narrowed.

'Your father owns the tavern. How can that be stealing?' she demanded.

'I don't know,' Paul confessed.

'Maybe I should just have Therese do it, if you are too scared,' sighed Keren.

'No, I'll do it, I'll get some bread,' Paul hastily agreed. It was one thing if he got into trouble, but he did not want his younger sister to suffer their father's wrath. Keren smiled at the boy's easy submission.

THYSSEN KROTZIGK LISTENED to the children squabble, the smile again crossing his swine-like face. Truly the Dark Gods were watching over him, the sorcerer thought. It had taken only the slightest suggestion to the girl's mind to bend her to his intent. She was a naturally bullying and haughty soul, full of pride and arrogance, such easily manipulated qualities. It was indeed fortunate that they ran so strong in the girl's make-up, for, if Krotzigk admitted the truth to himself, in his present condition, he was beyond any but the most minor of evocations. The little sorcerer shifted his weight, trying to relieve the pressure from his twisted leg. Krotzigk bit down on the sudden pain, refusing to cry out and alarm his newfound patrons.

Memories flooded the sorcerer's mind as his hands tried to massage the torment from his mangled limb. Memories of Talabheim and his initiation into the priesthood of

Morr. Krotzigk smiled at the recollection. Even at an early age he had been what most people considered morbid. He had always been drawn to the dark side of things. It was this quality which had led him to the rites and rituals of the God of Death and then, in time, to the forbidden study of the ultimate darkness, Chaos itself.

He could not remember now how he had come upon the book, a vague treatise on all the dark and forbidden cults that lurked in the shadows of man's great kingdoms. The book had told of the foul worship of Morr's brother Khaine, the Lord of Murder, and Malal the Fallen. More, it had told of the great Ruinous Powers – Khorne, Nurgle, Tzeentch and Slaanesh, the Dark Gods who were the chief aspects of Chaos.

That simple book, meant to warn, to outrage its studious reader with such blasphemous and heretical rites, instead had ignited a sinister passion within Krotzigk's already morbid heart. Perhaps his superiors at the temple had sensed the change in their colleague for it was shortly thereafter that he received his transfer to an isolated way temple in the back-country of Stirland. It was little more than a shrine and a cemetery really, serving the scattered villages and towns for a dozen miles around when one of their denizens was called to Morr's kingdom. But if his new situation did not bring with it prestige and advancement, it brought with it something far more important to Krotzigk's darkening soul – seclusion.

Krotzigk could not remember for how many years he had practised the profane rites of Chaos in his blasphemously re-consecrated temple. From the peasants who sometimes visited the temple, he carefully recruited followers, more souls for the Dark Gods. He led them in the dark worship of Chaos in its most pure and absolute form, conducting them in blood rituals on Geheimnisnacht, sacrificing travellers his loyal following provided. More, he conducted them in sacrilegious rites on Death Night, twisting the rites of Morr into a celebration of the Great Powers.

And his zeal was rewarded, not with the paltry powers of one of Morr's adepts but with true sorcerous might. Krotzigk found that his aptitude in the magical arts had increased to a degree far beyond his wildest desires. True, there was a price to pay: a necessary humbling which the Chaos Gods inflicted upon Krotzigk even as his magical powers grew. His once handsome face twisted and distorted itself into that of a swine; a soft golden fur covered most of his body. His tongue had split like a serpent's and his body had shrivelled and shrunk into an almost dwarflike state. If Krotzigk needed any proof of the awful power of Chaos, he had only to stare at his own reflection. Worse would befall him, he knew, if he ever betrayed his new lords. They would not remain silent and inactive like Morr. To offend Chaos was to invite worse than death.

After years of isolation, there came an inspector from the temple in Talabheim. The wily old priest had at once detected the hideous rededication of the temple. It had not preserved his life, however, but it had been the beginning of the end for Krotzigk. In response to the vanishing of an aged and respected scion of the temple, the High Priest of Morr had despatched not another band of priests but the cult's templar knights, the feared Black Guard of Morr.

Krotzigk had been fortunate to escape with his life; none of his followers had been so lucky. The power of Chaos had delivered him, even if it had not spared him the agony of a broken leg. Perhaps it had been another lesson in humility, the sorcerer considered. And now, after weeks of dragging himself painfully across the wilds, almost at the very brink of death, the Ruinous Powers had again delivered their faithful servant from his suffering. Krotzigk turned his pale eyes on the squabbling children.

They had delivered him, that he might deliver unto the Chaos Gods a dark harvest of souls.

THE WIND HOWLED through the boughs that lined the small dirt road. It was the chill wind of late autumn that stirred the fallen leaves on their way, the chill cousin of the icy gales of winter. It was a time when travel was all but absent from the back-roads of Stirland, when only the few cities of that lonely province still drew wanderers to their gates. Still, a shadowy apparition made its way down the disregarded path.

Had anyone else been roaming along the lane, they would have been impressed by the sinister horseman that shared the road, and made the sign of Sigmar as they passed the silent wanderer. The steed was a magnificent warhorse, dark as the dead of night, a swarthy shroud-like caparison clothing the animal almost from head to hoof. The man mounted upon the horse's back was also garbed in black, ebony armour of forged obsidian over which he wore a heavy, monk-like habit of coarse sombre fibre. Etched upon the breast of the habit was a raven in flight, the sign of the grim god of death. The silent rider was no mere sellsword or freelancer, but one of the dread Black Guard of Morr.

The templar's head lay upon his chest as his horse slowly trotted down the path. The caparison and habit, which clothed the two, were torn and muddy, the man's armour soiled with the dust and grime of many weeks of travel on the back-roads of the Empire. A sudden bolster of the wind's strength caused the templar's hood to fall away from his head, revealing the hard, toughened visage of a veteran warrior. The man's nose was broad and splayed, the result of being broken one time too many. Between his brow and his close-cropped black hair there was the grey furrow of an old knife wound. His left cheek had puckered into a vile patch of withered flesh, through which his cheekbone and even his jaw and rearmost teeth could easily be seen. The withered edge of the templar's lip trembled and the napping guardsman awoke with a start. Immediately his right hand released the reins and clutched at his left arm, only to close upon the empty sleeve of his habit.

Ernst Ditmarr grimaced as his mind roused itself to full wakefulness. He released the empty sleeve that had once clothed his left arm and wiped beads of perspiration from his brow before awkwardly shifting his body in order to recover the discarded reins. The same dream, always the same dream. The templar had not passed an hour in slumber without suffering from its baleful intrusion.

He saw himself, once again leading his command of Black Guard to the way temple of Curate Krotzigk. Once again he saw the deranged Chaos cultists attack them, throwing themselves upon the guards' swords with a maniacal fervour. And once again he saw the hideously twisted thing that had at one time been a priest of Morr. He saw the monster hurl unholy power upon his knights, reducing men and horses to ash and slime. He saw himself charge the filthy sorcerer, leaping from his saddle to tackle the vile creature. He saw it writhe from his grasp, fleeing up the rough-hewn steps that led to the roof of the small temple. Finally, he saw himself, his great sword clutched in his hand, his skull-shaped shield held before him as he advanced upon the cornered cult leader.

Power danced about the bestial mutant as it summoned its last reserves of sorcerous might. Ditmarr raised his shield to protect his face even as he struck out at the beast with his sword. Searing agony enveloped him as a blast of green flame seared through his shield, knocking him on his back. The dark shape strode triumphantly towards his prone body, unholy power crackling in its hands, utterly unfazed by the templar's savage attack. The swinish head glared down at him and the sorcerer laughed as it sent a second blast of dark magic into Ditmarr's body.

No, that was not how it was. The sorcerer had not gloated over the templar as he lay writhing on the roof of the shrine. Dimly, Ditmarr seemed to recall seeing a black shape topple over the side of the roof even as he himself fell. Clearer memories provided the rest. His awakening in the back room of a healer's, the gruesome sight of his left arm, withered down to the elbow, every bone showing through the sorry parchment-like skin. He could see his second, Sergeant-Acolyte Ehrhardt, nodding grimly to the healer. He could see the serrated blade in the old man's hands as Ehrhardt held down the withered arm...

Ditmarr clenched his teeth against the memory of that pain; a dead arm cut from a living body. If it took him a hundred years, he would find the blasphemer who had taken his arm, his honour and his life. And when he did, Krotzigk would discover that the vengeance of a god betrayed was terrible indeed.

EDUARD THREW THE stick across the small yard that adjoined Marburg's tiny chapel. The little brown dog yipped with glee as it tore across the grass and damp earth in pursuit of the fleeing stick. Eduard watched the little dog race away, the smile fading from his face. The boy's breath came hot and short, his hands clenching and unclenching in a fit of nervousness. As the puppy ran still farther away in pursuit of the stick, Eduard began to tremble, shifting his weight from one foot to the other. The dog reached the stick and hesitated a moment. Eduard knew that the animal was just getting a better grip with its mouth, but he could not fend off the utter terror that brought tears to his eyes, the horror that the little dog would not come back. The dog always did, but Eduard could not overcome his fear that it would not. His parents had left him after all, left him alone. He had only himself to blame, it was true, for he had been such a sickly little boy. Perhaps they had been afraid that he would make them sick. He knew that many grown-ups were like that, avoiding the ill so that they would not fall prey to the same infirmity. The only one in the village who had been kind enough to take him in was the priest, Father Hackl, but the old cleric was too dour and demanding to make a real parent for the boy, and did little to ease his loneliness.

It did not help that none of the other children seemed to like him. None of them would play with him. Keren Mueller in particular seemed to despise the boy. Whenever she saw him, she said the most horrible things. She called him names like 'worm' and 'pig's slop' and told him horrible lies about his parents being dead because he had made them sick. It was because of her that no one else liked him, Eduard was sure of that. Although Father Hackl had taught him that such thoughts were wrong, sometimes he secretly wished that Keren would die for saying such mean things.

The boys were almost standing next to Eduard before he saw them. The young orphan turned as they approached, prepared to run away from a new barrage of taunts and small stones. To his surprise, the boys were smiling at him, wide friendly smiles.

'Do you want to play with us?' Paul asked the bell-ringer. Eduard stared at the boy, almost refusing to believe his ears.

'We found a great new place to play,' added Rudi, the shifty eyed son of Marburg's wainwright. Eduard just continued to stare. Paul stepped forward to grip his hand.

'Come on, I bet we beat you there,' the boy challenged Eduard. He waited a moment before racing away, Rudi following him. Eduard continued to stare at the pair of boys.

'Wait for me!' Eduard cried, hurrying after Paul and Rudi, all thoughts of dogs and sticks abandoned.

The boys led Eduard on a merry chase through the paths and game trails in the woods. Eduard joined in their laughter; running and giggling just like a real little boy. He could not believe how good it felt to be playing with other children, to have friends. The boy did not dare to question his good fortune, to ponder the sudden change that had come over two members of Keren's mob. Some distance ahead, Paul called out for Eduard to hurry. They were almost at the secret place.

It was an old, run down building, larger than the chapel but smaller than Marburg's tavern or town hall. It was almost hidden by the trees and undergrowth that surrounded the derelict structure. The sight of the eerie building brought Eduard's run to a sudden halt.

'Th-there?' the boy stammered. Paul grabbed his hand and started to pull him toward the yawning, cave-like door of the old mill.

'Come on, Eduard, don't you want to play?' The criticism had its desired effect. Eduard's resistance slackened and Paul led him through the doorway and into the dark, shadowy interior of the building.

There were many children inside the mill, all of them wearing garlands of flowers and smiling faces. Most of them were watching the doorway as Paul and Eduard entered, but others were looking up at the wooden platform that rose from the earthen floor. Eduard followed their gaze and his eyes grew wide with fright.

The figure on the platform was imposing, despite its short stature. It was a monstrous creature garbed in a robe of black. The beast's hands were horribly human in shape, though covered in a soft golden fur, each finger tipped by a brown claw-like nail. The monster's head was like a young boar's, a pinkish snout rising from the centre of the face. To either side of the snout, sunken deep in the monster's skull, a pair of pale blue eyes gleamed. There was intelligence in those eyes, evidence of knowledge forbidden, corrupt, and unholy. Indeed, a malevolent energy seemed to emanate from the twisted beast as it looked at Eduard.

The monster rose from its sheepskin-cushioned chair and walked toward the boy. One of its legs was crippled, but it served well enough to allow the beast to hobble down the few steps separating the platform from the floor. The limping, scuttling gait only added to the creature's unnatural image. Eduard's body trembled as the monster stopped a few paces away from him.

'Welcome, Eduard,' the monster said with a soft, soothing voice. 'We've been waiting for you.'

Eduard let out a piercing scream, turned and ran for the door.

DITMARR EMERGED FROM the small ranger's hut, his armoured boots sinking into the soft mud outside. He awkwardly began to redress his black steed in its midnight-hued caparison when a sound arrested his motion. The

Black Guardsman of Morr spun around, caparison discarded, his hand on the hilt of the sword at his side. Standing not twenty paces away was a figure in black.

'You are far from where you should be, kaptain-justicar,' the voice behind the great helm that enclosed the man's head intoned.

'That depends upon how far from me my prey is lurking,' Ditmarr replied, his eyes covering the other Black Guardsman with an icy gaze.

'You know the decision of the Temple,' the other templar said, reaching up and removing his helm. The face revealed was weathered, hardened beyond its years by a life spent roaming from battle to battle.

'You were there, sergeant,' Ditmarr stated. 'You saw the thing that did this to me.' The templar flicked the hem of his empty sleeve with a steel finger. 'You saw the heresy and sacrilege it committed in the house of Morr itself.'

'Yes, and I was there long ago when you and I sold our swords to whichever border prince or Tilean merchant paid the best. I was there when we fought the orcs in Mad Dog Pass, when you pledged your sword to Morr if he would delay your death and allow us victory over the greenskin horde,' Sergeant-Acolyte Ehrhardt returned.

'Then you understand why I cannot abide by the Temple's decision,' Ditmarr stated. 'I pledged to fight the enemies of Morr. It is all I have.'

'I too made that oath,' Ehrhardt reminded his old comrade. 'Are you so certain that priests do not fight their own battles to honour Morr?' Ditmarr laughed at the templar's argument. It was a dry, sardonic sound, lacking in joy or merriment.

'Can you see me living the life of a cloistered priest? Ministering to the souls of the dead and ensuring their entry into the gardens of Morr?' Ditmarr sighed. 'No, I know only the path of the sword. That is how I can best serve Morr.'

'You pursue this Krotzigk for yourself, for revenge,' Ehrhardt sneered. Ditmarr was silent for a moment.

'Perhaps I do this for both of us.'

'You have been declared apostate by the Temple,' Ehrhardt said with a grave voice. 'For what? Because you hunt a monster that has probably already crawled into a hole somewhere and died?'

'It is my choice, even if it be a fool's errand.' Ditmarr stared closely at Ehrhardt. 'You have come to take me back? I have seen your swordarm in battle, many times. I will conduct you to Morr before you conduct me to his priests.'

Ehrhardt returned his helm to his head and nodded sadly. 'I did not find you this day. You were not here.' The Black Guardsman turned and started to walk away. 'I hope you find what you are looking for, Ernst. I hope it brings you peace.'

THYSSEN'S PORCINE TUSKS noisily cracked the sheep bone in his mouth and his supple tongue began to probe the fissure in search of marrow. Almost absently the sorcerer patted the head of the little shepherdess who had undergone a beating to bring one of her father's flock to the sorcerer's cooking pot. The sorcerer considered the child's devotion, favouring her with his most benign smile before returning his attention to the cowering boy who thought to report him to the village priest.

'My dear, dear Eduard,' the swine-headed creature clucked. 'You have been very bad, haven't you?'

And I ought to blast your filthy carcass into a thousand pieces and hand feed them to the crows, Thyssen thought. But that would not be good. Such a display of discipline might upset his other young followers. After all, flight from the stern discipline of their parents was what had brought most of them to him in the first place.

The boy was young; his impressionable mind still a thing capable of being moulded into Thyssen's desire. Yet, the children needed to be reminded that it was no light thing to try and run off, to let an adult know about him and their little sanctuary in the woods. Thyssen cast his gaze about the old mill as he pondered how best to proceed.

Already the children were gathering, the dozen who had completely broken away from the village, spending day and night with Thyssen at the ruin and the twenty or so others who lived still with their parents. They were the biggest threat to Thyssen, these transient disciples who came only when they could slip away unseen and left when they would be missed by their elders. It was necessary; they were Thyssen's sole source of supplies and information about the village beyond the mill. It was also dangerous: there was always the chance that one of them would betray the sorcerer, as little Eduard had thought to do.

Thyssen watched as the last few children returned from playing outside. True Chaos, the sorcerer thought. No concern for labour or stricture, only the pleasure of the moment. It was a testament to how greatly the children enjoyed his lessons that he did not have to collect them from their romps but that they came of their own accord. They sat, mostly quiet, mostly still, awaiting the beginning of Thyssen's story of the day. Thyssen noted the eager young faces and a cruel smile played about the edges of his porcine mouth.

'You have been bad,' the sorcerer said softly, 'and for that you will not be allowed to listen to the story today.' A twinkle of malicious mirth gleamed in Thyssen's eye as he noted the sudden look of loss that masked the boy's features. One of the many lessons of Slaanesh, the ecstasy of experience and the torment of its denial.

Thyssen waved Kurt and Paul forward. The boys lifted Eduard from the floor and carried the boy over to a large wooden barrel resting in the farthest corner of the mill. He should be just out of earshot, the sorcerer mused as he watched the boys force Eduard into his small prison. He was certain that this blatant exclusion of Eduard from the other children would have the desired effect, upon both the would-be turncoat and the other children. Still, it would pay to ensure his strategy.

'Keren,' the sorcerer hissed softly. The girl took her place at his side and Thyssen whispered into her ear.

'I understand that young Eduard has a little dog,' Thyssen smiled as he saw the wicked grin growing on Keren's face. What an eager student. 'When we let him out of the barrel, tell him that if he ever runs off again, something bad will happen to his dog.' Thyssen waved away the girl and hobbled his way to the front of the platform.

'Today, children, I will tell you a story about Sigmar.' A hush of excitement crept across the assembly. Thyssen choked on the loathing their excitement evoked, reminding him that he had much nonsense still to remove from their young minds. *Let them have their heroic delusions, I will correct them soon enough. And until then, I will exploit their naïve faith.*

The sorcerer began his tale, telling of great and noble Sigmar and his struggle to found the Empire. He told of how hordes of orcs forced Sigmar and his mighty army away from the places known to men, past even the icy lands of Kislev, until Sigmar came upon the border of a land of wonder and magic. The sky sparkled like diamond and the ground was paved with gold. And, just as Sigmar would have entered this land of fantastic beauty, he found the way barred by four mighty figures.

'One was a massive man encased in a suit of ruby armour, a blazing axe in his powerful hand. The second was a beautiful woman, her armour sparkling like the diamond sky so that whenever the eye fell upon it, it was a different colour. The third was a tall, keen-eyed wizard garbed in a brightly coloured robe and the air around him shimmered with magic. The last was a great fat warrior, whose coughing laugh boomed across the horizon.

'They were the Four Princes and Sigmar recognised them as his equals, beings worthy of his respect. He knew that it would be best to not raise arms against them and turned to return and face the overwhelming orc hordes. But the Four Princes would not allow the armies of men to fall, and they returned with Sigmar and together they scoured the land until all the orcs had been driven beyond the mountains.

It was late in the evening when Thyssen finished his tale. Not one of his young audience had lost interest, not one youthful head bowed in slumber despite the late hour. The sorcerer was pleased with his success. *Soon, soon I will teach you more than fables. Soon I will show you the Four Princes and you will love them.*

'THE OLD FOOL!' Thyssen roared, throwing the clay cup across the mill, spilling goat's milk on his black robe. A young girl hurried forward and began to sop the milk from his robe with the hem of her dress. Thyssen smiled at her and turned his head to look at the boy who had brought him the news. He should have expected something. More and more of the children had been coming to him, his permanent base now consisting of thirty with only another eleven still acting as his eyes and ears in the village. It had been a month since that fat idiot Bassermann had convinced the village leaders to hire a hunter to discover the beast that was carrying off their children. Thyssen smiled as he recalled the hunter's demise, how he had fixed it to look as if the man had fallen into his own steel-jawed trap. Kurt had helped him with that. Sometimes the boy's bloodlust alarmed even the sorcerer. Still, all gods looked with favour upon the zealous.

'So, the old priest wants to send a petition to Altdorf and bring witch hunters to Marburg?' Thyssen snarled. Rudi nodded his head with a bird-like bobbing motion.

'The village elders don't want him to, though. They say that witch hunters find witches even when there aren't any around.' The boy grinned at Thyssen. 'So it isn't really bad, because they told him not to.'

The smile Thyssen directed at Rudi was not a friendly one, though the boy foolishly took it to be. It was the same ignorant naivety that made the boy think Hackl would listen to what the village elders had to say. Truthfully, he was surprised that the old priest had taken this long to act. He had certainly been upset enough two months ago when Eduard had 'disappeared' to join Thyssen's full-time students. No, the old priest would be sending for witch hunters. Which meant that it was time to attend to the meddling fool.

'Keren,' the sorcerer said, 'bring the others inside. Today, I will tell you all about the Four Princes a little earlier than usual.'

The girl raced outside to bring the children from their play. Thyssen knew it would not be long before his little students were assembled before him, their attentive faces looking up at his own as he continued the epic tale he had started so many weeks ago. Thyssen had achieved much in that time. Sigmar had gone from the equal of the Four Princes to their exploiter, cravenly allowing the Four to fight his battles for him. Thyssen told of how it was the Four Princes who defeated the Great Enchanter Drachenfels and brought to an end the savage dragon Mordrax, how it was they who truly conquered all the horrible enemies the children had once been told Sigmar himself had vanquished. Slowly, carefully, Thyssen had recast Sigmar in their imaginations, changing him from hero and saviour to coward and manipulator. Now, today, it would be time to add a new sin to Sigmar's crimes, a new title to attach itself to his name. It was time for Sigmar to become the betrayer.

Thyssen looked out on the hastily assembled children. He smiled as he saw their eager faces. Tonight he would put that eagerness to use. Tonight he would allow some of them to show their devotion to the powers of Chaos.

The sorcerer began his tale, relating how a numberless army of the undead had arisen in the blighted south, slaughtering all in their path, adding their victims to the host of death. Their tireless advance brought the army of skeletons and wraiths to the very edge of the Empire the Four Princes had conquered for the sons of men. A great army of men had been assembled; no household in the Empire failed to send at least one of its number to face the terrible invasion. Yet large as it was, before the tide of undead it was nothing. Sigmar saw the mammoth force of his enemy and was seized with dread. He turned to the Four Princes and ordered them to lead the attack on the undead, claiming that here was a foe unworthy of an Emperor. Sigmar retreated to a nearby hill to watch the battle while the Four Princes led the mortal army against the overwhelming numbers of the dead.

It was a fierce and horrible struggle. Not one in ten of those who fought the undead survived. The battle looked hopeless until the Four Princes forced their way to the very heart of the undead host. Before them stood a hideous giant encased in magic armour black as the darkest pit, his face a leering skull. He was the general of the terrible army, the Supreme Necromancer, Nagash the Black. The Four Princes did not hesitate before the terrifying foe, for they knew that without Nagash, the evil army would return to their graves and the lands of men would be saved. It was a terrific fight, even for the powerful Princes, and when at last they broke the evil necromancer's body and cast his black soul to the wind, they were weary and wounded.

From his hill, Sigmar had watched the battle progress. Seeing Nagash defeated, he descended to the battlefield, striking down the remaining skeletons and zombies as he found them, rallying the tattered remnants of his army to his sparkling banner. At last Sigmar found the Four Princes, half-dead from their terrible battle. Sigmar saw their weakened state and seized upon their infirmity. He turned to his soldiers and told them the Four Princes were evil daemons, that it was they who had brought the undead up from the Southlands to destroy them all. The men heard his lies and believed them, driving the weakened Princes from the Empire and making of their names the vilest of curses.

Thyssen listened to the whispers of outrage that slithered amongst his assembly, the muttered oaths against a name they had once worshipped. His porcine lips pulled away from his fang-like teeth. Yes, tonight would be the night to deal with a priest of such a loathsome being.

FATHER HACKL AWOKE with a start. The old priest looked about the darkened cell which held his bed and the few possessions the cleric allowed himself, his mind trying to accustom itself to the benighted surroundings. What had intruded upon his slumber, the priest could not recall. He wiped the crust of sleep from his eyes, and coughed as the chill night air flowed into his lungs. Then Father Hackl's head slowly turned toward the door of his room. Yes, he had heard a sound that time, a furtive scrabbling in the temple room itself.

Eduard's little dog must have got loose, the old priest decided. The priest had been taking care of the puppy in the weeks since the boy had disappeared. It was an act of denial, the priest reasoned, a refusal to accept Eduard's disappearance. Father Hackl thought it strange that he had not realised how much the orphan had come to mean to him until the boy was no longer around. The old priest missed the boy greatly; with him gone, there was an empty spot in Father Hackl's life. Perhaps that was why he kept Eduard's little dog. By keeping the puppy, he was defying whatever evil had befallen the boy, declaring to the darkness that the boy would return. A tear welled in the priest's eye as the thought crossed his mind that he was clinging to an impossible hope.

Still, whatever his reasons for attending the animal, he could not have it scampering about in Sigmar's holy shrine. He would have to catch the dog and return it to the anteroom. He doubted if the dog would bother to chew through its rope twice in a single evening. With the tired weariness of age,

Father Hackl rose from his bed, letting the chill air shock his body into full wakefulness before opening the door and entering the dark hall of the chapel. The old priest made his way along the ranks of rough, wooden pews, softly calling for the dog, as though he did not wish to wake Sigmar at this lonely hour with any undue noise. Father Hackl's eyes swept the expanse of the temple, seeing little beyond shadows. Then his gaze strayed to the altar itself. It took the old priest a moment before he could recognise the change that had taken place there.

With an impious oath and a quickness in his step, Father Hackl made his way down the empty ranks of pews toward the altar. The hammer, the holy symbol of Sigmar, had fallen from the altar, lying like a piece of refuse on the floor.

The priest could not imagine how the little dog had managed to topple the heavy iron hammer from its place, but he would not have it lying in so disrespectful a state. Father Hackl bent over to retrieve it from the floor, ignoring the creaking of his old bones, ignorant of the dark shape which rose from the pews behind him.

A thick, animal stench struck Father Hackl a moment before the attack. The cleric's head rose ever so slightly as he detected the foul odour. Then the sinew cord wrapped itself around his throat. Once, twice, thrice, the Chaos worshipper wound the grey strangler's cord about the priest's neck. Thyssen's porcine jaws clamped down on his tongue as the sorcerer drew the cord tight, pushing his body back and pulling the old priest to his feet as the noose did its work. Father Hackl's hands rose to the garrotte, feebly trying to thwart the restricting cord. After a moment, as the priest's face grew flush and a hideous gargling noise began to form in his throat, the man's arms flailed about wildly, striking the swine behind him. For an instant, the crippled sorcerer lessened the tension, allowing the priest to draw breath into his starving lungs.

Father Hackl did more than simply draw air into his lungs, however. With the momentary respite, the priest sent his elbow smashing into the throat of his unseen attacker. The attack did more than damage the assassin's windpipe; the crippled monster's twisted leg gave way, spilling the sorcerer on the cold stone floor, dragging the priest down with him.

Thyssen kept a death grip on the garrotte, even as he gasped and hawked on the phlegm building in his own damaged throat. The small, twisted creature desperately tried force the priest's body around, that he might plant his one good knee in the cleric's back. The priest resisted with all of his being, his aged frame contesting with Thyssen's crippled one. In the course of the struggle, Father Hackl nearly succeeded in forcing the sorcerer's furred fingers away from the constricting sinew cord. It was a very near thing when Thyssen at last managed to bring his knee crashing into the small of the priest's back. The monster began to pull with all his might, the extra support of his knee adding to the choking pressure. The fiend could feel the life leaking away from his prey with every moment. But the fight was not yet decided, and Thyssen could feel the body beneath him beginning to roll onto its side, threatening to spill the sorcerer once more on the stone floor.

From the shadows came small figures, figures Father Hackl was horrified to recognise. As the cord continued its deadly labour, a huge boy Hackl remembered as the brother of some foresters grasped his left arm, restraining it completely. Keren, the miller's daughter, and another boy gripped his right arm, allowing him to move it only with the greatest of efforts. Father Hackl struggled to raise the arm to his throat, succeeding by the slightest of degrees, when his fading vision settled upon another small figure standing behind the altar. Father Hackl tried to read the expression on Eduard's face, but he could not decide if it was a look of shock, concern or simmering hatred. The priest's eyes were still locked with those of Eduard when Thyssen Krotzigk finished choking the life from the cleric's body.

'Such very good children,' Thyssen said as he released the sinew cord and let the corpse's head strike the floor with a dull thud. The sorcerer rose to his feet and then sank into one of the pews to recover from the strain of his efforts. He noted with pride the hate and loathing with which his pupils regarded the expired priest.

'Paul has everything ready in the bell tower,' Keren offered, looking pleased with herself. The boys looked proud as well, their eyes straying from Thyssen to the sorcerer's handiwork. They had every right to be, the Chaos worshipper decided. As much as any soldier, this had been their first battle, and they had performed valiantly.

'Then let us take this filth there,' Thyssen said, rising from his seat and resting a furry hand on Keren's shoulder. Kurt and Paul lifted the corpse and followed Thyssen into the bell tower. Thyssen reached out and tugged on the noose at the end of the bell rope. He smiled as he imagined the spectacle when the villagers discovered their priest hanging in his own temple, dead by his own hand. He was still smiling when he noticed that one of his pupils was missing.

'Where is Eduard?' the sorcerer hissed, twisting Keren's arm in his sudden terror. The girl winced from his grasp, alarmed by her master's harsh tone.

'He was with us,' she protested. Thyssen turned from her angrily, roaring at the boys to leave their macabre chore.

'Find him! Now!' Thyssen hobbled after the children as they raced back into the temple. Thyssen watched them as they rushed through the double doors of the anteroom, visions of witch hunters lending speed to his limping gait.

Thyssen found the children standing in the anteroom, all of them staring at the gory spectacle strewn across the floor. Eduard rose from the butchery, smiling at Thyssen Krotzigk. The sorcerer returned the smile and placed an arm around the boy. He looked again at the gruesome offering, the sigils drawn in blood upon the walls and floor. Such zeal, but Eduard's initiative was inappropriate just now. Thyssen turned to Keren.

'Clean this up,' he said in a soft, low voice. 'This is not a fitting place for an offering to the Four Princes.' Thyssen turned away from the girl and led Eduard away from the profaned temple. He looked down at the boy.

Soon, I will let you make another offering to the Dark Gods. A proper offering.

* * *

THERE WERE THOSE in the village of Marburg who had believed their suffering was a punishment visited upon them by the gods, that they were paying for their prosperity with their own children. Yet even these pious individuals were at a loss to explain the horrible suicide of Father Hackl. In this time of crisis, many had come to rely upon the priest for both leadership and comfort. A menacing pall had settled over the village, and none could say when the dawn would come.

A week had passed before another omen of doom presented itself to the simple people of Marburg. A shadowy horseman slowly stalked down the narrow lane through the village; a silent twisted figure on a midnight steed, man and beast clothed in black. Men watched the horseman pass and made the sign of Sigmar before retreating behind the shutters of their cottages. The horseman's gaze strayed neither left nor right, seemingly oblivious to the existence of the small community until he drew abreast of the tavern.

Ernst Ditmarr turned his head and regarded the plain building for a moment before the one-armed man awkwardly dismounted. The Black Guardsman advanced upon the tavern, pushing open its oaken door with his armoured fist. The tavern was nearly empty at this early hour; only the blacksmith Rudel was keeping Otto Keppler company at present.

The two men watched the templar stride across the room, seating himself at one of the rearmost tables. A deep sepulchral voice addressed Otto, asking for water and bread as the black-garbed figure situated itself. Otto continued to stare at the Black Guardsman for several heartbeats before remembering his business and hurrying into the back room to comply with his strange patron's request.

'Father, who is that man?' Keppler's son asked as the elder Keppler opened the small larder and removed a loaf of dark-coloured bread and a wedge of cheese.

'A templar,' the tavern keeper explained over his shoulder. 'One of the Black Guard of Morr.' Otto Keppler hurried back into the main room of his establishment, concerned by the grim figure occupying one of his tables. The dark templar was not the sort of patron Otto wished to keep waiting. He did not see the crafty look which entered his son's eyes. Nor did he hear the opening and closing of the rear door of the tavern.

THYSSEN'S BESTIAL FACE split as a peal of malevolent laughter wracked his wasted form. Truly, none could predict the Chaos gods. First, they spared the man who had destroyed his former cult, allowed him to strike down their trusted and loyal servant. Then they delivered the same man into his power. A gift from the Realm of Chaos. Thyssen laughed again.

'You have done well, Paul, very well.' Thyssen grasped the boy's shoulder as he praised him. The sorcerer spun around and addressed his assembled cult.

'Tonight, I will teach you how to truly honour the power of Chaos! I will show you how to make an offering to the Four Princes, a testament of your undying love and loyalty to them. They have delivered into our hands a worthy and fitting sacrifice to anoint you in the service of Chaos!' Thyssen turned from the excited mob of children and spoke into Paul Keppler's ear.

'As we did with Bassermann's hunter,' the sorcerer chortled. 'Lead the guardsman here, to the mill.' A fire of madness blazed within Thyssen Krotzigk's eyes as he contemplated the execution of his commands. 'Bring the cripple to me,' the fallen priest hissed.

'WHAT BRINGS YOU to Marburg, lord templar?' Bernd Mueller nervously asked the seated knight. As Marburg's chief citizen, it had fallen upon the miller to act as spokesman to the village's sinister guest. The wealthy man did not relish the appointment.

The black-garbed knight looked up from his simple meal, the living side of his mouth still working on a sliver of cheese. Mueller retreated a few steps from the lifeless gaze of the Black Guardsman. The eyes remained fixed upon the retreating villager.

'Have you come to claim the priest's body?' Mueller asked, desperately hoping Ditmarr would lose interest in him. Instead the templar's gaze became even more penetrating.

'I came because of rumours of missing children,' Ditmarr's hollow voice stated. The templar rose from the table, causing Mueller and the half-dozen villagers at his back to tense and cast sidelong glances at the tavern's door. Ditmarr took a step towards Mueller, his armoured footfall echoing on the wooden floorboards. 'What is this about a priest?' There was venom behind the dirge-like tone, a fire slowly creeping into the templar's dead eyes. The Black Guardsman took another step towards Mueller.

'Our priest hung himself seven nights past,' Mueller said, raising his hand to wipe sweat from his brow. Some of the fire seemed to leave the templar's eyes as the miller spoke.

'Where is the body? I would see it.'

'We left it in the chapel,' stammered the fat wainwright Bassermann from over Mueller's shoulder. Ditmarr did not waste further words on the villagers, turning on his heel and striding from the tavern. All of the tavern's denizens took a deep breath as the sinister knight departed. The sense of dread which had gripped them seemed to have lifted, and the unnerving stench of the grave that had impressed itself upon them had finally cleared away.

DITMARR WALKED WITH purpose toward the small chapel devoted to Sigmar. He had nearly reached the small path that wound its way to the isolated shrine when a soft voice called to him from the shadowy space between two of the closely packed villager huts. The guardsman spun around, his hand grasping the hilt of his sword. A young boy greeted the templar's gaze.

'Thank Sigmar I have found you!' Paul Keppler said, his pockmarked face smiling at the templar. 'I have seen one of the missing children.'

'Have you?' Ditmarr asked, his hand releasing the hilt of his weapon.

'Yes, not far from here. In the woods,' Paul elaborated. He began to step back into the alley, motioning for Ditmarr to follow. The templar did as the boy asked, following him across the field behind the huts and towards the stand of trees beyond. The templar studied the boy's bright, excited face.

'How is it that you are not afraid?' Ditmarr asked, drawing closer to the boy.

'I am brave, like you,' the boy answered.

The hunter had asked the same question and been satisfied by the same answer. The templar manoeuvred still closer to the boy.

'Why didn't you tell your father or the other men in the village?' Ditmarr's eyes zeroed on the boy's back as the youth stopped and stood still.

Paul hadn't expected that question. With the hunter he had said he wished a part of the reward, but even his young mind knew the templar was not motivated by greed and would be suspicious of anyone with such desires. Paul decided it would be better to lead the knight into Thyssen's trap a different way. If he ran, the templar would be certain to give chase, and that pursuit would lead him straight to the sorcerer.

The boy started to bolt, to race away from the templar. Only one thing prevented his flight – the heavy, black-clad hand that closed upon the neck of Paul's jerkin at the first sign of motion. The boy was pulled off his feet and Ditmarr lifted him from the ground.

'Suppose we tell your elders about what you have seen?' Paul's furious kicks impacted harmlessly against the knight's armour as the Black Guardsman carried the struggling boy back to Marburg's tavern.

THE MEN OF Marburg stood in the common room of the tavern, silent, all eyes focused upon the small door which led to the tavern's kitchen. No disquieting sounds came from behind the door now, and somehow their absence was even more unsettling. The door slowly opened and the ashen-faced figure of Otto Keppler emerged, followed closely by the black-garbed templar of Morr.

'There is corruption here,' the guardsman's grim voice declared. 'Chaos has touched your town.' The templar's malformed face regarded each of the silent men in turn. 'Now you must be strong. Now you must deny the Darkness its victory.'

ERNST DITMARR PUSHED open the rotten door of the decrepit mill. Within all was darkness and shadow. A smell like that of a kennel overcame the faint traces of burnt kindling in the air. Furtive, creeping sounds rustled from the shadows, suggesting much but revealing nothing. That someone was here, Ditmarr knew, but in what numbers, the darkness kept to itself. Slowly, sword in hand, the templar made his way into the building, his vision struggling to pierce the all-encompassing gloom. The templar had advanced nearly to the centre of the structure before any sign of life manifested itself.

'It is you!' a soft voice chortled from the darkness. Ditmarr turned to face the unseen speaker. A small globe of blue flame sprang into life, illuminating the bestial creature standing upon the flimsy platform. The witch fire danced in Thyssen Krotzigk's hand, shaking with the sorcerer's every laugh.

'I have come to fulfil my duty,' Ditmarr's cold voice intoned. The Black Guardsman of Morr took a step towards the Chaos worshipper.

'Ah, still serving feeble old Morr?' Thyssen sneered. 'I fear you will once again disappoint your god.' A stone raced out of the darkness, smashing the sword from Ditmarr's hand. A horde of small, wiry figures leapt upon the knight, forcing the man to his knees through sheer weight of numbers. As Ditmarr struggled against the assault, Thyssen sent the witch-fire speeding from his hand to put to light the wood and bracken piled at the centre of the old millstone.

The sudden dispelling of the darkness revealed a mob of dirty children clutching and punching the templar. Their young faces wore expressions of savagery as they leeched the strength from Ditmarr's struggling limbs. At last the templar sagged limp and helpless in their grasp. When the fight had left his foe, Thyssen Krotzigk slowly hobbled down from the platform.

'Refusing to defend yourself against innocent children?' The beast's mouth yawned as he shook with laughter.

Thyssen leered into Ditmarr's face. 'Shall I tell you of that innocence? Can you imagine the ecstasy of corrupting such fertile fields as these?' Thyssen gestured to include the frenzied throng gathered about the two old adversaries. He crooked a clawed finger and motioned for one among them to come forward. Ditmarr looked at the young, blank faces of the sorcerer's fold. Even the huge boy who broke away from the other children had about him an air of confusion. The children knew that they were changing, but they had no understanding of what they were becoming. At once, the Black Guardsman's loathing of their corrupter increased tenfold.

'This is Kurt,' Thyssen beamed. 'A more worthy instrument of the Blood God has never been seen by these old eyes.' The sorcerer reached into his dark robe and withdrew a filthy, blood-encrusted knife. He handed the weapon to Kurt. Ditmarr stared into the boy's expressionless face, his eyes a soulless window into Khorne's domain of carnage.

'You are just in time to witness Kurt's devotions to the Blood God,' a vile grin spread across the sorcerer's face. 'Or participate in them, as the case may be.' The sorcerer's words were answered by a rasping, choking sound. It took Thyssen a moment to realise that the templar was laughing at him. 'You will scream for me, cripple, when your blood feeds Khorne!' Thyssen snapped, glaring at Ditmarr. The templar raised his head, letting his cold eyes stare into the sorcerer's own.

'I wonder how Morr will receive you?' the Black Guardsman said. 'What is the justice earned by a heretic priest?' Thyssen continued to glare at Ditmarr, a snarl upon his face. Suddenly, the sorcerer's eyes grew wide with alarm.

'Where is Paul?' the sorcerer roared, his head bobbing about trying to spot the boy he had sent to lure his enemy here. Thyssen had been too lost in gloating over his enemy to notice the flaw in his plot. Now the alarmed sorcerer was trying to recover the situation.

'Keren!' Thyssen shouted. 'Look outside. Our guest may not have come alone.' The girl released Ditmarr's shoulder and ran to the doorway of the mill.

'It's Keren!' gasped Bernd Mueller from his position in the trees outside the ramshackle mill.

'Aye,' agreed Otto Keppler. The tavern keeper lit the torch in his hand and made ready to cast it. Mueller grabbed the man's arm before he could cast the firebrand.

'You know the guardsman's orders,' Keppler said, his voice as cold and lifeless as that of the templar himself. He tore his arm free of Mueller's and threw the torch at the mill's rotting roof.

'But my daughter is in there,' sobbed Mueller.

'As is mine,' Keppler whispered.

'They're setting the mill on fire!' Keren's shrill voice shrieked as she retreated away from the door. The other children stared at her for a moment, as if uncertain how to react to Keren's cries when the first crackling flames licked downwards from the ceiling and the first tendrils of fire danced at the mill's broken windows. Panic gripped the coven and they disintegrated into a frantic mob, racing about the mill, seeking refuge from the growing flames.

Thyssen shouted at his followers, trying to calm them. He did not see how few had retained their hold upon the templar, or how, their numbers lessened, Ditmarr seized the opportunity to free himself of their clutching grasp. His arm free, the Black Guardsman groped within the seemingly empty sleeve of his habit. A small silver dagger appeared in the knight's hand. As Thyssen Krotzigk turned to observe the templar's sudden motion, Ditmarr lashed out with the dagger. The blade passed cleanly through the sorcerer's left eye.

Thyssen recoiled, a furred hand clutching at his face in a vain attempt to staunch the flow of blood and jelly. Ditmarr brought an armoured boot crashing into the sorcerer's twisted leg, pitching the villain to the floor.

'Rot in the gardens of the damned,' Ditmarr snarled, crouching over his enemy. As the templar raised his dagger to slit the throat of the heretic, a powerful grip closed around his wrist and jerked him off the sorcerer's body.

Ditmarr swung at his attacker, arresting his weapon when he found himself looking into the youthful face of the boy Thyssen had called Kurt. The boy stared back with eyes that were pools of crimson, windows into the gore-soaked domain of the Blood God. A slight smile tugged at the boy's lips as he backhanded Ditmarr and sent the knight flying across the mill. Ditmarr struck his head hard against the floor. As he raised himself from the ground, he shook his head groggily from side to side, trying to clear his vision.

Something was not right. Amid a rain of blazing thatch, the boy was slowly walking towards him. But with every step the child seemed to be growing larger, rippling muscles swelling on his arms and chest. The boy's flesh was turning leathery, taking on a red sheen. When Kurt reached the stunned templar, his features had grown sharp and inhuman; the teeth within his smirking mouth were long ivory fangs. Again the boy struck Ditmarr, crumpling his breastplate, the dented metal stabbing into the flesh beneath and sending the knight hurtling across the burning mill.

Ditmarr landed, his back striking the burning hulk of a fallen beam. The templar's habit caught fire and Ditmarr hurried to tear it from his armoured body. As he freed himself of the blazing garment, Ditmarr felt a monstrous hand close about his neck.

Like a rag doll his armoured body was lifted from the floor.

There was no trace of Kurt in the thing that held Ditmarr. The daemon that had entered the boy had now completely possessed Kurt's body. The hands that held Ditmarr ended in long, razor-sharp claws. Monstrous black horns protruded from the abomination's elongated head while a stink of old blood oozed from the daemon's scarlet hide. The Bloodletter licked Ditmarr's face with a long, sinuous tongue. The obscenity's free hand touched itself to Ditmarr's chest and slowly raked its claws downwards, slicing through armour and flesh as though both were made of butter.

Ditmarr screamed against the searing agony of the daemon's touch. With a tremendous effort, he took his hand from the claw choking him and smashed the daemon's grinning mouth. The fiend's head snapped back and it dropped Ditmarr to the ground. The Bloodletter worked its jaw for a moment and then snarled at the templar.

Blood streamed from the gaping wounds in his chest, flowing through the rents in his armour like a cataract of gore. Despite the hideous wounds and his own fast failing strength, Ditmarr lunged at the Bloodletter. The Black Guardsman's armoured body struck the daemon of Khorne head on, knocking beast and man through the weakened wall of the fiery mill.

The daemon rose first, grabbing Ditmarr by the leg and hurling the templar a dozen yards, the warrior landing with a crack that bespoke of broken bones and internal injuries. The monster hissed and strode away from the inferno that blazed behind it, intent upon the filthy creature that sought to deny its bloodlust. At one point, the Bloodletter stopped in mid-step, its body frozen. For a moment, it seemed to shrink, to wither, before a sudden surge of unholy power caused the beast to swell again and continue its advance.

Ditmarr crawled through the brush, every motion heralding unspeakable agony. Somewhere in his body a rib had shattered, its bony shrapnel skewering the knight's lung. Blood trickled from his mouth and nose with every breath. The Black Guardsman could barely feel the familiar inhuman grip that closed about his arm and wrenched his body from the ground. His bleary vision could barely discern the leering daemonic face that leered into his own. But he heard the cry of terror that sounded from behind the fiend.

The Bloodletter turned, still retaining its grip upon the templar and regarded the obese man with the rusty axe who had been fool enough to attack it. The daemon reached out towards Bassermann even as the wainwright struck at it again. The blade failed to pierce the fiend's flesh, a fact which caused the fat man's eyes to grow even wider with fear.

The Bloodletter licked its fangs at the prospect of still more blood to satisfy its hunger.

Suddenly, the monster's form began to tremble. Ditmarr found himself falling to the ground as the Bloodletter's arm began to wither and fade. The daemon let out a howl of rage and fury as its body shrivelled. Soon only the echoes of its scream and a pile of smouldering ash remained as testament of the daemon's intrusion upon the realm of man. Ernst Ditmarr coughed weakly as Bassermann rushed to the templar's side.

DITMARR STIRRED WEAKLY as one of the villagers drew near. Blood seeped through his bandages as he moved. Try as they might, there seemed to be no way to stop the wounds inflicted by the daemon of Khorne from bleeding. It had been a marvel to the villagers that the templar had endured through the night.

'Have you found him?' the Black Guardsman asked, his voice the barest of whispers. Bernd Mueller looked down at him.

Ever since the fire had settled, the templar had been asking them to find the twisted remains of the Chaos sorcerer. In the darkness and now, in the light, the men of Marburg had undertaken the hideous task. Now Bernd Mueller stared at the dying templar.

'Aye, we found his filthy carcass,' the miller declared. 'Pinned beneath a fallen support. He must have burned to death in the fire.' The templar sighed as Mueller finished his report. The sigh slowly trailed off into the knight's death rattle. The taverner and miller watched as the mangled body twitched for a moment and was still. Otto Keppler leaned down and pulled the heavy wool blanket which had been wrapped about the dying knight and drew it over Ditmarr's sightless eyes.

'We found nothing,' the tavern keeper whispered. Mueller smiled feebly at the man.

'If it allows him to pass the portal of Morr easier, of what harm is that?' Mueller did not await an answer, but slowly started the long, lonely path home.

THE BLACK-CLOAKED FIGURE rose from the shadows and limped to the corpse lying on the other side of the hedge. Carefully, a furred hand pulled the crude stone knife from the forester's still warm body. The creature's single eye studied the simple blade for a moment. He did not give any sign that he heard the furtive sounds of motion at his back. Slowly he rose, turning to observe the even more twisted and grotesque figures emerging from the trees.

Thyssen Krotzigk smiled as the beastmen began to circle him. The swine-headed sorcerer dropped the knife in his left hand and the blood-caked dagger in his right. He studied the malformed, animal faces, their brute eyes gleaming with hate, their fanged mouths dripping saliva as their bloodlust rose. The beastmen began to grip their crude weapons more tightly, testing their weight with practice swipes, displaying brutal strength capable of crushing skulls.

And all is the laughter of the Four Princes, thought the sorcerer, as the beastmen closed upon him.

THREE KNIGHTS
by Graham McNeill

DARKNESS WAS APPROACHING as the three knights neared the outskirts of the village, their horses' hooves thumping on the rain slick timbers of the bridge. Below them, the river foamed white, swollen by the recent rains washing down the flanks of the Grey Mountains. The roadway led within a badly constructed wooden palisade wall and lamplight from behind shuttered windows cast shafts of light in their path. The air was thick with the smell of woodsmoke.

A wooden sign nailed to an empty guard booth at the end of the bridge proclaimed the village's name as Gugarde. An ugly name for an ugly town, thought Luc Massone as he and his two companions rode through the broken gateway into town.

Luc knew that Bretonnian towns were never the most aesthetically pleasing places at the best of times, but this was a particularly offensive example. His father's estates to the south of Couronne were much more attractive to the eye. Luc was a powerfully built figure, with a thick mane of black hair and darkly handsome face. A long, white scar trailed from his right temple to his chin, giving him a cruel, sardonic expression.

As they rode deeper into the town, he knew they were being watched. Fitful slivers of light, as tattered drapes were drawn aside behind barred windows, told him as much. Luc knew that three armoured knights on horseback would not pass unnoticed in a squalid little town like this.

'This place reeks of fear,' said Fontaine, Luc's second brother, riding on his left. 'They hang witchbane and daemonroot above their doors. Mayhap the stories were true.'

Luc smiled at the unmistakable edge of anticipation in Fontaine's voice.

'Did I not tell you so?' answered Luc. 'We shall find the dark ones soon, I am sure. Evil like theirs does not die easily.'

'Then are we three enough?' asked Belmonde, Luc's youngest brother. 'If the nightwalkers have truly returned should we not have come in greater numbers?'

Luc sighed in exasperation at Belmonde's foolishness. His brother would never learn. 'And if we brought an army and smashed down their keep stone by stone would that make you a knight? Where would the honour be? How then would you prove your manhood to father with a horde of screaming peasants at your back? No, if we are to do this, we do it alone. Only in this way can you become a knight of the realm as I am.'

Suitably chastened, Belmonde did not reply. Luc reined in his horse before a low-roofed building, the odious stench of unwashed bodies and boiled vegetables emanating from within. A faded sign above the door bore a crude etching of a many turreted castle below which were carved the words, 'The Manor'.

Luc laughed at the inappropriateness of the name as the brothers dismounted, tethering their horses to the inn's only hitching rail while Belmonde did likewise with their pack mule. Casting a distasteful glance at the establishment, Luc and his brothers ventured within.

* * *

Three Knights

THE STENCH OF the inn was an almost physical thing, all-encompassing and overpowering. The sweat of hard labour, poor food and stale beer mingled into a pungent aroma that caught in the back of Luc's throat. The inn was surprisingly full and, conspicuously, none of the bar's patrons raised their eyes to the knights. A surly looking barkeep sat behind a trestle bar at the end of the room and Luc's annoyance rose as he moved through them. Did these peasants not realise the honour he brought them merely by deigning to enter their stinking establishment? He drew a gold coin from a purse hanging from his sword belt and dropped it onto the bar.

'There are three horses and a pack mule outside,' he stated. 'See to it that they are fed, watered and stabled adequately for the night.'

The innkeeper's eyes bulged at the sight of the coin, more wealth than he would normally see in a year, and snatched it up in his meaty fist. His eyes darted suspiciously around the room, frightened that others might see his sudden good fortune. He smiled and barked, 'Antoine! Move your worthless carcass and take the lords' horses to the stables! Hurry now!'

In response, a harried looking youth scurried quickly from the inn.

'We shall also be requiring rooms, food and wine,' continued Luc. 'This should ensure that they are of the requisite quality...' He dropped another coin on the wooden bar, its clatter causing heads to turn throughout the inn.

The innkeeper scooped up the second coin as quickly as the first.

'You shall have the very best, my lords!' said the man. 'The best in all Bretonnia!'

'I somehow doubt that,' replied Luc airily, 'but do what you can.'

He turned his back on the man and made his way to an empty table next to the window. Conversations that had been low and subdued before now ceased altogether and every man in the bar stared into his tankard as though fascinated by its contents.

'Luc,' whispered Belmonde urgently, 'do you know how much you gave that man?'

'Of course,' answered Luc. 'It is only money, and a Bretonnian knight needs not money.'

Fontaine smiled, thinking he understood his brother's intentions, and said, 'Yes, one must always be prepared to help the lower orders. You must learn this, Belmonde, if you are to be part of this, the brothers Massone's quest...'

Silence filled the expectant gap left hanging by Fontaine's words and he struggled to conceal his anger as no one in the bar took the bait of his statement. Belmonde, finally grasping his brother's vain theatrics, said, 'Yes, Fontaine. To destroy the evil blood drinkers that dwell in Blood Keep we must be true to the vows we swore in the Lady's Chapel in Couronne. We must...'

His words trailed off in the face of Luc's stare. Unaware of Luc's chagrin, Fontaine continued, 'Indeed, brother. For such is our quest, to do battle with the creatures of the night that plague these noble people, that carry their children to Blood Keep and drain them of their souls. To face the vampires!'

Fontaine sat back in his chair, the barest hint of a self-satisfied smirk playing around the corners of this mouth. A throat cleared at a table beside the fireplace and his grin widened as an aged voice began to speak.

'If you are truly heading to Blood Keep then you are even more stupid than you look.'

Fontaine's grin vanished and he surged to his feet, face scarlet and his hand flashing to his sword hilt. A blur of silver steel and the blade was in his hand.

'Who dares insult my honour?' he roared, eyes scanning the wary crowd. A single pair of eyes rose to meet Fontaine's. A man, bent by age and toil, his skin worn and leathery, whose eyes, despite the twin ravages of time and alcohol, were clear and blue, haunted by a wisdom that belied his appearance.

Fontaine's resolve faltered as he met the old man's gaze, but his pride would not allow him to back down now. He held the sword at the old man's throat and said, 'Were you a worthy foe I would challenge you to a duel. But I am a man of honour and will not strike one so venerable.'

The man shrugged, as though the matter was of no consequence, saying, 'You are a fool to think you can defeat the Blood Knights. They are warriors beyond compare. I know. I stood in the ranks when the Duc de Montfort fought them at Gisoreux. He was a great man, but the vampires cut him down like a child.'

Luc stood and gently lowered Fontaine's sword arm.

'I am also a warrior of no small repute, old man,' Luc began. 'In Kislev they called me Droyaska – blademaster – and in the Northern Wastes, the Chaos beasts know me as the "One who walks with Death". It is the night stalkers who should be wary of *me*.'

Fontaine spun his sword, sheathing it in one smooth motion and sat down as Luc stood before the wizened figure.

The old man fixed Luc with his piercing gaze, looking deep into the young knight's eyes. He leaned forwards and whispered, 'There is fierce pride within you, boy. I see it plain as day, but do not travel to Blood Keep. If you do, you will all die. I can say it no more plainly than that. Heed my warning, leave this place and do not return.'

Luc smiled and turned his back on the old man, addressing the bar's patrons, 'Know this, people of–'

'Gugarde,' whispered Fontaine.

'Gugarde,' continued Luc smoothly. 'We travel on the morrow for Blood Keep and the vampires. That my name shall be remembered is reward enough.'

His speech over, Luc spun on his heel and strode in the direction of the stairs to the upper floors.

'Innkeeper!' he barked. 'Show us to our rooms and I demand you bring us the finest wines you possess.'

* * *

A THIN MIST hung over the muddy road as the three knights led their horses from the gloom of the stable into the weak morning sunlight. Luc tethered his black gelding to the hitching rail again and slid his sword from its oiled scabbard. He moved to the centre of the road, swinging his weapon in easy arcs around his body, loosening the muscles of his shoulders. He slowed his breathing and held the blade before him, the quillons level with his face. Suddenly he lunged, spinning and twisting, the blade a sweeping arc of silver as it spun in a glittering web before the knight.

Luc's bladework was flawless, every movement perfectly balanced and controlled. Cut, thrust, parry and riposte, Luc's sword became an extension of his flesh. He finished his exercises by making one last, neck-high cut, spinning the weapon by its pommel and scabbarding it.

Luc returned to his horse, examining the beast's legs and hooves. The stable lad, Antoine, had obviously looked after the horse. Its flanks were clean and groomed and the leather saddle had been given a fresh coating of oil. He crouched beside the gelding and tightened the saddle cinch before climbing onto the horse's back. He stared up into the soaring mountains and felt a thrill of anticipation surge through him. He was so close to his goal he could almost taste it.

High above him, the blackened fastness of Blood Keep awaited him. All his years of questing and battle had led him to this point and now that he was here, he was faintly amused to discover that there was a tremor of fear mixed with his excitement. Would he prove worthy? Almost as soon as he formed the thought, he chided himself for his lack of faith. Had he not fought the mightiest foes and vanquished them? The real question should be, was this quest worthy of him?

He twisted in the saddle to make sure his brothers were ready and saw the young lad, Antoine, standing by the stable door, casting hopeful glances at the armoured warriors. Luc fished in his purse and drew out a copper coin, flicking it in the boy's direction. The boy scampered forwards and caught the coin, hesitantly approaching Luc. He smiled nervously, exposing yellowed stumps of broken teeth.

'Sir knight?' he began.

Luc scowled. 'I have no more coin for you, boy.'

'No, sir,' said the boy shaking his head. 'I don't want no more of your money.'

'Really?'

'Really,' said Antoine. 'I want to come with you, to fight the vampires.'

Luc laughed and slapped his thigh with mirth. 'You want to fight the vampires, boy? How old are you?'

'Not sure, sir knight. I think maybe thirteen. I can be your squire. I can carry stuff and I can cook and clean swords and stuff. Please?'

'It takes more than that to become a squire, boy,' said Luc sternly. 'Years of training, noble spirit and the right heritage. Can you match up to that?'

Antoine's head dropped and he muttered, 'I know a short-cut up the mountains to the keep as well.'

Luc's interest was suddenly piqued. He could see the boy was close to tears at the thought of being left behind and sighed. He didn't need this, now of all times. But if the boy knew a quicker route through the mountains then perhaps he might be useful after all.

'Very well,' said Luc, 'you may ride the pack mule and will do exactly as I say when I say it. You displease me even once and I will send you back here. Do you understand me?'

Antoine nodded enthusiastically. 'Yes, sir! I do! You won't be sorry, I promise.'

'I'd better not be,' snarled Luc, in what he hoped was a suitably fearsome voice.

Fontaine walked his horse next to Luc and whispered, 'Luc, are you sure about this? Do we really want this boy travelling with us? We will not be able to protect him properly if we are to go into battle.'

Luc nodded. 'The boy claims to know a short-cut through the mountains. I shall let him lead us to the pass then send him on his way. He'll be in no danger and I'll look out for him if things turn vicious. You worry too much Fontaine. We are on the road to glory, brother. Have faith.'

Fontaine shrugged, 'You know best, Luc.'

'Yes,' agreed Luc, 'I do. Now come on, I want to get as far up the mountains as possible before it gets dark. Even if the boy's short-cut is genuine, I do not believe we will reach Blood Keep before nightfall, but I want to be sure we'll get there while it's daylight the following day.'

Luc touched his spurs to the horse's flank and the small group headed north along the mud-choked street, Antoine swaying on the back of the pack mule. At the edge of the village, next to the village cemetery, the group passed a small, ill-kept shrine to the Lady of the Lake. A few flowers and a pile of mouldy grain were the only offerings within the alcove and the three knights bowed their heads as they passed. Overhead a carrion bird circled, black wings spread against the struggling sunlight.

THE SUNLIGHT BURNED through the mist within the hour and the ground began to grow noticeably steeper. The day had warmed and Luc removed his helmet. It was warm now, but he knew that once they climbed higher into the mountains, the temperature would plummet rapidly. The short-cut Antoine had shown them had cut nearly seven miles from their journey and Luc was in fine spirits. The air was clear and Luc breathed deeply, enjoying the sense of freedom he suddenly felt.

The morning passed uneventfully, the path up the mountains allowing them to make good time. The miles were covered quickly, though the horses were tired and Luc called a halt to their climb as the sun reached its zenith. Antoine walked and fed the horses as the knights rested and ate a light meal of black bread and cheese accompanied by a bottle of Estalian wine. Luc leaned back against a boulder and peered into the snow capped mountains, their tops wreathed in ghostly grey clouds.

Separating the land of Bretonnia from the heathen land of the Empire, the Grey Mountains towered above him. Blood Keep nestled in a narrow pass that connected the two lands and had once been a mighty fortress, home to a noble order of warrior knights that had protected the lands hereabouts from harm. The knights had been renowned for their honour and martial skills, the very sight of their banner enough to send cold jolts of fear through the servants of evil.

Legend told that one day a warrior had presented himself at the gates and demanded to join the order. It was said that this had been the deathless knight known as Walach of the Harkon family and that he had, in one night, infected the order with the curse of vampirism. The knights took the ancient name of the Blood Dragon order as their own and years of terror and bloodshed were unleashed on the lands surrounding their fortress. It had taken the combined might of four orders of Empire knights to stand against the vampires and drive them back to their fortress. After three years of siege, the gates were finally breached and the castle put to the torch. The knights and witch hunters slew the vampires and the evil legacy of Blood Keep passed into history. To this day, it was believed that their evil had been defeated, but Luc knew that the bloodline still lived.

Deep in the northern Chaos Wastes he had fought one of the soulless vampire knights and cut the head from his body in a battle that almost cost him his life and left him with the long, white scar on his face. Luc had gazed upon the seraphic face of the vampire and watched in amazement as his youthful face had aged centuries in a matter of seconds before disintegrating into ashes. The vampire's blood-red armour, exquisitely detailed with intricate scrollwork and moulded muscles, was all that remained of the creature. It was a work of art and Luc could tell that it was incredibly ancient. The vampire must have been hundreds of years old, yet looked no different than Luc's youngest brother, its youth prolonged for all eternity!

Luc shook his head at the memory, remembering the feelings the vampire's demise had stirred within him. He finished his bread and pushed himself to his feet. They set off again and continued further up the mountain, the air becoming colder as they went higher and higher into the peaks. The sun dropped behind them, bathing the Loren Forest in a golden glow as the day wore on.

'Luc?' said Fontaine, startling him from his thoughts.

'What?'

'It is getting late. Should we not send the boy home?'

Luc glanced round at Antoine, cursing as he raised his eyes to the darkening sky and realised that it was too late to send the boy back.

'No, he will need to make camp with us tonight. I will send him back tomorrow. Where we go he cannot follow.'

'Where shall we make camp?'

Luc scanned the horizon, spying a circle of jagged boulders perhaps an hour's ride uphill. He pointed to the spot he had selected. 'There, we'll make camp in the rocks yonder.'

NIGHT DREW IN swiftly and it was dark long before they arrived at the circle of boulders. A wolf howled in the distance and the knights paused in their ascent. An answering chorus of howls echoed mournfully across the darkness and the horses whinnied in fear, eyes wide and ears pressed flat against their skulls. Antoine once again took the horses as they reached the rocks and Belmonde began preparing a fire in the lee of a flat-sided boulder. Satisfied that all was well, Luc walked to the edge of the camp and stared into the inky blackness, his thoughts on the castle above them and the beings that were said to have returned to dwell within it.

The mountains were a different place at night. Where earlier he could see for hundreds of miles in all directions, now he could barely see his hand before his face. The fire behind him illuminated a pitifully small area, its fitful light a tiny island of life in the night's darkness.

Luc returned to the fire, the reflected heat from the boulder beginning to warm him now. He settled down on his haunches, watching as Antoine unpacked a pot, some chopped meat, vegetables and oats from the panniers on the pack mule. Luc suddenly realised how hungry he was, his mouth watering at the thought of a hearty broth.

'You'll need some water for that pot,' pointed out Fontaine. 'There's a stream about twenty yards or so that way.'

Antoine glanced fearfully in the direction Fontaine had indicated, unease plain on his features. Luc sighed, 'Take a torch from the fire, boy. And don't be long, I'm so hungry my belly thinks my throat's been cut.'

Reluctantly, Antoine took up a burning brand and picked his way over the uneven ground in the direction of the stream. The brothers chuckled as they heard the boy cursing as he slipped on the uneven shale. Fontaine followed the bobbing torch as Antoine made his way towards the stream. A sudden sense of premonition made him glance uphill from the lad's position as he caught sight of sinuous movement at the edge of the torchlight. He sat bolt upright, reaching for his sword as he saw more shadowy forms with red coals for eyes surrounding the boy.

'No!' he yelled as the first wolf attacked, a bolt from the darkness with gleaming fangs and claws. The boy barely had time to scream before the giant wolf's jaws closed on his head, tearing his face off in a spray of blood. Claws like knives raked down his chest, laying him open to the bone. The creature's body was briefly illuminated by the torchlight as it attacked, rotting skin and bone glistening wetly through mange ridden fur.

Antoine's body spasmed as he died, his hand swinging around and thrusting the torch into the wolf's body. It howled as long-dead flesh and fur ignited spectacularly. The sudden flare of the wolf's death cast a wider ring of illumination and Luc had a brief glimpse of over a dozen undead wolves closing on them. The knights drew their swords, Luc grabbing Fontaine's arm as he made to rush to Antoine's aid.

'He's dead!' he snapped. 'There's nothing we can do for him now!'

Fontaine nodded curtly, and stood back to back with his brothers, the fire at their centre. Antoine was dead for sure. All they could do was avenge him and fight off these devil dogs as best they could. Their warhorses reared and stamped the ground as the wolves circled them, hooves lashing out as the beasts came in range. One wolf pounced forward, jaws wide. An iron shod hoof smashed its skull to shards with a single blow.

'Don't leave the firelight!' yelled Luc as a wolf leapt at him. He ducked, swinging his sword in a short, brutal arc. His blade disembowelled the wolf, decaying entrails spilling from the wound. Its carcass landed on the fire, sparks and embers flying.

Howls echoed as the wolves attacked en masse. Luc drew his dagger and thrust the blade between the fanged jaws of another hell beast. It howled and rolled away, tearing the weapon from his hand. He side-stepped and swept his sword down, beheading another wolf. Fontaine staggered from the fire, his shoulder guard torn away by powerful claws. He dropped to his knees, a wolf's jaws snapping shut on his vambrace. The armour held and Fontaine grunted in pain as the metal compressed on the flesh of his forearm. Luc thundered his boot into his brother's attacker, feeling ribs break under the impact. He stabbed with his sword and another beast was silenced. Luc pulled Fontaine to his feet, dragging him back to the fire.

Belmonde swung wildly with his sword and a burning torch. The wolves snarled, wary of the flames. The three brothers regrouped at the fire, their breathing shallow and laboured. The pack mule was down, screaming as blood pumped from its torn belly. Again the wolves charged, to be met by the steely defences of the knights. Keen blades flashed in the firelight and blood splashed the rocks. Luc slashed and cut, killing wolves with every stroke. The carnage continued until the first cold, grey slivers of light began spilling over the high peaks. With a howl of defiance the wolves melted into what darkness remained, leaving their slaughtered kin behind. Belmonde slumped to the ground, his armour streaked in gore, his face lined with exhaustion.

Fontaine sat next to him, wiping the blade of his sword clean on a dead wolf. Like his brother, he was covered in blood. Luc stared up the mountainside, grinning fiercely and raised his sword to the lightening sky.

'I am Luc Massone!' he shouted, 'and I am coming to Blood Keep!'

He turned to his brothers and walked to where the warhorses stood, their flanks heaving and nostrils flared. The animals bled from scores of wounds, but they were alive. It was not for nothing that Bretonnian warhorses were renowned as the finest cavalry mounts in all the realms of man. He sheathed his sword and gently stroked each animal's head, calming them with soft words. Finally he allowed himself to sit next to his brothers.

'Well done,' he said. 'You fought well. I am proud of you both.'

For long seconds no one spoke until Belmonde's head snapped up.

'Antoine!' he groaned, standing on weary muscles and limping across to where the boy had died. The burnt corpse of the wolf lay where it had fallen, a pile of stinking ashes, the wood of the brand lodged in the remains.

But there was no sign of the boy's body, just a wide crimson stain on the rocks.

THE BROTHERS DIVIDED the supplies from the dead mule and set off with the dawn's light. Luc knew Fontaine and Belmonde had been shaken by the wolves' attack and he couldn't blame them. Such beasts were feared throughout the Old World, but Luc had faced horrors a hundred times worse and prevailed. A pack of mangy wolves would not stop him from achieving his destiny.

The journey became slower as the ground became more treacherous and icy, the path vanishing as they climbed past the snowline and the weather quickly worsened. Several times their horses stumbled on the slick rocks and the knights were forced to dismount, leading their horses over ice-covered ledges. All three were well wrapped in thick furs, yet still the wind leeched the heat from their bodies as it knifed through them. Hours passed in a white haze, swaying with exhaustion, the freezing temperature robbing them of strength.

'Luc! We must turn back!' implored Fontaine, moving alongside his eldest brother.

Luc shook his head violently, 'No! We go on. It can't be far now.'

'You said that two hours ago.'

'I know what I said, damn you!' snarled Luc. 'We're almost there. I feel it in my bones. We cannot stop now! I will not stop!'

Luc dragged his mount onwards, ending the discussion.

Another hour of frozen misery passed before they crested a snow covered rise and a vast shape emerged from the whiteness. At first Luc wasn't sure what he was seeing as he stared into the flurries of white before him. Then, gradually, shapes began to resolve themselves from the blizzard. Jutting from the rocks, shattered walls and breached bastions loomed out of the falling snow. Smashed turrets and broken merlons, all that remained of the ruined fortress-monastery, reared vast and bloated, like jagged and blackened teeth. Before them lay the rotting carcass of what had once been one of the mightiest citadels in the Old World. Splintered gates hung on sagging hinges and the air of desolation was palpable.

Luc turned to Fontaine and smiled in triumph.

'Blood Keep,' he said.

A SINGLE, LONELY path wound its way over the rocks towards the broken gates and the knights directed their horses towards the remains of Blood Keep. Luc smiled, breaking the ice that sweat had formed on his skin. He was here! Nothing could stop him now. He glanced over at his brothers and his smile faltered, but as he imagined the rewards of success, he put such thoughts aside.

'I dislike this place,' said Belmonde as they entered the cold shadow of the keep's walls. 'We should not be here.'

Luc said nothing, urging his mount further up the path. The walls soared nearly sixty feet above him, the stonework blackened by fire and the rubble infill spilling from holes blasted long ago by Empire cannon. A shiver passed through Luc as he entered Blood Keep and though he told himself it was the cold, he only half believed it.

They found themselves within a wide, granite-flagged courtyard, drifts of snow piled high against the walls. Wind whistled through the stables and lean-to's around the walls, a ghostly lament to the warriors who had once occupied this place. The main keep of the fortress squatted against the sheer rock face of the mountains, its main gateway also splintered and broken. Blackened loopholes in the wall gaped like empty eye sockets and Luc could not help but feel he was being watched.

He gently patted his horse's flanks. The beast was exhausted and frightened. Something about this place had spooked the beast; looking round he saw that the other horses were similarly wary. His brothers moved to stand alongside him.

'What now?' asked Belmonde, staring at the inner keep.

'We find the vampires,' answered Luc, untying his shield from his warhorse. 'Come on.'

His brothers shared an uneasy glance and also took up their shields, following Luc as he walked his horse towards the inner keep. Fontaine looked into the sky as Belmonde tied the horses to a broken timber spar. He couldn't see the sun and wondered how long it would be until nightfall.

The three brothers stood together at the gate and drew their swords.

'Come, brothers,' smiled Luc. 'The vampires await.'

* * *

THE DARKNESS WITHIN was absolute, as though light itself were afraid to venture too deeply. Two skeletons lay inside the gateway, slumped against the wall and still clutching rusted spears. Luc crouched before the nearest cadaver, tearing two lengths of cloth from its tattered tunic. He snapped the shaft of the dead sentinel's spear and wrapped the cloth around one end, passing the other half and some of the cloth to Belmonde. Fontaine dug out a tinderbox and lit the dry fabric, the light from the torches illuminating the passage with a flickering glow.

Luc set off without a backward glance, advancing down the wide corridor with his torch held before him. Murder holes pierced the ceiling and arrow loops punctuated the walls. Luc could imagine the horrific casualties the Empire knights must have suffered attacking down this hallway. The passage ended at a sharp right turn, ascending a spiral staircase into the cobwebbed darkness. Luc swapped the sword into his left hand, knowing that the turn of the stairs would prevent him from using the sword effectively in his right. He slid along the outer wall of the stairs, his weapon extended before him, having learned to use either hand with the same deadly skill.

The knights emerged into an echoing cloister, the air musty with the stench of decay. Hundreds of skeletons littered the floor, clustered around an oaken double door, their armour rusted through and bones filmed with the dust of centuries.

'Do you know where you are going?' whispered Fontaine nervously.

'Of course,' hissed Luc. 'To find the vampire's lair.'

'Then should we not be looking for a way down rather than up?' said Belmonde. 'I was led to believe that vampires would make their lairs within underground crypts and sepulchres.'

Luc shook his head. 'The main hall will be where we shall find these vampires. I am sure of it.'

His brothers looked unconvinced, but Luc pressed on before they had time to contradict him, stepping carefully over the skeletal warriors towards the door at the end of the cloister. The door was splintered at its centre and he pushed it open, beckoning his brothers to follow as he slipped through into the main hall.

Golden sunlight filtered in through high windows, partially blocked with rotted velvet drapes, revealing a long banqueting hall with a gigantic wooden table running its length. Shields and suits of blood-red armour lined the walls, below crossed lances, unlit torches and faded tapestries.

Belmonde and Luc passed down one side of the table, Fontaine the other, lighting the torches set in the sconces as they went. Their armoured boots echoed loudly in the deserted hall.

'The table is set for drinking,' said Belmonde, nodding towards empty goblets placed before every seat.

'But not eating,' pointed out Fontaine. 'Where are the plates?'

'The vampire does not take sustenance as we do, brother,' answered Luc.

Fontaine grimaced and advanced towards the massive fireplace, bending his head towards the grate. He turned back to Luc and said, 'This smells of woodsmoke, a fire has been lit here recently. And look, there is fresh-cut wood here. Why would the undead require heat?'

Luc joined his brother at the fireplace. He shrugged. 'I do not know, Fontaine. Perhaps other travellers have passed this way recently.'

'And stopped for the night in Blood Keep?' blurted Belmonde. 'They must have been desperate.'

'Perhaps,' agreed Luc, watching as the thin strips of light filtering into the hall from behind the velvet drapes slowly crept across the floor as the sun descended behind the peaks.

Fontaine caught Luc's gaze and also noticed the dimming light.

'Luc!' he exclaimed, 'the light is going! It must be later than we thought. We must leave this place!'

'It may already be too late for that,' answered Luc, hearing the rustle of dry bones from the cloister they had passed through and noticing armoured figures cloaked in shadow on the balconies above them.

'Lady protect us!' prayed Fontaine as the oaken door burst open and the previously lifeless skeletons marched relentlessly into the banqueting hall, spears and swords raised before them.

'For the Lady!' screamed Belmonde, launching himself forward, his sword smashing the first skeleton to fragments. Dust billowed around the skeletons as they attacked. Flesh and blood fought dry, withered bone, the air filling with the crack of ancient skulls and ribs. Luc hacked a skeleton apart at the waist and smashed his shield into another. Fontaine kicked the legs out from under his assailant, breaking its skull open with his boot heel. Belmonde's sword rose and fell, the blade as much a bludgeon as a cutting weapon. The skeletal warriors were no match for the knights, but no matter how many the brothers killed, there were more to take their place.

Slowly but surely they were forced back towards the fireplace, the shadowed figures above them silently watching the battle. Fontaine screamed in pain as a spear point stabbed into his unprotected shoulder, where the armoured plate had been torn away by the wolves. The thrust pitched him off balance and he fell to his knees. A sword smashed into his temple, tearing the helmet from his head. His vision blurred as blood streamed down his face.

'Fontaine!' shouted Belmonde as his brother struggled to rise.

Bony fingers grasped at Fontaine's wrists, the press of numbers preventing him from rising. He roared as the skeletons held him down, struggling to free his sword arm and kicking out desperately. He had a fleeting, horrified glimpse of a wide spear-point plunging towards him before it was rammed deep into his belly below his breastplate. It tore upwards into his heart and lungs, bursting from his back in a flood of gore. His screams trailed into a bloody gurgling as an axe split his head apart.

Belmonde hacked his brother's killer down, screaming a denial. Luc was at his side, sweeping aside the undead with brutal sword blows, but it was far too late for Fontaine Massone. Backs to the wall, Luc and Belmonde kept the skeletons at bay with desperate skill, tapping reserves of courage neither knew they possessed.

As he destroyed another skeleton, Luc felt his fury building. This wasn't how it was supposed to end! He spared a glance up at the dark balconies and the warriors watching the furious battle.

'Cowards!' he yelled as he smashed his dented shield into the grinning face of another opponent. 'Where is your honour? I am Luc Massone and I slew one of your kind! I demand you come down and face me!'

Almost as soon as he had spoken, the skeleton horde ceased their attack and took a single backward step. The hall was silent, the sudden absence of noise more unnerving than the clash of arms. Belmonde rushed to Fontaine's side, cradling his dead brother's head in his arms. Tears streaked clear trails in the dust coating his face.

'Oh my brother, what have we done?' he wept.

'Belmonde!' hissed Luc. 'Stand beside me. Now!'

His brother ignored him until Luc grabbed him by the shoulder and hauled him to his feet. Belmonde's face was twisted in grief, his sword held limply at his side. Luc smiled weakly at him. 'Fear not, brother. This will all be over soon.'

He looked towards the balconies, watching as the armoured figures slipped out of sight. The metallic rasp of armour sounded as the watchers descended to the banqueting hall, emerging from concealed alcoves either side of the fireplace.

Three powerful warriors, clad in suits of exquisitely fashioned crimson armour stood wordlessly before the two brothers. The Blood Dragons wore no helmets, their pale, aquiline faces regarding the exhausted knights before them with expressions of faint amusement. Each carried a black bladed sword, its surface seeming to shimmer with an oily iridescence.

The knight on the left tilted his head to one side and raised his sword.

'You say you have killed a Blood Dragon?' said the vampire. 'You will forgive my scepticism, I hope?'

Like a striking snake, his sword lashed out at Luc's neck. Luc had been ready and swiftly parried, his riposte slashing towards the vampire's groin. The Blood Dragon barely had time to react, his sword flashing down to block the blow. Fast as quicksilver, Luc altered the direction of his cut and hacked off the vampire's head in a single, powerful sweep. The Blood Dragon toppled backwards, his body ashes before the armour hit the stone floor.

Luc pulled his sword back to the guard position.

'Anyone else?' he asked.

The dark haired vampire with deep violet eyes who faced Luc glanced at the empty suit of armour beside him and said, 'You are fast and skilful for a mortal. There are few alive who could have even scratched Grigorij, let alone slain him.'

Luc nodded. 'My skill with a blade is great.'

The vampire smiled. 'Where is your humility, knight? You are arrogant.'

'It is not arrogance if it is the truth,' pointed out Luc.

The Blood Dragon laughed. 'Here, in this place, you are a child amongst your betters. I could kill you in a heartbeat. You cannot hope to vanquish me. Surely you must know that?'

'I know that,' nodded Luc.

'Then why are you here?' asked the vampire. 'You have not come to slay me?'

'No,' admitted Luc as Belmonde stared at his brother in horrified fascination.

'Then why?'

Luc altered his grip on his sword and shouted, 'Because I have come to join your order!'

His blade slashed and blood geysered as Luc Massone spun round and beheaded his brother. Belmonde's corpse swayed for a brief moment, then slowly crumpled to the floor, slumped across Fontaine's lifeless body.

Luc faced the Blood Dragon and planted the sword, point first, on the stone hearth, his face alight as he met the vampire's stare.

'The blood of innocents is on my hands and I am a warrior beyond compare. Where in the mortal world can I find my equal?' hissed Luc. 'I bring you this offering of my own flesh and blood as proof of my desire. I am one of you and I demand you grant me the boon of immortality!'

Hot excitement pounded through his veins. Luc's skin flushed red, his scar a livid white line across his face. It was done. He had reached the point where all mortal laws ceased to bind him. He would become one of the ever-living, destined never to die, destined only to become the greatest warrior of the age!

The Blood Dragon watched the blood pump from Belmonde's neck and raised his eyebrows in puzzlement.

'Demand...' he said as though he had never heard the word.

'Aye,' snarled Luc. 'It is my right. I deserve this.'

The vampire knight grinned, exposing razor sharp fangs.

'Very well. you shall have what you deserve,' he promised.

THE VILLAGE OF Gugarde echoed to screams of pain and fear. Dark horses with red eyes carrying crimson armoured knights stalked the streets. No one had really believed the three knights boasts of defeating the vampires of Blood Keep when they had passed through the village some six months ago, but perhaps there had been tiny embers of hope stirred in a few hearts. That hope was now ashes on the wind as black armoured skeletons dragged the screaming inhabitants from their beds to the slaughter.

The knights laughed as peasants ineffectually waved bundles of daemonroot before them. A venerable human with a rusty sword had been the only one prepared to fight, but there had been no honour in slaying one so old. The vampires would feed, but would not lower themselves to trade blows with those who were not worthy of their blades.

Undead warriors in rusted armour stood motionless as their masters began feeding on the villagers, zombies picking themselves up from the mud as the vampires raised the newly dead to swell their ranks. Bats flapped noisily overhead as snarling wolves padded soundlessly through the village, seeking out those who had chosen to hide from the vampires. There would be no escaping the killing.

In the walled cemetery at the village's edge, stooped creatures hugged the shadows, scrabbling at the wet ground. Pale, blotched skin hung loosely from their emaciated frames as they dug the dead from the ground. Perhaps a dozen of the vile ghouls pawed furiously at the earth, the hunger for cold, dead flesh driving their efforts. At last the group dragged out a simple casket, the largest of the fiends wrenching the coffin lid off and howling in triumph. Clawed hands reached within, desperate for the taste of human meat, but the largest creature snarled and the rest pulled back hissing.

It reached inside the coffin, tearing out the dead heart and ripping great chunks of rotten meat from the bones of the corpse. It scuttled to the cemetery walls to devour its horrific meal, unnatural hunger in its eyes.

The moon emerged from behind a cloud and the degenerate beast blinked in its unforgiving glare, noticing a small shrine lying on its side where the Blood Dragon's charge had knocked it. It stared at the shrine as a faint memory stirred, as though the sight should be familiar to it. But the memory was gone and the beast shook its head, biting deeply into the cold heart it carried and scratching idly at the long, white scar that ran from its right temple to its chin.

THE ROAD TO DAMNATION
by Brian Craig

LUIS QUINTAL WATCHED admiringly as Memet Ashraf turned in the saddle and drew back his bowstring. The Arabian took aim as carefully as he could, given that his horse was at full gallop. As soon as he released the arrow the bowman turned to regain full control of his mount. It was left to Quintal to note that the arrowhead flew straight into the breast of an exceptionally ugly orc mounted on a giant boar.

'One more down!' the Estalian cried, exultantly. Then he raised a fist into the air, and said: 'They've finally had enough! They've given up!'

The remaining orcs were bringing their boars to a halt, and their goblin companions encouraged their wolves to do likewise.

The two human riders reined in without delay, knowing that they had to preserve the strength of their animals. Their horses gladly slowed to a canter, and then to a walk.

'They haven't given up,' Ashraf growled. 'Orcs never give up. They're playing a game. It's a wise move – no pig, however monstrous, could outrun a horse over a short distance, but even a running man can out-stay one if he's prepared to keep going day and night. If they don't lose our trail they'll catch up eventually – the orcs might be too stupid to work it out, but their goblin friends will put them right.'

The ill-assorted band that had been chasing the two companions since dawn was by no means large: numbering no more than eight orcs – two of which had been killed or disabled by Ashraf's arrows – and half a dozen goblins. But Quintal knew that he and the Arabian would soon be overwhelmed if they had to fight at close quarters. A long career as a pirate had given Ashraf a useful education in many kinds of fighting, and Quintal was unmatchable with a sabre, at least by any greenskin. However, the two men could not defend themselves against twelve mounted enemies save by a very careful war of attrition.

'Surely we're not worth that much effort?' Quintal asked, dubiously. 'If we were worth robbing we'd hardly be deep in the Badlands following rumours of treasure.'

'That's the kind of calculation a man would make,' Ashraf told him, 'but orcs think differently. Even if I hadn't shot two, they'd still come after us. It's not the means to an end for them: the murder of a human is an end in itself, an accomplishment worth every effort.'

Quintal shook his head. He found it difficult to credit such an absurdity. 'It's not as if we are trespassing in their territory,' he said. 'This desert is incapable of supporting any kind of life. No orc tribe would bring its herds through here.'

'That's not a concept that all men would understand,' Ashraf observed. 'Estalians think in term of territorial rights, but in Araby we have more than our fair share of useless land and we are born to a life of piracy. We're not nomads because we seek grazing for our herds; we're predators, who must live off the herds of others. These orcs don't care that this useless land is shunned by the majority of their kind – they're outcasts, forced into the margins of their own society. Whatever purpose they had before they stumbled across our trail is forgotten. Now they have but one: to hunt us down. Their goblin hangers-on might give up if the task becomes too challenging, because their wolves will find it very difficult to hunt in these parts. But remember orcs and their boars can go without food, water and rest for far longer than humans and horses.'

'Suppose we were to double back behind them, and try to pick them off one by one,' Quintal suggested. He felt uncomfortable proposing a plan that the bowman would have to execute virtually single-handed.

'Impossible,' was Ashraf's judgment. 'That would be playing into the goblins' hands. Countering sneak attacks is one of their skills. We have no choice but to go on, and hope that we can find a way to give them the slip.' His tone suggested he didn't believe they could do it.

Quintal looked at the terrain before them, and knew exactly why his companion was so pessimistic. Like the deserts of Araby, this part of the Badlands was all sand and rock, and the sand was gathered by the wind into continually shifting dunes that limited their vision to a few hundred paces.

Although noon was long past the sand was still very hot and yielding; it was far from an ideal surface for steel-shod horses. Quintal and Ashraf had put leather socks over the hooves of their mounts, but that wasn't enough to save them from distress.

Quintal raised his water bottle and shook it. There was hardly any liquid left to rattle. He put it down again even though his throat was parched.

'If we don't find water by nightfall,' Ashraf told him, grimly, 'We'll be travelling on foot tomorrow. And if we don't find water tomorrow... it might be a blessing if the greenskins were to catch up with us.'

'So we keep going forward,' Quintal said. 'The one thing to be said for these dunes is that there's always high ground ahead.'

'And more dunes,' the Arabian muttered.

Quintal guessed that the odds were perhaps a thousand to one in favour of that judgment, but to his surprise, Memet Ashraf challenged it almost immediately. 'There was a road here once,' he said, pensively.

'I see no sign of it,' Quintal admitted.

'You're not desert-bred,' the Arabian reminded him. 'It is far older than any I've seen before, but it's definitely a road. The orcs are desert-bred, but they're probably too stupid to see it, so we'll lose nothing by following it. I wonder where it leads to?'

'To the city!' Quintal exclaimed, feeling a sudden surge of exultation. 'Elisio was telling the truth!'

'To damnation, more likely,' was Memet Ashraf's grim verdict. 'Even so, we have no choice but to follow it. There comes a time in every man's life when all roads lead to damnation.'

It was obvious to Quintal that Memet Ashraf had lost whatever faith he had had in their mission, and that even the discovery of the all-but-obliterated road could not reignite it. The Estalian could hardly blame him, for he had lost faith in the informant who had sent him on this mad expedition, and he could find little comfort in the news that there was a road here only detectable by an Arabian.

Even so, he thought, we might as well pray that Elisio was right, as we've little else to offer us hope.

Quintal was a native of Magritta, where noblemen were exceedingly proud of their naval traditions, and made great heroes of their explorers and privateers. Mindful of the bad example set by the smaller neighbouring city-state of Almyria, whose royal family were perennially engaged in murdering one another, the Magrittan nobility had found it conducive to political stability to put their younger sons in charge of ships commissioned to undertake expeditions to distant and dangerous parts of the world. A few returned very rich, but a greater number never returned. An even greater number brought their vessels home in ignominious states of disrepair, with nothing to show for their adventures but tales of treasures *almost* captured and battles *almost* won. These tales were usually discounted, but when one of Quintal's cousins, Elisio Azevedo, whom he had been careless enough to worship in his youth – assured him that no one but loyal Luis should hear the tale of what happened to his lost ship, Quintal had been very eager to believe him.

When the time came for him to take his own ship south, Quintal had been determined to take advantage of the knowledge that he alone possessed – if Elisio could be trusted. His cousin, alas, had suffered a fatal accident a few months after telling him the story. In spite of being warned of the dangers, Quintal had matched his cousin's losses. He had found himself stranded on a distant shore along with the sole survivor of the foundered ship that had sent his own to the bottom.

Had Memet Ashraf been an orc, they would doubtless have continued to fight one another until one of them lay dead. But Memet Ashraf was not an orc, and the two of them had been sensible enough to make a truce – which had turned quickly enough into a firm compact. Ever since they had stolen the horses they were now riding, Quintal had been happy to think of the other man as a fast friend – although he knew that he would never be able to introduce him as a dinner-guest to any inn or home in Magritta.

At the moment, that was the least of his troubles.

Quintal wondered whether Memet Ashraf had ever believed a word of his second-hand tale of a city of roseate stone, almost buried by desert sands and so far south in the Badlands as to be perilously near the borders of the Land of the Dead. Probably not, he decided, but the Arabian had no destination of his own – however fanciful – and he was a desert man by birth.

At any rate, he had consented to be led into the desert, presumably thinking it was a place they were least likely to run into the orc and goblin tribes that were the curse of the Badlands.

Alas, it had not been unlikely enough.

'Perhaps we should have stolen boars instead of horses,' Quintal said, when they crested yet another rise only to see yet more dunes before them. 'Perhaps, if we're very careful, we still could.'

'An Arabian does not ride a pig.' Memet Ashraf's reply was hoarse but scornful.

Quintal looked back at the way they had come. Earlier in the day there had been a wind blowing, which meant that their tracks in the soft sand might be obliterated, but the evening was utterly still and the route they had followed could hardly have been marked more clearly. It could not be helped. There was nothing to do but continue until the horses collapsed – then there would be nothing to do but continue on foot, until he and Ashraf became incapable of moving on.

Quintal would be the first to fall, and he knew that however firm his new friendship was, Memet Ashraf would then go on without him, perhaps cutting his throat so that he would not fall into the hands of the orcs and goblins alive. Goblins had a reputation for ingenious and effective torture even in Estalia, whose inquisitors were legendary throughout the Old World.

Well, Quintal thought, at least I shall never have the opportunity to pass the tale on to some younger cousin in Magritta who knows no better than to take it seriously. What could I have been thinking? Buried cities older than the desert sands! Temples raised to evil gods when the Land of the Dead was still the Land of the Living! Horned idols with enormous gems mounted in their foreheads! How could I have been so gullible? And yet... my desert-bred friend says that we are following a road. It must lead somewhere solid, even if it is to damnation as well.

Memet Ashraf's raw voice cut into his reverie: 'Look there!'

For a moment, Quintal's carefully-balanced cynicism fell away, releasing a flood of delirious hope. But then he saw that the pirate was pointing up towards circling vultures, and his optimism faded again.

'Have they come for us already?' he moaned. 'Is the odour of death already upon us?'

'Not yet,' the Arabian croaked. 'They have more urgent work to do. There's something up ahead which is not quite dead.'

'And if we get there first,' Quintal said, 'we can hold the birds at bay and claim the prize for ourselves!'

'Perhaps,' said Memet Ashraf, urging his horse to one last effort.

Quintal made to follow him, but his horse made no response at all. The sun was setting, and the twilight would not last long. His horse was finished, and the Arabian's mount was almost as bad, although it was slightly ahead. There was no danger that Quintal would be left far behind.

The dunes were smaller and steeper here than they had been before, and the low ground between them a little stonier. Even Quintal could see signs of a road now, it was no longer straight – but it made good sense for Quintal and Memet Ashraf to follow the meandering course of the ancient path, even though they could hardly see thirty paces in front or behind.

Ten minutes passed before they came in sight of the vultures' quarry. Quintal's first reaction was to groan in disappointment. He had been hoping to find another human traveller – preferably a pretty woman who had fainted from the heat even though she still had a full water bottle – or, better still, a barrel in the luggage borne by her sturdy and patient packhorse. Instead they found a boar bred by the orcs for transportation, milk and meat. It carried no saddle or harness, but it was almost certainly an escapee from orcish domestication rather than a natural inhabitant of the region. It was lying down, presumably stricken by thirst and exhaustion. Its eyes were open, and they fixed upon Memet Ashraf as he rode forward. The creature seemed incapable of movement, save for a reflexive spasm in one of its hind legs.

Trying to look on the bright side, Quintal told himself that the animal was meat. But meat was not what he needed most; water was. He wondered, briefly, whether horses could be persuaded to drink boar's blood, and whether they would benefit out of it if they did. Having failed to convince himself in respect of the horses, he then wondered if he could drink boar's blood, and whether it would benefit him.

He was surprised that Memet Ashraf was a great deal more excited by the discovery. 'Is it really worth fighting the vultures for?' he asked.

'Boars have good noses,' the Arabian told him, briefly. Quintal, looking down at the animal's incredibly ugly four-horned snout, and realised that *good* evidently did not mean *handsome*. 'Look at its tracks!' the Arabian went on. 'Its path has converged with ours. I don't know where it started, but I do know that it would not have come this way if there were a better way. If there's water anywhere, this is the signpost that will lead us to it.'

'If it's more than a few hundred paces off, it might as well be on the other side of the world,' Quintal said.

Memet Ashraf had dismounted now. 'But it's not!' he said. 'It's right here, but the poor creature couldn't get to it. It's a well, my friend. A covered well! That's why the road suddenly became so round-about.'

The Arabian was using his booted feet to brush the sand away from a rounded stone. Its emerging shape declared clearly that it was no mere boulder. It was a sculpted capstone – and what could it possibly be capping, if not a well?

'Help me!' the Arabian demanded.

Quintal was not slow to oblige. The capstone was heavy, but its weight had been carefully judged so that one man alone would be able to slide it away in case of dire necessity. They shifted it together without undue difficulty.

Night was falling, but they would not have been able to see far into the pit even in full daylight. Memet Ashraf picked up a pebble no bigger than a knucklebone and dropped it into the darkness. The splash was somewhat delayed, but clearly audible and satisfyingly sonorous; it promised reasonable depth.

'We don't have a bucket, but we do have a rope,' the Arabian said, exultantly. 'One of us can let the other down, with a bottle in each hand. It might take four or five trips, but we should be able to bring up enough to put new life into the horses.'

'I'm lighter,' Quintal said, 'and you have the stronger arms in any case. But the water's a fair way down – is the rope long enough, and will it take the strain?'

'Only one way to find out,' his companion told him, rummaging in his saddlebag for the rope.

Quintal took off his belt, his sheathed sword and his pouch, and passed them to his companion.

'These are all my worldly possessions – everything I have and everything I am is in this belt,' he said. 'Look after it, I beg you.'

Ashraf nodded, and muttered: 'You'll be back in three minutes.'

Alas, it required only two minutes to ascertain that the rope was not quite long enough, and that it would not take the strain of Quintal's weight. As he reached its limit, bracing himself as best he could against the walls of the well, a worn section of the rope snapped where it was looped around his chest, and he fell out of the noose.

He could not find a handhold or a foothold in the wall, and scrabbling after them only served to bloody his hands. He told himself that he could not have far to fall, and that he would not hurt himself because he was falling into deep water.

He was right, although the second part of his conviction had better grounds than the first. He fell less than three times his own height, scrambling at the walls as he went, but when he hit the water the impact seemed adequately cushioned.

He was astonished to find that the water was cold – and more surprising, had he only had time to consider the matter – it was far from still.

Before Quintal hit the water, the circle of light at the well mouth had shrunk alarmingly. Then he was immersed in total darkness, and by the time he had struggled back to the surface the current had carried him away.

He was not at all disappointed to be wet, or to have filled his mouth with water, but he knew that he was in dire danger. At any moment the flow might dash him against a rock or carry him into a bottleneck where he would stick fast and drown. He gulped as much air as he could, knowing that he might not have the opportunity to do so for much longer. He fought to swim against the current, hoping to bring himself to a safe pause if not to get back to the well shaft. But he was weaker than he had imagined. Magrittans were famed in Estalia as strong swimmers, but even the strongest of them would have floundered had he been brought as close to dehydration and exhaustion as Quintal.

So far as he could judge, the tunnel through which he was being carried was almost level, and there was at least an arm's-length of clearance above the surface. It was filled with stagnant but breathable air. He was wise enough to know that water does not flow as fast as this along a level course unless there is a cataract ahead. He could already hear the cascade. It might be as high as a man was tall, or it might descend half way to the centre of the world; all he could do was make ready for the drop and hope.

The water hurled him over the edge, and for a moment he almost came clear of the stream. Then he hit the pool below the waterfall, and the breath was knocked out of him.

The pool was even colder than the flood that had dumped him into it, and he was grateful for the slight additional shock. He was grateful too that the pool was relatively still once he had drifted away from the cascade. It must have an outflow somewhere, but it was relatively tranquil.

He was able to swim now, albeit weakly. He dared not make haste in any case. He had to be wary of swimming into an unforgiving rock face or catching an arm or leg on a jutting spur.

When his hand finally touched something solid, it felt like a ledge. In fact, he soon discovered, it was one of a whole sequence of ledges arranged in series.

No! he thought, feeling another resurgence of optimism. Not ledges – but steps!

He was right: a flight of stairs had been cut into the rock that lead down into the water. He was able to stand up, albeit very shakily, and climb out. Once clear of the water he sat down to rest. He squeezed the cloth of his shirt to release the water it had trapped. The pain in his hands as he increased his grip told him that he had lost a good deal of skin.

I'm in a bathhouse! Quintal thought.

He scrambled up the whole flight of steps feeling steadier on his feet. The water he had taken in had made him feel slightly sick as well as slaking his thirst.

He began to walk away from the head of the staircase, taking one careful step at a time with his hand extended in the darkness before him, wary of meeting a wall. He found one eventually, but it was not set squarely across his path. It was set aslant, as if the area at the top of the steps was triangular rather than square.

Of course it narrows, he told himself. It leads to a corridor of some kind. And if I follow the corridor carefully, I shall find more steps... steps that will eventually lead me all the way to the surface, for I must be in the cellar of a building – a building in a roseate city lost for thousands of years in the worst of the Badlands, where even orcs and goblins will not go. Oh, Luis, Luis, how could you ever have doubted dear Elisio's word?

Quintal was shivering now, and his teeth were chattering. He would have been very glad to find another flight of steps at the far end of the corridor into which he came, but it opened out instead into another wide space, of which he could see not a single detail.

Rather than marching forwards he followed the wall, running his hands along it even though his fingers became thickly beslimed with something horrid. He paused to wipe them on his trousers, but the slime was difficult to dislodge even on the wet cloth.

When he came to another narrow opening he had no way of knowing whether the tunnel would lead him up or down, but he tried it anyway. There was a wooden door at the further end, which seemed to have been barred. He could find no trace of a handle or a lock, but it would not yield to a tentative push. What gave him hope, though, was the fact that the invisible surface seemed to be covered in slime and fungal nodules. He concluded that it must be rotten, and if he could find its weakest point he might be able to make a hole. If he could not dislodge the bar after that, he could probably gradually widen the hole, until it was large enough to crawl through.

It was hard work for a man in his depleted condition. When the wood finally began to splinter it produced dagger-sharp pieces. They would have been easy enough to avoid had he been able to see them, but under cover of darkness they stabbed his hands and forearms, reopening the cuts he had sustained in the well and making several new deeper ones. Even so, such was his desperation and determination that it took him less than an hour to break through.

The other side of the door was dry, so Quintal assumed that the air beyond it must be contiguous with the desert air through which he had been riding for days. The prospect of dry warmth suddenly seemed welcoming, so he set off with a will into the darkness, hoping for a glimpse of starlight.

The wall he was following took him right, then left, then right again, eventually delivering him into yet another open space. Here at last, he saw chinks of light far above him, let in by narrow horizontal slits unlike any window he had ever seen before.

In here the still air was much warmer, and so dry that the water began evaporating from his clothing.

Quintal might have felt less disappointed by the fact that the floor was still lost in darkness if his ears had not become active again. It was not the flutter of lazy wings that disturbed him, even though they probably belonged to roosting vultures; it was the sound of serpentine scales slithering on stone, and the click of insectile feet that might belong to scorpions. They seemed to be heading towards him, but when he froze and pressed himself against the wall he realised that they were just passing by. It was not the scent of his sluggishly flowing blood that had attracted them but the draught of cool moist air that had followed him from the broken door.

When he moved on, Quintal eventually came to a raised stone platform. Its slightly concave surface was as broad and long as a princely bed, and it seemed quite clean. It was a welcome discovery, for it seemed quite safe from snakes and scorpions alike, as they had no way to climb its smooth sides.

Desperately tired and weakened by the loss of blood from his hands and arms, Quintal hauled himself up on to the slab and stretched himself out. Utterly exhausted, but no longer wringing wet or frozen half to death, he fell unconscious almost immediately.

MEANWHILE, A FRUSTRATED and annoyed Memet Ashraf pulled the broken rope back up. It was only a couple of feet shorter now than it had been before, but there was no obvious place to secure the free end. He knew that if Quintal were alive and unhurt, the Estalian's curses ought to be clearly audible, but there was nothing. He must have been knocked unconscious, and possibly drowned.

It was a dire, uncomfortable thought. The chances of two men outwitting and outfighting six orcs and six goblins were not good. The odds against one alone were tremendous – and they would be astronomical if he could not bring up water for himself and the two horses.

Ashraf knew that he had to extend the length of the rope far enough to be able to dangle a bottle in the water. Eventually, he contrived a considerable extension by using his own belt, the sword-belt that Quintal had prudently taken off and the reins of both the horses. He found, then, that by leaning over the edge of the hole, with his arm at full stretch, he could get a bottle down to the surface of the water. But filling it up was a different matter. The only bottles he had were made of stiff leather, and they were not heavy enough to sink beneath the surface – and there did not seem to be anyone down there who could push them under for him.

In the end, the best Ashraf could contrive was to send down his shirt and bring it back wet. He was glad, though slightly puzzled, to find that the water was not at all foul or bloodied. But he did not have time to waste in wondering what could possibly have become of Luis Quintal. He wrung enough water out of the garment to fill his mouth twice over and moisten his head after only one immersion, but satisfying the thirst of the two horses was a task of a very different order. Having no alternative, he set to it with a will, as glad of the cloak of darkness as he was of the light of Morrslieb and the stars, which made it less than absolute.

When he finally felt that he and the two animals were capable of moving on, the Arabian carefully replaced the capstone on the well and concealed it as best he could. He buckled both belts about his waist, making sure that Quintal's sheathed sword and pouch were quite secure. Then he killed the boar. He dragged its body some distance away before butchering it. He loaded up the best of the meat, and left the rest for the vultures.

Ashraf did what he could to obscure the fact that he had lingered so long, but he knew that his pursuers would need to be unusually stupid not to realise the fact. If the orcs and goblins found the well, they could afford to occupy the spot indefinitely, and leave it guarded while they sent search-parties after him. He, alas, could not risk staying nearby. But there was a well here as well as a road, he thought, so there must once have been a village, or a town… or even a city like the one the crazy Estalian had heard rumour of. The dunes must have covered the ruins of its buildings hereabouts, but if it had been a big place there might be walls still standing only a little further on.

He was glad to have a reason to proceed, and a reason to hope that he might still evade his pursuers. Even a city fallen into ruin thousands of years ago might offer useful hiding-places. With luck, it might be a place where traps could be set, and a war of attrition waged with a chance of success, even by one clever warrior pitted against a dozen.

Ashraf found that there were walls a little further on. The sand had covered most of them, but the stumps of hundreds of fallen columns still projected from the rubble. What must once have been an arterial road was littered now with all manner of stony debris, but it was easy enough to pick a moonlit course towards the few distant buildings that seemed more-or-less intact.

There were far more signs of life here than there had been among the dunes, but the creepers that overgrew a few of the columns and the thick-boled trees beside the ancient highway were understandably parsimonious in the matter of putting forth foliage or fruit. The moon was not quite full, but its face seemed unusually large, clear and ominous as it sank towards its setting-place. Memet Ashraf was glad that he was heading south-east and did not have to look at it. The silence was oppressive. Any nocturnal hunters prowling among the ruins would take care to be discreet. But Ashraf doubted that there was vegetation enough to support a great many rats and lizards, which would in their turn support precious few snakes and jackals.

He headed towards the buildings because they offered the best chance of a hiding-place where he might safely sleep, but the closer he came to them the less welcoming they seemed. Their sand-scoured walls seemed uncannily bright and baleful by the light of the setting moon, and when the moon actually went down their dark bulk seemed even more ominous.

The Arabian reined in and looked back. For the last thirty paces or so the horses had been walking on smooth bare rock, leaving little or no sign of their passage, and there was more bare rock ahead. If the orcs and goblins followed him to this point, they would assume that he had gone straight on towards the buildings in search of shelter. Perhaps, he thought, it was time to make a detour.

He set off at right angles to his former course, sticking to the smoothest and hardest ground he could find until he had put a good distance between himself and the ancient roadway. Then he cast about until he found a convenient covert between two fallen columns, where even a man with two horses would be invisible to anyone more than twenty paces away.

Satisfied that he could not be found except by the most monstrous stroke of ill-fortune, Memet Ashraf unburdened the two horses and threw himself down on the ground to sleep.

LUIS QUINTAL WOKE with a start as a spider ran across his face. He could feel the warmth of a gentle ray of sunlight on his face, but when he sat up he lost the sensation. His eyes were glued shut and he had to rub them before he could begin to force them open. The knuckles he rubbed them with were covered in something glutinous, and when he finally got one eye open he saw that they were caked with a horrid mixture of blood and dried slime.

The light that filtered through a dozen high-set cracks was bright, but the space in which Quintal found himself was so vast and so cluttered that most of the rays seemed to be soaked up and nullified, so he paid it scant attention at first.

He inspected his hands and forearms more closely, then his clothing. He was a sorry sight. His shirt and trousers hung in tatters, and the bare flesh was scraped and cut wherever it showed through. The panic he felt when he saw that he did not have his sword-belt was only partly assuaged when he remembered that he had taken it off in order to make his brave descent into the well. He remembered that he had taken off his pouch, too, and that all his worldly possessions – such as they were – had been entrusted to the care of an Arabian pirate. He sighed, but he was not too dismayed – the Arabian in question was, after all, his friend

He forced the other eye open at last, and then looked around.

Quintal realised immediately that he was in some sort of temple. Two rows of fluted columns extended before him to either side of what must have been the area in which the faithful made their devotions. The floor had been covered in tiles; all but a few had been displaced – some, apparently, by violence, the rest by the upthrust of sprawling roots. The open space had been colonised by six gigantic thick-waisted trees of incalculable antiquity, their crowns remarkable for their patchiness. Wherever a beam of light shone through the broken walls there were leaves gathered to receive it. They formed arcs that mirrored the sun's path across the sky, but where no sunlight shone through, the branches were bare and shrivelled.

Quintal knew that trees needed water as well as light. If it was astonishing that these sprawling excrescences had grown so massive with such a meagre supply of light, how much more astonishing was it that their roots must extend deep into the ground to the underground river that had carried him here? He had opened a passageway by breaking a door, but these trees had enjoyed no such luxury: they obtained their nourishment the hard way, by burrowing through stony foundations and the rock beneath.

Between the pillars there were statues. They were almost totally obscured by the trees that grew around them, hugging them lovingly with their branches. They were certainly idols of some sort. It was almost impossible to make out their shapes, but Quintal got the impression that some resembled squatting toads with heads and horns like cattle, while others were like seated apes with the ugly heads of pigs, and horns on either side of their snouts. All of them, however, had a disturbing look of humanity about them, as if they were chimerical hybrids of human and animal elements.

Quintal took particular note of anything that resembled a horn, however faintly, because his cousin Elisio had mentioned horns in connection with gems. Unfortunately, there was no trace of a gem in any of the places where the foreheads of these creatures might have been. All that Quintal's inquisitive eyes could discern among the labyrinthine branches was that each of these figures appeared to have a single huge breast. It was as if they were female on one side of the body only.

It would have been difficult to confirm this hypothesis even if he had been able to see the groins of the statues, and he did not try. Instead, he scanned the trees for signs of edible fruit, but he found none. Then he peered at the distant walls, his anxious gaze scanning for a doorway or low window. The temple appeared to be octagonal, although it was difficult to be certain with so much dead vegetation shielding the walls.

He could just make out the place where the main doors of the temple must have been, but it appeared to be blocked. It was easier to see where the windows had once been, but they seemed to be blocked off too, at least in their lower reaches. The shafts of daylight he could see were entering through gaps just under the eaves or actually in the fabric of the roof, at least three times his height from the floor.

He was not overly worried by this discovery, because the trees were extending their sturdiest branches to all those points of ingress. There were several that would be easily accessible to an agile and determined man, and there would be time later to consider the problem of getting down on the outside.

It was only after a while that Luis Quintal looked down at the shallow bowl in which he had curled up to spend the night. He guessed that it must have been an altar: a *sacrificial* altar, in which far more blood must once have been spilled than the few clotted droplets he had recently shed... He studied the mess he had made, and concluded those dried-up libations seemed a far from trivial loss.

Having realised that the platform was an altar, he turned around to look at the previously unseen figure that loomed above it – and this time, the panic raised was not so easily quelled.

Unlike the smaller figures in the colonnade, this vast idol was not overgrown, nor had its shape been eroded by the ages. The representation was of a clothed figure rather than a naked one, and it was more like a human in other ways. The outline of a single huge breast could be seen on the right side of its body. It was only partly hidden by an open-necked jacket intended to resemble a knitted garment, or perhaps chainmail armour. The left half of the torso was, however, unmistakably masculine in its musculature. Residual flecks of colour suggested that the carved clothing might once have been painted in vivid pinks and blues.

Its face was strangely beautiful, in spite of its asymmetry; it was surrounded by a lush mane of hair. The forehead bore two pairs of horns, and again there was no jewel set between them. On the other hand, there was a cluster of red gems decorating the head of the sceptre set in the idol's right hand. The shaft seemed to be made of green jade.

Quintal was instantly avid to possess those gems, but he could see that the sceptre would not easily be snapped off, nor the individual gems easily prised loose. Nor could he help wondering why the sceptre had not been snapped off long ago, or the gems broken away if this temple had been here for thousands of years.

There were, in any case, more urgent needs to be attended to before he could make plans to improvise a sledgehammer or a lever, and a platform from which to work. Most important of all, he needed something to drink. He knew that abundant water was not far away, and he had no alternative but to grope his way towards it in the dark. He could have made up a bundle of dead twigs easily enough, but he had no means of lighting it because his flint and kindling-wool were in his pouch.

Quintal let himself down from the altar, and looked around for the entrance to the corridor that would take him – if he could remember the turns he had made – to the door that he had broken. He saw his footprints easily enough, limned in blood and slime, but one of the shafts of light that illuminated them winked out – and then another.

He looked up at the holes and saw to his dismay that two of them were partly occluded by broad green heads with exceptionally ugly faces. Half-hidden though he was, the orcs saw him almost immediately, and began calling to one another in triumphant excitement.

Quintal realised, to his horror, that the same branches that he could climb up might easily allow the orcs – or their leaner companions, at least – to climb down. Given that he had no weapon, and had been so badly bruised when he fell into the underground river, he could not possibly make a stand against them.

For once, he could not rouse his previously-indomitable optimism to a new effort.

It seemed that he was doomed.

MEMET ASHRAF HAD left the horses hidden when he found the tracks along the highway at first light. He cursed, realising that the orcs and goblins must have travelled through the night, determined that their prey should not escape. What was worse, he could only find traces of four wolves and two boars; two wolves and four boars must have been left behind – almost certainly at the well.

The discovery that the enemy forces were evenly divided would have been encouraging had Quintal been there, but the odds against him would need whittling down before any fight came to close quarters. It was the fact that those at the well would be on their guard that made Ashraf turn towards the buildings whose pink roofs were already catching the sunlight.

His approach was a model of stealth, but he cursed when he found that the attention of the orcs and goblins was directed elsewhere. A great deal of sand had been piled up against the west-facing wall of a large building – an octagonal structure markedly different from the architectural styles of Araby. There was so much sand in fact, that Ashraf assumed there must have been a substantial amount of rubble there already, perhaps to seal doors and windows. One of the orcs and one of the goblins had climbed to the top of this treacherous slope, where there were cracks that allowed them to peer through. They were calling excitedly down to their friends, and demanding tools with which to make the cracks wider.

What can they see there, Ashraf wondered? What could distract them from their vengeful hunt of him?

He remembered what the Estalian's cousin had said about idols encrusted with gems, like eyes in their heads. It was the standard stuff of travellers' tales – he had heard dozens of similar tales in the souks of his native land. But there were cities buried in the desert sands, even in Araby. The world was ancient; it had been inhabited long before the rise of human civilization, perhaps long before the rise of elvish civilization. The abandoned cities of Araby had been looted long ago. The Badlands however had long been the province of orcs – whose rise to civilisation had yet to begin. These goblin allies would know the market value of gems, as their ancestors had learned their value from humans, perhaps less than a dozen generations ago. It was just conceivable that this temple had been here for thousands of years, and that its existence was known only to uncaring orcs who had insufficient brains to make them efficient looters.

This is foolish! he chided himself. There is only one reason why treasures remain unlooted, even by scavenging scum like the greenskins – and that is that they are well-guarded. But Elisio Azevedo had sworn – again, after the invariable fashion of tale-telling travellers – that although he had clearly seen the gems, he had been quite unable to reach them, for fear of venomous snakes and monsters like crocodiles that walked. The last, at least, had to be false –

not so much because Ashraf had no reason to believe that there was any such thing as a crocodile that walked erect, but because there was every reason to believe that there was no water here to support such creatures even if they did exist.

Whatever their motive, the orcs and goblins seemed to be making a concerted effort to widen the cracks, in order that some of them could pass through. Memet Ashraf was glad to observe that his earlier calculation had been correct – there were two orcs and four goblins, and each had a mount appropriate to its kind. Ashraf was pleased to note that if four contrived to get inside, only two would remain without.

Given that he had all the time in the world to pick his spot, the Arabian was confident that he could put arrows into two orcs before either had a chance to reach cover. Within minutes, however, his plan was upset by the fact that one goblin had scrambled down the slope, mounted his wolf and rode off in the direction of the well.

Ashraf was not unduly worried. Reinforcements would not arrive for some time, even if they came in a hurry, and the cracks were almost wide enough now to allow the remaining goblins to squeeze through. Well, he thought, I hope you step straight into a nest of horny asps, or spitting cobras.

He moved swiftly to his selected position. He wasted no time once he was there, bending his bow to secure the string before taking an arrow from his quiver.

As he had anticipated, one goblin slipped through the gap into the temple – though not without difficulty – followed by another. The two orcs hardly paused before renewing their assault on the ancient cement that had bedded down the roof of the huge stone building.

Memet Ashraf took careful aim, and let fly.

The shot was perfect: the arrowhead ploughed into the target's back, tearing through the orc's tunic and scaly skin.

The greenskin fell backwards and rolled down the slope.

Had the other orc turned round to see what had become of its companion it too might have slipped back, but at that very moment it scored a success in his own task. An entire roof-block fell away, its supporting structure having been fatally weakened. It must have caught the makeshift digging-tool that the orc was using, and the greenskin was pulled through the hole it left behind, into the building.

What does it matter? Ashraf was quick to reassure himself. *It'll be dead anyway.*

But he could not be sure of that until he looked.

Before climbing the slope, Ashraf cautiously approached the place the orcs and goblins had tethered their mounts. The wolves snarled at him and the boars watched him malevolently, but he had Quintal's blade in his hand now, and they did not attack. When he released their tethers and menaced them, they were quick enough to run away, scattering in three different directions.

Fortunately, the goblins had unloaded their packs, and their water bottles were still full. Ashraf took a long draught from one of them, then attached the fullest to his own belt. His waist was rather crowded now, but not inconveniently so.

When he looked closely at the slope, Ashraf saw that his earlier surmise had been correct. It had, indeed, been contrived by several sets of human hands – or humanoid hands, at any rate. It seemed, if his analytical eye could be trusted, that this had once been a solid and carefully constructed barrier – stone blocks positioned to barricade the doorway of the edifice. More recently, the ancient debris had been disturbed; apparently hastily rearranged, and piled up to form a steep ramp. Had Elisio Azevedo and his companions been partly responsible for that work? Perhaps – but if so, those companions had not survived to tell the tale.

Ashraf regretted leaving the rope with the two horses, because it seemed now that it would have been useful to have once he reached the top of the slope. He wondered, briefly, whether he ought to return to the horses anyway, and redirect his violent attentions towards the guardians of the well. If more than half of them came back here with the goblin who had gone to summon help, he might win the supplies he needed to make good his escape.

After considering the matter briefly, he decided that he must at least take a look at the interior of the temple. Sheathing Quintal's sabre and making sure that his bow was secure, Memet Ashraf began to climb. He went warily, keeping the gap in view at all times in case one of the goblins should have been called back by the sound of the orc's fall.

The slope was harder to negotiate than it looked, but even a seaman can climb a face that a clumsy orc can negotiate, and Ashraf reached the top soon enough. There was no goblin there, but when he looked down into the gloomy interior he could see no fallen orc either.

He paused for a moment to take advantage of his lofty viewpoint, and looked out over the sand-drowned ruins. From here it was much easier to make out the contours of the dead city. He could see other octagonal shapes sketched out in the sand and he could trace the remains of vast colonnades. He saw now that the structures which protruded furthest from the dunes were stepped pyramids and the stubs of broken statues.

Beyond the city was a further expanse of barren plain that stretched as far as the eye could see. That plain extended into the Land of the Dead, where armies of bleached skeletons, animated by liche priests, were said to march under the command of Tomb Kings, accompanied by giants and chimerical monsters. Ashraf knew of no one who had ever fought such an army and lived to tell the tale, but the stories were persistent and had grown more urgent of late. He wondered whether the empire ruled by the Tomb Kings had ever extended as far as this – and, if so, whether the city that he looked down on was an outpost of the Land of the Dead. But more urgent matters demanded his attention, and he turned to peer into the temple's interior again.

A huge tree had directed the strongest and leafiest part of its crown towards the crack, and some of its branches had provided a safety net for the falling orc. The lumpen creature must have crashed through, but his fall had been slowed and the branches had offered abundant handholds.

Instead of falling to its death, it seemed the orc had made a slightly more measured descent.

But where was it now?

It was difficult to see through the clustered foliage, but there seemed to be statues set between the columns supporting the roof, and one unusually large one set against the far wall of the building. It was impossible for Ashraf to discern the shape of the idol from his vantage point, but one hand was clearly visible. It held a sceptre whose gem-studded head was fiery red – not because it was reflecting a fugitive shaft of sunlight – but because it was glowing.

It was, Memet Ashraf thought, almost as if it were advertising its presence to anyone who might peep through this particular aperture.

LUIS QUINTAL MOVED into the dark corridor anxiously, knowing that he was likely to be at a disadvantage when his enemies came after him. The greenskins – who would outnumber him – were well-armed, and he had nothing with which to defend himself but his sore hands. They would also have the means to strike a light. When they followed him into the darkness, as they undoubtedly would, they would be able to see where they were going. He could not.

He went anyway, knowing that he had to find his way back to the pool from which he had emerged on the previous evening, to have a drink.

It's not so bad, he told himself. If they can light their way, then I shall see them coming before they see me. If these corridors are labyrinthine, they may split up – and who knows what might have been stored behind the door that I was the first to go through in a thousand years? There might be weapons.

He did not remind himself that there might be other things that Elisio had mentioned, such as poisonous snakes and monstrous crocodiles. Had he not already navigated the underground river and the pool in perfect safety, despite being unable to see? He groped his way along the wall, wincing at the friction on his cuts and grazes. He turned without hesitation whenever he came to a junction, but by the time he had made five such turns he knew he could not be retracing his steps.

He paused and took stock of his position, listening quietly and trying to detect a draught in the air. He could hear sounds, presumably from the temple, where the goblins had now made their descent along the tree-branches. But he could also feel a cool current in the air, which must surely be coming from the vaults below.

Quintal turned to face the airflow, and every time he reached a junction after that he paused to consider the possibilities carefully. Within a quarter of an hour he had found the door again, and had not yet seen a flicker of light behind him.

After that, it was easy enough to find the first flight of steps, and then the second.

He picked his way down very carefully, until his feet were in the water, and then he knelt to drink.

At that moment, nothing else mattered.

After he had drunk his fill, Quintal could hear loud sounds, which echoed strangely in the subterranean corridors. It appeared that his pursuers were arguing over something. He heard the clink of metal on stone, and guessed that the blades in question were being plied in earnest – perhaps against scorpions, or snakes, that he had been unable to see.

His eyes were straining for the first hint of torchlight – but that was not the kind of light he eventually saw.

It was a red spot, bright and by no means diffuse; a spot like a cyclopean eye burning with its own inner light. He had no doubt that it was looking at him, perhaps to taunt him.

He might have cried out but for the certainty of attracting goblins. As things were, he had no alternative but to hold himself very still and silent, waiting to throw himself into the water as soon as he felt a touch of any kind.

What would I give to have my sabre now, he thought? I'd give all the gems in that sceptre!

'The price is higher than that,' a voice whispered in his ear, making him start violently, 'but the reward is greater.'

Quintal raised his arm and passed it back and forth in an arc. It met nothing but empty air, even though the whisperer could not have been more than a hand's-breadth away from him.

Luckily, he had the presence of mind not to make a sound as he asked: *Can you hear my thoughts?*

'The first gift is sight,' the voice went on. 'The second... Well, you'll see what the second is when you have the first. But the fee you have so far paid is but a tiny drop of water in a large and thirsty throat. You must offer the rest freely... and you have no more than half a minute to decide before your pursuers appear. Be aware that you will not easily pass through the ranks of the ushabti for a second time.'

Fee? Quintal thought. What fee? And what in the world is a ushabti? But the first question was rhetorical, because he already had an inkling as to what the voice meant by 'fee', and because he knew that he had no time to strike a better bargain.

He did not have to frame his consent in words, even inaudibly. Before he had completely reached his decision, the red glow moved, dividing in two as it rushed upon his eyes, entering both his dilated pupils simultaneously.

Then the whole place was lit by an eerie red light, unlike any ordinary illumination and Quintal did not doubt for an instant that it was his and his alone to use, for the purpose of seeing.

What he saw by the power of this uncanny vision chilled him to the bone, more than freezing water could have done.

His eyes were level with the top step, and the floor-space beyond, which was some twenty paces wide at the stairhead. He had walked across that space twice, keeping near to the wall on each occasion, but it seemed impossible that he could have done so, for the space was littered with what appeared to be crocodiles – eighteen of them, every one half as long again as a man was tall. When he looked at them more closely, though, he saw that they were chimerical creatures, with as much human in them as crocodile. Although there was skin covering their skeletons there seemed to be precious little flesh between scale and bone.

Now I know what a ushabti is, he thought. They looked as if they had been dead for centuries, but they also looked as if they might be remarkably resilient if ever they were reanimated – and he had a horrid suspicion that might be at any moment. Obviously, he had stepped between them, and occasionally over them. They had not stirred, but they were not asleep: their eyes were open, glinting red. While he looked down at them, their heads began to move. They moved slowly, as if long unaccustomed to movement. Perhaps, Quintal thought, they had not been animate a few moments ago, but they were certainly awake and animate now.

Mercifully, the heads were not turning towards him. They were facing the opening of the corridor where a light was now beginning to show. The light seemed bright and sulphurous to Quintal's unnatural sight.

He saw the flame before he saw the first goblin. If the goblin saw him, it didn't matter, because its improvised torch was directed at the ushabti.

Quintal had always accepted the common rumour that goblins are cowards – cunning cowards, but cowards nevertheless. Perhaps this one was an exception, or perhaps his cunning was sufficient to outweigh his cowardice for a few vital seconds. The goblin howled in anguish, as any creature would have done, and did not linger, but it had the presence of mind to lower the torch before it fled. It placed the torch very carefully across the entrance, so that the flames swiftly spread along the whole length of the bundle, forming a barrier that no ordinary crocodile would ever have dared to cross.

But these were not ordinary crocodiles.

Irritated by the flame, the lean monsters reared up, standing on their hind legs. Their hides were black instead of green, to be sure, and their snouts were much longer than any orc's, and what their teeth lacked in mass they made up in profusion. There was definite malice in their eyes, which seemed to Luis Quintal to be entirely orclike.

None of the ushabti turned towards Quintal; instead, they moved as one toward the corridor where the goblins were fleeing. Their leader stamped on the burning twigs, extinguishing the flames with the hard pads of its hind feet.

All eighteen monsters moved after the three goblins, unhurriedly but with every appearance of steadfast purpose.

Quintal knew that he ought to feel relieved, and even thankful – but he could not. All he could do, for the moment, was wonder exactly what price he had offered for the privileges he now had, and how long it would take him, in what kind of occupation, to clear his debt.

ONCE MEMET ASHRAF's eyes had adapted to the dim light inside the temple he was able to make out the form of the limping orc, forcing its way through the tangled branches towards the idol behind the altar. It was almost as if the creature were drawn towards the glowing sceptre, although Ashraf thought it unlikely that any magic would be required to make that happen.

Ashraf touched his bow, but he did not have a clear shot from where he was. He knew that he would have to descend to the temple floor to find a better place from which to aim, but he hesitated when he saw the orc climb up on to the altar.

Although the greenskin was tall, with considerably long arms, the sceptre was still frustratingly out of reach. Even a goblin would have had difficulty climbing on to the statue's arm, so the orc had to formulate another plan. It unsheathed a heavy iron sword, with a blade just long enough to make solid contact with the sceptre.

Even an orc would realise that hacking at a solid object with a sword would ruin the blade irreparably, but greed could be a powerful motivator in those who were slaves to their baser appetites.

Why not let it dislodge the sceptre's head, if it can, Ashraf thought? He had been a pirate long enough to know that it was best to let others do the heavy, dangerous and tiring work, so that he could conserve his own strength and weaponry for the final moves in the game. So he leaned back on his heels and watched the orc swipe at the sceptre, trying to crack its shaft with a series of sharp blows.

The blows had no apparent effect. Ashraf even felt slightly frustrated, although he took some pleasure from the knowledge that the orc had ruined his blade for no obvious reward.

Then things began to go awry.

Ashraf realised that his patience had turned against him. He heard a cry from behind and looked back to see the other four orcs and their two goblin companions approaching as rapidly as their mounts could carry them. He had already been seen, and knew even as he slipped through the opening into the crown of the tree that it would not be long before he was followed. He cursed his carelessness.

While he moved from the gap in the eaves into the foliage he was mindful not to disturb any more masonry – for he had noted that the edges of the hole made by the orc were ragged, and that cracks were spreading from it. The roof of the temple had resisted collapse for a very long time, in spite of the external erosions of windblown sand and the internal corrosions of the patient trees, but now that the roof had been rudely breached it was distinctly precarious.

The orc on the altar was not yet aware of Ashraf's presence, but the possibility of getting to a position to put an arrow into the greenskin's back became remote when three goblins emerged from a dark doorway to the right of the altar, in a state of high panic.

Ashraf moved more swiftly then, knowing that he had to hide himself before the goblins discovered him. He had to find somewhere in the crowded temple where he could put as many of his enemies down before they combined forces to rush and overwhelm him.

The Arabian knew that his prospects of long-term survival were relatively poor, and they did not seem to have improved when the situation became still more complicated. The goblins were being followed by a scaly and skeletal monster – half-crocodile and half-human – walking on its hind legs.

The monster was unarmed, but when it was greeted by an arrow and a javelin in its lightly-armoured breast, it continued to waddle forwards regardless of its wounds. And it was not alone! A second came after it, then a third. Ashraf knew that the goblins would not be so panic-stricken if they had merely been surprised by the unnatural sight of a thin crocodile walking erect. There had to be a great many of the creatures, and they had to be uniquely terrible. He continued to scramble along a branch towards the heart of the largest tree.

Ashraf knew that there would be no point in trying to deploy his bow until he was securely positioned. But now he could not decide which sort of creature he ought to aim at. He lost count of the marching monsters long before they stopped emerging from the doorway. It made sense to put one or two of them down so that the orcs and goblins would stand a better chance of further reducing their number.

On the other hand, the Arabian thought, the crocodilian monsters were unlikely to be able to chase him through the crowns of the trees, like the goblins could, despite their ability to stand upright. Was it conceivable that they might be capable of gratitude, if he were to shoot down a few goblins on their behalf?

Meanwhile, the orc with the ruined sword had jumped down from the altar, and was ready to cut and slash with its blunted and twisted blade. The goblins were hurling everything they had at their new adversaries, who had formed an arc and were closing in on them. At least six of the scale-and-bone creatures had been struck and wounded, but there did not seem to be any blood flowing from their wounds. Not one had fallen. Their progress was measured but inexorable.

Ashraf reached a position which satisfied him: crouched on the broad back of one of the more batrachian idols, where he was half-hidden from both the altar and the gap in the roof by a barrier of branches. The goblins of the second party were now on the top of the ramp outside the temple wall. They could see what was happening well enough, but they were in no hurry to assist. Ashraf knew that the bonds of loyalty between goblins – even if they were brothers – were weak at the best of times, and the goblins confronted by the walking reptile-men were certainly not enjoying the best of times.

Not one greenskin had fallen as yet, but that was because the crocodilians had such short 'arms', and bore no weapons. They were showing their teeth now, snapping at the heads of their tormentors, but they seemed to be doing so merely by way of intimidation rather than with murderous intent. The orc was by far the tallest of their opponents, and he was wearing a spiked helmet that would make it very difficult to crush his skull. The goblins were trying desperately to reach the branches of the trees, so that they might make use of their agility. They had wasted too much time inflicting ineffectual wounds. The bony horrors were encircling them now.

Ashraf came to a decision. If he were to intervene at all, it would be best to do so on behalf of the greenskins. It was obvious by now that they needed all the help they could get.

The Arabian brought his bow from behind his shoulder, and reached back to his quiver for an arrow.

Then he froze, trying with all his might to be as still as the statue.

While he had been biding his time a tiny snake had coiled itself around his bow, and another had somehow contrived to wind itself about the shaft of his selected arrow. Each snake had reacted to its sudden displacement by setting its mouth threateningly agape, showing needle-sharp fangs moistened by the gleam of some viscous secretion.

Ashraf dropped both the bow and the arrow, but he had time before they fell away to see that each snake had two little horns on its head, above the eyes. He had never encountered such horny asps before, but he was not deluded enough to think that their miniature size would make their venom any less deadly.

Suddenly, the network of branches surrounding him seemed horribly unsafe.

Neither snake had struck at him fortunately. And he considered himself doubly fortunate because he could see no more of their kin in the branches above his head, but he had to move to a clearer space, and be far more vigilant in future.

He looked around for a more suitable location, forgetting the three goblins and the orc who continued to hack at their adversaries with desperate abandon.

They were inflicting cut after cut, but to no avail. The slender crocodile-men still did not bleed, neither did they fall.

As Memet Ashraf moved, he observed that the green-skins in the roof-cavity had begun to fire arrows of their own. The goblins were making their way through the canopy of the indoor forest, and the orcs were hacking at the crumbling fabric of the roof, so that they could follow two abreast, firing arrows as they went.

It was not bravery that impelled them, Ashraf realised, but the same greed that had brought the first orc to the altar. They too were trying to even the odds, because they hoped that the last survivor of the conflict would have a clear run at the glowing red sceptre.

The Arabian reached a far safer spot, close to the wall of the temple and far from the gap through which he had gained entrance. There were branches nearby, but they were all dead and desiccated, offering no useful cover even to subtle serpents. He had a clear view of the space around the altar, and of the conflict that raged there.

At long last the crocodilian monsters had been able to bring their forepaws into play – but they had no fingers or thumbs, so their 'hands' were exceedingly clumsy, and their blunt claws were no use for stabbing or tearing. They had struck the various weapons from the goblins' hands, and the sword from the orc's, but had inflicted no wounds. In the end, each of the four greenskins was seized by one of the crocodiles in what might have seemed in other circumstances to be a loving hug. They were held tightly, but they were not crushed.

No matter how extravagantly the greenskins wriggled, they could not get free. Like parents restraining unruly children, the creatures that held them quelled their struggles in a conspicuously gentle fashion.

The crocodile monsters that were still unburdened turned away from their kin, and directed their attention towards the newcomers. But two of them had finally fallen, disabled at last by their bloodless wounds. The four captive greenskins immediately began shouting advice to their free companions instructing them to aim at the eyes and the hind legs of the monsters.

Ashraf realised that the two snakes that had threatened him might have been adopting the same attitude as the crocodile-men were to the three goblins and the orc: they had not even tried to strike. Perhaps their real purpose had been to *capture* him, or to prepare him for capture. There was, after all, a sacrificial altar here, and there might also be a priest with a sacrificial knife, yet to emerge from the darkness.

Memet Ashraf had always laughed at men fearful of evil magic thinking that they took ominous delight in proclaiming that there were fates worse than death. Now, for the first time, he wondered whether they might be right.

This place was a trap. Its treasure was intact, because it was too well guarded to be taken away, but it was on display as a lure to tempt thieves and soldiers of fortune.

The Arabian took great care to remind himself that it was certainly not an inescapable trap... But he could not help wondering whether Elisio Azevedo had really *escaped*, even though he had found his way home to Magritta. The alternative possibility was, of course, that Quintal's cousin had been bait: bait better by far than a glowing sceptre that had long since ceased to be the stuff of legend, even in the world of men.

LUIS QUINTAL HAD no difficulty at all making his way back to the temple, now that he could see perfectly in the deepest darkness. Nor had he any fear of so doing, given that the ushabti had not made the slightest move against him. He did not suppose that the goblins posed any danger to him now, even if there were six of them waiting, with six orcs to back them up.

Even so, when he came to the doorway he hung back, content to remain in the shadows while he watched the progress of the battle.

He watched the ushabti close in with mechanical efficiency upon their immediate prey, not caring in the least whether they were cut about the belly. They did not act as individuals, but as components of the same intelligence. He deduced that they were not really alive; they were merely reanimate instruments of the evil god that had been worshipped here thousands of years before. Perhaps they were patchworks of the corpses of men and crocodiles, neatly sculpted into their new forms and placed in a state of suspended animation, like a kind of death without decay, from which they might be roused as puppets to do the bidding of their preserver.

I know you, Quintal said, silently, as he saw them remove weapons with clinical efficiency, from the greenskins' hands. The greenskins had not known what kind of battle they were fighting, and they had wasted their thrusts, realising far too late that no anatomical elements were necessary to the movement or the nature of their monstrous adversaries.

Quintal really did feel that he knew something of the being into whose untender care he had delivered himself. Estalia was a ragged patchwork of rival city-states, but its best ports had long histories of trade with a rich variety of nations. Elves of the kingdoms of Ulthuan had been entertained in Magritta, as well as elves of a darker kind, who were more inclined to gossip.

Quintal knew that there were many names attached to malign gods by their various and multitudinous followers. The names referred to a mere handful of great powers, each one of which reflected a different kind of primal force: violent wrath; self-indulgent greed; intellectual ambition; and bilious envy. He had often said that if all roads led to damnation – as they certainly seemed to do – then he would rather follow the one that took him by the most luxurious route. Now, he felt that his unholy wish had been granted.

The captive greenskins continued calling to their free companions, advising them how to fight their uncanny opponents. Quintal knew that they had no altruistic motive in doing so; they were hoping for rescue. The advice was nevertheless good. The second party of goblins and orcs had only two bowmen, neither of them as accomplished as Memet Ashraf, but they were working at close range and the thick hind legs of the ushabti were more sizeable targets than their lean bodies. None of the other four had yet released a spear, they were cleaving to the branches of the half-dead trees and using their javelins to stab at the eyes of the monsters.

This strategy was far better than the one the captive greenskins had unthinkingly adopted. Three more ushabti fell on all fours as the wiry ligaments in their legs were cut, and a further three began to blunder about as their eyes were blinded.

I had best not take my own eyes for granted, Quintal thought, for this new power of sight is a treasure to be carefully guarded.

He had counted the greenskins: there were four captive and seven still free. An orc was missing. It may have been left behind to guard the boars and the wolves, or even to guard the well. But it could have been killed before it had the chance to climb down into the temple. Quintal knew what an ingenious man Memet Ashraf was, and he was prepared to believe that the Arabian was also hereabouts, watching from a position of relative safety.

As he formed this hope, Quintal began to wonder whether his truce with the Arabian was still in force – or whether it could endure even if it were.

I suppose I am some sort of priest or a magician, now, Quintal said to himself. And Memet Ashraf might not be the kind of man to form alliances with the favoured servants of maleficent gods.

'There are only two kinds of men,' the tiny voice in his ear informed him, reassuringly. 'Great fools, and little ones. In either case, your friend is mine.'

Quintal knew that he had already bartered his soul, and was not in a position to ask questions, but he hoped that his protector might be the kind of god who would respect a proper measure of imaginative daring. Instead of having the temerity to wonder how an entity so powerful could have allowed an entire city of worshippers to vanish from the face of the Earth – leaving nothing behind but a snare for exhausted travellers and stupid soldiers of fortune – he boldly set out to find the logic of the situation himself.

If I were a god, he thought, with incalculable power and potentially-eternal existence, my greatest enemy would be boredom. If I were a god of wrath, I might take the edge off that boredom with never-ending orgies of violence. If I were a god of envy, I might become a connoisseur of disease, decay and all the other forms of catastrophic change. If I were a god of intellectual ambition, I might become a creator and solver of intricate puzzles and bizarre games. But if I were a god of lust and luxury, a proud creature dedicated to sensual self-indulgence, I would always be vulnerable to satiation. I would have no option but to give in to my boredom, again and again and again, amusing myself with every toy for a little while and then putting it away, but the advantage of the situation would be that whenever boredom struck, I would have a storehouse of old instruments of amusement available for resurrection. Any one of them might have regained its potential for amusement during the long years... or the millennia... of its neglect.

Satiation is, after all, a temporary thing, even for men. Hunger, thirst and lust, no matter how successfully they are appeased, always return; every appetite fed always gives way to an appetite renewed in the fullness of time. So it must be for the gods, with their vast appetites. I believe that this city has served its interval of neglect, and is making ready to be born again – in which case, I am no mere priest or magician, but a veritable redeemer, whose role will be a thousand times more glorious than that of my silly cousin.

Quintal noticed that the balance of the skirmish in the temple had altered yet again. The three goblins and the four orcs were tumbling from the branches where they had had the advantage of height. It was as if they had been frightened half to death by some invisible menace. They were all on the floor now, close to the surviving ushabti, who had already grabbed two of the orcs in their unloving embraces.

The other two orcs were stabbing wildly at the monsters' faces and feet, but it was the agile goblins who were doing the most damage as they had got the measure of the fight. One had been knocked down and hurt, but the other two had easier targets now that the ushabti were not so seamlessly massed into a single organism.

Quintal knew that it was time to take a hand. He moved out of the dark mouth of the corridor and picked up a brace of discarded weapons: a light sword and a mace. The single-edged sword was far cruder than his own sabre as well as shorter, but it had been nicely honed. He had never wielded a mace, as he considered such weapons far too brutal for a gentleman's use. But he had picked it up in preference to a javelin because he was even less of a gentleman now than he had been before.

He moved smoothly to support the undead crocodilians, aiming to take on the two goblins who still had weapons in their hands. They must have been astonished to see him coming, and they were genuinely uncertain as to whether he had come to attack them or to attack the unnatural monsters assailing them. They were not long in doubt. As soon as he moved to engage them they were quick to retaliate, making rapid progress away from the groping ushabti in order to concentrate their attentions on him.

The Estalian parried their blades easily enough, and thumped one over the head before either of them had time to organise another thrust. When the second thrust came from the one still standing, he met it easily with the shaft of the mace, and smashed the blunt side of the swordblade into the side of the goblin's head. That one went down too, stunned, but by no means dead.

Ushabti gathered both of them in.

The larger of the two orcs, howling with anger, broke off his engagement with a ushabti to come at Quintal in a berserk rage.

Quintal's only anxiety was that he might have to run the ugly brute through in order to stop it, but he need not have worried at all. The ushabti lifted up one of its feet and swept its tail along the floor to trip the charging greenskin. The orc fell so heavily that the impact seemed to make the floor shake.

The fight was over; every single orc and goblin had now been seized, although there was not a single effective pair of scale-and-bone arms to spare.

Every one of the green-skinned invaders was ready for sacrifice.

Luis Quintal dutifully looked around for a blade even sharper than the one he already held.

MEMET ASHRAF WATCHED in fascination as his erstwhile ally took up a position behind the altar. Quintal looked to be in a parlous state – as might be expected of a man who had fallen down a well – but he was moving with an alarmingly mechanical sense of purpose. His clothes were in tatters and he seemed to be carrying at least a dozen superficial but bloody wounds. On the other hand, his eyes were gleaming with a fervour that could not be entirely explained by the light of sunbeams flooding through the damaged roof.

It seemed to Ashraf that there was a peculiar redness to Quintal's eyes, more profound than if it merely reflected the glow of the sceptre as well as the glare of the sun.

Ashraf's first impulse on seeing his companion had been a glad one, but when he saw the way Quintal had tackled the goblins he was not so sure that he had any reason to be delighted.

Whatever miracle had preserved the Estalian's life seemed also to have transformed him – as his cousin might also have been transformed.

Ashraf had always been too cautious to entirely trust his enemy-turned-friend; it seemed safer now to proceed on the assumption that he could not be trusted at all. So the Arabian remained hidden in the shadows, watching carefully to see what would happen next.

One of the monsters came forward to the altar, clutching a terrified goblin. Its forepaws were woefully inefficient as hands, but once they had a grip they maintained it. The creature had been cut in a dozen places, but it had not lost a single drop of blood. It lifted the goblin on to the altar, and carefully changed its grip to hold the greenskin, stretched out in a supine position.

Luis Quintal cut its throat, and stood over it as if mesmerised. He watched arterial blood rise up in a fountain before falling back into the shallow bowl. Ashraf knew that goblin blood was dark green, but this was so dark as to seem jet black in the uncertain light. While it gushed extravagantly the black blood bathed the Estalian's face and breast, but once the flood had slowed to a trickle every drop had drained into the concave surface of the altar.

Until this point, Ashraf had not heard any of the chimerical monsters emit the slightest sound. But now they sighed in unison, opening their mouths wide to display unnaturally white teeth and sturdy grey tongues. Even the ones that could no longer stand erect, and those whose eyes had been put out, so that they could not see, joined in the sigh.

'My faithful ushabti,' Quintal said, in a voice whose timbre was unfamiliar to Ashraf, 'this is a new beginning. Greenskin blood is by no means rich and by no means sweet, but as the old saying has it, "every great crusade must start with a single step". Blood is blood, after all, even if it is black – and had I not shed a little of mine, voluntarily, into this same avid receptacle, we might have contrived nothing here today but a petty massacre. While we are celebrating the wisdom of ancient proverbs, we might also take note of the one which observes that even the greatest treason tends to begin with a single petty act of self-betrayal.'

The creatures that Quintal had called ushabti made no reply, but they sighed again when the first goblin was cast aside, the blood having been wrung from its body by the monster's patient massage. Another was brought forward to supply a second dark fountain.

'You have been bloodless far too long, my patient pets,' Quintal went on. 'We have all become thirsty while the desert was our bed, but the roads will soon be clear, and the traffic will come again, as warm and wet and foolish as ever. Nothing is ever lost, my cryptosaurian soldiers; every favourite that has been set aside becomes beautiful again. Periods of absence renew her lovely unfamiliarity.'

Again, the bipedal crocodile-men made no reply, but they sighed again when the goblin was replaced by an orc, which bled blackly with astonishing generosity. Its unusually powerful heart stubbornly refused to admit that it was dead.

Ashraf could not see what was happening to that portion of the orc's blood that flowed into the shallow bowl. Not a drop spilled over the sides and when the used-up corpses were thrown aside, their clothes were by no means soaked. The Arabian could see well enough, however, that even though Luis Quintal had been liberally bathed in exceedingly dark blood, he did not seem to have been significantly stained. Only the red glow in his eyes had become more glaring.

If Quintal did not come here by the same route as the rest of us, Ashraf thought, there must be a passage of some kind connecting the bowels of the temple to the bottom of the well. If it is navigable in one direction, it must be navigable in the other. If the trees are infested with snakes, no matter how hesitant to strike they might be, there is probably no safe way back to the hole in the roof. But the dark doorway from which Quintal emerged would be easy enough to reach if there were fewer monsters in the way. *What I need is a distraction that would give me time to make a run at it.*

While the fourth victim was donating his blood to the thirsty altar, Ashraf took stock of his remaining equipment. He still had Quintal's sabre, but there was little to be done with it. Apart from the sabre, his own dagger, quiver of arrows and the stolen water bottle, all that he had was Quintal's pouch, whose exact contents he had not yet bothered to ascertain.

As the crocodiles sighed yet again, Ashraf took the pouch from his second belt and tipped out its contents to ascertain the sum of Luis Quintal's worldly goods.

There was an embroidered handkerchief, the key to a lock that was presumably more than six hundred leagues away, a device for extracting stones from horses' hooves, a mummified hare's foot, a small pair of scissors, a tangled ball of thread but no accompanying needle, a spare belt-buckle, a screw of tobacco but no pipe, a whetstone, an ill-made flintlock with a wispy hank of kindling-wool, a short length of twine and three brass rings which could be used for the attachment of various items to bridle and harness.

Memet Ashraf was a simple man, who did not believe in carrying clutter, but he was suddenly glad that Luis Quintal took a different view of the accumulation of personal possessions.

'If I get out of this alive,' Ashraf muttered, 'I'll never laugh at another effete Estalian, no matter how many of them I might have to murder in the course of my piratical pursuits.'

So saying, he took up the flintlock and the kindling-wool, then moved sideways until he was in close proximity to a substantial aggregation of ancient branches, that had been dead and dry for hundreds of years. He struck a spark, which immediately set the kindling-wool alight – and when he set the kindling-wool among the branches, they caught fire with amazing alacrity. It was as if they had been as hungry for fire as the altar had for blood.

Ashraf retreated from the gathering blaze, making his way swiftly to an empty angle of the octagonal temple, which was almost as far from the cramped and twisted foliage of the ancient trees as the dark doorway was.

There were two possible routes to that doorway from where Ashraf now crouched, neither of them quite straight. He could go to the left of the altar or to the right. There was far more space to the right, but that area was crowded with emburdened ushabti. Behind the altar there was, for the moment, no one but Luis Quintal – who might well have moved by the time Ashraf made his dash, and might not be inclined to stop him even if he had not.

While Ashraf made ready to run, the fire made rapid headway.

Not one of the six trees that had taken root in the temple's interior had been growing for less than a thousand years. Each one had fought long and hard for every drop of water its questing roots had dragged from the stony earth below. Their patterns of growth had been built into their seeds, and they had had no alternative but to put forth branches in every direction, even though those which could not find sunbeams to nourish them had withered and died in consequence.

Trees have no eyes with which to see, and no minds with which to plan, so they had continued putting out new branches wherever there was space, even if they would never find a ray of light to bring forth leaves from their living heart.

The fire leapt from one branch to another with an appetite that would have been incredible in a man or an orc, perhaps even in a god. White smoke billowed out in churning clouds, but could not choke the flames, which hurled themselves upwards and outwards: towards the roof-space filled with warm and moistureless air, and towards the gaps where more air could be sucked out of the desert sky.

The gaps were not easy to reach because of the living and leafy wood that clustered about them, but the fire was burning hotter with every second, and nothing could stand in its way.

The ushabti were dead and dry too. The stricken ones that were stretched out horizontally lay close enough to the woody litter on the floor beneath the trees to be caught in the sudden rush of fire that swept across the paving stones.

Blades had not hurt the creatures, but avid fire could. The recumbent ushabti burst into flames first, followed almost immediately by the ones still standing.

Unfortunately for the goblins and orcs, the animate torches were too stubborn to release their iron grip upon their scaly captives, even though they were on fire. The greenskins had been silent while they waited churlishly for the knife, but they could not be silent now. They began to scream. Ashraf had always thought humans were good screamers, but he had never weighed up the opposition. He wasted no time in privately conceding that orcs were very good screamers indeed.

Five greenskins had already died on the altar, but it was obvious that the remainder would not be donating their blood to the ambitious idol or its zealous new disciple. It was obvious, too, that Memet Ashraf could not remain where he was for a second longer, else there would be nothing left to breathe in the smoke-filled air.

Ashraf began his dash with a blade in each hand, hoping that Luis Quintal would have sense enough not to get in his way. He might even abandon his recently discovered vocation and revert to his former career as an honest thief and plunderer.

IN ALL HIS twenty-three years, Luis Quintal had never felt better than he did when he plunged his borrowed dagger into the flesh of the first sacrifice. The good feeling began before the first drop of arterial blood touched his skin, but there seemed nothing strange in that. Common men, as he knew only too well, found it easy to distinguish between anticipation and fulfilment, but he was no longer a common man. Gods, he presumed, had sufficient will power to alloy intention and reward into a perfect whole, and this facility must be one of the echoes that resonated in the souls of their favourite acolytes.

The Estalian did not feel the black blood raining upon his face even when the huge-hearted orc was offered to him. It was already a part of him. He did not thirst for it because he did not need to; it had already undergone whatever process of digestion had been necessary to convert it into the fabric of his own being. The tattered remnants of his shirt did not become soaked, for the sacrificial blood – no longer bound by the common laws of fluid dynamics – passed right through the material and into his breast.

Quintal felt *wonderful*, and knew that it was because he was full of wonders. He knew, of course, that they were evil wonders, but he had never made any conspicuous effort to be a good man and his only regret was that he had wasted his whole life trying to embrace evil as it needed to be embraced. He knew now how trivial the record of his petty thefts, murders and treasons had been. Now he knew the luxury of wholehearted self-indulgence.

One consequence of Quintal's new-found inability to distinguish anticipation from fulfilment was that he had become incapable of surprise. Events could no longer astonish him, even when they were genuinely unexpected or inconvenient. He was above annoyance now, and beyond fear, so when the fire leapt up like a berserk giant to consume the paradoxical trees that were more dead than alive, the questions that sprang to his mind were utterly casual, though they did contain a measure of wonderment at the quirky ways of fate.

Did I request a holocaust, he asked, flippantly? Do I require an orgy of conflagration? Is this necessary to the renewal of my amusement?

Quintal watched, more bewildered than irritated, as the ushabti burst into flame. The excessive heat of their combustion caused the blood that was still confined in the intended sacrificial victims to boil, and then to degrade into odorous black tar.

The space behind the altar filled up with cloying smoke, but the clouds did not obscure Quintal's new power of vision. His blood-fed lungs drank in the particles without difficulty, as if they were a mere spice lightly sprinkled on the healthful air.

Something came hurtling out of the shadows to the right of the altar: something blind and mad, impelled by panic and determination. The thing had two arms and two legs, but it was too long-limbed to be a crocodile and not green enough to be an orc. It carried a blade in each hand, one of which bore an uncanny resemblance to the sabre that had once been Quintal's most prized possession. But neither hand made any attempt to cut him down. The racing form seemed quite content to knock him out of the way so that it could run past, heading into the shadows on the opposite side of the altar.

A human, obviously, Quintal thought, as he landed flat on his back, feeling neither jarred nor bruised, nor even unjustly insulted by the tumble. What else is human life but a blind flight from one shadow to another, impelled by helpless panic and mistaken determination, supported by borrowed weapons in whose use one is woefully inexpert?

But when Quintal rose to his feet again he remembered that even humans were not *complete* fools. Sometimes, there were good reasons to flee madly from shadow to shadow. There may be adequate intellectual justification for an insane hope that the shadows might contain a safer exit than those they had forsaken. Sometimes – for example, when a temple roof began to fall – there were good reasons why even an acolyte of a god of luxury might forsake the altar upon which he had been reborn. There might be a kind of safety to be found in mundane shadows.

Quintal had to suppose, as he looked up at the falling roof, that only a miracle of sorts had kept it from collapse. It must have been considerably weakened by the passage of the centuries – and it was, after all, an item of human manufacture, however divinely inspired. Nothing built by humans could last forever; the miracle was that it had lasted any time at all. The orcs had obviously brought the ancient roof to the very limit of its endurance – and the unexpected holocaust that had so rudely interrupted his sacrificial ritual had administered the *coup-de-grace*.

So now the roof was falling.

Perhaps, Quintal thought, I ought to get out of the way.

Ordinarily, it would not have been the kind of decision that warranted careful consideration or in-depth discussion, but the Estalian did not move immediately. He formed the intention to move, but intention was still strangely entwined in his consciousness with fulfilment. He felt – oddly enough – that he had *already* moved.

He also felt – perhaps even more oddly – that there was something else that had yet to happen *before* he moved.

So he waited, and watched the stony fabric of the roof disintegrate as it fell, like a thundercloud turning precipitately to rain and hail.

He watched modestly sized blocks descend upon the statues in the crumbling colonnade, smashing their ugly heads and misshapen bodies. And he saw other blocks, of an altogether more immoderate magnitude, descend upon the huge idol which loomed above him still, pulverising its head and breaking both its arms – including the one that held the gem-encrusted sceptre.

When the severed forearm hit the stone floor the hand shattered into thousand shards – but the jade sceptre rolled away, seemingly immune to all injury.

Luis Quintal walked calmly away from his station behind the altar, ignoring the lumps of stone that were bursting like bombs as they hit the unforgiving floor on every side. He picked up the sceptre, and rested the glowing head on his right shoulder. Then he marched, with military precision, into the dust-shrouded shadows which concealed the doorway to the underworld.

MEMET ASHRAF HAD fallen twice in the pitch-black corridors, and had rapped his knuckles a dozen times against invisible and unforgiving walls, but he had kept on relentlessly and he had refused to drop either of his blades in order to liberate his fingers.

Had it not been for the fire he might have become irredeemably lost. The fire was so fiercely avid for air that it sucked a considerable wind from the underworld beneath the temple, and all that the Arabian had to do was keep his face to that wind. That was not a hard thing to do, given that the wind was so cool, so clean and so moist.

In the end, the draught brought him to the flight of steps that Luis Quintal had climbed in the wake of his misadventure in the well. Ashraf might have stumbled on the steps, bruising himself badly as he tumbled into the water, but luck was with him. Although he could not see anything at all he was able to set his blades safely down beside him, within easy reach. He seated himself on a step with only his booted feet in the water, so that he could scoop up water in his cupped hands and pour it gratefully upon his head.

He drank a little, but only a little – he had no wish to make himself sick.

He lost track of time while he sat there, exhaustedly, but he was glad to do it. Time did not seem to have been on his side in the last few days, and he was pleased to have an opportunity to set it aside for a while. Perhaps it was kind of time to let him do that – or perhaps the concession was one more trap to catch and torment him. Either way, he did not look up again until his eyes were stimulated by light.

As soon as the red gleam appeared Ashraf was seized by the fear that he had lingered too long. He ought to have plunged himself into the subterranean river immediately, no matter how desperate a move it had seemed.

The red light showed him the bare space which he had crossed in order to get to where he was, but it also showed him the walls that slanted towards the aperture from which he had emerged.

The walls were covered in fungus and strange dark-blooming flowers, whose blossoms were nests for scorpions the size of his hand. The scorpions seemed to be prey, in their turn, to the kinds of leeches that preferred insectile ichor to vertebrate blood. No part of this revelation could or would have frightened him, had it not been for the eerie quality of the red radiation. There was something about that glow which invited terror. Ashraf felt the beat of his alarmed heart increase, and knew that he was in trouble.

The light came from the sceptre that had formerly been held by the idol in the temple: the sceptre that had been adequately protected from theft for thousands of years. Luis Quintal had it now.

The artefact must have been heavy, but Quintal seemed quite comfortable with it.

The Estalian was resting the glowing head of the device upon his shoulder, but Ashraf doubted that he was doing so to obtain relief from its weight. It seemed to the Arabian that Quintal simply wanted to keep the glow as close to his face as possible, to maintain the light in his own glowing eyes.

'Memet Ashraf,' Quintal said, in a perfectly level tone. 'It's good to see you again. Do you have my sword and pouch?'

'Yes,' Ashraf said, rising slowly to his feet as he spoke and adjusting his stance so that he could face the newcomer squarely. 'The blade is as sharp as it ever was, but the pouch is a little lighter. I fear that your supply of kindling-wool is quite exhausted.'

'No matter,' Quintal said. 'We are partners in this enterprise, after all. We must pool our resources as well as our rewards.'

Ashraf was mildly surprised by this statement, but he was reluctant to take it at face value. He had a suspicion that Quintal was offering him more than a half-share in the gems that starred the sceptre's head, and he was not sure that the treasure would be easily divisible.

The Arabian stooped to pick up Quintal's sabre, taking hold of it by the blade so that he could extend it hilt-first to his companion.

Quintal accepted the offering, and waited for Ashraf to take off the belt, the sheath and the pouch as well. When Ashraf tried to pass them to him too the Estalian raised his elbows slightly to indicate that his hands were full. Then he turned slightly, using body-language to indicate that Ashraf might loop the belt around his waist and fasten it, so that the sabre would be safely sheathed.

Ashraf knew that this would be his last chance. If he intended to attack his former partner, the best thing would be to do it now; it would be far more difficult to do it later. There did not seem to be any urgent necessity to do so... but to what was he committing himself, if he accepted the resumption of their association?

The Arabian hesitated. 'You have the black blood of an evil god within you,' he observed, mildly. 'I saw you sacrifice the greenskins.'

'I suppose I have,' Quintal admitted. 'But it was only answering a thirst I already had... a thirst that all men have, though there are some who take perverse delight in refusing to give way to it. We came here in search of enrichment, my friend, and we have it. Are you not ready, after all we have suffered, to claim the entirety of your inheritance?'

'If you will pardon me for saying so, Luis,' Ashraf said, gently, 'you do not seem quite yourself since you fell into the well. I am not quite sure what to make of you.'

'You are not required to make anything of me,' Quintal countered. 'I am a self-made man, as all proud Estalians desire to be. The question is: what will you make of yourself?'

Ashraf glanced around at the walls that were a-swarm with exotic vermin. He remembered that he had passed his hand along those walls, and had come away with nothing worse than the slime of crushed fungus upon them. The scorpions had refrained from stinging him, and the leeches from sucking his blood, just as the horny asps had refrained from biting him. This was not the nature of such creatures; they were obviously operating under some alien influence.

Other men might have accounted that influence generous as well as kindly, but Memet Ashraf was a pirate; he had ceased to believe in kindness, let alone in generosity.

'I have never had the slightest ambition to be a priest or a magician,' Ashraf said. He had not known that it was true until he said it. But it was true. He had not known that it was irrelevant until he said it, either. But it was irrelevant.

'If you attack me,' Quintal pointed out, equably, 'you will need to be quick and clever. Perhaps you can run me through before I can bash out your brains, and perhaps not. I think not, but you might disagree so I shall not press the point. Instead, let us look calmly at the possible outcomes. In one case, I would die and you would live; in another, you would die and I would live; in the third, we would both die. Consider only the first and best: what will you do when I lie stretched upon the staircase, with the sceptre tumbled from my hand? Will you pick it up, or leave it where it lies? Perhaps you would be a hero if you killed me, and perhaps a fool – but in either case, what would you be thereafter? What will you become when you stand here all alone, with the sceptre at your feet?

'What will you make of yourself, Memet Ashraf? I make you no promises, although I could. I could promise you wealth, power, and luxury. I could promise you an empire – and more than that, all the joy and triumph of building an empire, of shaping its nature and future. I will not do that. I promise you nothing, except a chance to make something of yourself that is more than you are now.

'As for the fee you must pay... well, I shall play the honest trader and admit to you that it is exceedingly high, and it may not be haggled down.

'Now you know all that you need to know, and you understand more than most men are ever privileged to understand. So tell me, Memet Ashraf: what will you make of yourself?'

Still Ashraf hesitated, but he knew that the hesitation was only a display. He already knew what he had to do, and what he was. He supposed that he had known since the moment just before he had turned in his saddle to put an arrow into the breast of one of the pursuing orcs. That was the moment when he had first realised that there was a road of sorts across the desert: a road as yet invisible to Luis Quintal, but clear enough to a desert-bred man.

He had known as soon as he began to make out the ancient traces of that route that it was a road to damnation – and that every road he had ever followed in his entire life, by land or by sea, had been directed to intersect with it. He understood, now, that he had passed the crossroads, and that only a human capacity for self-delusion had kept him from knowing that the gap between anticipation and fulfilment is always an illusion of time and thought.

Memet Ashraf was not a hero – and if he was doomed to be a villain, he thought, why should he not play the part properly?

Ashraf placed the sword-belt around Luis Quintal's waist, and buckled it for him.

'We have no time to waste, my friend,' the Arabian said, as the Estalian sheathed his sabre. 'We have to find a safe way out of here as soon as we can. This crooked road has a great deal further to take us, and we had best be on our way.'

MARK OF THE BEAST
by Jonathan Green

TORBEN BADENOV SCOURED the smouldering remains of the peasant village for signs of life, but saw none. The settlement had been razed to the ground. The acrid odour of burning in the air almost masked another, more sinister reek. Torben knew instinctively what it was. His horse whinnied and snorted; she could smell it too, and it made even this hardy, steppe-bred warhorse uneasy. The musky odour was of something both animal and man, less than either but at the same time greater: the stink of beastman.

For ten days the border patrol, commanded by the highborn Captain Yasharov, had been hunting the beastman warband through the snow and ice of the coniferous forests, where the lands of the Taiga met the foothills of the World's Edge Mountains.

Torben ran fingers through his tangle of raven coloured hair and looked to where his men waited, as Captain Yasharov and his entourage rode up the wind-scoured slope in front of the broken posts of the settlement stockade.

Torben had been in the army of the Tzar for five years, first as a foot soldier and now as a cavalryman commanding fifteen men. He looked to each of them in turn. There was Oran Scarfen, a rat-faced, whiskered rogue from Talabheim; there was Vladimir Grozny, a huge, heavy-set bald-headed Dolgan. Adjusting the padded jerkin of his leather armour was Alexi of Nuln, one of the Emperor's men. Alexi was the oldest in the band. Next came the two Tolyev brothers, Arkady and Andrei. Absent-mindedly cleaning the blade of an ebony-handled knife was Manfred of Stirland.

Oleg Chenkov, named the 'Preacher' by the men, sat in an attitude of prayer. Under his chainmail shirt he wore a sackcloth habit. Like so many others, his family had been murdered by the predations of a marauding northmen tribe.

The experience had unhinged his mind, driving him into a sanctuary of religious fanaticism, and compelling him to find service in Tzar Bokha's army that he might smite the enemies of mankind with righteous vengeance. His constant muttering of holy scripture unnerved some of the other men. He was mumbling now.

'Be quiet, Preacher,' said a blond-haired giant, seated high in the saddle of the roan next to Oleg. Arnwolf's huge physique denoted his Norse ancestry. Beside the huge barbarian was Zabrov, a sallow-skinned steppes warrior. He rode saddleless and without reins, as if he had been born on a horse.

Mikhail Polenko was a member of an offshoot branch of the noble household of Praag and was quick to remind people of his proud and ancient lineage.

Then there was Yuri Gorsk who was practically a boy compared to the rest of them. The remaining four had been transferred from the remnants of a unit that suffered heavy casualties in an earlier skirmish. Kiryl, Evgenii, Cheslav and Stefan were their names.

The whole unit was uneasy. It had been only two days since they had last seen evidence of the beast horde's rampage. Their quarry must be almost within reach: Torben could feel it.

The young cavalryman commander looked at his captain and Arman Yasharov returned the stare with fixed cold eyes. His flat nose and chiselled features spoke of his noble heritage, as did the swathing ermine-lined cloak and fine leather boots he wore.

Torben despised Captain Yasharov, and he was not alone. He was arrogant, ill mannered, short-tempered and lacked any real battle experience. Even in a country with a reputation for raising mighty warriors, there were still those who attained high position by familial influence, money or favouritism.

The unit commanders held the captain in low regard, but none would dare disobey his orders. The only ones who didn't seem to share the general consensus were the captain's personal bodyguard, and Torben knew that their loyalty did not come cheaply. So it was that Captain Yasharov was secure in his position as general of one of the Tzar's armies.

However, Torben could well imagine that Yasharov had been given this border patrol to lead thanks to the machinations of a political rival of his father's. Somebody, it seemed, with influence even greater than Ramov Yasharov liked him about as much as his own troops did.

'It's definitely them,' Torben told the captain.

'We cannot be certain that this was the work of the horde we are hunting, commander. There are many such warbands infesting these forests.'

'I'm sorry, sir, but we can be sure,' Torben said, barely suppressing his frustration at his commanding officer's irritating incompetence, and pointed over the ridge behind him.

A gust of wind brought the slurry stink of the dung to the captain's nostrils before his eyes took in the scene. Excrement had been crudely arranged in moist piles to form a particular shape, one that they all now recognised. They had seen it many times since they had begun tracking the beastmen: torn into the bark of trees, daubed in blood on the rent awning of a pillaged wagon or made from the carefully-arranged bones of the warband's victims. The 'Mark of the Beast', some of the men had called it. It was a crude, almost runic, representation of a skull: two long, curved horns in the ascendant, two shorter horns framing the oval outline of a long-muzzled head. But they had never seen it on such a scale before. Here, the combined manure of the whole warband had been gathered together and moulded into a symbol that covered an area the size of a field.

The first signs they had come across of the warband had suggested a pack numbering somewhere in the region of twenty creatures. But it had taken more than twenty ruminating digestive tracts to produce this amount of excrement. Either the pack was growing in size or the first group they had encountered was only a splinter force of a much larger tribe, and one into whose territory Yasharov's army had now strayed.

Torben had heard a rumour that there were more beastmen in the world than men. It was a nightmarish thought and Torben put it down to being just that – an exaggeration. Now he wasn't so sure.

But something else troubled him. The corpses of several of the razed settlement's defenders lay amidst the ruins. But they had found no other bodies among the burnt out buildings. Where were the rest of the villagers?

GASHRAKK BLACKHOOF, BEASTMAN champion, Chosen of the Great Beast and leader of the Dark Horn tribe, fixed Cathbad with a piercing black stare that bore into the shaman's own blinking caprine eyes like a bone-tipped spear. Gashrakk was bigger and bulkier than the most formidable of his bestigor warriors. His whole body was corded with muscle and covered with a tough dark hide. Ridged horns rose proudly from his monstrous goat head. His flesh was pierced with symbols of his dark gods and he had a thick iron ring through his nose.

He was no mere blood-lusting beast. Of course, bloodletting and cruel violence had its part to play in sovereignty but Gashrakk was above those other chieftains who thought nothing of strategy and posterity. He had been blessed by the Chaos Gods, granted a malign, human intelligence combined with savage, animal cunning.

Cathbad the shaman wore a hooded robe that covered his body completely. It was decorated with esoteric sigils, painted with a mixture of blood and soot. Two long horns emerged from holes in the hood. The cloak-robe was tied at the waist with a gut cord and he held a long staff, adorned with animal skulls.

'You summoned me, my Lord Blackhoof,' the Dark Horns' shaman grunted in the guttural words of the beastmen's ugly tongue.

Gashrakk snorted gruffly, a gust of animal-breath turning the rancid air around him even ranker. 'I did. I want you to read the auguries for the sacrifice. I need to know if today is the propitious time.'

'I come prepared.' The shaman ushered two gor beastmen into the chieftain's hut. Slumped between them was a human prisoner, gagged and bound. Cathbad pulled a large saw-edge gutting knife from inside his robes, the prisoner's eyes widened in terror. The gor guards tightened their grip on the panicking man's arms and his desperate wailing penetrated the gag that stopped his mouth.

Cathbad thrust the serrated knife into the man's midriff. With a sharp tug the shaman opened him up from stomach to sternum. Eyes screaming, the man watched as the rent in his abdomen bulged and ejected his intestines, the viscera flopping wetly to splash onto the packed earth floor. The light in his eyes faded but the agonised grimace remained. The beastmen released their hold on the prisoner and the body crumpled to the ground.

The soothsayer stared at the pattern formed by the entrails and the pooling fluids.

'The omens, are they good?' prompted the beastlord.

'The gods smile on this day,' Cathbad said. 'The signs are auspicious for the sacrifice. Slaughter the prisoners this night and the Lord of Misrule, the Lord of Beasts, will be freed of his prison, to fulfil the ancient prophecy.'

At the shaman's words, Gashrakk considered the tribal herdstone, which stood on the highest ground within the camp, like some malevolent grey-black sentinel. The monolith was huge: three gors high, weighing as much as the whole herd. It was adorned with lengths of rusted chain from which dangled the tribe's trophies and remnants of offerings made to their bloodthirsty gods.

But what made the Dark Horns' herdstone unusual was the ancient prophecy that wound over the fractured faces of the rock. Carved countless seasons past in still-potent runes, it told of the Lord of Misrule, who had once held great swathes of land in the grip of his anarchic rule; a kingdom of confusion. It told how he had been conquered; how he now slept within a prison of stone, the Cave of Beasts; how he would one day be freed by a champion of the descendants of his tribe, to return order and civilisation to the natural bestial state of Chaos and wanton destruction, red in tooth and claw, where beast preyed upon beast.

Gashrakk's lips formed something approximating a smile. Then tonight it would be. It was Gashrakk's belief that if he sacrificed enough souls to the daemon-beastlord he would rightly be made the greatest of those champions, and thus rewarded. The Lord of Misrule's return would throw the lands of men into anarchy and the Dark Horns would rampage across the realms of Kislev and the Empire in a bloodthirsty orgy of killing.

'Beware!' Cathbad suddenly declared. 'I see an army marching on our camp, an army of the hu-men.'

'Hu-men,' Gashrakk growled. 'But the omens are good for the ritual to take place?'

'Of course, my lord.'

'Then nothing must be allowed to prevent its happening.' He turned to one of his guards. 'You! Take word to

Slangar and Barruk! Tell them to marshal their warriors. Nothing must disrupt the sacrifice. We will deal with these hu-men like the litter of runts they are, and paint our fur with their blood!'

IT HAD BEEN easy for Torben Badenov's scouts to follow the tracks left by the beastman horde. There had been nothing more the Kislevite soldiers could do for the nameless settlement and its lost populace, other than to avenge its memory and not rest until their chieftain's head adorned a stake outside the army's camp.

Torben spurred his steed forward, coming level with the sharp-eyed Yuri Gorsk and Mikhail Polenko. The other thirteen mounted men were spread out across the valley behind them. As Torben's unit scouted ahead through the wild, untamed hills, the bulk of Captain Yasharov's army trudged through the wilderness, several miles behind them.

Torben felt uneasy. He felt – knew – that something was waiting for them out here in the wilderness of the barren uplands. It was perfect ambush territory. He had not wanted to take this route and had suggested circling around the valley to come upon the beastmen from upwind to ensure a surprise attack. He suspected that the creatures already had the scent of the approaching army. Yasharov had rubbished the idea immediately, laughing at Torben's, 'inane understanding of strategy.'

'That could take days!' he had scoffed. 'The way to win this is to charge at the heart of the foe as quickly as possible, and rip it out!'

Torben guessed their captain was eager to return to hearth and home, at any cost. Torben scanned the rim of the valley. Its crest appeared almost black against the clouded grey-white of the winter sky. They would have to make the best of the situation. They could not return to Yasharov until they had at least sighted the beastmen.

And then Torben saw them.

At first they were no more than black silhouettes against the stark horizon, lank manes blowing in the wind, flint-headed spears in hand, taking their place in line around the valley sides. Then they were a pelting mass of leaping, bounding bodies. Torben's men cried out to each other, drawing their weapons as the beastmen set about them.

It was immediately apparent as the pack converged that Torben's scouts were greatly outnumbered. The horses whinnied and shied but the soldiers did their best to bring them back under control.

Darting glances from side to side, Torben saw four of the filthy, dark-skinned beastmen moving towards him. These were of the breed that some scholars and soldiers referred to as ungors, or un-men. Their bodies were thickly haired with contrasting-coloured fur covering their shoulders and descending the length of their spines to the scraggy tuft of a vestigial tail. Horns protruded from their foreheads, some no more than nubs of bone, others sporting crowns of several darkly ridged projections. All of them carried crude hide-stretched, wooden shields and deadly gutting-spears.

As the first ungor thrust at the mounted Torben, he was ready with a powerful down swing that batted the shaft of the spear away. The beastman stumbled forward on cloven feet, carried towards the mounted soldier by the momentum of its lunge. As a result, Torben's returning upswing caught the creature under the jaw. Half its face disappeared as the malformed mandible was torn free. The ungor fled, screaming through the ragged, gaping wound.

Torben turned his steed towards his other attackers, as all around him his men engaged with the hollering beast warriors. The reins clenched firmly in his left hand, Torben swept his sword at the stooped figure to his right. He caught the beastman across its shoulders, opening a bright crimson wound in the matted fur.

Another beastman jabbed at Torben's steed with its spear. The horse reared, whinnying, and Torben's second stroke missed. But the horse's hooves came crashing down on the injured ungor's head, hurling it onto the iron-hard, frozen ground and cracking its skull open.

As Torben despatched those others who had foolishly taken him on, he already knew his men were in trouble, despite the fact that many were holding their own against the ungor pack. Vladimir Grozny, unhorsed, his steed gone, stood drenched in the blood of the foe, with a mound of beastman heads and corpses at his feet.

Arnwolf was in single combat with a beastman that was taller and more heavily muscled than the human-sized ungors. This must be the pack leader, Torben thought. Beastman polearm clanged against Norse axe-steel as Arnwolf deftly parried a two-handed downward strike and then backhanded his opponent across the snout.

The Preacher was delivering divine retribution against the savages with a gore-splattered hammer gripped tightly in his white-knuckled fists. 'Begone, foul spawn of Chaos!' Oleg yelled as he shattered the spine of another beastman with his holy weapon.

The skirmish had split into two halves. Torben, Arnwolf, Oleg and half a dozen other soldiers had quickly broken the beastman charge on their side, although the dull-witted beasts had spread their warriors unevenly so Torben's half had met with the weaker assault.

The rest of his cavalrymen, caught unawares by the sudden ambush, had not fared so well. As Torben galloped to their aid he realised that the bodies of several men and horses lay twitching or motionless on the valley floor amidst the snow and scree. Zabrov lay curled around an ungor spear, which thrust vertically into the air from where it was sunk into his dead body. Mikhail Polenko lay half-crushed beneath the carcass of his own thoroughbred steed, desperately fending off three slavering brown-furred beasts.

At the same time, a number of the ungors, who had at first fled when their ambush had not immediately brought down Torben's cavalrymen, were regrouping at the other end of the valley, under a filth-encrusted banner that looked like stretched human skin, which bore the Mark of the Beast.

Oran Scarfen, however, was surrounded by more than half a dozen beastmen, and he wasn't dead yet. As Torben closed the distance between them he saw Oran's horse dragged down by the beastmen and his friend disappeared from view amidst the excitedly braying ungors.

With a shouted 'Yaaah!' Torben urged his panting mount on even harder.

He felt the rumbling through the vibrations of the rock-hard ground before he heard it, drumming like the cartwheels of a loaded wagon. Looking towards the head of the valley he saw the two chariots thundering towards them, bristling with spikes and slicing blades, iron-shod wheels gouging great ruts in the frost-hardened turf, and pulled by monstrous horned and tusked creatures that combined the very worst and most savage attributes of great boars and brutish rams.

The arrival of the chariots alone could assure the beastmen their victory. Turning his plunging steed to face the rumbling chariots, Torben prepared to break their charge.

'AND YOU'RE THE only ones who remain?' Captain Yasharov asked as he surveyed the survivors of Torben's unit. 'Half of you?'

'That's correct, sir,' Torben said. Only eight of them had rejoined the rest of the border patrol. Following the appearance of the chariots, despite Torben's men managing to wreck one of them, five of his fellows had been seized and carried off by the second tuskgor-drawn contraption – Oran, Manfred, Andrei, Evgenii and Mikhail. Three had died: the steppes warrior Zabrov, the untried Cheslav and Kiryl. 'We were ambushed.'

'And you failed to locate the horde's encampment,' Yasharov said pointedly.

'Yes, sir. We were down to half strength and needed to regroup to effect a rescue.'

'Your orders were to locate the enemy camp. That is what scouts are for, is it not?'

'If we had continued it is doubtful there would have been any of us left alive to return and tell you the location of the camp.'

'Well, no matter,' Yasharov said, smiling coldly, disdain visible in his eyes. 'Boris Bogdashka's infantry found it for you. And their scouting mission met with no such misfortune.'

Torben was fuming inside but he said nothing. His survivors had made their way back to the main force to find that the army had made camp, following news of the discovery of the enemy's stockade, to prepare for the final decisive push. That night the Kislevites would lay siege to the beastmen's stronghold.

'The beastman camp is within a stockade atop what remains of an ancient earthwork. It is not far from here, beyond a spur of the pine forest. Order your unit to ready themselves. We attack at dusk. Dismissed.'

Torben remained exactly where he was.

'I said, you are dismissed,' Yasharov repeated, fire creeping into his voice.

'Sir, we should mount a rescue to free my men. I also believe that the beastmen have other prisoners, taken from the villages they've raided. Why, I do not know, but I do know it is not the normal behaviour of the warped ones.'

'Why would you want to rescue them?' Yasharov asked, an incredulous look on his blunt features.

Torben's loathing for his commander was increasing by the minute.

'Other than to save my men from a horrible death, you mean? Men I value and respect, some of whom I consider my friends?' Torben retorted. 'Other than that, the beasts must be planning something, I'm sure of it, possibly some dark ritual. It could be dangerous negligence to let such a ritual take place. Who knows what the consequences might be?'

'We are fighting a war against these mutants and in war there are bound to be casualties. Your men, and any other prisoners the beastmen may have taken, are expendable.'

Torben's blood was boiling. 'Good soldiers are a commodity you should do your best to protect,' he rejoined.

'I have suffered enough of your insolence! It is time you learnt your place!'

'I am sorry, my lord,' Torben lied, 'but if you would only give me a few hours we could at least try to infiltrate the camp and free the prisoners before the main attack.'

'In a matter of hours we will be ready to attack the stockade and cull this tribe, dealing with them once and for all.'

'But by then it may be too late. They know we are coming. The prisoners could have been sacrificed before we can rescue them and who knows what dark blessings such a sacrifice might bestow upon the horde? It could be the difference between victory and defeat.'

'You cannot even be sure that the prisoners are still alive, if indeed there are any!'

Yasharov was silent for several long, agonisingly drawn out seconds.

'Very well,' the captain said at last. 'You have until nightfall. Then the rest of us go in.'

'LOOK,' SAID ALEXI, pointing excitedly at the hilltop from the party's seclusion within the pines. 'You can see quite clearly how the stockade has been planted around the top of the earthwork. Those contours aren't natural. Some long-dead tribe built up the hill and turned it into a fortification.'

Stripped tree trunks had been rammed into the hillside and the palisade strengthened at irregular intervals by massive granite monoliths. Rising above the sharpened points of the great sunken logs they could all see a huge wicker effigy that had been erected inside the camp. It reminded Torben in part of the figures woven from corn stalks at harvest time, only it was constructed from numerous wicker cages lashed together in the form of a colossal beastman. Even from this distance, Torben could clearly see the antlered skull of some Chaos beast mounted on the 'head'. From between the spars of the wooden cages hands and arms waved in pathetic supplication. Torben's suspicions had been correct.

'I see what you mean,' Torben nodded.

'And that could also provide us with a way in,' Alexi said, a wry smile forming on his lips.

'How?' asked Vladimir.

'The ancestors of your people often dug secret escape routes through the earth beneath their hill-forts as a way out in dire emergencies. Sometimes they emerge up to half a mile away from the earthwork.'

'What are you trying to say?' Stefan muttered.

'Isn't it obvious?' Yuri said, fixing their newest recruit with a harsh glare.

'A way out can also be a way in,' Torben explained.

On foot, avoiding the attentions of the beastmen above, it was not a difficult matter for them to get closer to the hill-crowning edifice and begin their search for a secret way into the camp.

'OI! SCARFEN!' A voice hissed. 'Are you awake?' Oran opened his eyes.

'Manfred?' Oran replied, trying to look round.

'Up here.'

'What's going on? Where are we?' Oran's wrists and ankles had been roughly bound and where the rope rubbed his skin was sore with red welts circling his wrists.

'Have a look for yourself,' came Manfred's disgruntled reply.

Turning his head, Oran saw that he had been squashed inside a wicker cage with several other people, all packed on top of one another. He was pressed against the crossed spars of one side of their prison. Squeezing around within the cramped cage, Oran tried to assess precisely where they were.

The cage was just one of many that had been fastened together to form a much larger structure. He found himself looking out across the entirety of what he realised must be the beast horde's camp. It was a stockaded hilltop. Beyond it the sun was setting behind the pine-forested horizon, painting the sky and distant snow-capped peaks orange and mauve.

The spaces between the bars of the cage were wide enough for Oran to push his face through. He looked down and immediately regretted the action. His head began to spin; he was over fifteen feet above the ground. He closed his eyes and swallowed hard, fighting against the rising vertiginous nausea.

He opened his eyes but this time looked straight ahead. As he took in more of the cages lashed together around him he began to see a definite shape to the structure. It was that of a giant figure and his cage was part of its trunk. The colossus stood on two pillared legs while other cages, hanging from broad-beamed shoulders, formed its arms. Stacked high around the structure's legs were faggots of wood. There was no doubt as to the intended fate of the captives.

In front of the bonfire stood the granite monolith of the tribe's herdstone. The menhir was festooned with human remains hung on rusted chains – some no more than skeletons, others still red-raw and glistening. His vision blurred and he felt his stomach turn over as cold sweat beaded on his skin. He had looked down again.

Twisting his neck, Oran was just able to look upwards. The monstrous wicker edifice was surmounted by an equally monstrous skull. He wondered what sort of warped beast had ever existed for there to be such a relic. Every part of the pyre was packed tight with human prisoners. Now he knew what had happened to the inhabitants of the villages. Some of those who were still able moaned and wailed their plight to the heavens, while others huddled together within the cage whimpering or remaining eerily silent.

'Are there any of the others in here?' Oran asked of his companion.

'I can see Polenko through the bars of the cage above me, but I'm not sure if he's even alive. I know that one of the Tolyevs was brought here with us – Andrei, I think – but other than that, I don't know.'

Despite his hands being bound Oran was still able to reach inside his jerkin and, with relief, found his dagger still secreted there. By manipulating the sharp blade with his fingers alone he was able to cut through the hemp with ease. However, he didn't fancy his chances with the blade against the wicker staves of the cage.

'Can you see any way out of here?' Oran asked.

'Yes,' Manfred's replied. 'There's a door. It wouldn't be hard to force it open, but we're not going anywhere trussed up like a couple of game birds.'

'Don't worry about that,' Oran replied, 'Just worry about forcing that door.'

As the last light of day leeched away, Cathbad the shaman began the ritual to reawaken the Lord of Misrule.

A hush fell over the assembled herd. Beastman rituals were usually raucous, unruly affairs, but this night the assembled tribe understood that what was occurring was more momentous than anything they had ever witnessed before. They were summoning their god.

Gashrakk gripped the burning brand tightly in a great hairy paw, fingers as thick as a man's wrist curled around the wood ready to ignite the pyre and make the sacrifice. The flickering flames cast rippling orange shadows over the contours of his slab-muscled torso as Cathbad's guttural chanting intoned the incantation.

Gashrakk could feel the quickening power of Chaos coursing through his body. He snorted in excited anticipation. In moments the sacrifice would be made, the prophecy would be fulfilled and he would face his destiny, revelling in an orgy of unrestrained bloodlust against the forces of order. All would be returned to its primal, uncivilised state where the only law was to kill or be killed and the beast ruled supreme.

And unseen by Gashrakk, Cathbad or the tribe, high up on the structure of the wicker beastman, two figures emerged from the splintered door of one of the cages and began to scale the monstrous effigy.

THE NAUSEOUS REEK of the dung heap swept over Torben as he emerged from the tunnel. Thanks to Arnwolf's tracking skills and Yuri's sharp eyes, it had not taken the rescue party long to locate a half-collapsed opening overgrown by the straggling tangle of a bush, itself half-buried under a drift of snow. Twenty feet into the tunnel, they had discovered that it rose to the height of a man, the tunnel wall reinforced with slabs of rock.

Torben had led the way, a half-shuttered lantern guiding them through the dank darkness. More slabs of stone gave the shaft its form and also provided irregularly distanced steps, creating a rock ladder that led up to the earthwork above.

It had taken them longer than they had hoped to infiltrate the camp. A large, flat stone covered the earthwork end of the escape tunnel, which had itself become covered by the general detritus of the camp. They had smelt the mound of excrement that seemed to be the beastmen's privy, several feet from the top of the chimney. They now crouched behind it as they took in their surroundings.

'There's no fear of them smelling us coming,' Vladimir grunted disconsolately.

'Listen!' Yuri hissed.

Torben did so and realised how quiet it was. A lone braying voice came to them from the southern end of the camp, along with pitiful moans.

'We'll be outnumbered Sigmar knows how many-to-one but any time now the rest of the army are going to attack, providing us with just the distraction we need to free the prisoners,' Torben explained. 'When we see their torches we need to be in position.'

'It sounds like the beasts are too preoccupied and dullwitted to be on guard against an attack from right inside their own stockade,' Arkady suggested.

'Just the same, watch your backs. We don't know what sort of creatures they might have keeping guard for them.'

Cautiously, the party began to creep through the abandoned huts of the encampment. There was no need for the lantern now, the night was clear. The flicker of torches could also be seen beyond the solid black shape that towered over the camp.

How long did they have, Torben wondered, before the Kislevite attack came? They had best move quickly, if they were to have any chance of saving their companions. Then, as the party rounded the side of the largest hut, Yuri stopped them again.

'I hear something,' he said.

Torben scrambled up onto the crudely thatched roof of the hut. From his vantage point he could see the beastman herd thronged before the towering effigy. And then he saw them: dancing specks of yellow-orange light bobbing towards the hill-camp from the jagged, black silhouette of the pine forest in a snaking line.

Torben cursed. 'They're coming!'

'Let's pray that we're not too late to rescue anyone at all,' Oleg muttered.

GASHRAKK BLACKHOOF SAW the lights too and realised what must have happened. The ambush had failed. It could only have been a skirmish force that Slangar and Barruk's ungors had fought, not the whole hu-man army. But he wasn't going to let his plan fail now.

Snarling in rage and before Cathbad could finish the ritual, Gashrakk plunged the brand into the bonfire at the feet of the wicker colossus. Doused with tar, the faggots ignited with an incendiary roar. The shaman looked on in horror, the sacred rite climaxing too quickly, as the caged prisoners' screams drowned out the beastlord's triumphant bellow.

ORAN CLUNG TO the bars of the giant beastman feeling like he was going to vomit.

'Move it, Scarfen!' Manfred encouraged, only a few feet beneath him.

'I-I'm trying!'

It had been the only thing to do, Oran told himself, but now, as they climbed higher to escape the rising flames, they only seemed to be delaying the inevitable. It was hard to say whether the fire would claim them or whether they would fall to their deaths first, as vertigo threatened to overwhelm him.

Shrill cries cut through the night air, audible over the excited braying of the beastmen. The two soldiers had shown others a way out of their predicament and some of those who had shared their cage had begun to follow them. However, the prisoners were struggling to climb the wicker structure with wrists and ankles still tied. Some lost their grip, falling into the hungry flames below. Others were being picked off by spears hurled by the beastmen, as the tribe became aware of the prisoners' escape attempt.

'Scarfen, move it!' Manfred roared in desperation.

His whole body shaking, Oran continued his laborious ascent.

'For Kislev and the Tzar!' Torben yelled and flung himself, sabre drawn, at the monstrous beastman standing before the blazing bonfire. Before the creature knew what was happening, Torben had sunk his blade into the thick, corded muscle of its flank.

The monster roared, a sound born of pain and red rage. Torben tugged his weapon free as the monstrous beastman span round to face him. It was half as tall again as Torben, its long horns curving upwards from its ugly, distended goat-head, adding to his height. Its head was slung low, between broad, hunched shoulders and a shaggy mane of hair covered the muscular neck. Two great yellow tusks jutting from its jaw drooled thick saliva.

It wore a hide loincloth, trophies it had taken, as a champion of the beastmen, hanging from its waist, a macabre testament to its savage prowess in battle. Below the knee the creature's legs became backward-jointed animal limbs, ending in cloven hooves. No doubt to honour some primitive deity, the beastman had various parts of its body pierced by thick iron. Most impressive of all, however, was the huge ring through its snout. Everything about it spoke of ferocious strength: it looked capable of wrestling a bear and winning. The orbs of its caprine eyes burned with the reflected glow of the roaring bonfire.

The champion hefted its oversized, jagged-edged cleaver and, opening wide its mouth, bellowed. Torben didn't need to be able to understand the beastmen's language to know that it was a direct challenge.

The Kislevite needed no second invitation. Yelling his own battle-cry Torben flung himself at the beast.

His opponent was surprisingly fast and agile. Torben parried the beast's first ringing blow but staggered back under its force, his own muscles protesting as he maintained his position. Out of the corner of his eye Torben saw Arnwolf wrestling with the tribe's robed shaman, axe and bone-staff locked. Alexi and Vladimir were leading the others against the closest of the startled herd.

Any moment now, Torben told himself. Any moment now the rest of the border patrol would crash through the gates of the stockade like the Sea of Claws breaking against the cold coast of Kislev. But the attack never came – at least not as Torben imagined it would.

He heard the riders galloping past on the other side of the stockade, their horses' hooves pounding the frozen ground, but it took Torben a few moments to realise what the riders had done. Putting the stockade to the torch, Yasharov's knights had trapped the beastmen inside and Torben's rescue party along with them.

Hatred and fury burning in his heart, Torben realised they had been betrayed. Considered expendable by their captain, Yasharov had simply used them as a distraction, so that he could put an end to the beast horde once and for all, condemning the tribe's prisoners along with their captors.

Sudden, sickening doubt gripped Torben's stomach, as it became abruptly apparent that the outcome of the battle was no longer as assured as he might have at first hoped. Then steely resolve entered his heart. If it was his destiny to die here and now, then at least he would die fighting!

They traded blow for blow, Torben putting every ounce of his strength and every iota of concentration into the battle while the beastman's blood-lusting rage, relentless in its ferocity, drove it on against him. This was no scrawny, half-starved specimen but a true monster among monsters. Torben knew there was no way he could win this fight by brawn alone: the brute's massive body seemed to soak up every wound he managed to inflict against it. He would have to use his brains as well, something that from his experience most beastmen lacked.

The Kislevite and the champion fought on, Torben carefully manoeuvring them away from the heat and smoke of the conflagration towards the trophy-hung menhir. As he jumped backwards, to avoid a swipe of the heavy-headed cleaver, he felt the cold stone at his back and his hand touch the rusted links of a chain. Carried forward by the momentum of his swing, the beastman champion almost lumbered into Torben. This close he could smell its foetid reek, like a cowshed overdue a mucking out.

He thrust his sword forwards at the creature's unprotected midriff, but this was merely a diversionary tactic. The end of the chain in his hand, he swiftly pushed its hooked end through the iron ring in the beastman's nose and rattled it through with a strong tug. Snorting, the beastman lowered his horns, preparing to skewer Torben on their sharpened points.

Turning away from the beastman's goring attack Torben pushed the hook through another link in the chain, which was still securely attached to the herdstone. He backed off hurriedly as the champion swung at him with his brutal weapon again. Missing him, it lunged for Torben.

Torben clearly heard the sickening crunch of cartilage breaking over the roar of the burning wicker beastman, as the chain pulled on the great nose-ring. His opponent bellowed in pain and tried to free itself but the links of the chain remained strong.

Torben heard a crash and a screaming roar. Turning to the source of the pain-induced bellow he saw the robed shaman crashing into one blazing leg of the wicker effigy, its body a mess of red wounds dealt it by Arnwolf's rune-inscribed axe, as it recoiled from another mighty blow from the Norscan. The burning wood of the leg, already weakened by the flames, gave way, the shaman being swallowed by the white-hot conflagration. With one of its supports destroyed, the whole burning structure gave way.

Torben looked up to see the fiery body of cages, packed with roasted peasants, toppling towards him. Despite his wearying battle with the beastman champion, with an almighty leap Torben flung himself out of the way of the collapsing effigy.

GASHRAKK BLACKHOOF, CHAMPION of the Great Beast and chief of the Dark Horns, bellowed his anger to the heavens as the burning effigy of his god crashed down on top of him, a burning spar impaling his instantly combusted body.

ORAN AND MANFRED clung to the antlered skull-head of the pyre as it came crashing down in a blizzard of sparks and fiery smoke. Oran closed his eyes tight when he saw the sharpened tips of the burning palisade coming up to meet him.

Then he was falling, before scant seconds later he hit slushy snow and started rolling down the steep slope of the man-made hill. The head of the towering effigy had cleared the perimeter fence, throwing him and Manfred clear of the flames altogether.

TORBEN, ALEXI, YURI and Arnwolf raced through the blazing stockade, the air around them filled with swirling sparks. There was now nothing they could do for their fellows who had died valiantly, battling the beastmen. Oleg, Arkady, Stefan and Vladimir had all succumbed to their animal wrath. Now the four of them who remained could only hope to save themselves and with a pack of fire maddened beastmen at their heels, there was no only one hope for them.

Yuri was the first into the tunnel, diving into the hole by the dung heap. The others quickly followed, half scrambling and half falling down the shaft cut through the earth and rock. The first of the goatmen plunged headfirst in after them, only to become wedged in the narrow tunnel entrance, being so much broader than its quarry.

At the bottom of the hill again, the four survivors gathered reunited. The Kislevite cavalry who had launched the attack on the stockade were now mere flickering specks within the tree line once again.

The fire consuming the beastman camp lit the hills and forest for a quarter of a mile. As the flames rose high into the night sky, for a fleeting moment Torben fancied he saw a roaring antlered head appear briefly amidst the conflagration before vanishing.

Was it something being banished, he wondered, or summoned?

As the stockade continued to burn in the distance, back under the shelter of the trees, the survivors of Torben's unit found the other Kislevite soldiers gone, assured of the success of their captain's brutally effective tactics. As far as Captain Yasharov was concerned, the abducted villagers and even his own men could burn if it meant he achieved his goal, without putting himself at risk.

'I don't know who I loathe more – the beastmen or Yasharov,' Torben seethed.

'It was a massacre,' Manfred stated coldly.

'So what are you suggesting we do?' Alexi asked Torben. 'Desert?'

'Yasharov thinks we're dead already anyway,' Torben replied, the first hint of a grin creasing his face.

Yuri looked at Torben anxiously: 'What would we do then?'

'Do what we've always done. Live by the sword – as mercenaries.'

THE NEXT NIGHT the moon hung full and gibbous in the star-pricked sky over the Kislevite camp. Torben Badenov and his companions had watched and waited as their erstwhile fellow soldiers celebrated defeating the beastmen. But now, with half the night gone, the sounds of carousing had finally ceased as drink and sleep overcame Captain Yasharov's men.

'Are you ready?' Torben whispered to the foully grinning Oran.

'Oh yes,' the weaselly man replied, playing with the blackened dagger in his hands, 'I'm ready'.

'We won't be long,' Torben said, addressing Alexi, Yuri, Manfred and the burly Arnwolf, 'Then we can be on our way.' He lifted a heavy, bulging sack over one shoulder. 'We've got a delivery to make.'

With that, he and Oran slipped between the tents like fleeting shadows.

THE MORNING AFTER the attack was cold and frosty. Lev Kolenski stumbled through the tents, clumsily strapping on his sword belt, to take his turn at gate duty. The chill morning breeze was clearing his muzzy head and he began to gently whistle, his breath pluming into white clouds.

Reaching the entrance to the camp the soldier froze, the tune dying on his lips. His eyes widened in shock and he put a hand to his mouth to stem the bitter tasting bile that rose up his throat. He staggered backwards, his still unbuckled sword belt slipping onto the frosty ground, then turned tail and scampered back into the camp towards Captain Yasharov's pavilion.

BORIS BAGDASHA STEPPED quietly into Yasharov's tent after repeatedly failing to wake him from outside. He stopped abruptly, mortified by the sight that greeted him. Yasharov's bedclothes were twisted and rumpled, the pure white fur of the top blanket saturated with glistening red blood. Protruding from underneath the sheets was Yasharov's hand, his fingers bent into claws as if in a paroxysm of agony. His emerald signet ring winked balefully in the morning light. But the thing that lay on the deeply stained pillows made Kolenski double up and vomit violently onto the tent's lush carpeting. Staring back at him from burnt out eye sockets was the remains of a monstrous and unmistakably goat-like head, severed at the neck, with long curving horns protruding from its charred skull and a blackened tongue lolling from the side of its scorched mouth.

Bagdasha stooped out of the tent, nausea and shock making his head spin. He regained some of his senses when Kolenski, babbling incoherently, hared round from behind a tent and almost bowled him over.

OUTSIDE THE CAMP, just past the gates, a huge black rook settled gently on the bald, fleshy lump that sat atop a post driven firmly into the ground. It ruffled its oily coloured feathers and cawed, sharp eyes darting over the land. Then, with a powerful thrust of its neck, it buried its hooked beak into the juicy eye socket and tore free a lump of jellied fluid. The bird began to feast busily, as above more carrion birds began to circle.

And on the wind-blasted plains of Kislev, Captain Arman Yasharov's dead eyes wept red tears.

JAHAMA'S LESSON
by Matt Farrer

SOMETHING HAD ARRIVED on the shores of Bretonnia, a chill shadow that slipped into the Bay of Hawks under an empty night sky and through a still, quiet ocean mist. It was a thick, unseasonable fog that lay across the shore like a blanket of some parasitic mould, drowning the shingle beach and tangling itself in the trees beyond. On another night it would have had poachers or late-night fishermen muttering uneasily, but tonight the moon was in and nothing moved in the dimness. Out to sea it narrowed sharply to a spot in the centre of the bay: a spire of black rock, glistening like a rotted tooth, spearing into the air between the headlands. The spire had not been there at sundown.

Khreos Maledict, Lord of Karond Kar, master of the Black Ark *Exultation of Blighted Hope*, chuckled over the sound of lapping water and tugged at the cloak about his armoured shoulders. The night had been mild as they had sailed into the bay, but the sorcerous fog had brought a chill to the air.

'I confess I have often thought our sorcerers' interest in weather weaving and concealment foolish and effete, but I profess myself newly educated. Even lacking the skills of our soft-spined southern cousins, I can see how the techniques Skail and his apprentices were fretting over could be... profitable. I have never seen the *Exultation's* walls of mist extended so far from her, or so thick.'

He peered about him, trying to see the hills over the curve of the bay, but they were as smothered by the fog as the shape of the Black Ark behind them.

The young helldrake towing the landing-skiff was invisible in the whiteness ahead, although every so often he thought he could hear a crack or chink as the Drakemasters goaded their charge one way or another. Even the lines of his coach, almost close enough to touch, were grey and dreamlike, and the four dark riders behind it made ghost-shapes as their horses pawed at the skiff's broad deck. Khreos shot a look at the young elf next to him.

'You, nephew, are clearly still not convinced of this whole exercise. No matter. Truth to tell, Khrait, I do not believe you will be convinced until you stand at the foregate of the *Exultation* and watch the... feh, what's the creature purporting to rule this piece of the land?'

'The Duc d'Argent,' put in a pale shape from the gloom at the front of the skiff.

'Watch the Duc d'Argent being towed aboard by the witch elf hooks in his flesh. What do you think, Miharan? Gilded chains for the baron and his family, in honour of their station?'

Miharan Diamo, the diminutive witch elf elder, the one they called the Scorpion's Daughter, would not return his smile.

'Make sure your reach does not exceed your grasp, Lord Khreos. You have not yet made your cut – you are only just drawing the knife.' She gave a dismissive gesture of her hand. 'But when the Castille d'Argent has fallen, I will commission your gilded chains happily enough.'

Jahama's Lesson

Khreos kept his smile in place and made a polite bow of acknowledgement, as he narrowed his eyes and promised himself yet another time that the little albino bitch would be meeting with an accident as soon as he could find a foolproof way to arrange one. Ahead of them, splashing sounds came through the fog as the helldrake gained shallow water and was made to pull the skiff aground. The little vessel juddered as its bow was hinged down into a ramp, and Khreos and Khrait climbed carefully into the coach as Miharan stepped in on the other side. There was the sound of hooves and they were off, jolting up the beach until they reached the road into the hills, the Dark Riders taking up position around them as they emerged from the fog.

'Perfect,' declared Khreos, sitting back and smiling again. 'See, nephew? I told you the coach would cross the beach with no trouble. I selected this bay for its shingle as well as its roadway.' His nephew did not reply, and Khreos's gaze switched to the fourth figure in the coach, a silent patch of black against the wine-and-gold colours of the seats.

'And you, Jahama, you are to be the knife we draw tonight, the core and pivot of my stratagem.' He leaned forward to the figure – but not too close. He had heard stories about the assassins who emerged from all those years under the witch elves' tutelage, and of what happened to those who got too trusting toward them. 'Miharan has sung your praises, sir. I don't doubt that when we ride upon the Castille d'Argent tomorrow we shall find you greeting us at the gate, knife-blade wet, eh?'

'I understand my orders, lord.' The assassin spoke well enough but his voice was oddly soft and flat, as if reciting unfamiliar words by rote. He would not meet Khreos's eyes.

'You'd best leave him, Lord Maledict. He has a hard night ahead of him, and he must prepare himself.' Khreos snorted at the sound of Miharan's voice, making less effort to hide his displeasure now, and sat back to watch the trees shadowing out the stars over the road. The road was entering woods and the sounds of hoofbeats slowed as the coach-horses moved onto rougher road and the Dark

Riders began weaving in and out through the trees, watchful for movement in the dark around them. There was something oppressive about the evening and for a time the only sounds were hooves and the wind until the coach slowed and they heard the driver's voice murmuring through the little window:

'Lord, we are at the place. Beyond here the patrols from the Castille begin.'

With what Khreos considered unseemly haste, Miharan flicked open the coach door and vaulted easily out of the howdah and down to the ground, Jahama a moment behind her. But when Khrait went to lower the little folding steps and follow them Khreos put a hand on his shoulder.

'Don't look so puzzled, nephew. Just bide your time. We wait for the Lady Miharan to kiss her throat-cutter goodbye and come back aboard, then we return to the *Exultation*. In the meantime, try turning your wits to what we're actually about here.' His eyes turned to the two shapes outside in the clearing. 'Let's see if you can realise what I have planned.'

ON THE GROUND below them, Jahama shrugged his shoulders and adjusted the hang of his cloak. His hands flickered pale in the dimness as he tested the draw on each of his weapons.

'You need no final advice, Jahama. Remember only what it is you have to achieve. I will greet you again on the Black Ark.' Miharan gave a small tilt of her head, and Jahama swept back into a deep kneeling bow. The witch elf placed her hand on his head. Then they both straightened and stepped apart.

As Jahama scanned the hills and got his bearings, Miharan leapt lightly onto the running board and slipped into the coach. He ignored the sound of its wheeling and moving away, but one of the Dark Riders paused long enough to look down at Jahama with an odd expression. Jahama met the other elf's gaze for a chilly moment before the rider wheeled his mount and disappeared after the rest of the party. His face still expressionless, Jahama looked around the clearing again.

The stiff wind blew at ground level too, crumpling the treetops and sending gusts between the trunks. Night-eyed as he was, Jahama had to crouch in the shelter between two thick roots and strike one of the little tapers the assassins used, designed to burn for just a moment and to be easily shielded with a cupped hand. It showed him the piece of yellow parchment, the one with the forest, the road, the little river-bridge, the village, and the Castille d'Argent on its hill. In the seconds it took for the taper to burn down and extinguish he had fitted the map to the clearing he stood in; tucking it into his belt he could turn and look into the night in the direction he now knew the castle lay.

'I understand my orders, lord.' he said again, and now his voice was full of a soft, easy amusement. His cloak sat warm and close about his shoulders as he began a gentle jog away through the woods to the killing ground.

SEATED IN THE coach, Khrait Maledict sprawled his legs out in a finely calculated pose of carelessness and listened to the sparring between his uncle and the Scorpion's Daughter. He hooded his eyes and tilted his helm forward a little to obscure where his gaze was resting, and idly rested his head on his hand in such as way that he could grin without it showing. This was interesting.

'And so, my Bride of Khaine, was your assassin ready? Had he prepared himself adequately? He needed no further tutelage from you?' The lord's tone was heavy and bantering, more so than it would normally have been. Dark elves, particularly their nobility, never conversed – the most trifling exchange of words was always a subtle, studied contest of insult and counter-insult as each tried to saw away at the other's composure. Khrait knew it irritated his uncle that the game didn't seem to work with witch elves, whose manners tended to the simple and brutal. Miharan didn't seem to have the wit to feel the barbs that Khreos had constantly thrown at her on the *Exultation's* voyage out – but that fact nettled the lord so intensely that Khrait couldn't believe it wasn't a deliberate gambit by Miharan herself. He wondered why his uncle hadn't picked that up. Perhaps the old fool really was starting to lose his edge.

'He is the equal of the task you have set him and more, my Lord Maledict. When you came to me at Naggarond, you demanded the finest assassin under my tutelage. I promised I would provide no less. I was sent for that night and told to bring Jahama to your docks. My finest pupil. I could hardly have sent anyone less.'

'You do credit to yourself, Daughter of the Scorpion.' said the lord. 'Your reputation, your skills as a tutor...' Miharan waved a hand airily as the coach bounced over a rough spot. They were moving faster now, the driver more sure of himself and their cargo delivered.

'It takes a certain eye, lord, and the providence of Khaine. I took Jahama personally, of course. A small manse over Karond Kar harbour. I understand they were master shipwrights of some kind.' She shrugged. 'Their blood was as red as anyone else's.'

Khrait suppressed a shudder. He had wondered, as had everyone he knew when they were young, whether the eyes of the witch elves would ever fall on him. How could they not when sometimes on the dazed, shattered morning after Death Night houses were found with the families and retainers butchered, even the animals cut apart, but the children not dead just simply gone? And then years later, as an army drew up for battle, one might hear among the witch elves' battle-cries the particular voice of a girl not heard since childhood, or move to let an assassin take his place among the soldiers and glimpse for half a second under a cowl the features of a playmate vanished a quarter of a lifetime before...

Jahama had seemed about his own age. Khrait shuddered again and wondered if the assassin would have been someone he would have grown up to know.

* * *

Jahama's Lesson

THE WIND HAD been Jahama's friend. It gusted and eddied and stung the skin in a way that reminded him of the training grounds outside Ghrond. And it would also break up his scent and stop more than a scrap of it reaching the giant hunting-hounds that seemed to be tethered outside every farmer's cottage he passed. He had rubbed his tunic and plastered his hair with the oil that Bretonnians used on their leather jerkins and tack, and that confused them further: he had triggered nothing more than the occasional puzzled, hesitant bark. Had this been Naggaroth, these ones would have been dead in their sleep at their own brothers' hands five times over, with guards that soft.

Deep night though it was, the countryside was not as deserted as the bay and forest had been. Not long after the road left the forest for farmland he had come up behind a pair of wagons pulled by great slab-muscled horses, decked with lanterns and with men-at-arms jogging beside them. Whatever was urgent enough to have such a cavalcade out at night Jahama did not try to guess, but they created a useful commotion, setting dogs barking and flocks of geese honking and making the farmers more likely to ignore them. He had shadowed them for the time it took to pass by the village, then peeled off and flitted away through the vineyards.

'DOUBTLESS JAHAMA HAS profited by his... change in circumstances.' Khreos said silkily. 'Quite an upbringing! A life among the Brides of Khaine – stepchild of the Lord of Murder, as it were. A respectable lineage, even by proxy. And to have excelled in the deadly arts as he has... If, of course, you have described his abilities properly.'

'You seem satisfied enough with my claims about Jahama's capabilities, my lord. You accepted him to be your agent tonight, after all.' Khrait smirked at the lord's questioning of her truthfulness being elegantly turned on its head. If Khreos doubted her confidence in Jahama, she was saying, then to have picked him anyway for this mission was doubly foolish. Oh, she was sharp. No drug-addled beast-woman, this one.

Lord Khreos, glowering, shifted tack.

'The Shades I sent to spy out the land were unable to approach the castle, you know. The peasants are loyal and tenacious. They keep vigils of their own at night, with dogs and wardens, and are quick to answer an alarm from the castle walls – why, you saw for yourself that we could not go even halfway through the forest before we had to leave Jahama to go on by himself. This is a troubled part of the coast, you see, and its people are well prepared. Two of my Shades tracked a warband of Gor that came out of the swamps to the south and into the Duc d'Argent's lands, and the Duc's response was well marshalled indeed. If he should make it to the castle, he had best be careful when he flees it. I expect the yeomen will be combing the countryside for him. Perhaps we should have warned him that our last three spies were all captured.'

Miharan's face betrayed nothing.

'I would not concern yourself. Jahama was sent last year beyond the Watchtowers and into the east where the Chaos tribes wander. His mission was to poison the wells of a tribe that had been harrying our border. The land was alive with roving warbands – there was some great strife between the Marauder chieftains that had them hunting each other and everything else they found – but Jahama slipped by them all. None found him. Watchful or no, the Bretonnians will not find him either.'

AROUND THE VILLAGE Jahama began to see the wardens and slowed his pace. In country like this the Duc's patrols would be no idle night-wanderers, podgy with the bribes they took from the poachers they were supposed to catch. The first he found were on a little footbridge near the village mill, three men in ducal livery leaning on the bridge wall with a brazier between them. Jahama did not think of taking chances; he moved in a wide semicircle around them and soon found their two companions. Two more yeomen in a grove thirty paces from the bridge, dark capes over their surcoats, easy to overlook if an intruder were intent on the lanterns and conversation of the guards around their little fire. Safely out of reach of their inferior human night-vision Jahama eyed them balefully, fighting down the urge to put a blowpipe dart into each of them. Sentries who knew enough to set up a twofold guard like this would also know enough to keep regular contact with each other, and the instant anyone found any of these men gone there would be an alarm raised. It was not the time for that yet.

It took him ten minutes to circle about them, triple-checking every bush and shadow for a third hidden watcher. There were none. Jahama shrugged out of his cloak and bundled the thick material into a parchment-thin hide envelope – wet, it would cling to him and weigh him down. Then he slipped into the water and darted eel-quick across to the far bank, pulling his cloak about him again as he listened intently. His breathing had not quickened; his face showed nothing but quiet concentration. There were fresh horse tracks on this side of the river, meaning night-time patrols, but he could hear no hooves and so he began to move again. The hillside below the Duc's castle was bare and he was grateful for the lack of moonlight: invisible in the dark, he looked up at the black bulk of the castle and grinned.

'I AM PLEASED to hear it,' declared Khreos. 'The quieter and more skilled he is, the greater his chances of catching the Duc in his bed. The advantage of surprise would be crucial, I imagine. The Duc has something of a reputation as an opponent. Were he to face Kouran of Naggarond himself, I might still hedge my bets.' Khreos kept his voice carefully casual. 'My spies' accounts of his battles against the bestigor war-chief were really quite chilling to read, and he has by all accounts bested vampires, trolls, greenskins of all–'

'Jahama is unmatched at all the assassin's arts. As I told you.' Miharan cut him off, sounding impatient – or was it defensiveness? Miharan's expression was still unreadable above the fur she had wrapped around herself, but Khrait thought he was going to give his uncle this one on points – she seemed rattled.

'I hope for his sake he is.' They were back on shingle again and Khrait realised with mild surprise that they were back at the bay – they had been moving faster than he had realised. Next to him, his uncle was letting his smugness show. 'Jahama will not have the assassin's usual advantage for too long. There will only be a few soldiers he will be able to take by surprise; the rest he must fight while looking them in the eye, and with no others to support him. Or not for many hours, at least. I know he can pounce like a cat, but should he have to fight the Duc toe-to-toe, blade against blade... well, we must have hope, eh?'

The lord cocked a triumphant eyebrow. Miharan's gaze was stone.

GUILLAUME SHIFTED FROM foot to foot and eyed the brand guttering in the bracket above him. From the castle rampart he could just hear the singing and the banging of goblets on tables from the feasting hall. Jacqueline would be in there, he supposed, carrying the big jugs of coarse red wine back and forth. If he hadn't been bullied into taking Marcel's watch tonight he could have worked his way in, and he was sure that tonight he would finally have found the courage to talk to her. His grandmother in the village had told him that the west wind knew all about love, if you said the name of the one you loved just as you held a burning torch up high and watched the sparks...

He looked about again, didn't see anyone, switched the halberd to his left hand and started trying to wrestle the torch out of its bracket. If the sparks blew straight, it meant your love would be returned, but if they corkscrewed in the wind... Guillaume frowned. He must have strained a muscle or something – there was a sharp pain in his neck. And then his legs crumpled under him.

Jahama fielded the halberd before it could clatter on the stones and slid his stiletto free of Guillaume's body, then took a deep breath of chilly air. The moment in a mission when there was no more need for secrecy and he was free to kill was always the most delicious one. He flicked the blood from his knife, selected a broader, heavier blade for his other hand and looked around.

The wooden roof inside the gatehouse, that would be the stables. Important work: a little poison dust scattered there and any surviving knights would be without mounts come the dawn. That tower to the left: he knew that was the quarters of Sir Roland, the Duc's adjutant, and of Jules the Rash and the brat pack of knights-errant that he led. Important men. That should be his next stop after the stables, to deal with any who had retired early and then lie in wait for the rest as they came in, rolling on their feet and flushed with drink. The gatehouse itself, of course, must not be overlooked: there would be the capstans and counterweights for the drawbridge and portcullis, to make sure that the Lord Maledict could march straight into the courtyard upon his arrival.

Hours until dawn, but not that many. Jahama looked up and down the wall, saw no other sentries, then went leaping down the stairs and through the shadows, away from the gatehouse and stables and straight past Sir Roland's tower to the servants' quarters.

THE EXULTATION WAS nothing like the quiet bulk against the stars that it had been when the skiff and its coach had left. Now the lower reaches of the Ark were strung with lamps, and the air rang with shouts and splashes as boat after boat was lowered to the water and dark elves thronged at the docks to board them. Cold ones were being hooded and shoved into longboat corrals and bundles of crossbow-bolts passed from shoulder to shoulder from the armouries. Lord Khreos surveyed the activity and gave his nephew an indulgent smile as their own skiff was hoisted from the water.

'Nearly time now, Khrait. You are already in armour, of course, and our mounts are prepared. We will move straight to begin our march. Enough bickering over our little assassin friend, eh, Miharan? We shall find out if he has done his work soon enough.' The Lord laughed, and Khrait could tell he considered the argument with Miharan over, but the little elf was talking again.

'A pity our trip ended so soon. I had hoped to have time to tell you another story of Jahama before we marched. The manner in which he was made a full assassin is not known to many outside our cult, but the tale is a good one.' She stretched inside her fur cloak, indifferent to the way the skiff hung fifty feet over the *Exultation's* marshalling yards.

'The year Jahama reached his final training the winter was bitter and the stars in a vile alignment, and Hellebron was in an ill humour. Decreeing a special test for the assassins, she stationed her own master assassin Hakoer beside her, the one they called the Breath of Ice for his coldness.'

'No one I have ever heard of.' Khreos was inspecting the back of his gauntlet, feigning indifference.

'Oh, you will have heard of him, my lord. All Naggaroth has heard of him, simply not his name.' Miharan allowed herself a smile as the implication sank in. The air turned grey as the Ark's shield of enchanted fog swirled around them.

'Jahama was barely six-score years and scrawny with youth. No one else would be his patron, but I knew I had found a quality in the boy. The test was simple. Hellebron locked her palace. Her best artisans set their traps in every room, her own assassins and her guards hunted through her tower with orders to strike down any elf they did not know as one of their own. And to Hakoer she handed her own blade, the Deathsword, to use on any that approached them.

'All they had to do, you see, was make their way to Hellebron's audience chamber, and pluck from Hakoer's neck his silver collar with its single ruby. Then Hellebron would declare it a gift to them and we would have our newly anointed assassin. She laughed as she told us that she would see the hearts of our pupils on Khaine's altar by the next sunrise, and that if any got close enough even to set eyes on Hakoer's silver collar she would reward his trainer richly.'

The skiff came to a gentle landing on its rest, and servants hurried to roll a ramp into place. Dotted with baleful lamplights, the Black Ark's spires skewered the night sky around them.

'But I have wasted time, lord, I apologise. I am sure you have better things to do than listen to old tales of a simple functionary of yours.'

Miharan walked past the two nobles, ignoring their glares, and stepped lightly down to the deck where her handmaidens waited. The lord watched her for a moment, then shrugged her off and turned back to his nephew.

'Well now, Khrait. If you ever wish to take a place in the great hall of House Maledict I trust you have learned from what you saw tonight. We could have followed the urgings of your infantile friends, marched ashore from the *Exultation* as soon as we came to the bay and tried to smash our way inland. Within a day we would have been surrounded by those ham-handed human knights and brought to battle. By the time we had felled them, what then? Our energy dissipated in barbarous hacking-matches with a foe beneath our dignity.

'Attend! See the way that the edge, the steel, the very spear-point of our army is assembling and moving to shore. Our cold ones are waiting, our retainers and lieutenants. But as we advance through the night, as we move like armoured shadows along the road, our first strike will come sooner still! Like the tongue flicking out ahead of the snake, Jahama is stealing ahead of us. Like the night wind he will pass into the baron's fortress and descend upon the sleeping knights like Khaine himself, Blade and venom throughout the halls and walls and chambers!' Khrait, leaning insolently against the rail, rolled his eyes – his uncle's penchant for melodrama had slipped its reins again.

'Tomorrow when we reach the castle, there will be nothing! A gutted husk, its gates standing open before us, its knights lying naked in their beds, their throats open, the watchmen struck down in their towers with never an alarm sounded! And then – attend, nephew – then we shall turn to the countryside at large, to the farms and villages. Then the slavers will bring out their shackles and whips, then the cold ones can gorge, then we shall have our hunts and our fights. And those animals will scurry and cry, "where are our knights, where is our Duc?" but their defenders will have been cut from the tale before it begins! By the time messengers can reach any other castles, the *Exultation of Blighted Hopes* will be sailing for Karond Kar, and our holds shall groan with slaves!'

'The crashing invasions and battles that you youngbloods seem to favour are well enough in their way. But save them for those repugnant little inbreeds on Ulthuan! Why waste warriors against these sweaty, hairy savages? Brute force is one thing, Khrait, but this is House Maledict. And a plan like this has...' he matched the words to the closing of a fist, '...elegance.'

THREE HUMANS IN the little cobbled yard around the well: a pair of servants drawing water and a valet relieving himself against the wall. Running and leaping, Jahama passed over the well and between the two servants who dropped without ever seeing the blades that had cut them. A twist in mid-air and he rolled into a lunging double thrust that caught the valet in sternum and throat as he turned. The man fell with his hands still tangled in his breeches and Jahama was away.

Light and noise emanated from the windows of the servants' hall, and Jahama flicked the stiletto back into his sleeve and grabbed a little wooden stool sitting by a wall. A sweep of a long arm sent it crashing through the shutters and the first of them came milling out of the door a moment later, silhouetted sharp against the firelight. Jahama could have dropped five of them in as many heartbeats with throwing-blades, but he was already bounding up the steps to the walkway that led to the Grail chapel. Its heavy doors stood ajar, throwing out candlelight, and two figures stood outside them, hands on sword-hilts. One grey head, one blond. Harsh human syllables grated on Jahama's ears.

'An argument or something. It's the servants. Shall we finish our prayers, father?'

They peered out, eyes adjusting to the gloom. The old one was no threat, but the young one would be one of the Duc's warriors. There was power in his frame and he held his sword with casual ease.

He ran at them and pirouetted by the young knight to take his father with a low, flat backhanded stroke. The old knight fell to his knees, wheezing in agony and as the son turned to try to swing Jahama made a dainty slash just above his eyes. The cut was shallow but the flow of blood was blinding. The knight staggered, wiping his face with one hand and roaring as Jahama neatly finished his pirouette, leapt straight up and swung onto the chapel roof.

He must have knocked over a lantern in the servants' quarters; the firelight was much brighter and people were running with shouts and wet sacks. One or two had even come to the door of the main hall where horns and loud singing were still blaring. In front of the chapel, the young knight was screaming. Jahama knew enough Bretonnian to catch 'Father!' and 'Murderer!' before he slipped a noose over a roof-gable and slid down the thin cord to the cobbles on the far side.

A boy was peering out of a high window at the commotion, and Jahama took the opportunity to flick a throwing-needle up and into him. The motion caught the eye of someone at the servants' hall – the fire was all but out but the crowd was growing – and at the first shout of 'Who goes there?' Jahama was running again, flitting sparrow-quick past the open door to the feasting hall with his blowpipe rising to his lips.

'Marius?' from behind him, then, more urgently, 'Marius? Marius!' In motions so practised they were unconscious, his left hand stowed his blowpipe back at his thigh and re-drew his cleaving knife. His other sheathed the stiletto and tugged the cord that opened a pack at his hip and sent a dozen small steel caltrops tinkling onto the steps behind him. The man at the hall's entrance had dragged his crumpled companion away and now more figures were pouring out, from the hall and the tower, and shouts were going around the walls. Jahama grinned; now things would begin in earnest.

FOR THE FIRST time since the skiff had set off from the Ark, Khrait spoke aloud. 'The assassin was expensive to procure, uncle. And his success–' he shot a look over his shoulder, but Miharan had passed out of earshot '–his success will bring kudos and rewards to the witch elves at the expense of ourselves. All things considered, uncle, is it really wise to hand Morathi and her followers a gift like this? All that anyone will know when those two return is that House Maledict are so under Miharan's thumb that we're freighting a load of slaves back for her for free.'

Khreos turned to look at his nephew as they sauntered down the ramp to the Ark's lower keep. Scorn, smugness and exasperation fought for position in the curl of his lip and the arch of his eyebrows.

'Return? Return with us? Don't be stupid, boy.'

THERE WAS A howl behind him: someone rousted out of bed had been the first to cross the caltrops and hadn't put on his boots. Jahama laughed loudly for a few moments to give them his location then hurled himself down the cloister alongside the hall and through the first door he found.

A stifling kitchen, cooks banking the coals in the roasting-pits now that the feast was finally done. Good. Jahama's arm described a curt quarter-circle and two fell back with slivers of steel in their necks, then he vaulted a chopping-block, plucked the cleaver from it and drove it into a serving-man's shoulder. Almost without thought his fingers picked a loose-weave sachet of Tuern's Curse – one of the few poisons he had bothered to bring – and tossed it into the stewpot as a surprise for them later, then he turned as the knights poured in behind him.

All were unarmoured, but all were armed: a dozen drawn swords and perhaps half that many axes and maces. All weapons needing a wind-up and space to swing. If he could get in among them, getting back out to the courtyard would be an easier matter.

They were rushing at him, the young one he'd cut in front of the chapel in the lead wearing a mask of blood and tears. Jahama took a moment to wonder how he looked to them – a head taller than they but slender even with his cloak and cowl about him, narrow-faced and steel-eyed even by Naggarothi standards. The dying fires seemed to give everything a lushness, a depth, and turned his assassin's cloak into a pit that drank the light. Then Jahama stopped thinking, gave a nonchalant flick of his arm that threw a line over a roofbeam, and swung neatly up over their heads.

They were quicker than he expected and a sword-point caught the hem of his cloak, but it was too light a touch to slow him and he somersaulted in the air to land lightly behind the men who had run at him. Someone cannoned into him and for a moment he almost lost his balance, but it was no real difficulty to turn and trap the man's leg just so. The knight's knee snapped as he fell forward into the others.

Jahama whipped the edge of his hand expertly into the next man's jaw, sending him choking as another bared his teeth and swung a mace. In the second it took the assassin to shift his balance inside the swing, the haft had caught him above the ear and with a snarl to match his attacker's, Jahama arced his knife up and lunged. His reflex was to take out the man's throat before he could balance for another swing until he remembered what he was here for, just in time to reverse the stroke and smash the weighted pommel into the man's temple. He would live.

Jahama placed his hands on the staggering knight's shoulders as though he were about to deliver a double-cheek Bretonnian kiss of comradeship, then he spun the man about, pushed off and drove both his feet into the face of the first of the squires to come running through the far door. The boy went down unconscious or dead and Jahama turned the movement into a backward roll, swiped a knife through the hamstrings of the second squire and ran through into the great hall.

Almost empty, now, a handful of cowering servants the only ones left. A great bestigor head leered from the wall and captured banners hung from the ceiling. Jahama thought of looking for any he recognised but there was no time. Horns were blowing outside, and the counterpoint of booted feet was everywhere. The knights were on his heels again, far too many to fight now – Jahama was starting to think he had done his work a little too well.

'Do you think she knows we've sent her star pupil on a suicide mission, uncle?'

'Knows? I don't see how she can. She's too sure of the massacre her pet is preparing to deal out, for all the taunting I gave her.' Forgetting his dignity, Khreos spat on the deck. 'Oh, he'll do his share of damage, I don't doubt. That's why I sent him on ahead to begin with. We'll march into the Duc's lands in a few hours and find the castle boiling like an ants' nest that someone has kicked. But you've read the reports of the Duc and his men. One elf destroy them single-handedly? Even one elf whose smug little mistress loves to spin such stories about him? Hellebron's challenge, indeed! Have you ever heard of that Hakoer fellow? Of course not!

'My speech about Jahama emptying out the castle was for Miharan's benefit, Khrait. If you believe it you're as gullible as she – Jahama will never leave that castle alive.

Shadowblade himself would be lucky to silence the Duc's entire household. Think about it, Khrait. If one assassin were able to achieve that, or even a dozen, why are there any knights left in Bretonnia at all? He'll never kill them all, certainly not the Duc himself. From what I know of our human friend I think he'll swat Jahama like a gnat when they face off. Face off they will, of course, since that's what I had Miharan tell him to do. But Jahama will kill enough of them for the Duc to be preoccupied with lamenting his comrades, not watching for more attackers. We arranged for our spies to be captured to teach the Duc that dark elves only ever sneak into his lands alone. Just as he's writing off this as another solitary intruder, albeit a more vicious one – there we shall be!'

The lord's steward was standing nearby with a golden tray. They watched carefully as the aged elf had a mouthful of wine from each goblet before they picked them up.

'What will Miharan do when she realises?'

'Oh, I hope she tries to avenge him, Khrait.' Khreos chuckled as he swaggered away. 'Oh, I hope she does.'

Khrait took a last swallow of wine as he watched his uncle go. But even as he was dismissing his uncle's vainglory and walking away to prepare for the march, his thoughts turned back to his last sight of Jahama's cloak parting as the assassin had bent to step out of the coach, and the gleam he had seen at the assassin's neck: a collar of dull silver plates with a single deep red jewel.

'ASSASSIN!' THE VOICE filled the room and seemed to thrum in the stones. Standing on one of the long trestle tables, Jahama turned and stared. In the doorway, almost filling it, his knights assembled behind him, the man he had been sent here for. The Duc; his iron-grey hair flowed to his shoulders and his greatsword looked like a rapier in his hands. His scarlet and white tunic caught the torchlight.

'Only vermin stab and flee in the night. Can you not fight a knight of the Lady, you that hide in the shadows and murder children and old men? Let me look you in the eye. Do yourself one service in your degenerate life: die a proper death.'

The man had taken a step into the room and the knights were spreading out around him, watchful but not attacking. Jahama realised they were waiting for the duel between their lord and their invader.

The Duc had taken up a fighting stance. His bare arms were heavy with muscle: to an eye used to slender elf limbs he seemed to vibrate with power. Jahama's knives felt like sticks in his hands, felt like nothing. He took a deep breath.

Voices in his memory. *The Lord: you are to be the knife we draw tonight, the core and pivot of my stratagem. Lady Miharan: Remember only what it is you have to achieve.* He took a deep breath.

Then he swept his arm in a single, careful throw that drove his last throwing-blade through the heart of one of the damsels huddling by the fire, gave the Duc his most winning smile and polite bow, and was gone into the courtyard.

TWO MEN-AT-ARMS RAN to block him. Jahama flew by them without seeming to slow or even to strike until one after another they dropped to the cobbles. Everywhere he looked in the courtyard there were soldiers closing about him, he fixed his eyes on the gate and opened his stride to the longest. For one agonising moment he thought he would have to climb back to the parapet and back down the line he had cast to scale the walls, but then he saw the little gatehouse door. Instinct made him swerve and jag as he ran at it, and the archers on the walls sent their arrows down to crack against the cobbles. Then the bar to the little inset gate clattered to the ground behind him – one last move to make.

He worked it loose from his belt and dropped it just where they would run in pursuit of him. Then he ran, swerved, and made a long dive that carried him almost to the far edge of the moat. A single stroke and he was surging up the far bank, a shadow among shadows even as the first rumours of dawn began to touch the eastern sky.

I have put my neck down across the block and lifted it away clean, he thought. The wind now gone, he heard voices behind him from the gate and allowed himself a single backward look. He could just make out one man peering after him and another standing hunched over, staring at something on the ground. The little waterproof pouch with the parchment map inside. Jahama laughed then, almost doubling over before he heard the horns behind him and sped up again. He thought they would have better things to do than hunt him now.

It would be dawn very soon. Khreos did not like to admit it, but he was finding these lands less detestable than he used to. The sunlight that had scorched his white skin intolerably when he was younger now brought a not unpleasant glow to old bones that felt older in the Naggaroth winter. He put the thought from his mind and hefted his lance – he hated the way he never seemed to be able to concentrate when they were due for battle.

He turned in the saddle, settling into the swaying gait of his cold one, and looked around him; there behind the ranks of his personal guard, Khrait was riding with his own little retinue. To either side, blocks of warriors quick-stepped to keep pace with the cavalry, crossbows slung on shoulders. The sea dragon scales on the corsairs' cloaks and banner caught the pale pre-dawn light.

A noise nagged at the edge of his hearing and he turned his head this way and that, trying to place it. Cries? No. Birdsong? Too harsh. The only thing it sounded like, it couldn't be. Miharan's assassin had seen to it. He craned around again trying to see the little witch elf, but her palanquin had fallen further behind as they rode out from the Ark. As far as he could tell she was still back in the forest that the road had just emerged from.

His cold one raised its head and grunted at the air, and he turned to grab the goad from its saddle-clip. Only then did he see what his soldiers were staring at, and understand the noise he had heard.

The war-horns on the hilltop ahead of them gave another blast, and the glittering ranks of armoured knights sent up a shout as the scarlet and silver grail banner of the Duc unfurled over their heads. Khreos, gaping, could only clutch at his lance as a babble of orders rose behind him, cries as his corsairs milled about into fighting ranks, as the crossbow regiments scrabbled for bolts, as his champions tried to awaken the Blood Banner to bring their cold ones to full frenzy.

And then hissing clouds of arrows flew high into the air, line after line of yeomen and squires rounded the base of the hill and the Bretonnians were thundering down the road toward them like a floodtide.

KHREOS MALEDICT, LORD of Karond Kar, Master of the Black Ark *Exultation of Blighted Hope*, was dying. He could still feel dim fire in his crumpled leg where his cold one had fallen on it, but he had to lie on that leg because lying on his side was the only way he could drag himself along after a Bretonnian mace had crushed his other shoulder even through his armour and sea dragon cloak. His lungs felt full of splinters and when he coughed he coated the ground in front of him in a fine red spray.

He had to find Khrait. He couldn't see his nephew's black-and-cobalt surcoat anywhere in the drifts of dead dark elves that choked the road. He was sure that Khrait would never have fled like the last remnants of his army had, the triumphant Bretonnians scattering them into the forest and riding them down.

He had to find Khrait, or someone that could get him to hiding and then to the Ark, get him somewhere he could heal before the last of his energy ran out or the Bretonnians came back to make sure the battlefield had no survivors.

His vision greyed out and he lay there for a time until another coughing fit ripped unconsciousness away from him. He still lay alone in the road; he was still surrounded by his dead. He was clear of the dead cold ones now: the big beasts had still been blinking stupidly as the lance-points drove at them, their nostrils only just twitching with the Blood Banner's scent. Their corpses were jammed and piled together like sacks, the bright blood of their riders mixing with the dark reptile ichor.

Khreos was under no illusions that any of his guard might still be alive. For a moment he thought he saw one of the cold one carcasses breathing, but it was just the shimmer in his vision as another wave of grey broke over him.

Reach, drag. Reach, drag. The gravel of the road was washed red under his fingers, and the dust by the roadside was a bloody slurry.

He was in among the infantry now, piled high atop one another after the knights-errant had crushed the formations as they had tried to plant their spears ready for the charge. Beyond the heaped corpses lay the second, more scattered lines of bodies where his crossbow ranks had died under Bretonnian arrows, scrambling to get their own weapons strung and loaded. The bodies thinned out towards the treeline – those were the ones who had tried to run as they realised what was happening and had been chased down.

There were none of the stirrings and cries that he was used to after battles – Bretonnian fury had made the killing far too efficient for that.

Reach, drag. Reach, drag – his world had shrunk to the pain of his broken body and the sun beating on his armoured back.

He lay in between a dead corsair whose name he couldn't remember and a warrior he didn't recognise. He tried to see which regiment's badge the warrior wore, before he realised through the fog of pain that the elf wore no armour at all. The body was not lying in a death-sprawl but reclining lazily on the grass at the roadside twisting a flower-stem in his fingers. Finally he was able to focus his eyes on the red gem in its silver collar about the other elf's neck.

'I'm sorry, lord, was this not what you had planned?'

Khreos managed a single dry croak that would not become words. He could think of nothing to say.

'I would give you your map back, my lord, except that, oh, I seem to have misplaced it. Perhaps that was careless of me, but then who would have expected that a clumsy brute such as the Duc – with his castle full of sleeping babes that a single assassin could kill – would be able to read a map that showed the road by which you would be marching to his castle? Perhaps I should have memorised the land and the rendezvous position, rather than carry a map that showed me how to find my way... right... to... you.'

Khreos groaned and closed his eyes. Jahama was paring his nails with a knife.

'Oh, yes, after I'd finished dancing with them I was sure the Bretonnians would have been too stirred-up to read anything, let alone a map. But then how would I have delivered my lesson?'

The assassin rolled over onto his stomach, his face next to the lord's. 'You are so fond of your lessons, my lord, always so intent on giving instruction. Haven't we done you a service, my mistress and I? Think of the lesson you will be remembered for! Imagine it! Anyone who thinks of the kind of stupid, clumsy little ruse...' Jahama had started to spit his words, and controlled himself. 'Anyone who thinks to treat myself or my brothers or the blessed Brides of Khaine as their sling-stones, their expendable pawns, will remember the lesson we have made of you.'

He sprang to his feet. 'My mistress could have refused you, you know. She discussed it with her sisters, discussed this petty noble who thought he could make her dance on his strings. But then... then you would have gone on in your tricky little ways, believing you could try to betray the Scorpion's Daughter and never be the worse for it. So why not fall in step with you, sir, dance on your strings until we could turn about and strangle you with them? I don't have your mincing subtlety and I must be blunt. It's important that you understand just why you die as you do.'

The lord's face was twisted in despair, and Jahama nodded in satisfaction.

'I'd offer to make sure, sir, that you aren't alive by the time your enemies return to the field. But I want to give you plenty of time to think about my lesson. And for my part, well, the sun is up and the Ark must sail soon, with or without you at the helm. If your nephew has survived, I'm sure he'll be happy to give the order. Excuse me, lord, I believe there's a boat waiting for me at the bay.'

And Jahama the assassin turned away and left Khreos Maledict weeping in the dust as he disappeared into the forest, as the bright sun slanted down between the trees and the birds sang from the branches.

A GOOD THIEF
by Simon Jowett

Is THAT IT, François Villon wondered? The polite applause that greeted the end of his performance failed to rise above a ripple and was quickly drowned out by the babble of his erstwhile audience taking up conversations that had been interrupted by the Graf's call for silence, which had also served as Villon's cue to begin.

This evening's poem had been Villon's most ambitious work: the product of a week's pacing through the town's muddy streets and along the marshy banks that bounded the tributary of the Reik that provided Wallenholt with its connection to the civilised centres of the Empire. A week spent honing every line, shaping every verse and memorising each new version. And for what? To flatter the ego of his patron, Bruno, Graf von Wallenholt, and to interrupt the drinking of those townsfolk and travelling traders who made up what passed for 'society' in this boggy backwater.

Sigmar take them, Villon shrugged inwardly. It still beats working for a living. He reached for one of the wine-filled goblets on a passing servant's tray, drained its contents and reached for another from the tray of a servant passing in the opposite direction.

Yes, he reminded himself as the blood-rich wine slid easily down his throat, it was better to live as a pampered pet in this out-of-the-way place, than to rot in chains in one of Marienburg's danker oubliettes – which was where he would have spent the last months, had certain friends and drinking companions not warned him of the warrant that had been sworn against him by that hypocritical prig, Gerhard von Klatch.

Hypocritical prig or not, Villon would not have deliberately made an enemy of one of the Merchant Princes of Marienburg. It was just that everyone knew about the extra-marital activities of von Klatch's wife and, when set against von Klatch's pompous pronouncements on the subject of 'family values', they seemed the perfect subject for a rhyme. Or, they seemed so to Villon's wine-fuddled brain at some point in the midst of a week-long binge, financed by the 'acquisition' of the collection money from the temple of a middle-ranking deity near the pleasure gardens.

Had he been sober – or even within hailing distance of sobriety – Villon might have thought twice before extemporising the poem that later saw print as 'Madame Klatch's Menagerie'. A number of his other drunken satires had been transcribed and circulated around the docks and lower quarters of the city, but he would never have imagined that a transcript of his latest opus might find its way from the pages of Marienburg's yellow papers – scurrilous rumour-sheets printed on stuff better suited for use in the privy than for the absorption of ink – to those of a more respectable journal, more usually associated with political and economic news. Obviously, von Klatch had enemies and Villon's rhyme was a convenient weapon to hurl against the old windbag's political ambitions.

'The Heroic hexameter,' the voice came from behind Villon as he waved to a flagon-bearing servant with his now-empty goblet. 'An unusual choice.'

Villon turned. The speaker was a stranger to Wallenholt – one of a small group of visitors in whose honour the Graf had ordered this soirée. Villon had assumed them to be of greater-than-average wealth and power to warrant the full deployment of the Graf's hospitality, though the man he found himself looking at, as the servant refilled his goblet, showed very little outward sign of wealth or power. Dressed from head to toe in close-napped black velvet, he was over average height and build. His features, though edging on the handsome, were pale grey eyes, a narrow nose, a black beard, neatly trimmed and peppered with grey – a description that might apply equally to an uncountable number of men.

What marked this man out to Villon's eyes, eyes which had years of practice in judging the relative wealth of potential victims and/or patrons, was an absence of certain details: he wore no house, guild or family insignia.

And he recognised the Heroic hexameter, a six-beat rhythm that had passed out of poetic favour centuries ago.

'It was an experiment,' Villon replied, adopting his most refined accent and most polite form of address. 'I heard La Rondeau de Sigmund when a child and the six-beat metre struck me then as very strange and beautiful. And very challenging to those like us who are more used to the pentameter that is the fashion of today's verse. You are a man of rare sensibilities, sir, to recognise it.'

'I have no use for poets,' the stranger cut across Villon's attempt at flattery. 'The Graf tells me that you cannot read or write. Is that true?'

'There is more to writing than the mere act of making marks on paper,' Villon shot back, more forcefully than was seemly. Despite his privileged status within the Graf's household – he had no other duties than to compose verse to flatter his lord's vanity and act as a living example of Wallenholt's rising status within the Empire – he was still a servant. And the man whose aesthetic sense he had just insulted was an honoured guest.

Mouth running away with you again, François, he scolded himself. He cursed the third goblet of wine and searched for a form of words to ease the situation.

'But I... I know enough to make my mark,' was all he could find to say. That 'mark' was no more than a shaky 'V' which could be found on the very few documents he had ever been required to sign – mostly papers recording his appearances in court to answer charges of street theft, swindling and burglary. When one had been born in the gutter and set to thieving almost as soon as one could walk, the learning of letters was not a priority.

The stranger cocked an eyebrow. To Villon's surprise, he seemed amused.

'An illiterate poet,' he murmured. Villon was unsure whether he intended anyone to hear him. 'An interesting contradiction.'

At that moment, the Graf swept up to them. Villon's heart jumped – had he heard that his pet poet was arguing with one of his guests? If so, the best he could hope for was to be escorted beyond the town walls to return to the sorry state in which he had fetched up in Wallenholt after fleeing the warrant in Marienburg. Villon didn't relish the thought – day upon day of muddy roads, eating roots and berries and sleeping up trees to avoid roaming predators.

'Magister,' the Graf began without sparing Villon a glance. 'There is someone I have been meaning to introduce to you...'

Villon's heart resumed a more sedate rhythm as the Graf led the stranger away. Villon took this as his cue to quit the evening's festivities; the longer he stayed, the more he would drink; and the more he drank, the more likely he would be to say something else that he would regret.

He moved towards the doors to the hall unnoticed and unmolested by any of the other guests – proof, he believed of the regard for poetry among Wallenholt's elite. He had been lucky, shortly after arriving in the town, to hear that the Graf had a taste for verse. What was it about men of power that they desired some recognition of their finer sensibilities? The Graf had begun to talk of a printed collection of Villon's verse – calf-bound, subscription only – though the von Wallenholt name would be the only one to appear on its pages.

At the doors he paused and looked back into the hall. He spotted the Graf and the stranger; they were talking to, or rather being talked at, by another of the out-of-towners. Probably a travelling representative of the Nuln Cheesemakers Guild, Villon chuckled to himself. Now, perhaps, the stranger would feel more appreciative of the conversation of poets.

'VILLON!' HE WAS back in the Blind Monk, on Grosse-festenplatz, down by the docks. He had drunk far too much cheap wine to be sure of exactly how long he had been in the tavern – longer than a day, not so long as a full week.

'A verse!' the cry went up around the room. 'A verse from Villon!' The cry was repeated; a steady drumming of tankards and fists upon the tavern's tables beat against the fetid, belch-ridden air.

This was how it always happened: such was his reputation that, if he spent long enough in one tavern and drank enough wine, one of his fellow drinkers would think to call for a verse. And, because he had spent enough time in that tavern and had drunk more than enough wine, he would, after a moment's thought, oblige:

'I rhyme of the lady, von Klatch...'

'FRANÇOIS!' THE YEARS had fallen away; he was in Brother Nicodaemus's study. A bitter winter breeze was slicing through the shutters of the room's single window.

'François!' the old priest repeated. He was the only adult the young urchin could remember taking the time to repeat an instruction. More usually, his lack of attention was rewarded with a slap about the head.

'Yes, father,' Villon looked at the priest. He had been thinking about how cold he felt. Nicodaemus never seemed to feel the cold, not did any of the other priests –

though Villon could tell by their expressions whenever they saw him that his presence in their monastery was as welcome as the stench of an over-full privy pot.

'I asked you to explain the pentameter, François,' Nicodaemus told him. The old man had caught the young Villon trying to steal from the vegetable garden within the monastery walls. He was surprisingly nimble and strong for an old man and, despite his gentle demeanour, more than willing to administer enough of a beating to pacify the struggling young thief.

But that had been the last time he had touched Villon. Nicodaemus, it seemed, had certain theories about the training of the young and, before he died, he wished to test them. Villon had appeared at just the right time and presented quite a challenge.

'A pentameter is a line made up of five feet,' Villon parroted.

'Very good. And what is a foot?'

'A foot is a poetical unit of two syllables,' Villon replied. 'The Gothic pentameter is the most popular of these, in which the stress is placed on the second syllable.'

'Very good!' Nicodaemus smiled. He had not asked Villon to explain the Gothic pentameter, but he could see that, of all the subjects he had introduced to the child, poetry was the one that most drew him in. It seemed that his theories might bear fruit after all.

'Extemporise upon the Gothic pentameter for me,' Nicodaemus continued. Villon had already begun to exhibit his peculiar gift for creating verse on the spur of the moment and the priest regularly used this as a means of maintaining the boy's interest. 'I shall beat time.' He began to stamp rhythmically upon the flagstone floor. Villon began:

'The twin-tailed comet crossed the sky, Bright Sigmar's birth to prophesy...'

'VILLON!' THE VOICE was louder, rougher, more insistent. The drumming had also changed. No longer the slapping of the old monk's sandals on the bare flags, it had the demanding, heavy quality of a fist on wood.

'Villon, in the name of the Graf, open this door!'

Villon opened his eyes. He was in his small room in the servants' wing of the Graf von Wallenholt's manor house. Weak, early morning sunlight leaked in through the room's high, narrow window, running in a shaft to the door. The door jumped and shuddered with each impact from the other side.

This, he quickly realised, was not a dream.

HIS ROOM MIGHT have been small, Villon reflected, but it had been dry and private – unlike the space he now found himself in: set well below ground level, it was broader than his room, but the moss-covered stones of its walls ran with damp, it stank like an open sewer and a set of bars, each as thick as a man's wrist, ran from floor to ceiling, bisecting the space and standing between Villon and the door.

Nor was he alone. A rotund imbecile, who Villon decided looked more toad than man, squatted in the dampest corner of the cell. He hadn't moved since Villon had arrived: thrown through the then-open gate in the bars by the constables who had burst into his room the moment he opened the door, bullied him into his clothes and dragged him down seemingly-endless flights of stairs, each one darker and damper than its predecessor.

'A new friend for you, Tobias,' one of the constables shouted after the gate had clanged shut. His fellow lawkeepers laughed. Tobias the toad-man regarded Villon with eyes that bulged so far from his face that Villon expected them to burst like water-filled bladders thrown by mischievous children. And while he stared at the new arrival, Tobias licked his lips.

For all Villon knew, Tobias might still be licking his lips. The constables had taken their lanterns with them and left the dungeon in complete darkness.

This wasn't a new experience for Villon. Incarceration was a hazard he had lived with since he stole his first loaf, at the age of four or five; not knowing his exact date of birth, he couldn't be sure. Every one of his companions had likewise spent time in various cells, but Villon, a better thief than most, was rarely spotted in the commission of his crimes and was caught less often still. Even when the constabulary or militia knew he was the culprit, he was usually able to evade them in the narrow maze of Marienburg's rookeries – sprawling acres of close-packed slums into which a wanted man could disappear and into which the officers of the law would not enter unless equipped as if for war.

There were taverns in the rookeries, buyers and sellers of stolen goods and women who were more than happy to entertain a man flushed with loot from his latest job. By the time his money was spent, the constables would be occupied with other crimes and the way would be clear for Villon to set about refilling his pockets.

But, since his arrival in Wallenholt – or since the Graf decided to become his patron, at least – Villon's conduct had been exemplary. The allowance he received from the Graf, though not extravagant, was sufficient; he ate with the servants, when not performing for the Graf, and avoided indulging in prolonged bouts of drinking, hence the poetry he had composed since his arrival had been of the most proper and decorous type. In fact, the three goblets he had drunk the night before his arrest had been the most wine he had consumed for close to a month...

That had to be it. The guest in black. Monsieur 'I have no use for poets'. The pompous lick-spittle must have taken offence at something in Villon's tone after all. Not for the first time, he cursed the foibles and caprice of the wealthy, then set to thinking about how best to effect his escape from this pit. His accuser would be gone in a few days' time – he might already have left Wallenholt. All Villon would have to do was re-establish himself in the Graf's favour. Knowing the Graf, a poem of the most astonishing and shameless flattery would do the job. Vanity was one of the foibles of the wealthy he had used to his advantage many times in the past.

He had begun to sift through possible subjects for his verse when he heard a soft scraping from the far side of the cell. This was followed by a wet-lipped, child-like giggle, then the scraping resumed. It sounded as if something soft and heavy was being dragged – or was dragging itself – across the rough stone floor.

'You want to keep those bloated guts inside your scab-ridden skin, Tobias,' he spoke into the darkness. 'You'll stay exactly where you are.'

VILLON WAS ON his feet as soon as he heard the door opening. 'Ah, good constable, at last,' he began. 'There has clearly been some egregious error, but I believe I know a way to solve the problem and smooth any ruffled feathers. If you would only take a brief message to the Graf, this unfortunate affair will soon be at an end.'

'You may have received little schooling, but you have certainly mastered the art of buttock-kissing.' A lantern's shutter hinged back with a clank. Villon blinked in the sudden light until, as his eyes grew accustomed to the lantern's glow, he was able to make out the features of the speaker: fine, but not quite handsome; regular, but unremarkable.

'Kind sir, we meet again,' he adjusted his approach, determined not to give his accuser further offence. 'I had hoped to find a way to mend any injury I had caused you when we last met. Though doubtless I deserve the time I have spent in this darkness, cut off from the light of those such as your good self and my lord the Graf–'

'Enough, poet, enough.' Villon again heard amusement in the stranger's voice. 'Your over-honeyed words are wasted on me. I had nothing to do with your fall from favour. It seems your past has caught up with you.'

'My past, lord?' Despite his innocent tone, Villon's guts had suddenly started to churn. 'By my troth I don't...'

'Keep your troth to yourself and stop treating me like the kind of preening idiot who gives a good damn about how others think of them.' What sounded like genuine anger had replaced the amusement in the stranger's voice. 'Does the name von Klatch mean anything to you?'

'Von... Klatch.' Villon's stomach had stopped churning and had begun a tumbling free-fall.

'Madame von Klatch, it seems, has several brothers,' the stranger continued. 'One of whom attended the Graf's soiree. His family name, and that of Madame von Klatch before she married, is Liebermann. The name Villon was well known to him before he came to Wallenholt.

'Herr Liebermann has told the Graf much that he was unaware of regarding your past. He was surprised to learn that you have a reputation as an accomplished thief. However, when you begin your journey back to Marienburg tomorrow, you will be going to answer for the insult you paid Madame von Klatch. The Graf von Wallenholt knows better than to cross one of the Merchant Princes of Marienburg.'

'This... This Herr Liebermann is mistaken,' Villon stuttered. 'He has mistaken my name for that of the thief of which you speak. Perhaps he is called Villain, or Villette, or–'

'I do hope not,' the stranger interrupted. 'If that were the case, I would have no reason to help you escape.'

AFTER AN UNGUESSABLE amount of time in the dark, they came for him, manacled his wrists and ankles and led him up into the dawn.

A donkey cart was waiting for them in the stable yard. They all but threw Villon aboard and clucked the donkey into rattling motion through the still-quiet streets. Villon was left to roll painfully about in the bottom of the cart, receiving a kick every time he rolled too close to the feet of one of the constables that had climbed aboard after him. It was, unfortunately, a very small cart.

The slow-running Kleinereik fed into the Reik several leagues to the west and served as Wallenholt's main trading route to the Empire. But the boat moored at Jetty

Number Four, a river cutter that was flying a crest Villon assumed to belong to the Liebermann family, had more to do with politics than trade; it was going to take Villon back to Marienburg.

Villon was able to swing his feet under him as he was rolled off the cart and, with the aid of an inelegant stumble-and-shuffle, he managed to stay upright. However, the over-zealous prod in the back he received from the chief constable's short club almost pitched him into the dirt. With a constable keeping pace on either side, he shuffled towards the jetty.

Looking about him, he saw that the quayside was not much busier than the rest of the town at this early hour. Another cutter had finished loading and its crew were in the process of casting off; another, two jetties along, was still being loaded. The door of the Rudderless Cutter, the tavern that catered night and day to dock workers and rivermen, stood open, though the lack of noise from within suggested that business was slow this morning.

'It'll be a long time before you see the inside of a tavern again,' the chief constable snarled in Villon's ear, then prodded him again with his club. 'Get a move on. Your carriage awaits.'

Villon continued to glance up and down the wharfside as he shuffled along the short wooden jetty. At least he didn't have to invent some pretext for slowing his progress towards the cutter. He wanted to give the stranger – what had the Graf called him? Magister? – as much time as possible to make good on his promise.

But, when his foot touched the lip of the gangplank that angled between the jetty and the cutter, Villon had to admit the possibility that the Magister had reconsidered his plan.

'Curse you, man! I'll not have anyone say that about my sister, even in jest!'

'Get back, you blackguard, or I'll do to you what I did to her – but you won't enjoy as much as she!'

'That's it! You're going to eat those words!'

The sounds of an argument exploded into the still air. There was the sound of heavy footsteps on wood. Villon, one foot on the gangplank, craned to look over his shoulder.

There were five of them, rivermen judging by their clothing. A couple of them still held flagons in their fists, though Villon had the impression that they had come from the opposite direction to the Rudderless Cutter.

They were already on the jetty. The last of them to speak shoved another in the chest, forcing him to stumble backwards towards Villon and his escort. The aggressor chased after him; the others crowded onto the jetty behind him.

'You men, stop that!' the chief constable stepped away from Villon and pointed at the men with his club. 'By order of the Graf, go home and sleep off whatever idiocy it is that you're arguing about!'

'You calling me an idiot?' The riverman who had been pushed backwards along the jetty had regained his balance and turned to face the chief constable. Villon noted that he held a flagon down by his hip.

It didn't stay there for long. The crack of its impact on the chief constable's skull was as loud as a musket's report. The chief constable staggered, came close to stepping off the jetty's edge, but recovered. Clearly the metal skull cap helmet that was regulation wear for the constables of Wallenholt had absorbed a good deal of the blow.

The chief constable's attacker stared for a heartbeat at the dented drinking vessel before hurling it aside. The constables were pounding towards him; his companions were racing to meet them. Villon didn't envy him his position at the meeting point of the two opposing forces...

The riverman dived at the constables' feet, clearly hoping to trip them. Ready for him, they leapt over his sprawling body and continued their forward rush. Rolling to his feet, he looked around for another target. Unfortunately for him, his first target found him.

Stepping close behind the riverman, the chief constable hooked his club under his chin and levered backwards. To avoid strangulation, the riverman managed to half-turn towards his assailant and they grappled, staggering back and forth across the width of the jetty, each trying and failing to hurl the other into the river.

Behind Villon, the cutter's crew looked on, unsure of whether or not their duties included going to the constables' aid. Villon imagined that, if their sympathies lay anywhere, it would be with their fellow rivermen. Past the struggling figures of the chief constable and his attacker, one of the chasing group had already been launched into the river, courtesy of a well-timed blow from one of the constables, but the remaining two were meeting every one of the constables' blows with one or more of their own.

As yet, none of cutter's crew had thought to complete Villon's transfer to their vessel and Villon wanted to be far from the wharf before the thought occurred to them. The manacles made swimming impossible. There was only one way off the jetty: past both sets of combatants.

Nervously, Villon shuffled away from the gangplank. Ahead of him, the chief constable seemed to be getting the upper hand. He paused, hoping to spot a chance to ease past them unnoticed.

'You! Stay!' the chief constable had succeeded in applying a head-lock to his opponent that looked at least halfway secure. Both hands occupied, he was relying upon the authority in his voice and the threat in his eyes to root Villon to the spot. Not about to be frozen like a frightened rabbit, Villon took another manacled step towards the wharf's end of the jetty.

'I said *stay*!' The chief constable shot a clawed hand at Villon, who jumped backwards more vigorously than the manacles were designed to allow. Suddenly, he was falling, feet tangled in the manacles' chains, hands clutching at air.

The river folded itself around him, pushing foul-tasting water up his nose and down his throat. Eyes still open, the world suddenly lost focus and took on a greenish tinge.

Arms and legs pumping as best they could, he somehow broke the surface long enough to gulp down barely half a lungful of air. Then the weight of the manacles dragged him back under. As he kicked and clawed at the water around him, desperate to regain the surface, he had the dim sense of a sluggish current carrying him away from the jetty.

Grey mist edged his vision as he redoubled his spastic, frog-like swimming stroke. This time, he managed to take a whole shuddering breath before the manacles' dragging mass reclaimed him for the river.

HE HAD NO IDEA how long he had been unconscious. He woke to the sensation of being lifted clear of the river's dank embrace. Was he being carried to stand before Morr's dark throne and be judged? He struggled to breathe, then coughed and what felt like a barrel's worth of river water jetted from his throat. Somehow he didn't imagine that his final journey would feel like this.

'Alive then.' Now he was flat on his back in some kind of rivercraft. Cracking his eyelids he could see the sides of the wooden hull rising over him. Something was hanging over him, he noticed. Fixing his bleary gaze upon it, he made out a face: pale eyes; black beard, neatly trimmed.

The stranger moved away from Villon, who struggled into a half-supine position. He seemed to be in a smaller craft than the trading vessel moored at the jetties: narrow, shallow and fitted with a single sail, which the stranger was in the process of trimming, though there didn't seem to be much point in raising a sail on a windless morning like this.

Raising his head above the gunwales, Villon was surprised to feel that a wind had indeed sprung up and was filling the small sail. He also realised that, rather than heading downriver with the current, the stranger was steering the craft back towards Wallenholt. Hauling himself into an unsteady position somewhere between kneeling and crouching, he stared ahead: there was Wallenholt; there was the ship that was to return him to Marienburg; and there were the constables, standing on the jetty, waving as if they expected the stranger to steer his boat towards them. There was no sign of the argumentative group who, deliberately or otherwise, had facilitated his escape.

'Master!' he rasped out through a throat made rank by river water.

'Magister,' the stranger corrected, without turning his head. He seemed to be looking for something further upriver, past Wallenholt.

'Magister,' Villon added. The stranger seemed to be very particular about titles and Villon saw no profit in antagonising him. 'While I am in your debt for rescuing me from the river, I confess I am surprised to find us returning to Wallenholt. Given our conversation in the cells, I had formed the understanding that you wanted to help me escape.'

'We're not returning to Wallenholt. Our path lies in this direction.' The Magister pointed upstream. Wisps of river mist clung to the banks further upstream.

'But the constables...' The boat was close enough for the shouts of the frustrated law officers to reach it. Villon saw that the chief constable was engaged in animated discussion with a man Villon took to be the captain of the river cutter. The chief constable jabbed a finger at the craft in which Villon sat, feeling particularly vulnerable. The captain thought for a moment, then nodded.

'They're coming after us!' The cutter's captain was barking orders to his crew, orders which were answered at a run by his crew. On the jetty, the constables began to unfasten the cutter's mooring ropes. 'They'll run us down!'

'Not if they cannot find us,' the Magister answered calmly. He pointed upstream. 'It seems the river mist is especially persistent this morning.'

'What?' Villon couldn't understand why the Magister should give a damn about the weather – until he looked past the low prow of the boat and saw that what had, only moments earlier, appeared to be faint wisps of mist had thickened and grown into a bank of dense white opacity that stretched from bank to bank. Nor was it simply sitting there. It was moving downriver towards them.

The Magister's craft had passed the Wallenholt wharf. As it left the town behind, it seemed to be picking up speed, as if the wind that filled its sail was growing stronger. But, if the wind was blowing upstream, Villon realised, what was propelling the bank of mist downstream?

Villon had no time to ponder this further. The combined speeds of the Magister's boat and the mist brought the two together more quickly than might be considered entirely natural and Villon's world turned white.

'IN CENTURIES PAST, the Kleinereik was known for the peculiarity of its weather.' The Magister handed Villon a key and nodded at his manacles.

'Really.' Villon got the impression that his rescuer didn't really care whether or not he believed him. He got on with fitting the key to the thick metal cuffs that bound his wrists and ankles. They hit the soft, slightly boggy soil of the river bank with a muffled clank.

The grey mare that had been waiting, tethered, on the bank – the opposite bank to that on which Wallenholt stood, at least a day's ride downstream – shifted its weight and whinnied softly at the sudden noise. Villon offered the key to the Magister, who took it – then tossed it into the river.

'Do likewise with the chains,' he instructed Villon. 'I prefer to leave no trace.'

By the time Villon had gathered up the manacles and propelled them as far away from the bank as possible, given their weight and awkwardness, the Magister had reached into the boat and lifted out a set of saddle bags. He handed the bags to Villon.

'In there you will find a map, some provisions and a small purse,' the Magister said without preamble. 'The map will guide your through the Reikwald Forest to a backwoods town which, I am informed, has become the base of operations of one Gerhard Kraus. Kraus is a bandit, nothing more, though he has ambitions towards respectability.' He broke off to snort derisively.

'I commissioned Kraus to acquire a certain... artefact,' the Magister continued. 'This he did, but subsequently reneged on our agreement, preferring to keep it for himself. In return for your liberation, you shall acquire that artefact from Kraus and deliver it to me.' The Magister had turned his pale gaze on Villon. It was clear that he did not expect Villon to object.

'What is it that you want me to acquire?' Villon asked.

'Oh, you will know it when you see it,' the Magister replied. 'It has a certain quality that you are sure to recognise, given your poetic sensibility'. It was impossible to miss the weight of mockery the Magister loaded upon the word 'poetic'.

'Kraus is a vain man who enjoys the flattery of poets. That and your talents as a thief shall be his undoing.'

The Magister turned and stepped into the boat, unhitched its mooring rope from the overhanging branch to which he had tethered it and pushed away from the bank. As the boat began to drift downstream, this time obeying the river's natural current, he looked up at Villon.

'I shall travel to Altdorf and stay there for the next seven days,' he said. 'You will find me at the Broken Bough, on Karl-Ludwigplatz. 'Do not disappoint me. Do not try to run. I will find you.'

'I believe you,' Villon replied – but the Magister had already turned to set his sail. That done, he settled into the stern of the boat, hand on the tiller. He didn't look back and was soon lost to sight around the first bend.

VILLON HAD HEARD his destination before he saw it: the sound of hammers, saws and shouted instructions.

A wall of stakes, taller than two men, was being erected around the town. A closer look at the labour force over the next couple of days would show that the townsfolk were building the walls of their own prison, supervised by the bandits who had taken possession of their home.

'Welcome to Krausberg,' The taller of the two gatekeepers growled. Like his fellow, this man was heavily armed, heavily bearded and just plain heavy. He held out an open palm and growled again: this time informing Villon how much it would cost to enter the town.

Villon paid the toll and was allowed to enter. He knew little about military matters, but the fortifications looked sturdy enough – though, he noticed the wall of stakes had yet to completely encircle the town. He made a mental note of the locations of the open sections, then made enquiries about the availability of a room for a weary traveller.

With surprising shrewdness, Kraus had barracked his men in the homes of the townsfolk and left the town's two lodging houses and its single inn open to accept paying guests. After visiting both guest houses, thus providing himself with an excuse for wandering through the streets, setting in his mind the locations of the gaps in the wall, he took the cheaper of the two rooms available at the inn.

IT WAS SOMETHING Villon had done hundreds of times before: pretend to become the friend and drinking partner of someone he fully intended to fleece. The only difference this time was that he was pretending to become the friend and drinking partner of somewhere between fifty and seventy men simultaneously, in the hope that his hurriedly-assembled reputation would reach the ears of Gerhard Kraus.

In the three days that had passed since his arrival in Krausberg, the man after whom the town had been renamed had not left the confines of what used to be the mayor's house at the far end of the main street. Direct questions regarding Kraus had met with hostile, suspicious glares, so Villon had concentrated on entertaining his new friends with verses that had proved popular in the stews and taverns of Marienburg. Ironically, 'Madame Klatch's Menagerie' proved to be the most popular of all.

* * *

'KLATCH! KLATCH!' VILLON wasn't sure what the time was, but he was pretty certain that he had already recited that particular verse once already this evening. His audience, however, had decided what it wanted to hear.

Holding up his hand for quiet, Villon prepared himself. Sweeping his flagon from the bar, he took a long draught, making sure to spill most of it down his shirt front in the process. Had he swallowed a fraction of what he appeared to have drunk, he would have been insensible hours ago. Placing the empty vessel on the bar, he took a breath.

'I rhyme of the lady, von Klatch...'

'Not again, poet!' At the sound of this voice – one Villon did not recognise – all eyes turned to a corner, a short way from the door. A heavy-set, red bearded man stood there. Where the bandits wore the rough fabric and oiled leather harnesses of professional cut-throats, he wore velvet and linen which would have been more suited to a merchant's salon. The mere fact that he would dare to wear such clothes in the company of the inn's other patrons left Villon in no doubt that this was the man he had been sent to find: Gerhard Kraus.

'Bawdyhouse rhymes are all very well,' Kraus declared, 'and you have some facility with them, as I have been told.'

'Thank you, my lord.' Villon bowed. He didn't imagine that Kraus would be too pleased to see the mocking smile that cracked his face. 'Some facility' indeed! This from a man who was better acquainted with the pleas of his victims and the screams of the dying than with meter, scansion and rhyme!

'But there are forms of verse capable of stimulating man's higher functions, rather than merely pandering to his baser tastes,' Kraus continued. Villon thought he was going to laugh out loud at the bandit's slab-tongued attempt at literary critique.

With an absurdly foppish flourish Kraus produced from a pocket of his tunic a small book. It almost vanished in his ham-like grasp as he brandished it before the crowd.

'Perhaps you would care to hear one of my most recent efforts?'

'I'd be honoured, lord,' was all Villon trusted himself to say; the urge to laugh in the bandit's face was almost too great.

That urge died the moment Kraus began to read.

The subject matter – an episode from the youth of Sigmar – was traditional, unsurprising; but the seven-footed meter in which it had been composed, as well as being much older than the Heroic hexameter, was used with a flexibility that one in a hundred poets might hope to achieve after a lifetime's practice.

This alone left Villon in no doubt: whoever had composed this poem, it was not Gerhard Kraus.

And the effect the poem had on its audience made Villon doubt the unknown poet's humanity.

Every drunken thug in the place had turned his attention to the verse; they leaned forward, anxious to catch the next word, the next line, as if they were collegium-trained aesthetes in a Marienburg salon, not bandit scum, drunk out of their minds in the middle of nowhere.

And though he couldn't have described it in words, Villon knew why.

It was there, in the back of his mind: a tingling, like an inaccessible itch. Not a voice. Something softer, more insidious, something that made it impossible to turn away. Villon felt as if he had gone without water for days and the words that fell from Kraus's lips were droplets from a mountain spring. A quick shake of the head cleared his mind long enough for him to take in the rapt expressions of those around him. Looking towards the back of the room, Villon saw the effect it was having on Kraus.

He could have been a different person. Though physically unchanged, everything about him was different: his posture, his expression and, most of all, his voice. Kraus's rough bass had become a delicate, flexible instrument, capable of octave-wide leaps and swoops. The verse sang through it, through Kraus's entire being.

'You will know it when you see it...' Villon remembered the voice from somewhere. It had sent him here to find something.

He struggled to recall the vague outlines of a face – a beard? – but the name eluded him. Had he been asked his own name, he realised, he would be hard put to provide an answer.

He was being drawn back, drawn back into the verse, whose words filled the tavern, filled the minds of everyone present...

THE SILENCE WAS deafening. Villon had no idea how long it had lasted, or how long it had taken him to realise that it was over. Looking around, he saw several of the tavern customers were shaking their heads and blinking stupidly, as if emerging from a deep sleep. At the back of the room Kraus hung between two of his bodyguards like a limp puppet; the power and elegance that had possessed him while reading was gone. He jerked his head drunkenly towards the door and was half-carried, half-dragged out into the night.

Villon waited as long as he dared then moved across the tavern and cracked open the door. The retreating silhouettes of Kraus and his bodyguard were already halfway down the street. Easing the door open further, Villon slipped after them.

AS FAR AS Villon had been able to ascertain during his evenings at the inn, the town's original inhabitants were not under curfew. Evidently, the back-breaking work on the fortifications and the type of person one was likely to meet of an evening in Krausberg were enough to keep them indoors after sunset. The main street was empty as Villon made his way through the shadows towards the former mayor's dwelling. He hung back in the lee of a barber-surgeon's shop until they had bundled Kraus inside, then made his way cautiously around the house, looking for a way in.

A small outbuilding leaned against the rear wall of the house. A running jump gained Villon a finger-hold on the edge of the roof and he hauled himself up. The roof inclined towards a narrow window; Villon edged towards it, wary of the roof's stability. Overconfidence – usually as the result of over-indulgence – had delivered him into the hands of the local law or more than one occasion. Should that happen tonight, he doubted that he would be lucky enough to spend any time in a cell.

Upon reaching the window, he drew a short, thick-bladed knife that had been among the articles he found in the Magister's saddlebags. A few minutes work with it between the rough-fitting window and its frame and he was able to flip the catch and slip silently inside.

He found himself in an unlit corridor, where he paused to take in the sounds of the house. Muffled conversation reached him from one end of the corridor; he edged towards it, careful to keep to the middle of the passage and thus avoid banging into furniture or ornaments. A corner revealed the house's main staircase. Dim light reached the landing from below, as did the voices; they faded as he listened – probably the bodyguards heading for the kitchen.

A table stood at the head of the stairs. A lit candle in an ornate wooden candelabrum stood on the table. Villon took it with him as he padded softly down the corridor that led away from the staircase at an acute angle.

The first door was unlocked – a linen cupboard. The second was locked, but the latch was not the work of a craftsman. A few seconds' work with the knife and the latch gave. After a glance back down the corridor, Villon cupped his hand around the candle flame and stepped inside.

ONE LOOK AT THE figure sprawled across the bed told Villon that he didn't need to worry about the candle light waking the room's occupant. Kraus might have been dead drunk but Villon hadn't seen him take a drop. His performance at the inn had robbed him of all but the strength required to maintain the shallow breathing that barely lifted his over-fussy shirt front.

And there, under one out-thrown arm, was the book.

Tucking his knife back into his boot, Villon reached out and prepared to gently ease it free.

Nothing could have prepared him for the shock of touching the book. It felt as if he had placed his hand into a bucket of freezing water. The chill ran quickly up his arm, hitting his chest with enough force to make him gasp involuntarily, then seemed to dissipate, leaving Villon at first shivering then sweating profusely.

Villon glanced at Kraus. The bandit hadn't so much as twitched at the sound of Villon's gasp. Villon took a breath, then eased the book from under Kraus's arm. Again, the bandit didn't move. Villon stepped away from the bed and stared down at the slim volume's plain calf-skin cover.

Had it been real – the racing chill he felt when his fingers touched the soft brown cover? It was just a book, probably a privately-printed volume of the kind von Wallenholt had planned for Villon's verse. And the Magister was just a collector of such volumes with too much money to spare and a sideline in parlour magic.

But Villon knew this was untrue. What had happened in the tavern was not natural. The chill that shot up his arm had been real. And there was something else about this book: it felt heavier than it should for a volume this slim, as if something had found a way to slip between the words, conceal itself among the fibres of the parchment pages, but could not prevent its weight giving away its presence.

The Broken Bough, Altdorf. He should already be on his way, not standing here staring at the book he had agreed to steal. He should be heading for the door, then padding down the corridor, past the stairs and on to the window over the outbuilding.

But he remembered what had happened in the tavern. The audience had been unable to turn away. Even he had been sucked into its world. What kind of verse could do such a thing?

He didn't remember putting the candle down on the table beside the bed. His hands might have been moving under their own volition as, with something approaching reverence, they opened the book.

Words. Page after page of marks in faded ink on slightly yellow parchment. Words that Villon could not read.

Villon sucked in a deep breath, surprised to find that his chest felt as if it had been squeezed tight since he had first touched the book. Something had withdrawn from him, leaving only a vague sense of disappointment floating on the air.

He shook his head, closed the book. Definitely time to go.

The sound of creaking bed boards and rustling fabric told him that he had waited too long already. There came the smooth rasp of a sword leaving its scabbard and Villon threw himself away from the bed – a heartbeat before the heavy cavalry sabre cleaved the air where he had stood.

Villon landed and rolled into a half-crouch in the middle of the room – and cursed his luck for not taking him closer to the door. Kraus was off the bed and standing between Villon and the door. At least, it looked like Kraus…

The bandit seemed to sway as he stood there, like a puppet held too slackly on its strings. The sword, which he had drawn from a scabbard propped against the other side of the bed, hung in a loose, almost careless grasp. His head lolled unpleasantly and, in the flickering of the candle, Villon saw that his eyes, though open, had rolled back in their sockets. The candlelight played across the exposed whites.

Villon backed away from Kraus, mind racing, eyes flicking about the room, seeking a way out. Slack-mouthed, Kraus stared after him, the tilt of his head giving him an air of detached curiosity, as if he were an astrologist studying the movement of the heavens. Villon began to entertain the hope that he might be able to step gingerly past the immobile imbecile and slip out the way he had come.

Then he heard it, rising in volume: a reedy ululation, that seemed to come from Kraus's mouth without any effort on his part. It echoed from him as if from the distant recesses of a mountain cave – a mountain cave in a very cold part of the world.

Villon had heard it before – as an undertone to the verse Kraus had performed in the tavern. Villon felt again a rising chill in his bones. Without the poetry to sweeten it, the sound was repulsive, but this did nothing to dilute its effect: as he had been drawn into the world of the verse, Villon felt himself being drawn into the world from which the sound emanated. Somewhere cold and dark.

Instinct saved him again. Some animal part of his brain knew that, after rooting his prey to the spot, Kraus would strike. It was only a stiff-legged stumble, but it took him backwards and out of the range of the descending sword. The sound of the heavy blade biting into the floorboards jolted Villon back to proper wakefulness.

After jerking the sword free of the floorboards, Kraus came for him again. Villon had snatched up a chair and used it to fend off the attack.

Kraus hacked at the chair, severing one of the legs – whatever power motivated him had endowed him with strength beyond the human. He might well carve his way through the chair even before Villon tired of holding it.

'Boss!' the shout from the other side of the door was accompanied by the sound of running footsteps. 'Boss! You all right in there?' Whoever was in the corridor didn't wait long for a reply. There was a loud thump. Luckily, the catch which Villon had refastened after entering the room held. But it would not hold for long. Still backing away from Kraus, and now holding a two-legged, one-armed chair, Villon risked a glance behind him, judged the distance between himself and the chamber's heavy, diamond-leaded windows.

Kraus drew back his sword-arm, ready for another hacking strike and Villon hurled the remains of the chair at him. The impact would have knocked a normal man to his knees. Kraus took two steps back, then came forward again.

Villon still did not dare turn and work at the window latches. He had already pulled his knife from his boot for the purpose, but, as Kraus charged towards him, he knew he'd have to use something else to open the windows.

Kraus swung for Villon with all the force he would have used against the chair. Villon ducked beneath the neck-level swing of the blade, then rose and slammed the knife into the bandit's right eye. For the first time since he woke, Kraus uttered a human sound – a low grunt of pain – as his sword fell from his suddenly nerveless grasp and he keeled over, landing heavily on the floor.

At this, the shouts and thumps from the other side of the door increased in volume and frequency. The door creaked, began to give way.

Leaving his knife in Kraus's socket, Villon once again hefted the chair. This was no time for subtlety, or for struggling to free his knife, should it have wedged itself into Kraus's skull.

The window exploded into fragments of lead and glass as the chair flew through it. Villon was halfway through the resulting gap when he heard movement and something approaching a groan. He looked back into the room.

Kraus was halfway to his feet. With one hand he scrabbled after his sword. With the other – his right – he reached up to his face.

'I'D NOT HAVE believed it if I hadn't seen it with my own eyes.' Villon paused to smile ruefully at the unintentional pun. 'He – Kraus, whatever it was – just pulled the knife free as if it were a splinter in his thumb.' He took a long swallow of the wine the Magister had ordered before ushering him into a small private room at the rear of the Broken Bough.

Villon wiped his lips and continued: 'The door gave in at that moment and I decided it would be much to my advantage if I was elsewhere. I had to drop to the bare ground, but it's not the first time I've done such a thing – I know how to land to avoid sprains or breaks.

'On my way to the livery stables, I stopped off at the tavern to raise the alarm and sent Kraus's men to the mayor's house to defend their leader from a monster with one eye. It was all nonsense but, fortunately, those in the tavern were very, very drunk.'

'You got away unseen.' The Magister had barely touched his own goblet. The well-banked fire that burned in the grate seemed to have no effect upon him, while Villon was beginning to sweat.

'Yes. The livery was close by the gate, but the guards had answered the general hue and cry. And anyway, I doubled back along the inside of the fortifications until I came to a gap. Kraus's men will have assumed I took the track from the gate. Thanks to your map, I was able to follow a less obvious route. I didn't want to risk missing you, so I rode as hard as I could for Altdorf. I took a room and stabled my – I mean your – horse and came straight here.' Villon decided not to mention his brief visit to the collegium library en route to the tavern.

'And the artefact?'

'You mean this?' Villon withdrew it from his tunic and placed it on the table between them. 'It seems a strange thing to risk one's life for.'

'Many have lost more than their lives due to its malign influence,' The Magister replied. He picked up the book and flung it into the fire. Villon leapt up, reaching involuntarily towards the flames.

'Leave it!' The Magister commanded. In the grate, the fire had already begun to consume the book's old, dry pages.

'You will already be aware that it was no ordinary book of verse.' The Magister seemed to be enjoying Villon's surprise as he took his seat again. 'It is the last surviving copy of the work of a damned poet – his name is of no matter, since it belongs in the lists of those lost to the darker powers. Some say he was a sorcerer, others that he was possessed, a mere conduit through whose verse those unseen powers sought to render other men susceptible to corruption, possession and eventual damnation. From what you say, they had already seized control of Kraus's soul and was beginning to twist the minds of his men. You will have felt something of its power when he read from the book.

'Kraus fell victim so quickly after acquiring the book for me because he could read. The power behind the verse could reach out to him directly from the page.' The Magister smiled. 'Who would have predicted that of a wandering cut-throat?'

'That's why you were so interested in me at the Graf's reception,' Villon interjected. For the first time, he had the sense that he understood at least part of the Magister's actions. 'Because I cannot read.'

'Your ignorance was to you as armour is to a warrior on the battlefield.' the Magister smiled again. 'Why else would I bother to save you from trial in Marienburg? I have no time for poetry and no use for poets.' He dropped a heavy purse onto the table, motioned to Villon to take it.

'Thieves, however, always have their uses.'

'THIEVES, HOWEVER, ALWAYS have their uses!' Villon parroted the Magister's final words to him as he strolled back towards his lodgings – a tavern tucked under the city walls. He felt the weight of the purse inside his tunic, next to the slim calfskin volume that had nestled there since his arrival in Altdorf. He had slipped the book stolen from the collegium next to it before making his way to the Broken Bough, where the Magister had helpfully disposed of the evidence of the theft.

The Magister had never seen the book he had gone to such lengths to acquire, therefore he'd not know if the volume Villon handed him was the right one. Villon could hand him any book of verse and receive his reward.

Enchanted or not, there were bound to be others willing to pay handsomely for the volume he had, after all, risked his life to acquire.

Why get paid once, when you could get paid twice – or, if you played your hand well, more than twice?

Why indeed? Villon chuckled to himself. Why indeed?

HE DIDN'T HEAR them coming. Admittedly, he had been drinking non-stop for close to a week by the time the City Guard broke down the door of his room at the Well-Paid Wanton. His companion had been handed her clothes and sent packing and he had been dragged naked through the streets to the nearest holding cell. No doubt the landlord would take the remainder of the Magister's money to pay for a new door.

'It would seem that the good burghers of Marienburg will have their satisfaction after all.' As he had sat on the cell's damp flagstones, with only a length of lice-riddled sack cloth for warmth, Villon had been waiting to hear that voice.

'How did you find me?' he asked the Magister, who stood on the other side of the barred cell door. 'How did you know?'

'How did I know?' The Magister addressed Villon's second question first. 'Most of my life has been spent working to protect the Empire from the encroachments of the Outer Dark. I sometimes work alone, I sometimes employ agents such as yourself. It is a loose, collegiate organisation. An invisible college, you might say. During that time, I have developed something of an instinct for the truth of a situation. On reflection, I did not feel that about our last meeting.

'As for finding you, that wasn't hard. You enjoy your reputation too much and once again it has landed you in a cell, awaiting transportation for trial. If my opinion means anything to you, I do believe you to be a good poet, but you know what little use I have for them, good or bad.'

Villon knew what was coming next, the way a condemned man knows the next thing he will feel will be the bite of the executioner's axe.

'Thieves, however are another matter,' The Magister continued. 'I have a job for a good thief. Would you be interested?'

Defeated, Villon could only nod.

WHAT PRICE VENGEANCE
A Brunner the Bounty Hunter story
by C. L. Werner

THE RAGGED GROUP of riders slowly made their way through the craggy grey piles of jagged stone. The men wore dirty, unkempt clothes, their armour soiled by grime and fresh blood. Mud caked the legs of their steeds. The horses themselves moved slowly, their tired limbs rising and falling with an almost machine-like cadence. The animals were too tired even to protest the continuing march. Their masters, too, sagged in their saddles, fatigue wracking their bodies. They were no less spent than their animals, but, unlike the horses, a greater need urged them forward. In each of the bleary eyes that stared from the riders' haggard faces there burned an ember, a tiny coal that kept their weather-beaten bodies in the saddle.

The line of riders manoeuvred past an old, half-dead tree, its skeletal limbs pawing at the dark, rain-laden sky. Soon, the clouds would again unleash the storm.

The riders hoped to achieve their destination before the rain came upon them once more, but rain, or no, they would take no shelter save that offered by the castle of

Claudan de Chegney, son of the Viscount Augustine de Chegney.

The men rode around the dead tree, their horses barely protesting the abrupt change in the tedium. The next to last horseman paused as he jerked his steed's head about with the reins. He paused, then fell, his body crashing into the mud beneath him. The man lifted his arm, reaching toward the stirrup of his saddle, his hand trembling from cold and fatigue. He pulled on the stirrup for a moment, then his hand dropped back into the mud and he was still. From a rent in his brigandine, dark crimson seeped into the mud.

'There goes Tonino,' the rider in line behind the fallen man reported, his voice expressionless. He was a swarthy man, his moustached face split along one side by the grey slash of an old scar. The riders ahead of him turned in their saddles, tired eyes staring at the comrade who lay bleeding in the mud.

The man at the head of the column nodded his head grimly. It was encased in a dark steel helmet, plated chin guards framing the man's sharp features. The leader of the riders sighed, sagging a little more in the saddle as he made the sound. One hand released the reins to make the sign of the goddess Myrmidia in the air. Then, the leader turned about once more. After a moment, his men followed suit. Soon, the entire column of twenty had marched on, leaving the body in the mud, the horse to go where it would.

'We shall just add Tonino to what is owed us,' the leader of the riders declared, his voice low, harsh, and murderous. The tiny ember of vengeance burned a little more brightly in his eyes.

GOURMAND, STEWARD TO the Comte de Chegney, stared from the window of the watchtower that loomed above the gate of the foreboding castle that had once been home to the deposed House of von Drakenburg. For centuries, the barons von Drakenburg had guarded the pass through the Grey Mountains, protecting Imperial interests from the ambitions of their Bretonnian neighbours. But such was in the past. For five years now, the lord of the Schloss Drakenburg owed fealty not to the Emperor in Altdorf, but the king in Couronne. Or more precisely, the viscount in the Chateau de Chegney.

Gourmand leaned a little forward from the window, looking over at the armoured man-at-arms by his side. He pointed with a knobby hand at a number of riders slowly making their way down the slope of the pass through the mountains.

'Bandits?' the soldier remarked, straining to make out more than the general outline of the men and their steeds.

'Keep a watch on them,' he said, clapping the soldier's mailed shoulder. 'They appear to be heading towards the castle. I will inform the comte and see what he wishes to do.'

When Gourmand returned to the West Tower with his master, a young, dark-haired man who sported the rakishly short beard and moustache currently favoured in the great courts of Bretonnia, the riders had drawn much nearer indeed. Even the steward's tired old eyes could make out the battered armour and bloodstained clothes, the mud-caked tack and harness, the wearily plodding steeds and swarthy skinned men.

'Bandits, my lord,' stated the sentry Gourmand had charged to keep an eye on the approaching riders.

'Bandits thinking to storm a castle in the middle of a storm?' the Comte de Chegney shook his head. 'Mercenaries, more likely.' As he made the observation, the nobleman peered still harder at the approaching men.

'Whoever they are, they've seen some swordplay,' said Gourmand, still covering the riders with a suspicious gaze. 'Recently too. A few of them look as though their wounds are still fresh. Perhaps they are some free-company that thought to raid villages and found the knights of Bretonnia more than they counted upon.'

'By the Lady, I think I recognise them,' the comte declared. 'When last I was at my father's house, he was engaging a band of Tileans. That man below I seem to remember as being their leader.' Claudan de Chegney waved at the men below. The leading rider, a man in a tight-fitting steel helm, returned his greeting.

'Call the archers off,' Claudan told his steward. 'I'd not turn away any man in such a state with the Grey Mountains in such an ill humour. That these men are of my father's house makes it doubly my duty to shelter them.'

'Your father would not think so,' grumbled Gourmand, still regarding the riders dubiously.

'I am not my father,' the Comte de Chegney snapped, a brief flash of fire in his eyes.

THE COMTE DE CHEGNEY was below in the courtyard when the gates opened and the motley group of haggard horsemen entered the Schloss Drakenburg. Two men-at-arms flanked him, each in the de Chegney livery, and by Gourmand. A scabbard and sword had been donned by the comte, but he wore no armour, the blade at his side more a facet of tradition and decorum than any foreboding of danger on his part. These men had already been in a battle, they were tired, and seemingly wounded to the man. Even were they not loyal to his father, men such as these could hardly pose any manner of threat in their condition.

'Hail and well met,' the leader of the troop called out to the Bretonnian noble, his words deeply accented as he translated the Tilean greeting into the softer tones of Bretonnia.

'I welcome you to the Schloss de Chegney,' Claudan said, though even he still thought of the castle as Schloss Drakenburg. 'You may rest here, and shelter within my walls until the foul mood of the Grey Mountains has passed.'

The leader of the horsemen smiled at the Comte de Chegney's words. 'Well, that is indeed kind of you, my lord. We were seeking cover from the rain when we sighted your castle. I hope that our presumption is forgiven.' The man's tones were the well-tutored semi-servile voice favoured by the mercenaries of Tilea, accustomed to deferring to the mad whims of the ruling merchant princes, while inwardly sneering at the idiocy of these same employers.

'How came you to be abroad with a storm in the air?' interrupted Gourmand. He stared past the leader's sharp features, casting his gaze across the entire company. He noted the blood-caked weapons and armour, the tightly bound injuries. 'And how came you to be in such a condition? Set upon by orcs, perhaps?' It was bait; anyone familiar with the region knew that there had been no orcs in this part of the Grey Mountains since the death of the Great Enchanter many long years past.

'Your castle seems a bit shabby,' the helmeted Tilean commented, ignoring Gourmand's words. 'Not like your father's.'

'I asked what happened to you,' the steward repeated, stepping forward. A glower from the massive Tilean beside the leader made the elderly servant retreat past the closest man-at-arms. The brute favoured the servant with a gap-toothed grimace.

'That's the problem with wealth and position,' the leader continued. 'Someone always has a little more than you do.'

'My steward asked you a question,' the Comte de Chegney said, his voice flat. Now he too was becoming aware of the aura of menace about these men. He had almost forgotten that trickery and treachery had claimed the lord of this castle once before. Now they would do so again.

'Still,' the leader sneered, 'that is the only problem with wealth and position.'

The comte's eyes were locked on the right hand of the Tilean mercenary, waiting for the villain to reach for his sword. Even as the Bretonnian drew his own blade, his eyes were still focused upon the right hand of his chosen foe. Claudan de Chegeny never saw the blade that whipped downwards to slash his throat. He would have understood the means of his death even less, the cunning Tilean device secreted in the sleeve of the mercenary captain, a coil of steel clenched between metal braces, triggered by pressure on a button-like contrivance to shoot a long-bladed dagger from the sleeve of the man's tunic into the grip of his hand.

As the Comte de Chegney fell, the other mercenaries sprang into action. A crossbow bolt from a weapon that had already been armed before entering the castle and was now aimed with terrible speed and accuracy skewered the throat of the man-at-arms to the left of the dying count. The other soldier was trampled by the powerful warhorse of the brutish hairy Tilean that had seconded the leader even as the Bretonnian raised his pike to ward off the sudden and vicious charge. The hairy Tilean roared like a blood-mad bear as he brought his heavy cavalry mace crashing downwards at the cringing, horrified steward. The old man raised his arm to ward away the blow. The steel weapon snapped the man's arm, but did no more than graze the old man's head. Gourmand fell, groaning. On the verge of unconsciousness, he could do no more than roll away from the hooves of the horsemen as they charged up the steps that led from the courtyard into the castle itself.

'Inside, everybody!' the leader shouted. 'Don't give their archers a clean shot!' As if to punctuate the mercenary's words, an arrow flew from the window of a tower to strike one of the rearmost riders in the back. The man fell with a garbled scream. More arrows flew downwards, striking the stone steps and walls as the Tileans charged into the safety of the keep itself.

Ursio looked at his men. Eighteen, there were only eighteen of them now. He had started with fifty-four when he had been engaged by the Viscount de Chegney. Six had fallen when they had seen to the capture of the viscount's neighbour the Marquis le Gaires's annual tithe of gold to

His Majesty King Louen Leoncoeur. The others had died when the viscount's own men had ambushed the Tileans, seeking to silence these pawns of their master. Ursio vowed that his treacherous former employer would pay for every man he had lost.

'Spread out!' Ursio roared. 'Search every room! Every hall!' There was a strangled cry and a man-at-arms who had been storming down the stairs toppled down the remainder of the flight, a black bolt of steel and wood protruding from his chest. 'We find the boy, we get paid! The mercenaries roared their approval of their captain's words, many of them tearing away the bandages they had tied about their bodies, for few in the company were as injured as they appeared. The smell of vengeance and the promise of gold lent their fatigued bodies a new vigour. As if sharing in the vitality of their riders, the horses offered no protest as the mercenaries spurred their steeds down hallways and up stairs.

Betraying us, thought Ursio, is going to cost you dearly, viscount.

IN THE NURSERY, Mirella de Chegney and her son's nurse cowered together. They could hear the sounds of battle and bloodshed echoing throughout the castle all around them. A brave woman in her own right, a part of Mirella desperately wished to race from the protection of the as-yet undisturbed nursery to see what had befallen her husband. But a newer and greater concern ruled her thoughts and enthroned a new fear in her heart. A fear for the small, fragile little life she clutched against her body, trying to stifle its crying wail in her bosom.

Suddenly, the door burst inward. A massive brown stallion, flanks caked in mud and dried blood, froth dribbling from its mouth, smashed through the heavy Drakwald timber. The steed whickered in a mixture of protest and pain as the rider upon his back straightened. The man was no less horrid in appearance than his warhorse. A powerful, brutish looking man, his face encased in a mangy black beard, his head sporting a mane of black hair as caked in blood and mud as the flanks of his steed. The man cast blazing brown eyes at the cowering women. With a snarl that was only half laughter, the man dropped from his saddle, shuffling towards the women with an almost hound-like lope.

'The boy,' he grunted, his words as thick and heavy as his voice. The man's huge hands closed about the tiny crying shape pressed against Mirella's body. The Tilean began to pull the baby from its mother, his bestial strength overcoming the noble-woman's desperate hold. The Tilean stared at his prize with hungry eyes, jostling the wailing infant in his hands as if to hear the clinking of golden coins.

'Unhand my son, scum!' Mirella screamed. The Tilean turned his burning eyes at the woman. He saw the bright flash of metal in the firelight as Mirella drove a knitting needle into the soft flesh of his groin. The improvised weapon was deflected by the metal of the mercenary's codpiece, but stabbed into the tender flesh of his thigh with scarcely impeded force. With the reflexes of a professional soldier, the Tilean ignored the pain and smashed a meaty fist into the blonde woman's face. Mirella staggered away as the mercenary ripped the needle from his thigh, ignoring the wailing child he had dropped to the fur-laden floor.

'You dropped this,' the Tilean spat as he rushed the reeling Mirella. The woman's hands left her broken nose as the Tilean drove the knitting needle into her midsection. The butcher wasted no further thought on the dying noblewoman, but turned his attention back toward the wailing baby. He saw the nurse clutching the crying child, trying to soothe its pain and terror, while casting horrified eyes on the Tilean's advancing bulk.

'Thinking of killing them too, Verdo?' a cold voice rasped from the doorway. The Tilean looked over to see his captain framed in the entrance of the nursery. 'We need the child, and unless you think you can nurse a baby, we need the girl too.'

'I can wait,' Verdo growled, snatching a fistful of the nurse's hair and pulling her to her feet.

GOURMAND GROANED AS another sharp pain rasped against his flesh. 'Don't die on me,' a voice snarled. Gourmand recognised those cold tones, that mocking sneer. It was the leader of the mercenaries, the man who had killed his master. The stricken steward groaned and forced his eyes to settle upon Ursio. The man scowled down at him.

'I have a message for you to deliver, messenger boy,' the mercenary captain tossed a leather packet down, letting it settle on the wounded man's body. 'You take that to the Viscount de Chegney. You tell him what happened here. You also tell him that we have his grandson.' Ursio gestured to the courtyard, once again filled with Tileans, and now joined by the mounted figure of the nursemaid and the swaddled form she held in her arms. 'If he doesn't want his line to die out with him, he will follow those instructions to the letter. Now on your way, messenger boy. And don't die until you deliver that to the viscount.' Ursio's face twisted into a cold, murderous leer.

'For the boy's sake.'

THE CENTURIES HUNG heavy within the great hall of the Chateau de Chegney. For a thousand years the de Chegney family had dwelled in the massive brooding stone fortress, guarding the narrow pass through the Grey Mountains that linked the Kingdom of Bretonnia with the sprawling Empire. The lands ruled by the viscounts de Chegney had alternately prospered or suffered under their lords, accepting the justice and tyranny alike with the dogged stoicism and subservience of the Bretonnian peasant, but seldom had they bowed their heads in fealty to so terrible a man as he who now sat brooding within the castle's great hall.

The Viscount Augustine de Chegney was no longer a young man, yet his build bespoke an animalistic strength and vitality. The man was not tall; indeed his stature was somewhat squat, slightly below that of the average

Bretonnian. But the viscount's shoulders were broad, his head rising from those shoulders on a thick bull's neck. The head perched atop that neck was likewise massive, the viscount's forehead sloping immediately from his thick brows to join his steel-grey hair, cut in the bowl shaped fashion of the Bretonnians. The man's nose was broad, his mouth a thin gash above his scarce chin.

The viscount lounged in his high-backed chair wearing a tunic of scarlet trimmed with the fur of a wild cat, a bejewelled dagger thrust through the leather band of his belt. His leggings were tucked into a set of high leather boots, their toes shod in steel and silver. A trim of wolf-skin had been sewn to the mouth of the boots, the grey fur exactly matching the cold eyes of the viscount's face.

It was the eyes of Viscount Augustine de Chegney that unnerved those who met them. Like the wild cat and the wolf, there was a ferocious cunning and ruthlessness about them, a quality of vicious determination that offered no quarter to those who might stand between the man and his desires. Even the closest of the viscount's associates dreaded the steely gaze of their master, more so when the fire of emotion crept into them and glared from behind the icy grey pools to strike with the force of a basilisk's stare.

Elodore Pleasant was facing such eyes at this moment, nervously adjusting his weight from one foot to the other. Pleasant was Augustine de Chegney's oldest and closest crony, and had become his master's seneschal following the sudden and unexpected death of Augustine's father. A slender, haggard-looking man, Pleasant's pate was bald, a thin mane of unkempt white hair fringing the back of his head. The merest suggestion of a moustache struggled in the shadow of Pleasant's sharp, bird-like nose. The man wore a long black robe fringed in gold, his hands heavy with over-sized rings. Indeed, if Augustine de Chegney suggested some feral predator, then Elodore Pleasant suggested a vulture. Only in the eyes were the two men similar, for both viewed the world through cunning orbs, though the craftiness behind Pleasant's pale blue eyes was akin to that of the fox.

'Tell me,' the viscount mused, sloshing the last mouthful of wine about the bottom of his crystal glass, 'why do they call you "pleasant"?' The grey eyes narrowed and the nobleman rose from his seat. Angrily the viscount hurled the glass against the wall, its gleaming debris scattering across the hall. 'For as long as I have known you, I have heard only ill tidings from your mouth!' the viscount snarled.

'It is better that a friend deliver such news,' Pleasant replied, trying to keep his tone even, not let any anxiety cloud his words. 'One who knows your heart and might better council you in such matters as these.'

'Was it not your council that advised I let that dolt Norval deal with Ursio and his men?' challenged Viscount de Chegney, his tone low and full of menace.

'Yes, my lord,' agreed Pleasant, bobbing his head like the carrion bird he so resembled. 'We have employed him for such matters before, and never had cause to regret...'

'My son is dead!' roared the viscount, clenching his fist in anger. 'And now this foreign rabble have my grandson as hostage, demanding I pay them twice the fee for their services as payment for his safe return!' The viscount scratched at the hairy growth on his throat and jowls. 'Tell me, Pleasant, what do you advise that I do? Hmm? Shall I pay these animals for killing one heir to ensure the return of another?'

'Begging your leave, my lord,' the black-garbed seneschal stuttered, 'but I do not think that paying them will achieve anything. They have been betrayed, and seek more than gold as compensation.'

'Do you think that thought has not occurred to me?' snorted the Viscount. 'But what other choice do I have? I have spent a lifetime expanding the realm and fortune of the de Chegneys, I shall not see it fail for want of an heir! We shall pay these vermin ten times what they ask, but I will have my grandson returned!'

'There is another way, my lord,' Pleasant said, not daring to let his eyes settle upon the viscount in his present humour. 'We could recover the child ourselves. That would ensure his return and not force you into a compact with this mercenary rabble.'

'These men are not morons,' snapped the viscount. 'I would not have engaged them in the first place if they were. If Ursio even thinks my men are close to finding him, he will kill my grandson.'

'Then we shall not use any of your men,' Pleasant offered. 'I agree, the Tileans would certainly discover an armed force sometime before they themselves were in peril. But a single man? One man could discover their hiding place, infiltrate it and recover the child.'

'Know you of such a man?' the viscount asked, his tone dubious.

'Our smuggler friends in the Empire speak of a bounty hunter, a man named Brunner,' Pleasant answered. 'They say that once he is on a man's trail, he will follow them to the Wastes themselves, and return with his prey.'

'A bounty hunter?' scoffed the Viscount. 'You would entrust the safety of my grandson to a bounty hunter?'

'They say that this Brunner is of noble blood, that when he takes a commission, he always sees it through to the end,' the seneschal responded, somewhat defensively. 'His reputation is quite terrible amongst our friends, and in this case, that is to our benefit.'

The viscount considered Pleasant's council for a moment, his feral eyes narrowing as he thought. At last he turned his gaze back upon the vulture-like seneschal. 'Very well, Elodore, if you can find this bounty hunter, engage him. Tell him to bring me my grandson. Or Ursio's head.'

Pleasant bowed before his master. 'As you wish.'

ELODORE PLEASANT AND his hulking bodyguard pushed their way past a gang of drunken farmers and entered the cave-like gloom of the Braying Ass, the most disreputable of Albrechtsburg's taverns. Pleasant brought a perfumed handkerchief to his nose, trying to blot out the vile mixture of cheap beer, unwashed humanity and dry urine that wafted out of the tavern. Beside him, the bodyguard rolled his eyes, annoyed that his charge had already broken his advice to keep a low profile in this thieves' nest. Pleasant did not pay his protector the slightest notice but arrogantly pushed his way into the darkness.

Pleasant doubted if the rumours about the man's nobility could be true. How any person of note could allow themselves to be surrounded by such filth and squalor was beyond the Bretonnian's ability to comprehend.

Pleasant scanned the room, his eyes lingering on every dirty bearded face, his gaze taking in the large oak bar, its surface nicked and pitted by countless brawls and endless games of mumbeley-peg. The burly Bretonnian man-at-arms beside Pleasant nudged the seneschal's arm, drawing his master's attention away from the antics of a fat coachman and a serving wench. Pleasant's gaze settled upon the dark corner his henchman indicated. The two Bretonnians headed toward the isolated table and its sole occupant.

The man seated at the table was an unnervingly grim sight. In build, he was a well muscled man, displaying a quality of strength such as might grace a professional soldier rather than the brawn of a common labourer. The man's legs were enclosed to just below the knee in black leather boots with steel toes, while dark steel cuisses encased his upper legs, a faded eagles rampant visible on each piece of armour. A suit of brigandine armour protected his torso, a breastplate of fabulously rare gromril fastened over the cloth-and-metal armour. The dull tan of coarse fabric shirtsleeves was largely obscured by steel vambraces that encased his arms. His hands were clothed in black leather gauntlets, the knuckle of each glove sporting a tiny spike-like stud of metal. The man's head was covered by the rounded bowl of a sallet-helm, the face of the helmet concealing the man's features as completely as an executioner's hood. Icy blue eyes regarded the

Bretonnians from behind the visor of the helm, while the exposed mouth below the armour sipped from a wooden cup.

'Do I have the distinction of speaking with the gentleman known as Brunner?' Pleasant said in his most fawning manner as he approached the darkened corner.

'Who wants to know?' came the guarded reply.

Pleasant's dour face broke into a wide grin. 'I am Elodore Pleasant, seneschal to his lordship the Viscount Augustine de Chegney,' the man said, lowering himself into the chair opposite that of the bounty hunter.

'I don't recall asking for company. Who invited you to sit down?' There was a note of challenge and warning in the bounty hunter's voice that froze Pleasant in mid-motion, his rear inches from the seat of the chair, his face inches away from the killer's. It was as if he had come face to face with a snarling wolf. Beads of perspiration gathered about Pleasant's brow. The hulking bodyguard took a step forward, hand falling to the pommel of his sword.

'Before he can draw that frog-stabber of his,' the bounty hunter's menacing voice rasped, 'I'll have your throat slit.' In the second it took the bodyguard to digest the threat, the bounty hunter erupted into action. A silver flash of metal caught the tavern's dim light, then was pressed against the skin of Pleasant's throat, a bead of crimson surrounding the point.

At the same time, the bounty killer's other hand rose from beneath the table, a small crossbow gripped in his gloved fist.

'We don't want any trouble,' Pleasant declared, rising slowly from the chair, the bounty hunter's dagger rising with him. A sidewise gesture of his hand made the seneschal's henchman sullenly back away. The bounty hunter set the crossbow pistol down upon the table, its lethal dart still pointing at the bodyguard, and removed the dagger from the chastened functionary's throat.

'Why are you looking for me?' demanded Brunner.

'I understand that you hunt men,' Pleasant stammered, dabbing at his bleeding throat with his perfumed handkerchief. 'And that you are the best there is to be had in that line of enterprise.'

'That much is obvious,' Brunner looked across the dingy tavern. 'It would take quite a reputation to bring so fine a gentleman as yourself to a place like this.' The bounty hunter lifted a small wooden cup to his lips. 'What's the job?' he asked before sipping at the schnapps.

The anxious look on the Bretonnian's face eased somewhat and Pleasant smiled. 'The castle of the viscount's son was ransacked by mercenaries discharged from my lord's service,' the seneschal began. 'They killed my master's son and his wife, as well as very nearly every living thing in the place.'

The bounty hunter slowly set the cup down, his cold eyes locking on those of the functionary. 'I have already heard news of the unpleasantness across the border.' Pleasant was visibly shocked by the bounty hunter's words. 'I make it my business to be well-informed,' Brunner explained. 'A man's life sometimes balances upon the merest shred of information.'

'The brigands have taken the viscount's grandson with them,' Pleasant continued. 'They are demanding ransom for his safe return.'

'I collect bounties, not children,' Brunner replied, lifting the wooden cup to his mouth again.

'The viscount is prepared to pay you very well,' Pleasant reached into the breast of his tunic and withdrew a large leather pouch. 'Two hundred gold crowns,' the Bretonnian said, setting the bag down on the table.

Several sets of eyes turned toward the scene as the distinct report of coins jostling against one another insinuated itself into the clamour of the tavern's atmosphere. Brunner reached a hand toward the bag, running his gloved digits across the cool leather surface. 'One hundred now, the rest when the viscount's heir is safely returned.' Brunner turned his helmeted head away, leaning back in his chair so that his back rested against the tavern's peeling plaster on wood wall.

'A fair price,' the bounty hunter admitted. 'But I am not interested.' Brunner bolted the rest of his schnapps and set the cup down upon the table.

'I could speak to the viscount,' Pleasant said, his tone desperate. 'He would surely agree to any reasonable sum.'

Brunner sucked his teeth and stared at the Bretonnian. 'I don't want your money,' he said, his tone menacing. 'I've had more than enough of you Bretonnians and your lordly ways. I am my own man, not some foppish snail-eater's errand boy.'

Pleasant's mouth dropped in disbelief as the bounty hunter's crude words impacted upon his ears. The functionary trembled in outrage, wishing he had more of the viscount's men with him so he could teach this villain some manners. The seneschal's tongue worked itself to voice a retort but all that emerged was a feeble croak. The bounty hunter turned away, motioning for a serving wench to bring him another drink, his would-be patron already dismissed from his attention. Balling his fist in outrage, Pleasant rose and stormed away from the table.

'This has been a fool's errand,' Pleasant snapped as he passed his bodyguard. The other Bretonnian took his place at the seneschal's side. The two men marched their way toward the feeble light seeping under the tavern's door. Neither man noticed the scruffy figures who had preceded them into the street, or the two rat-faced men who followed after them.

Elodore Pleasant's face was a mask of sullen, brooding rage as he stomped through the dirty streets of the township. The seneschal dabbed his handkerchief against the cut the bounty hunter's blade had left on his throat. The outright audacity of the scum! Pleasant wondered if he might not use some of the funds he had quietly diverted from the viscount's coffers towards seeing some justice meted out upon the arrogant vermin. But such thoughts of revenge were for another day. For now, there was still the matter of rescuing the viscount's grandson, or seeing his abductors dead.

Pleasant was so lost in his thoughts that he did not notice the darkened lane his steps had carried him into, nor the warning hiss of his bodyguard. It was only the sight of three men standing in his path that snapped Pleasant from his dark humour, bringing his attention back to his surroundings. Pleasant looked at the men, their dirty, grimy clothes, their unwashed faces and gap-toothed grins. The Bretonnian's face wore an expression of contempt as his eyes met those of the men, but the flesh that hung from his cheeks trembled with nervous anxiety as he noticed the clubs and blades the men gripped in their dust-blackened hands. He chanced a look back at his bodyguard, noticing for the first time that the soldier's sword was drawn, and that two more ruffians had closed upon them from the opposite side of the lane.

'I am on my master's business,' Pleasant said in a voice he hoped conveyed more authority than the fear that was building within him. 'Give me space to pass.'

One of the ruffians swaggered forward, a short-bladed sword clutched in his hand. He flipped a strand of dirty blond hair from his forehead as it fell into his eyes. The man grinned, exposing a set of yellow and pitted teeth. He spat a glob of phlegm into the dust.

'We 'eard 'bout yer little errand in da Brayin' Ass,' the ruffian said, his voice raspy. 'Two-hunert gold fer retrievin' some wine-swiller's brat.' The ruffian clucked his tongue. 'That's a pretty price, no mistake.'

'I am afraid that I am not at liberty to offer that particular commission to anyone but the man my master considered skilful enough to accomplish it,' Pleasant tried to keep his cool, but was all too aware of the beads of sweat trickling from his brow.

'Is that so?' the blond-haired man sneered. 'So we can't take this little job from yer? Can't earn us the two-hunert?' The man cast a mock regretful look at his companions and sighed. 'Well, I guess we'll just have to settle fer the hunert yer carry'n!'

The men laughed as they advanced toward Pleasant. The hulking Bretonnian bodyguard was soon beside the seneschal, trying to interpose himself between both the three men closing upon his charge and the other two quietly advancing from the rear. All five robbers were chuckling under their breath, their eyes gleaming like those of a wolf pack lighting upon a tethered horse.

'Easiest money I ever done made,' the leader of the thieves snorted as he closed upon Pleasant, drawing his sword back for a sideways swipe at the Bretonnian. The man's chuckle trailed off into a gurgling death rattle as a spike of steel impacted into his throat. The sword clattered from his hands and he fell to his knees, dirty hands fumbling at the crimson tide gushing from the hole in his windpipe where the crossbow bolt had torn its way through his neck.

The other muggers were thrown into confusion and disarray by the sudden death of their leader. It only lasted a moment, but even so slight an instant was enough. The hulking Bretonnian smashed his shield against the leg of one of the club-wielding men closing upon the Bretonnians from behind. The bone snapped under the impact and the ruffian fell to the dirt street, howling with agony.

The bodyguard lashed out at the other robber with a downward stroke of his blade, the thief barely managing to raise his own sword to parry the blow.

The men facing Pleasant snarled and made to leap at the seneschal, determined to claim the weighty purse of gold before making good their escape. But even as they sprung into action, a new player introduced himself into the fray. A heavy falchion sword ripped through the spine of one of the men as the steel blade was thrust through his body from behind. The man didn't scream, his eyes instead staring in incomprehension at the bloodied steel that protruded from the gory ruin of his belly. The eyes had glassed over by the time the blade was withdrawn and the robber's body fell into the dust.

The other thief turned, glaring at the black-helmed figure that had seemingly materialised from nowhere to spoil their game. He raised his stout club, its fire-blackened wood further enhanced by a cluster of iron spikes driven into the cudgel. With an oath that might be voiced by any cornered animal, the robber charged at his foe. The face below the visor of the sallet-helm smiled as the ruffian came towards him. With one hand, he raised the falchion sword, notching the thief's wooden weapon as he swung at him. The robber spat a second curse and renewed his attack. Again the armoured man parried the robber's attack with his bloodied sword, but this time the man's other hand leapt into action. As the thief was again repelled by the man's guard, the armoured fighter's left hand smashed into his face, plunging the blade of the dagger it held into the robber's eye.

The robber dropped to the ground, screaming and writhing in agony, burying his bleeding face in the dirt. Brunner smiled as he strode towards the thief and calmly raised his falchion. There was a final cry of pain and the crunch of breaking bone as the bounty hunter plunged his sword between the wounded robber's shoulders.

Pleasant stared about him, his mouth gaping open at the carnage he had witnessed. He had seen many combats in his time, but seldom had he seen a conflict begin and end with such swift dispatch. He looked for his bodyguard, finding the man already walking back towards him, wiping blood from his blade. The seneschal then turned his gaze back upon the bounty hunter. He watched as Brunner withdrew a rag from his belt and wiped the blood from his sword before sheathing the weapon. The bloodied dagger he returned to his gloved hand as he advanced toward the Bretonnian.

'We were lucky you came along,' the nervous seneschal stammered, the corners of his mouth twitching. 'It would have been a near thing. I am no warrior, and all five of these men against my bodyguard might not have turned out so well for me.'

Brunner didn't speak, instead his eyes turned toward the blond leader of the robbers, his breath still gurgling from the wound in his neck. 'Let's not be all day about it,' the bounty hunter's harsh voice hissed. Leaning over the dying man, Brunner raked the dagger across his throat, letting the new-made corpse pitch forward into the street.

'There was no luck in my finding you,' the bounty hunter said, turning his eyes toward Pleasant. 'I followed you from the tavern.'

'Followed us?' Pleasant asked. 'Then you have reconsidered the commission from the Viscount de Chegney?' Hope flared in the seneschal's devious heart.

'Reconsidered?' there was actually a suggestion of mirth in the bounty killer's voice as he repeated the Bretonnian's comment. 'I intended to take the job the moment you sat at my table.'

Pleasant's eyes sharpened, his face screwing into a suspicious leer. 'Then why did you refuse my offer?'

Brunner rose and stalked toward the other side of the lane. The ruffian the bodyguard had smashed with his shield was trying to crawl away. Brunner set a booted heel against the man's broken leg, pinning him in place and bringing a fresh cry of pain from the robber.

'You made yourself a target, showing your wealth in such a den of jackals,' the bounty hunter shook his head. 'I had to see what sort of rats would scurry out of the shadows to relieve you of that fat pouch of gold.' Brunner looked down at the groaning man at his feet. 'Though I must say I am less than impressed by the results. I doubt if I shall get more than thirty silver for these sorry cut-throats.'

'You used me as bait!' howled Pleasant. His earlier glee at the bounty hunter's acceptance of the viscount's commission had once again been overtaken by a fervent desire to see the arrogant commoner painfully put back in his place.

'I would prefer to think of it as seizing an opportunity that presented itself.' Brunner returned his attention to the man at his feet.

'I trust that you will show more expediency in retrieving the viscount's grandson,' Pleasant declared, choking down the more choice words that threatened to explode from his mouth. 'Time is of the essence in this matter.'

'I just have a few things to finish here,' Brunner said, still considering the man at his feet. 'If time is so valuable, I suggest you attend to effecting your return to Bretonnia. You can give me the details I will require on the road.'

Pleasant bristled under the bounty killer's tone. He, a viscount's seneschal, was being dismissed by a hired sword? Perhaps there was truth in the rumours of Brunner's noble birth; Pleasant had never encountered such audacity in anyone that did not have some manner of breeding in their background. With a sharp word to his bodyguard, the fuming seneschal turned away from the bounty hunter.

'Oh, messenger,' Brunner called after the Bretonnian. Pleasant turned to face the killer again. Brunner held a gloved hand in the Bretonnian's direction. 'The hundred gold crowns.' With a muttered oath, Pleasant savagely dug the pouch from the pocket within his tunic and tossed it to the bounty hunter. Brunner caught the jingling sack one-handed and tucked it into his belt.

THE BOUNTY HUNTER casually set a few more sticks into the circle of his campfire and unlimbered his packhorse of its tack and harness, hobbling the animal's legs to keep it from wandering too far. His riding horse, a magnificent bay, he left untethered. There were few things the bounty hunter placed any trust in, but the fealty of his Bretonnian warhorse was one. He could be certain that the animal would stay by his side, come fire or sorcery. Brunner patted the great horse's muzzle with a black gloved hand and returned to preparing his camp.

As Brunner continued to arrange his packs and blankets, the bounty hunter's attention was only minimally upon his task. This was the place Pleasant had named as the rendezvous with the kidnappers. Brunner had a deep knowledge of this region, certainly a more intimate familiarity than a rabble of Tilean mercenaries could acquire in a few months of employment. He had counted three men watching the barren glade from supposed places of concealment. He could have easily disposed of them but he had no way of knowing what other precautions the ransomers might have made against any treachery on the part of the viscount. Brunner had thus ridden into the lurking mercenaries' supposed control, and prepared to let the Tileans make the next move.

Brunner settled himself down upon a blanket, propping his back against his saddle. The killer faced the fire, seemingly unconcerned by what might be transpiring in the trees all around him. But the bounty hunter's steely gaze was all the time scanning the edges of the clearing, all the time his ears were listening for the sharp crack of a twig or the rustle of a branch. Beneath the cover of his blanket, Brunner's hands kept a loose grip upon his weapons.

'Hallo to camp,' an accented Tilean voice shouted from the darkness. 'May I share your fire?' There was a note of question as well as suspicion in the Tilean's voice. Brunner allowed himself an inward smile. His elaborately staged calmness and unconcern had disarmed the men. They were unsure if he was the man they were expecting or just some chance wanderer who had muddled along into their affairs.

'Provided you be no Ulricite zealot, please yourself,' the bounty hunter called back.

That reply should further disorder the villain's mind, Brunner thought.

The Tilean strode forward, the fire revealing his olive-hued features. He was a young man, a bright slash of a duelling scar across his cheek, a thin moustache worming its way across his lip. The mercenary wore a suit of loose fitting armour, a broadsword at his hip and a crossbow slung over his back. Even as the man strolled forward with a seemingly casual swagger, he rested a hand on the pommel of his blade.

'I might be spending a cold night in the crook of a tree,' the Tilean said, his eyes taking in Brunner's figure, a smile flickering on his face as he saw the sword and other weapons resting near the reclining man. Near enough to reach should any visitor to his camp think to cause him any trouble, but not near enough to reach should that visitor have friends lurking in the dark with crossbows trained upon the warrior before that trouble began.

'Then, by all means, warm yourself,' Brunner offered, inclining his head towards the fire. The Tilean advanced, making a display of warming his left hand above the dancing tongues of flame. His other hand still hung at his side, casually resting on the pommel of his sword.

'It is by Taal's grace that I saw your fire,' the Tilean commented, his eyes still studying what he could see of the face below the visor of his host's helm. 'How come you to be in this blighted place?'

'I should ask you the same question,' Brunner replied, his gaze piercing that of the mercenary.

'My horse threw me,' the mercenary answered. 'I was acting as an outrider for a wine merchant who hopes to establish a new route through the pass to sell his grapes in the Empire. I must have ridden too far out for them to hear my oaths as the wretched pony unseated me and ran into the hills. You can be sure I will have some words with the man who sold me that gangly brute.'

A smile appeared on Brunner's face. He had been listening to the creaks and cracks emanating from the dark, gauging the position of those who made the sounds. His watchers had drawn closer, eager to catch every word of the exchange.

'Strange,' Brunner said, spitting into the dust. He fastened his eyes on the Tilean once more, the mouth below the black slash of his helm split in a mocking smile. 'Do you not find it strange that a wine merchant would employ a foreigner as an outrider, rather than a man native to the region?'

An angry snarl appeared on the Tilean's features. An accomplished liar the man might not be, but to be caught in a lie was insulting to him all the same. The blade at his side flew from its sheath, the firelight dancing in the exposed fang of steel.

Thunder and smoke rose from the reclining figure on the blankets. Fiery pain blazed into the Tilean's chest, pitching him backward with such force that he crashed upon his back in the campfire. The mercenary's body rolled from the flames, his armour smoking, a wail of suffering rising from his throat.

The violent flash and boom of the discharge of the blackpowder gun the bounty hunter had fired through the fabric of the blanket momentarily startled and disoriented the two crossbowmen in the trees. The veteran killers did not hesitate for more than a breath before snapping the strings of their weapons, sending two steel bolts slamming into the target they had carefully marked. But in the thick grey smoke, the Tileans were not able to see that their would-be victim had thrown himself into motion even as the crack and boom of the gun's firing resounded across the night. Brunner had flung his body to the side at once, rolling away from the blankets and the saddle, away from the carefully laid out weapons to the left of his previous position. One bolt impacted in the centre of the blanket; another struck midway between the blanket and the weapons.

Brunner kicked aside the pack of provisions, lifting the strange crossbow he had secreted beneath the leather bags. A long black box sat atop the weapon and, unlike the weapons of the Tileans, the implement of death the bounty hunter now hefted bore not one but two taut steel bowstrings. Brunner sent one missile crashing into the chest of the crossbowman to his left before the mercenary even had time to register the fact that his prey had escaped his carefully prepared shot. The second man had a single moment to react as Brunner spun the weapon in his direction. Panic seized the man and instead of dropping to the ground, the Tilean fumbled at his weapon, trying to reload it. The second bolt from Brunner's repeating crossbow punched through the wooden stock of the Tilean's weapon and embedded itself in the man's lung. The mercenary fell then, a fraction of a second too late to save his life.

Brunner strode across the clearing, fetching up his sword from the display of weapons and calmly walked over to the still writhing man he had peppered with the blast of his firearm. The Tilean was cursing freely, his body wracked with pain. As he sensed his enemy drawing near, the Tilean stretched a bloodied hand towards his sword. Brunner set his boot on the mercenary's hand. He flipped the mercenary onto his back with his other foot. The armour was flecked in blood and pitted by the small steel pellets the bounty killer's gun had disgorged.

'You're lucky,' Brunner observed as the Tilean's face twisted into a grimace. 'The armour stopped most of the impact. The shot barely nipped your skin.' In truth, Brunner had been thankful for that armour. He needed one of the men alive.

'In case you are wondering,' Brunner said, turning his eyes from the wound in the mercenary's chest to the man's face, 'Viscount de Chegney did send me.' The information brought a groan not entirely of pain from the Tilean. 'He wants his grandson back, but he prefers to pay for him with steel instead of gold.' The bounty hunter put all of his weight to the boot crushing the man's hand, bringing a new cry of pain. 'Perhaps you would like to tell me where the viscount's heir is?'

'If I tell you, how do I know you won't kill me?' the Tilean snarled through clenched teeth. Brunner favoured the man with a frigid smile.

'Because if I killed you after you lied to me and made me lose the bounty the viscount is offering for his grandson, I wouldn't be able to kill you later for lying to me.' Brunner ground the mercenary's hand under his heel, twisting the broken bones against one another, wrenching another cry from his prisoner. 'So, where are your friends hiding?'

UNDER COVER OF night, Brunner replaced his gear on his packhorse and threw his saddle onto the back of the towering bay. He spared a single glance at the man he had tied to the trunk of the gnarled old tree the locals called the Wizard's Bones. The Tilean glared back at him from above the linen gag the bounty hunter had shoved down his throat.

'You seem to harbour me some ill will,' Brunner commented as he lifted himself onto the back of his charger. 'Perhaps you have called down all manner of curses on my head.' Brunner smiled beneath his helm. 'But consider this. If your friends kill me, do you think they will come back here looking for you? Do you think anybody is going to happen along here before hunger or thirst does for you? Or perhaps a pack of wolves will decide to pick your bones clean before that.'

Brunner clicked his tongue and turned his steed's head away from the clearing.

'Just something to keep your mind occupied,' the bounty hunter said, as he disappeared into the night.

THE LONELY GREY tower stabbed into the night sky like the defiant fist of some fallen giant. Brambles and weeds encircled the structure, choking doorways and windows with dry brittle limbs. Massive grey stones littered the ground all about the forlorn tower, falling prey to the same verminous growths that had surrounded the fort from which they had fallen.

Cold, hard eyes gazed at the tower from the shadows of the forest. Brunner noted the faint flicker of firelight in one of the lower windows of the tower. The captured ransom collector had told the bounty killer the truth, but, then, Brunner had never doubted that he would. Perhaps the bounty hunter would even hold to his part of the bargain and return for the man before the wolves made a meal of him.

Brunner considered the tower. Once there would have been a scarlet pennant flying from the now broken roof, displaying the drake rampant that was the device of the Baron von Drakenburg. Once there would have been four sentries patrolling the rampart that peeped from below that roof, each dressed in the von Drakenburg livery, each a veteran marksman, for the Baron von Drakenburg would hire only the most capable of men. The face beneath the black helm smiled mirthlessly. Perhaps the baron had not been such a good judge of men, for he had been betrayed in the end, after all. Although, it had to be admitted, that even the traitor had been very capable.

Brunner studied the rampart again, satisfying himself that only a single man patrolled the roof, a weary looking Tilean with a crossbow who barely spared a glance towards the forest as he made his regular sweep of the battlement. Brunner watched the mercenary, studying his regular, unvaried movements. The sentry was slipping into that dire, inattentive boredom that always threatened to dull a sentinel's wariness. With the man's mind wandering away from the tedium of his duties, his eyes might miss a dark shape emerging from the cover of the forest. No doubt his watchfulness was not so far-gone that he would fail to see that same figure creep to the base of the tower itself. But there would be no need for the bounty hunter to test the guard's capability that far.

Brunner made his way to a large overgrown bush, a massive thorny brute that promised no berries or leaves to any that might show interest in it, only the sting of dagger-like nettles. Brunner grabbed the bush, pulling it back from the small rise it leaned upon. As the bush moved, a dark opening revealed itself, a hole that dug its way into the rubble-strewn plain. Without hesitation, the bounty hunter worked his body past the unwholesome plant and into the darkness of the narrow tunnel. A predatory smile crossed Brunner's features. The Tileans might have made the fortalice their lair, but they would soon discover that they knew very little about their temporary stronghold.

THE MERCENARY WIPED the crust from his eyes and refocused his attention on the dim landscape beyond the fortalice. The narrow window afforded only a slight view of the terrain, but Ursio had wanted a man stationed here just the same. He was taking no chances that any party of the viscount's knights bent on revenge would fall upon the mercenaries without warning. Hence Ursio had placed two watch-points, one atop the tower, in the ruin of its roof, and a second here, in a damp room mid-way up the tower's height. The wily captain was always a careful man. Men sneaking up on the tower might see the sentry above, and hide themselves from his vision, but having seen one sentinel, they would not think to look for a second and would perhaps reveal themselves to the concealed watchman.

It was a sound theory, but it did not change the fact that the Tilean's post was a cold, dreary and boring one. Not for the first time, the Tilean began to recite old ballads to himself, imagining the times when he had first heard them, carousing with his comrades through the taverns of Luccini after a successful campaign.

The mercenary's soft humming ended in a ghastly gurgle as blood bubbled into his throat. He toppled forward, his body sliding off the dagger blade that had neatly punctured the back of his neck.

'You were off key,' the grim figure of the mercenary's killer stated, wiping the blood off the dagger with a bit of rag. Brunner turned away from the corpse and made his way back to the far wall of the chamber. His gloved hand caressed a worn stone several inches above the height of his head. Soundlessly, the wall sank inward. Brunner waited a moment, then slipped into the darkness from which he had emerged to kill the watchman.

BRUNNER EMERGED FROM the shadows that claimed the collapsed section of tile and timber which sagged across the greater portion of the roof. He watched the Tilean crossbowman making his rounds for a moment. The bounty hunter had finished scouting the tower. He had found that there were nine villains within it. Three were bivouacked in a long chamber that had once served as a barracks for the tower, busily playing at dice, gambling with the ransom money they had not yet earned. Another had been keeping watch over the horses, though now the horses were keeping watch over his body. Three others, one of whom he took to be the leader, were with the child and a nursemaid, busily plotting a triumphant return to Tilea and the strengthening of their depleted band. The other two had been the watchmen, the dead one below and the man death now stalked.

The drowsy sentinel finished his circuit and turned to retrace his steps. His mouth dropped open in shock as he found himself face to face with an armoured figure, its face hidden within a helmet of blackened steel. Icy eyes burned back into the young Tilean's stunned gaze.

A sharp stabbing agony shot up the left side of the mercenary's body and the crossbow clattered to the stone floor. The bounty hunter withdrew a bloody fang of steel, the same he had already used to send two of this man's companions to Morr's realm this night. The young mercenary gasped as the pain seared into his vitals and blood seeped from his side. The bounty hunter's gloved hands gripped the wounded man's body. He turned the sentry towards the crenelated wall. Stealth had played its part. Now it was time to let the sheep know that the wolf had arrived.

'Scream for me,' the bounty killer's murderous voice hissed into the Tilean's ear as he flung the injured man from the top of the tower.

THE SENTRY'S WAIL of horror echoed through the corridors of the fortalice in the brief instant before it was silenced in a dull crunch of bone. Cries of surprise and alarm sounded from the two rooms still occupied by the Tilean kidnappers. Ursio met the gaze of the foremost man from the former barracks.

'Find out what is going on!' the mercenary captain snarled. 'And kill it!' he added, slamming the door shut after him.

The trio of mercenaries crept up the stairway, swords held before them, making their way to the roof. They had already discovered the body of the lower watchman, removing any question that someone was loose in the tower. The men were wary, cautious and more than a little enraged. At least one more of their comrades gone, another debt of blood to be collected in this vendetta with the Bretonnian viscount.

The rearmost of the Tileans was only a few paces behind the leading pair when he paused. He had heard a sound: the scrape of stone against stone. He turned, facing a dark opening in the wall that had not been there a moment before. He opened his mouth to shout, but found his words silenced as a length of steel tore into his gut.

'Aren't you pleased you found me?' Brunner asked the dying man as he pushed him off his sword. The bounty hunter turned his body as he emerged from the concealed passage and made ready to meet the attack of the other Tileans as they reacted to the sound of their companion's demise. Brunner smiled to himself. The men would join their friends soon enough.

URSIO STARED AT the door of the room that had once served as the quarters for the commander of the tower. The sounds of combat, the ring of steel on steel and the gasping cries of dying men had sounded from beyond that now closed portal. The mercenary captain cast a nervous look over at his remaining men. The wiry, scar-faced Vernini nodded at his commander, hefting the loaded crossbow in his hands. Vernini was the best shot among all his men. Whoever opened that door would be rewarded with Vernini's quarrel in his heart.

The brutish mass of Verdo glowered at Ursio. The homicidal thug was still chafing from the violent reprimand his captain had given him. When they had discovered that there were intruders in their hideout, a fit of rage had consumed the black-bearded mercenary. Before Ursio could stop him, Verdo had snapped the neck of the abducted nursemaid with his bare hands and was lumbering toward the basket that contained the baby before a blow from the hilt of Ursio's sword had restored some degree of reason in the thug's murderous mind. Verdo stood, his heavy cavalry mace clenched in his hands, his chest heaving, every muscle in his body tensed in anticipation. Ursio thought his brutish comrade was not unlike a hound straining at the leash, or a Norse berserker working himself into a frenzy.

Ursio's roving eyes rolled to the basket and the crying form within. The mercenary captain had lost everything because of the Viscount de Chegney's treachery. The small life in that basket represented the only way Ursio could make his deceitful former patron suffer. The Tilean's face settled into a snarl. He pulled his long-bladed dagger from its sheath and moved toward the woven basket.

Just then, the heavy door swung open, its rusty hinges groaning. Vernini did not hesitate. The sharp snap of his crossbow discharging drowned out the creaking sound of the old hinges. The bolt sped into the shape that filled the doorway, smashing through leather tunic, flesh and ribcage. The body jerked as the bolt impacted, then fell forward as it was pushed into the room.

Brunner wasted no time discarding his cadaverous shield, shifting to the right as the body pitched to the floor. Vernini was already hastily reloading his crossbow, swinging his body about to bring the still unloaded weapon to bear on Brunner. Ursio froze above the basket, dagger in hand; his eyes locked upon the black-helmed figure that had slain so many of his men.

'Blood of Khaine!' the mercenary swore as recognition came to him. 'Brunner!'

As if to punctuate the Tilean's oath, the bounty hunter fired the smouldering weapon gripped in his left hand. The shot from the black powder pistol smashed into Vernini's forehead with a force far greater than that of the marksman's crossbow. The mercenary's face disappeared in a red ruin as the shot punched through the Tilean's skull and the man was dead before his body finished falling. Brunner let the spent pistol fall too, dropping the weapon and drawing the heavy falchion from the scabbard at his side.

As the roar of the firearm began to fade, it was replaced by a thunderous bellow no less violent. Verdo charged forward like a maddened bull, swinging his mace at the bounty hunter as if it were the avenging maul of Ulric himself. The bounty hunter managed to dodge the powerful but clumsy blow, kicking the brute in the knee. Verdo grunted, but did not stagger. Howling his wrath, the Tilean lashed out at Brunner again, this time finding his weapon blocked by the intercepting steel of the bounty killer's sword.

Ursio cursed again, gathering up the child from the basket, heedless of the wailing infant's cries. Keeping the baby pressed against his chest, the mercenary captain circled around the duelling figures of Brunner and Verdo. He did not favour his thuggish comrade's chances against the notorious bounty hunter, but perhaps Verdo could keep the hunter occupied long enough for Ursio to effect his own escape. As if to speed Ursio's flight, as he neared the doorway, he saw Brunner's blade slip past Verdo's guard, slashing the man's left arm almost to the bone.

The Tilean was running when he passed from the chamber of death and into the corridor outside. His steps were heavy and swift. He did not see the tiny glittering objects strewn about the floor, the sinister little steel spiders that met his weighty footfalls. They were caltrops, metal spikes designed to cripple warhorses, dropped by the bounty hunter to maim any escaping prey. As Ursio's booted foot encountered its first caltrop, the metal spike pierced leather and flesh, gouging a hole through the sole of his foot. Ursio cried out in pain, flinging both child and blade from him as both hands instantly sought to arrest his fall. The mercenary captain landed badly, another caltrop punching through the palm of his hand, three others digging into his chest and legs as he impacted against stone, another puncturing his right cheek.

Ursio writhed in pain, trying to dig the caltrop from his face with his uninjured hand. The sound of boots scuffling against flagstone brought a new horror to the Tilean. Ursio looked up to see Brunner framed in the doorway, wiping the lifeblood of Verdo from his sword with a rag torn from the mercenary's tunic before sheathing his blade. Ursio saw the bounty hunter cast a glance at the small swaddled object that lay against the wall, now silent and unmoving. The face below the visor of the helm was unreadable as Brunner strode toward Ursio's prone form.

'Wait!' the mercenary stammered. 'I'll go with you! I won't try to escape!' Ursio knew who had set the infamous bounty hunter on him, he knew that he could expect slow death and torture when he was delivered to the sadistic Bretonnian viscount. But it would take days to reach the viscount's castle, and Ursio was desperate to gain even so small a respite from his journey to the gardens of Morr. 'You can take me to the viscount. I won't resist!'

Brunner leaned over the pleading sell-sword. 'I will take you to the viscount,' his cold voice stated. Ursio's eyes grew wide with fright as he saw the bounty hunter draw a large serrated knife from its sheath. 'But the viscount is only paying me for your head.'

'MY GRANDSON IS dead then?' the question emerged from Viscount Augustine de Chegney's mouth like the forlorn growl of a wretched and dying wolf.

Brunner looked up at the seated nobleman upon his raised throne-like chair. He could imagine the man sitting there – not as he was, a morose creature who had seen his last chance for posterity taken from him, who knew that his long and noble line would now end with his last breath – but as a cruel and sadistic brute, resplendent in treacherous triumph. He could imagine the viscount sitting there, slowly sipping his wine as a sobbing maiden with long golden hair washed his feet with her tears, begging with the beast that had become her father to spare the battered and broken man whose blood still stained the stones of the hall's floor. He could almost hear the viscount's words of conciliation, of acquiescence to the pleas of his daughter-in-law. He could almost see the shabby, lice-ridden shapes of the slavers standing in the shadows of the room, there to ensure that every promise the viscount made to the maiden would become a lie.

'They never had the boy,' the bounty hunter's cold voice said. 'After leaving the castle, they killed the nurse and the baby, feeling that their prisoners would be too much of a burden to maintain. They never intended to return the child to you,' the bounty hunter concluded. He reached over and carefully unwrapped the small knotted cloth bundle that sat at his side upon the floor. The soiled cloth unfolded itself and the head of Ursio cast its sightless eyes upon the viscount.

The viscount trembled with emotion, one hand rising to conceal his face from the bounty hunter. With his other hand the nobleman gestured to his seneschal. 'Pay the man,' the viscount spoke through his fingers.

Elodore Pleasant shambled forward, withdrawing a leather pouch from the breast of his tunic. Brunner rose, opening his hand, letting the heavy sack of money sink into his palm. The bounty hunter bowed slightly to Pleasant.

Brunner favoured the viscount with a final icy stare. The viscount looked back, seeing only the hired killer his henchman had engaged. Brunner bowed again, leaving the viscount to consider all that he had lost.

THE ARMOURED TRAVELLER emerged from the rear room of the tavern, leaving the young woman and the quietly sleeping baby behind. He turned his black-helmed head towards the innkeeper, a slightly balding man in early middle age. The merchant gulped as he met the icy eyes of the bounty hunter.

'When I brought the child here three days ago,' the voice beneath the helm rasped, 'I promised you gold if you would care for him.' The man's gloved hand placed a leather pouch upon the counter of the bar, the sound of clinking metal whispering across the tavern as the bag came to rest. The innkeeper stepped forward, placing a protective hand on the bag of money.

'Rest assured, sir,' he said, his voice betraying his nervousness, 'I shall look after him as though he were my own.'

'You will do better than that,' the warrior said, his tone slipping still lower. 'Look after him as though his life were your own.' The bounty hunter strode towards the door. 'Because it is.'

'I shall return from time to time,' Brunner said over his shoulder as he opened the door of the tavern. 'To check on my grandson, and to bring you more gold. Take good care of him, Wiedemann.' The bounty hunter's last words seemed to linger as he closed the door.

'I'll find out if you don't.'

ABOUT THE AUTHORS

Brian Craig is the author of the three Tales of Orfeo – *Zaragoz*, *Plague Daemon* and *Storm Warriors* – and *The Wine of Dreams*, as well as the Warhammer 40,000 novel *Pawns of Chaos*. He has also contributed short stories to a range of anthologies. He is 28, and only looks older because his troubles have aged him.

Matthew Farrer has been writing since his teens, and was first printed in *Inferno!* He has published a number of short stories and was shortlisted for an Aurealis Award in 2001.

Jonathan Green works as a full-time teacher in West London. By night he relates tales of Torben Badenov's Kislevite mercenaries and the adventures of the Underhive bounty hunter Nathan Creed for *Inferno!* magazine.

Simon Jowett has written scripts for the comic book incantations of James Bond and Young Indiana Jones. He is currently writing scripts for animation, short stories and children's novels.

Robin D. Laws is an acclaimed designer of games. He has also worked on computer and collectable card games and is currently a columnist for *Dragon* magazine.

Graham McNeill. Hailing from Scotland, Graham is a Black Library regular who works full-time for Games Workshop. As well as three novels, he has written a host of short stories for *Inferno!*

Simon Spurrier has become a frequent contributor to *2000AD* and the Black Library whilst attempting to reconcile the zany partying lifestyle of a neurotic writer with the sombre, lonely existence of a student. This is harder than it sounds.

C. L. Werner has written a number of Lovecraftian pastiches and pulp-style horror stories for assorted publications. Currently living in the American south-west, he continues to write stories of mayhem and madness set in the Warhammer World.

More Warhammer from the Black Library

REALM OF CHAOS
An anthology of Warhammer stories edited by Marc Gascoigne & Andy Jones

MARKUS WAS CONFUSED; the stranger's words were baffling his pain-numbed mind. "Just who are you, foul spawned deviant?"

The warrior laughed again, slapping his hands on his knees. "I am called Estebar. My followers know me as the Master of Slaughter. And I have come for your soul." – *from* **The Faithful Servant,** *by Gav Thorpe*

THE WOLVES ARE running again. I can haear them panting in the darkness. I race through the forest, trying to outpace them. Behind the wolves I sense another presence, something evil. I am in the place of blood again. – *from* **Dark Heart,** *by Jonathan Green*

IN THE DARK *and gothic world of Warhammer, the ravaging armies of the Ruinous Powers sweep down from the savage north to assail the lands of men. REALM OF CHAOS is a searing collection of a dozen all-action fantasy short stories set in these desperate times.*

More Warhammer from the Black Library

LORDS OF VALOUR
An anthology of Warhammer stories edited by Marc Gascoigne & Christian Dunn

THE GOBLINS SHRIEKED their shrill war cries and charged, only to be met head-on by the vengeful dwarfs. In the confines of the tunnel, the grobi's weight of numbers counted for little. As they turned and fled, Grimli was all for going after them, but Dammaz laid a hand on his shoulder.

"Our way lies down a different path," the Slayer said. – *from* **Ancestral Honour** *by Gav Thorpe*

MOLLENS SNARLED WITH surprise. The hulking Reiklander advanced towards him, his own glistening blade held downwards. With a speed and grace which belied his hefty frame, the Reiklander leapt with a savage howl. Mollens twisted and struck. For one terrible moment the two men gazed helplessly into each other's eyes, then the Reiklander collapsed into the cold mud. – *from* **The Judas Goat** *by Robert Earl*

FROM THE PAGES *of Inferno! magazine, LORDS OF VALOUR is a storming collection of all-action fantasy short stories that follows the never-ending war between the champions of darkness and light.*

More Warhammer from the Black Library

LAUGHTER OF DARK GODS
An anthology of Warhammer stories edited by David Pringle

ONCE MORE THE lightning flashed. Exultation filled him. He stood untouched and unafraid in the elemental landscape. It seemed that part of him had come home at last. Kurt raised his sword to the sky. Its runes glowed red as blood. He laughed aloud and his voice was merged with the thunder. – *from* **The Laughter of Dark Gods** *by William King*

THE OGRE RAN a rope-like finger over the tip of his club. 'Shall I brain you,' he growled, 'before throwing you into the sea?' His shoulders moved in a grotesque shrug. 'Why make a mess?' And he laid his club delicately on the ground and advanced on me, hands spread. – *from* **The Song** *by Steve Baxter*

SATURATED BY THE *fell magic of Chaos, the Warhammer world is a dark and dangerous place, where dead things walk, and nothing and no one is ever quite what they appear. First published in the early 1980s, these classic tales of action and adventure have been brought together in a new, revised edition which should appeal to all lovers of fantasy fiction.*

INFERNO!

INFERNO! is the indispensable guide to the worlds of Warhammer and Warhammer 40,000 and the cornerstone of the Black Library. Every issue is crammed full of action packed stories, comic strips and artwork from a growing network of awesome writers and artists including:

- William King
- Brian Craig
- Gav Thorpe
- Dan Abnett
- Graham McNeill
- Gordon Rennie

and many more

Presented every two months, Inferno! magazine brings the Warhammer worlds to life in ways you never thought possible.

For subscription details ring:
US: 1-800-394-GAME   UK: (0115) 91 40000

For more information see our website:
www.blacklibrary.co.uk/inferno